PENGUIN BOOKS
THE SRINAGAR CONSPIRACY

Vikram A. Chandra is one of India's best-known TV journalists.
He anchors prime time news on the Star TV network, and is
news editor of NDTV, India's leading TV news organization. He
reports extensively from Kashmir.

Educated at St. Stephen's College and at New College, Oxford
University, Vikram lives in New Delhi. This is his first book.

THE SRINAGAR
CONSPIRACY

VIKRAM A. CHANDRA

PENGUIN BOOKS

Penguin Books India (P) Ltd., 11 Community Centre, Panchsheel Park, New Delhi 110 017, India
Penguin Books Ltd., 27 Wrights Lane, London W8 5TZ, UK
Penguin Putnam Inc., 375 Hudson Street, New York, NY 10014, USA
Penguin Books Australia Ltd., Ringwood, Victoria, Australia
Penguin Books Canada Ltd., 10 Alcorn Avenue, Suite 300, Toronto, Ontario, M4V 3B2, Canada
Penguin Books (NZ) Ltd., Cnr Rosedale and Airborne Roads, Albany, Auckland, New Zealand

First published by Penguin Books India 2000

Copyright © Vikram A. Chandra 2000

10 9 8 7 6 5 4 3 2 1

Typeset in *Sabon Roman* by SÜRYA, New Delhi
Printed at Chaman Offset Printers, New Delhi

This is a work of fiction. Names, characters, places and incidents are either the product of the author's imagination or are used fictitiously and any resemblance to any actual person, living or dead, events or locales is entirely coincidental.

To the memory of Nandini Chandra

CONTENTS

AUTHOR'S NOTE

Many of the incidents described in this book are based on true events, though I have taken liberties with them for the sake of the narrative. A number of books helped me get the backdrop for my story, in particular, *The Lost Rebellion*, *Kashmir: A Tragedy of Errors* and *The Bear Trap*.

A special thanks to all my colleagues at NDTV, especially Radhika Roy and Ayesha Kagal who spent hours revising the manuscript.

Thanks also to all my friends from Kashmir; and to those who helped me time and again but who cannot be named. The advice of Sanjiv Saith, Sunil Sethi, Om Arora and Ravi Singh was invaluable.

I am thankful to my parents, my family and my friends, who were always there for me.

Above all, this book owes everything to Seema, who insisted that I write it, and to Vedant, who tried to retype it with his one-year-old fingers.

Prologue

JANUARY 2000

Jalauddin shifted his position slightly. They had been waiting for over two hours, and the thorns were beginning to get through his clothing. The crisp dawn breeze whispered past his ear; it was early January, and a thin curtain of mist hung dreamily over the horizon.

Next to him, Mohammed Karim spat out the stalk of grass he had been chewing. 'There it is,' he grunted, shading his eyes and standing up.

Through the trees they could make out a speck in the sky, growing steadily: the morning Indian Airlines Boeing 737 from Mumbai, losing height as it approached the Indira Gandhi Airport in Delhi. Jalauddin and his men were hidden in a copse of sheesham trees in the gardens surrounding a small farmhouse in Nangal Deri, a short distance away from the airport. A sympathizer had bought the farm for a fat sum of money a couple of years ago, and had erected a high brick wall around it to discourage those who would peek inside.

As the aircraft approached, there was a flurry of activity, Karim bellowing orders punctuated with his trademark Pushtu obscenities picked up at the mujahideen camps where he had spent most of his life. Two men pulled aside a muddy tarpaulin, and Jalauddin lifted out the one thing that made him more than just another grubby foreign militant.

The Stinger missile had originally been sent to Afghanistan to destroy Soviet helicopter gun-ships. After that war, the Stingers were so many time bombs ticking away in irresponsible hands. One such pair of hands now caressed the smooth metal.

Jalauddin stood up swiftly, slotting the disposable firing tube onto his shoulder with a practised motion. 'Attach it,' he said, searching through the viewer for the green image of the aircraft.

The spot had been well chosen; the trees would ensure that they couldn't be seen from the air, but without obstructing their line of fire. As the plane screamed overhead, its undercarriage extended, Jalauddin carefully lined up its shadowy image in the centre of his viewer. Immediately the Stinger reacted with a joyous warbling in his ears, a leashed falcon waiting to fly.

'Go, my friend,' he whispered. '*Khuda hafiz.*'

He made as if to jab the trigger but stopped his finger just in time. In his mind's eye, there was a spurt of flames and the missile streaked towards its target. But for the moment he straightened slowly and lowered the Stinger to the ground before turning to face his jubilant cohorts.

'Call them up, Karim. Tell them that we are in position, ready to strike. We wait now for the correct moment.'

* * *

The message was received in a small house tucked away, across the border, in one corner of a 190-acre campus at Muridke, about thirty kilometres north of Lahore. This was the headquarters of the Markaz-ul-Dawa-wal-Irshad, the parent body of one of the world's most lethal terrorist organizations, the Lashkar-e-Taiba.

The man sitting on a thin carpet in the main room had just finished his prayers. His head was wrapped in a white turban and his long beard was full of silvery threads that betrayed his age. He looked up as his aide tapped on the open door and then entered. '*Salaam aleikum*, Abu Fateh.' The man on the carpet was known to the world by a different name, a name under which he was hunted by the intelligence services of a dozen of the most powerful countries in the world. But he had recently assumed a new title, in keeping with the customs of the Markaz-ul-Dawa.

His dark hooded eyes gazed unblinkingly at his aide. 'Speak,' he invited quietly.

'Abu Fateh, we have received the message. Jalauddin is in position. They carried out the dummy exercise this morning and there were no problems. They are now in hiding, waiting for your command.'

'It is good,' came the reply, uttered so softly that the aide had to strain to catch the words. 'But tell Jalauddin that he may have to wait for months. The others have tasks that are even more difficult. It will take us time to organize them. In any case, there is still no word on Clinton's schedule, is there?'

'No, Abu Fateh. All we know is that he plans to go to India in the spring.'

The man on the carpet rose slowly to his feet, and then turned his back to the aide in dismissal. 'It is good. We will wait, *inshallah*.'

* * *

Winter came early to Kashmir that year. The wind swept angrily down from the mountains, nipping at exposed skin and rustling through the piles of dead chinar leaves on the roads.

In Maisuma it was a winter of despair. An air of defeat hung over the courtyards and homes, so heavy that it was like a tangible burden on the shoulders of those who called this their home. For years they had given themselves to the cause. Hours on *dharna*, shrill slogans and fists pumping the air. Police firings and tear gas. But it was all for nothing.

Habib Shah nursed a cup of *kahwa*, gazing into the depths of the yellow sickly-sweet liquid, his slight frame shivering from the cold.

The past few hours had been the most mortifying experience of his life. Nothing had felt this bad, not the interrogations in stinking basements, not the long years of captivity and exile, not even the shame of the monthly abasements at the courts in Delhi.

'Fucking bastards,' hissed the man sitting to his right, slumped against a sack of wheat. Iqbal Qasim, Habib Shah's childhood friend and his companion through the struggle. The only man he trusted with his life.

'Goddamn cattle, gutless sheep. They deserve what they get.'

Habib smiled a sad, weary smile. The smile of a prophet who had called his people and they had not answered. There was nothing, really, to say.

That morning Habib had given a call for a statewide *hartal* to protest the arrival of the Indian Prime Minister in Srinagar. The high point of the hartal was to have been the march to the United Nations office. All of Srinagar had been asked to turn out for the procession.

'Forty people. Did you count them? Forty goddamned foot soldiers of revolution, while the sheep hung from their balconies and gaped . . .' Qasim stubbed out his cigarette and immediately lit another. 'Remember how many we used to get on the roads in 1990? I swear to you—on one day alone, one million, perhaps two. A quarter of our people on the roads, screaming for our rights . . . Forty people. Where have we gone wrong?'

*   *   *

The cameraman splashed water onto his face, standing close to the sink to prevent stray drops from wetting the floor. He had always been a fastidious man, and now he squeezed paste onto a toothbrush to brush his teeth for the third time that morning. Then he examined his face in the mirror. There were faint worry lines at the corners of the eyes, but otherwise the face that stared back at him looked normal and relaxed.

He used the toilet, and then unlocked the door, stepping out onto the somewhat frayed carpet that lined the floor of the hotel room. The correspondent was still sprawled in a chair, watching the latest news bulletin on the small fourteen-inch TV set the hotel management had magnanimously sent up to their room.

The cameraman smiled at the journalist as he walked towards the equipment piled in one corner of the room, pausing at the window to yank the curtain aside to let in the soft sunlight of a winter morning in Srinagar.

'Poor bugger,' thought the cameraman. 'He doesn't deserve this. But then, neither do I.' Speaking aloud, he said, 'When should we leave?'

Without taking his eyes off the TV set, the journalist sipped his Coke and replied, 'We should set off now, the Republic Day parade starts in about two hours. I've called for the cab, we can leave as soon as you get your stuff ready. And don't bother taking a tripod, it's not worth the hassle trying to get it through the security checks. You'll have to shoot hand-held.'

The cameraman nodded and began to put cables into a black leather bag. He put in a shotgun microphone, then a small case carrying a pair of lapel mikes, and three digital videotapes, each barely the size of a music cassette.

The camera itself was perched on the bedside table; it was the latest digital Sony, small and powerful without being too heavy. In fact, the heaviest part of the camera seemed to be the chunky Anton Bauer battery fastened to its rear end.

'Will a couple of spare batteries be enough?' asked the cameraman.

'Sure,' came the reply, 'I don't think we are going to get too much this morning.'

The cameraman lifted a battery off the charger where it had been humming quietly, and made room for it inside the bag. Then, without too much fuss, and with just a brief nervous look at where the journalist sat unheeding, he reached into his suitcase for a second battery. It looked like all the others, a black Anton Bauer with gold lettering on it, weighing more than a kilo and with three shining contacts protruding at one end. But unlike the other batteries, only the front one-fourth of this one was filled with nickel cadmium cells. If connected, it would provide enough charge for the camera to be switched on, allaying the suspicions of any security official.

The rest of the battery contained pure Semtex explosive.

*   *   *

The Garhwal Rifles unit was garrisoned at the Badami Bagh cantonment in Srinagar, a few kilometres from where Habib Shah sat. The cantonment was like a huge mini city, and after a series of suicide attacks on army camps in Kashmir, security was tighter than ever.

Civilians who wished to enter had to wait outside the fortified gates, submit to detailed checks and then proceed to a small room to state their business in front of an army officer who managed to appear both bored and sceptical with equal ease.

There was little to distinguish the scruffy young man in a worn and faded *phiran* from the other locals who had queued up that morning. But when he reached the room his expression of bovine resignation was replaced by something both imploring and insistent.

'I need to speak to Kaul,' he said to the officer who was eyeing him with suspicion. 'It's urgent.'

'What is it about?'

'I can't tell you, only Kaul.'

The officer's eyes flashed. 'What the—'

'Look, this is very important, I must speak to Kaul. You have to believe me and call him.'

'Kaul? Who is Kaul? And who the fuck are *you* anyway?'

'Major Vijay Kaul. The man with the moustache who raided the village near Rainawari two days ago. He is with your Psy Ops.'

The use of the technical phrase changed the officer's expression a little. He debated with himself and then reached out a languid hand and pressed four buttons on the phone next to him.

Twenty minutes later Vijay Kaul drove up in his jeep. He looked at the young man without a trace of recognition.

'Yes? What can I do for you?'

'Can I speak to you alone? Please, you have to listen to

me.' And then in a low whisper he added, 'Jalauddin.'

Vijay's eyes narrowed and he tightened his grip on his AK-47. He then turned to the officer behind the desk.

'It's okay, Sunil. Give him a card and I'll take him in.'

They walked in silence till they reached the interrogation hut a couple of hundred yards away, and then Vijay turned to the young man.

'Okay, what is it? What do you know about Jalauddin?'

'Jalauddin and his men are back in India, and within the next few weeks they will shake you and Kashmir like nothing before.'

'Bullshit. He's in Pakistan. He ran there after Chrar-e-Sharief.'

'Major Kaul, it is important that you believe me, so listen carefully. I was with Jalauddin when we broke your cordon that night in Chrar. I was with him when we crossed the Line of Control back into Pakistan. What I am about to tell you means that I could die, perhaps very painfully. So give me the courtesy of a patient hearing. It is going to start with an assassination, the most dramatic assassination the world has ever seen. But that is only the beginning.'

The young man spoke on for half an hour, lighting one cigarette after another, pausing briefly to warm his hands against the *bukhari* which stood in a corner of the room, giving forth both heat and noxious fumes.

Outside the wind whistled through the courtyard, piling the dead leaves against the veranda of the hut. Clouds gathered overhead, bringing with them the promise of the first snowfall of the season.

And in the hut, Vijay was frightened as he had never been before.

'What are we going to do? How can we stop him?'

Part One

Chapter One

ZAFAR BAGH, 1947

The state of Jammu and Kashmir is the crown of India, and the Kashmir valley the jewel in this crown. It is a land of almost unreal beauty, a landscape painted by God in an unusually mellow mood.

In the summer of 1947, in Zafar Bagh, a small suburb of Srinagar, Mohammed Shah looked out at the frantic activity outside his house, as tents were put up in his courtyard and cooks slaved over huge cauldrons to prepare for the evening's wedding feast, the *wazwan*. Next to him stood Jawahar Kaul, his neighbour and his closest friend.

For twenty-four hours the cooks had been pounding the choicest cuts of meats and fashioning them into smooth meatballs. These would be cooked in tomato for the delicately flavoured *rista*, and in yoghurt for the even more exquisite *goshtaba*. In one corner lamb ribs were being fried, and men were still staggering into the courtyard, bearing sacks of rice.

Jawahar Kaul was a short, round man, his shirt stretched tight over his paunch, the result of a lifetime of feasting. With his face already creasing in anticipation of the culinary delights to come, he sniffed the air joyfully and stuck a pudgy finger into the nearest pot.

'Say what you like,' he declared, licking his finger, 'the wazwan is the pinnacle of human civilization. I have but one complaint, that I have only one stomach to give to the cause.'

'Kaul, if you are done with drooling into the goshtaba, can you kindly go and ensure that my son and heir will be ready by the time the girl's family arrives?'

Mohammed looked fondly at the retreating figure of his friend as he called out instructions to the cooks on his way to the bridegroom's room, pausing every few steps to sample the dishes. Jawahar had been his friend from the cradle, and their families had lived and grown together for as long as anyone could remember. In some other parts of the subcontinent that summer, such deep friendship between Hindu and Muslim may have been Capulet and Montague, but not in Kashmir.

During the dark days of the Partition, Kashmir was like an oasis. Though whispers of what was happening elsewhere in the subcontinent filtered through into the valley like some poisonous miasma, by and large the people of Kashmir were immune to the communal virus.

Through that summer Radcliffe's scalpel carved its way across the map of the subcontinent, drawing the boundaries of a new Muslim nation, Pakistan. The biggest problems for Radcliffe were in Punjab and Bengal, the two largest provinces in British India, which would both have to be divided between the new nations.

But for the men who were to inherit power in India, an even greater problem was that of the princely states, all 500 of them, whose rulers had earlier acknowledged British suzerainty, and who were now being asked to join their destinies with either India or Pakistan.

By the middle of 1947, most of the states had signed instruments of accession to either India or Pakistan. But the Maharaja of Kashmir, a Hindu ruler in a predominantly Muslim state, had not made up his mind. And that summer the question of what would happen to their land was never very far from the minds of those who lived in Kashmir.

In Zafar Bagh, as evening fell, the wedding guests lined up at the Shah residence. The *nikaah* ceremony over, attention turned to the wazwan. Hands were washed in a copper bowl, using water from a giant copper *surahi*. Then all the men settled down in neat rows on white sheets placed on the floor, sitting in groups of four around *trambis* or large plates. Mohammed Shah and other family members piled up the plates with heaps of steaming rice, kababs and fried lamb ribs. Then the cook brought in cauldrons full of the seventeen dishes that made up the feast. All conversation came to a sudden end and the meal was given the full concentration it deserved.

As the men lit up their post-dinner smokes, Mohammed Shah's cousin turned to him.

'Did you go to see Gandhiji?'

Mohammed's eyes shone. 'Yes. It was marvellous, people on every street, hanging out of the balconies. I think it was also the sheer surprise of it all—with all that is happening in India, Gandhiji still finds time to visit the Valley.'

Across the room a young relative snorted, 'Of course he finds the time. If Muslim-majority Kashmir joins India it would make a mockery of the entire concept of Pakistan as a separate Muslim state. The Congress will do anything to make sure we tie up with them.'

'When is the Maharaja going to make up his bloody mind?' asked another guest.

'The decision should not be his,' said Mohammed firmly. 'He may be the ruler, but it should be *our* choice—the wishes of the people. And let me tell you, I think the people are fully behind Sheikh sahib. Our future will be better with secular India than with those clowns in Pakistan.'

There was silence in the room. No one there would question the decision of their leader, Sheikh Abdullah, the Lion of Kashmir. He had led an agitation against the Maharaja for years, and now the Pakistanis were sparing no effort to woo him, but with little success.

And that was the supreme irony. Sheikh Abdullah was a Muslim leader in a Muslim-majority state who had fought for years against a Hindu ruler. But that summer he stood like a rock for accession to India, thumbing his nose at Pakistan and the notion that Muslims could not live within a Hindu-majority nation.

The dinner wound to a close and the guests departed. Sitting in the courtyard under a brilliant full moon, Jawahar turned to his friend. 'Mohammed, I know you've always followed the Sheikh. But can I ask you something that I have never asked you before? Who knows what will happen in the future, what shape the India of tomorrow will take. Have you never considered the possibility that Pakistan may be the better option?'

Mohammed laughed. 'I've considered it, my friend, but never for long.'

'Why?'

'We may be Muslims, Jawahar, but our Islam is of a different colour from the Islam of some of the fundamentalists who will reign in Pakistan. Our culture is different, our ethos is different. We can't be independent, we are too small. But perhaps in India we will find tolerance and acceptance.'

Mohammed stood up and clapped Jawahar on the back. 'Now don't get me all worked up on my son's wedding day. And don't worry, we will join India, and there will be peace ever after in our land.'

Chapter Two

GROWING UP

Mohammed Shah's words proved prophetic, but only in part.

Soon after the Partition, Pakistan sponsored a tribal invasion into Kashmir, and the beleagured Maharaja signed the accession to India. Indian troops flew into the valley and drove back the Pakistani raiders, but before they could clear all of Kashmir of the invaders, the entire matter was taken to the United Nations. Secure in the friendship of the Sheikh and confident of the support of the Kashmiri people, India promised a plebiscite, but only after the Pakistanis fully vacated Kashmir. A stalemate followed, with India retaining two-thirds of the state and the rest under Pakistani occupation.

A couple of years later, relations between the Sheikh and Nehru soured, and the Lion of Kashmir found himself in prison. But the Kashmir assembly ratified the accession, and Pakistani attempts to wrest the valley through another war in 1965 proved unsuccessful.

By now, Mohammed Shah was aging rapidly. The cigarettes he chain-smoked had left their mark on his lungs together with a yellowish stain on his beard. But he was determined to hang on to see a great-grandchild. And on a warm July afternoon in 1965, Fatima, the wife of his eldest grandson, delivered an eight-pound-six-ounce screaming bundle of humanity into the world. As the doctors slapped and wiped him energetically, he bellowed his outrage for all in the maternity ward to hear. He was then wrapped up warmly and taken out to be placed in the patriarch's arms. Mohammed

Shah looked down at the screwed-up monkey-like face in his arms and said softly, 'We will call him Habib. Habib Shah.'

Jawahar Kaul was the next to hold the baby. 'May he always bring joy to those around him. And may he always find happiness.' Jawahar already had a great-grandchild, also a boy, born the previous autumn and now reaching the stage where he was just able to smile gap-toothed from his cot, reaching up with his tiny arms and murmuring in a language all his own. The baby had been named Vijay. Vijay Kaul. And his destiny had already been chalked out for him.

'You will be a soldier, my little warrior. And you will earn honours in the Indian army some day,' Jawahar had crooned as he began to teach him to walk.

Then, one day, it was time for the two boys to meet. Habib was carried into the Kaul residence at 12 Zafar Bagh Road. Vijay took one look at the interloper, and hurled a building block in his direction.

'Well,' said Mohammed with satisfaction, 'it seems they will be friends.'

* * *

For several years now, Kashmir had been relatively quiet and peaceful. If there was a storm brewing, there was no indication of it on the surface. Time, it seemed, had resolved the Kashmir issue. In 1971 India and Pakistan fought their third war, and the Indian army trounced the Pakistanis. In the aftermath of that triumph, a victorious Indian Prime Minister sat down with the Pakistani premier in Simla to thrash out a solution to the problems between the two countries. Among other things there was a secret understanding at Simla that the Kashmir dispute would be buried, with Kashmir partitioned along the Line of Control, but a magnanimous Indian Prime Minister did not insist on this being spelt out in black and white. That mistake would be bitterly regretted in the years to come.

But in the mid-seventies Kashmir was still a wonderful place for two young boys to grow up in. Vijay Kaul and Habib Shah were barely ten and nine when they first escaped with makeshift fishing rods to a tiny stream running not far from their homes. There they sat on the banks, dipping lines baited with a little moistened flour, looking at the reflection of the willows in the water. The sky was that special, brilliant Kashmiri blue, a few scant clouds scudding along in the heavens, the air crisp and scented.

There were few fish in this stream, and after some time both the boys began to shift restlessly. That led inevitably to a scuffle, as they turned their attention joyously to a quick trial of strength, wrestling on the grassy bank. Over the past few months, Habib's quicker movements had just begun to triumph over his older friend's bulk, but today they called an early truce and sat up, spitting soil and stray twigs from their mouths.

'The holidays are almost over,' said Vijay disconsolately. 'Arithmetic again in three days' time.'

'Did you have to remind me, Kaul? I had just begun to forget that school existed.'

A low whistle came from behind them, and another young boy slipped down the bank to join them. Iqbal Qasim was the son of the priest of the local mosque, and he did not go to the same government school as they did. Instead he attended a *madrassa*, a religious school run by the Jamaat-e-Islaami.

'What are you both looking so mournful about?' inquired Qasim with exaggerated politeness. 'Have the fish bitten off your genitals?'

'Arithmetic,' said Habib and Vijay in unison.

Qasim laughed. 'Thankfully that's something I don't have to worry about too much. But then, you don't have to deal with the mullah who teaches us—you know what he is like.'

There was silence as they all contemplated the long, thin visage of Maulana Abdul Lateef, with its flowing beard and pointed nose. There was hardly a child in the neighbourhood who had not run foul of his temper or tasted the cut of the cane he carried.

Then, with some relief, they turned their attention to more pleasant matters. Habib shook Vijay's arm excitedly. 'I hear that Rajesh Khanna is in Srinagar. They are shooting in the lawns of the Oberoi.'

'No!' gasped Qasim. 'Do you think we can sneak in once again?'

A couple of months earlier all three of them had been taken to see a film shooting in a nearby town, and they had stood transfixed at the sight of hero and heroine prancing around trees.

'I'll ask my father,' said Vijay, 'he's as fond of movies as any of us.'

Habib looked up at the sun, which was disappearing over the treetops. 'But now, I think we should head home.'

Qasim waved goodbye and walked off towards his own home, a tiny cottage located next to the mosque. The other two began to trudge back towards Zafar Bagh.

'Why don't you come over for dinner tonight?' asked Vijay.

'What's Amma making?'

'Meat *koftas* and rice, I think,' said Vijay, and Habib smacked his lips in anticipation.

*   *   *

The patriarchs of the two families had seldom been apart in life, and so it was in death. Habib was eleven when his great-grandfather's lungs finally gave up the unequal battle against the daily invasion of cigarette smoke. Jawahar Kaul did not weep at his friend's funeral; he knew that he would not have to live alone for too long. And so it proved to be, and Zafar Bagh was suddenly a less colourful place.

Chapter Three

YASMIN

'Amma, where are you?' Habib called, as he entered the Kaul residence, picking up an apple from the sideboard and polishing it vigorously on his sleeve.

He threw his satchel on the side of the sofa before hurling himself into its cushioned comfort. It was a large drawing room, panelled in wood like so many Kashmiri houses are, and decorated with impeccable taste. The sofa against one wall was upholstered in maroon fabric, setting off the beige curtains. On the floor was a dark rust silk carpet, 700 knots per square inch, with exquisite paisley patterns handwoven all over its surface, now just beginning to show signs of wear after decades of being trampled upon.

'How did it go, *beta*?' asked Sunita Kaul as she entered the room. 'This was the tough paper, wasn't it?'

'Yes, Amma, maths. But it wasn't quite as bad as we had feared.'

'And where is Vijay?'

'He'll be here soon, he went to the market to pick up a book we'll need for the exam on the seventeenth.' Habib stood up and stretched himself. 'Thankfully there is only one more to go, and then the boards are over.'

Though Vijay was several months older than Habib, they had manoeuvred their way into the same class.

By now, Vijay Kaul was determined that his great-grandfather's prophecy would come to pass. He would be an officer in the Indian army. In a couple of years he would leave for specialized training in a military academy, but for the moment he was content to spend as much time as possible with his friends and family.

Habib had charted an even grander destiny for himself. For decades, the de facto rulers of grass roots India had been the bureaucrats, the officers in the Indian Administrative Service, who passed a brutally difficult examination to enter the hallowed ranks of the service, but once in, reigned like mini potentates over their districts, dispensing favours and justice to their subjects. Hardly anyone from Jammu and Kashmir had ever got into the IAS, and Habib wanted to defy that trend.

'Come on, then,' said Mrs Kaul, 'you might as well start your lunch. There is no point waiting for Vijay, he could be quite a while. Does Fatima know that you are eating with us?'

'No,' replied Habib, reaching out hungrily for the nearest covered bowl, 'but I'm sure she will guess soon enough . . . Oh no, Amma, not *palak* again!'

'It's better for you than that oily meat you and Vijay live on night and day. And hurry up and eat. Yasmin will be here soon.'

'Who is Yasmin?' said Habib, chasing his food around in his plate disinterestedly.

'She sells pashmina shawls. The poor thing is an orphan, and the bravest kid you will meet. I knew her parents quite well before they passed away, her mother when she was just three and then her father seven years later. Then she lived with her grandparents in Gulmarg, where they had a shop catering to all the tourists, till her grandfather also died last autumn. She has now moved to Srinagar with her grandmother. The Siddiquis have rented them a tiny house not far from the Zafar Bagh square. She couldn't be much older than fifteen, but she is incredibly independent.'

'Hmm,' said Habib, giving up the hope that the hated spinach would miraculously disappear from his plate.

'But what do you need with another shawl?' he added, with his mouth full and a pained look on his face.

Mrs Kaul drew herself up to her full five feet two inches

and said in mock indignation, 'What do *you* know about these things? You never know when a good shawl could prove useful. Besides, I'm just looking forward to seeing Yasmin again.'

Habib laughed and grabbed another apple, just as the doorbell rang. He went to answer it and threw open the door just as his teeth met close to the apple's core.

All he saw at first were the eyes. Grey eyes. Huge eyes. Eyes with just a trace of kajal outlining the part where the lids met the long lashes that swept outwards. Eyes that were just beginning to crease with slight concern at the unblinking and silent scrutiny from the young man with his teeth deep in an apple.

'Umm . . . Is Mrs Kaul here?' she asked hesitantly.

'Come in, darling, come right in,' said Mrs Kaul, sweeping past Habib, and kissing the young girl soundly on both cheeks, before taking her hand to lead her indoors. 'No, leave that bag, he'll get it.'

Yasmin entered the drawing room, glancing at the still transfixed Habib nervously as she walked past him. Mrs Kaul made her sit down, and then turned to her with genuine affection. 'You've grown so much! It must be a year since I last saw you.'

'A little longer, Auntie', smiled Yasmin, glancing once again at Habib as he brought her giant sample bag into the room. 'Um, is this Vijay bhai . . .'

'No, no,' laughed Mrs Kaul, 'this is Habib, the son of Fatima and Javed Shah; they live just down the road, a couple of houses from here. He's Vijay's best friend.'

Habib sat down and smiled at the girl, 'Hello.'

'Hello,' she replied, suddenly feeling unaccountably shy, an emotion completely alien to her.

The door slammed open, and a burly figure walked in like a portable hurricane. 'Hi, mom. I'm home.'

'Yes, I can see that,' said Mrs Kaul, drily, 'but must you destroy the door—and must you call me by that name?'

Vijay Kaul grinned at Habib, and then caught sight of Yasmin. 'Hey, it's Yasmin, isn't it? How are you? I haven't seen you for years.'

'Yes, Vijay bhai, it's been about five years,' said Yasmin standing up. 'You had all come to the shop in Gulmarg, and I was just a little kid then.'

'Not that you aren't a little kid now,' thought Mrs Kaul and busied herself going through the shawls which Yasmin had brought with her.

Vijay and Habib stepped out into the garden. Though they were almost the same age, they were physically very different. Vijay had been working out with a set of dumbbells for some years, and now his arms and shoulders bulged with muscles. Habib was as thin as a rake, but unlike his friend he had to shave every day to keep his thick stubble under control.

'Shall we go and see what Qasim has been up to?'

'Okay,' said Vijay without much enthusiasm. 'But first, why don't you tell me all about her?'

'Who?'

'Yasmin, that's who. I thought your eyes were going to pop right out of their sockets.'

'Get lost, you bastard. She just seemed like a nice kid, and too young for all that she has been through. Perhaps we should introduce her to some nice people here in Srinagar.'

'Sure, Habib. Anything you say,' said Vijay with an evil smile, and fled as his friend tried to hit him.

*   *   *

Over the next year and a half the three of them became inseperable, often going out for walks in the early evenings.

On a hot July afternoon in 1984, sitting by the banks of the Dal Lake, Habib Shah was gesticulating wildly as he tried to explain his full outrage to Vijay and Yasmin. Farooq Abdullah, the son of Sheikh Abdullah, had been dismissed as chief minister by the Centre and a new government hastily sworn in. A storm had broken out in Kashmir.

'They say that India is the world's largest democracy . . . why is it that we in Kashmir don't get to see this democracy? Time and again they have rigged elections here, and when we are finally able to choose the leader we want, the state government is dismissed in this fashion. I tell you, the problem is that Delhi doesn't trust us Kashmiris.'

'Oh come on, Habib,' said Vijay. 'It's not as if state governments are not dismissed in other parts of India. And look at the overwhelming support that Farooq has got from opposition leaders all over the country.'

Yasmin spoke up hesitantly. 'I don't know much about politics, but I'm not sure that the Farooq Abdullah government was doing all that much for the common person.'

And the debate raged on. In the lake behind them were moored a number of wooden houseboats, which had become the accommodation of choice for tourists coming to the Kashmir valley. Little *shikaras* glided gently close to the bank. It was peak tourist season.

Kashmir was still a very conservative society, and normally it would have been quite scandalous for a young girl to be loitering around near the Dal with two boys. But Yasmin didn't have a family at home to worry about her, and in any case, Vijay had by now assumed the mantle of her protector and guardian. That afternoon, Yasmin turned to him, shyly. 'Vijay bhai, there have been so many occasions in the last year and a half since I returned to Srinagar when you have come to my help. I couldn't have asked for a more caring brother.'

Vijay smiled and patted her on the arm. Then, with a malicious grin at Habib, he asked her in an innocent voice, 'What about Habib? Isn't he a caring brother?'

Yasmin blushed a deep red and left hurriedly, muttering something incoherently about having to shop for vegetables.

Habib and Vijay sat on by the banks of the Dal, sharing a cigarette, their major new vice. 'Why don't you tell her how you feel?' Vijay asked.

'I don't know what you mean,' said Habib, taking a deep puff.

Vijay stood up, waving his arms in frustration. 'You have been giving me this same bullshit for the past year and a half. Any idiot can see it in your eyes whenever you are with Yasmin—but you never say anything, and I don't think you have even spent a minute alone with her. What the hell are you waiting for—she's seventeen now and the next thing you know, she will be married.'

There were several moments of silence, and then Habib said slowly, 'But I can't just go up to her and say . . . well . . . whatever. That's not how it works here. Surely the families should meet . . . or my mother should go to her house, or something like that.'

Vijay shook his head in disgust and sat back, thinking. Then he changed the subject. 'We haven't been to Chasme-Shahi for a while. Let's go across this Sunday.'

*   *   *

When spring comes to Kashmir, the residents of Srinagar gather in the gardens laid out by Mughal emperors which are scattered all over the city like so many emeralds.

On Sunday afternoon, Vijay picked up Yasmin from her Zafar Bagh house and took her on his newly acquired motorcycle towards the Dal. 'Habib said he would join us at the Botanical Gardens, and then we can walk up to Chasme-Shahi,' he explained over his shoulder to her.

The bike went past the thickly crowded Dalgate area and turned right on to Boulevard Road, which runs along the banks of the Dal Lake. To the left of the road were the houseboats and to the right, a number of shops and budget hotels. And then the buildings ended, as the hills which surround Srinagar sloped down to kiss the water of the Dal. After a kilometre or so, Vijay turned off the Boulevard onto a road which went up the mountainside. A few hundred metres ahead, he stopped the Enfield near a large iron gate. 'Where is that oaf?' he said in exasperation. And then, turning to Yasmin, 'We might as well take a quick peek at the Botanical Gardens.'

'No, there he is,' Yasmin said, pointing at a thin figure meandering up the road towards them. Vijay stifled a smile as he took in Habib's brand new shirt and trousers and his face, which had been shaved and scraped till it lost the bluish tinge that most Kashmiri men have.

'Do you want to walk up to Chasme-Shahi, or should we take the bike?' he called out to Habib.

'Let's walk,' came the reply, 'it's great weather.'

From the Botanical Gardens the road continued to wind up the hillside until it came to a large concrete square with a huge flight of stone steps at one edge. These steps led up to the gardens at Chasme-Shahi, with their fabled fountains and coloured spotlights. Small stalls at one end of the square sold everything from leather coats to soft drinks.

'Look at those phirans!' gasped Yasmin, drifting inexorably towards the shops. 'No,' said Vijay and Habib in unison and dragged her back towards the steps.

The road didn't end at Chasme-Shahi, but went on up the mountain towards the Nehru Guest House, where all the top politicians stayed when in Srinagar, and towards the ruined observatory at Pari Mahal. From the tiered gardens and crumbling walls of the Mahal, those who had the energy to climb this far could get the most spectacular view of the city as it slumbered on the banks of its numerous lakes and canals.

But the view from Chasme-Shahi wasn't bad either, and scattered all over the gardens were picnicking families; the men in their loose kurta-pyjamas fiddling with transistor sets or trying their luck with packs of cards, while the women clustered together giggling and gossiping as they dissected, with sharp black eyes, all those who passed by.

'There's a nice spot to sit,' pointed Habib, heading towards a bench under the shade of a giant tree. From here they could look over a concrete parapet at an extended lawn a few metres below them, and beyond that at the shimmering blue surface of the Dal Lake.

They had just started to munch on their snacks when Vijay slapped his forehead and jumped to his feet. 'Shit, I forgot all about Papa's documents. I was supposed to deliver them to the post office by lunch time.'

He turned to the others, 'You both wait here, I'll be back soon.'

And then he was gone, leaving Habib and Yasmin acutely aware of the fact that they were alone for the first time ever.

There were several long minutes of silence before conversation resumed. It started with polite inquiries about shawls and college, and then, suddenly, they were talking, really talking.

The snacks were finished, and Habib fetched some soft drinks. If either was aware that Vijay couldn't possibly have taken so long to deliver the papers, they didn't articulate that thought. The shadows were just beginning to lengthen when Habib brought up the question he had never dared raise before.

'It must have been very hard for you, fighting the world alone, without your parents.'

Yasmin was silent for a moment or two. 'My mother died when I was just a baby, so I never really knew her at all. Till I was ten, my entire universe was my father. He was the kindest of men, and we were so, so happy in those days. He used to insist that I go to school, where I was the only girl. He would dress me up himself, make some lunch for me to carry, and take me by the hand all the way to the school building. And then one day I came home from school and found that he wasn't with us any more. They said it was a heart attack . . .'

Habib slowly raised his hand, and gently touched Yasmin's shoulder. And then he let his hand drop to the bench, where his fingertips just brushed the side of Yasmin's palm.

'I don't remember much about the days which followed. But I do remember Vijay bhai's mother. She had known us in the old days, and had been going to my father's store for years—whenever she came to Gulmarg, which was very often. It was she who helped us, my grandmother and me, to rent a small store and also found us a place to stay.'

She smiled a watery smile at Habib, who said, 'Yes, Amma is an amazing lady. There are times when I almost forget that she is not my mother. She is normally the first person I run to when I have problems, when I have good news, or when I just want to gossip.'

And then he skilfully changed the subject. 'Hey, that's a new motorboat on the Dal, it looks far more powerful than the others. I'd love to go waterskiing behind it some day.'

They talked about tourism then, neither in a hurry to go back home. Habib's fingers continued to graze Yasmin's palm. And as he leant back and shifted position slightly, his hand moved too, just a little closer to Yasmin's. A slight flush of colour rose in her cheeks, and her lips quivered just a little. But she didn't move her hand away.

That's how they sat, as the sun came down over the Dal, painting it with orange streaks that rippled with the water. All around them, the Chasme-Shahi gardens came to life, as huge coloured spotlights came on, trying in vain to compete with the setting sun. The fountains had been going for a while, and their water reflected the coloured lights, drawing excited oohs and aahs from the tourists who had gathered in droves.

And fifty yards away from Habib and Yasmin, Vijay Kaul sat on a wall overlooking the gardens and watched the young couple, a smile of satisfaction on his lips.

Chapter Four

JALAUDDIN

Deep inside Afghanistan, several hundred kilometres to the west of Srinagar, a fifteen-year-old boy sobbed quietly to himself, as he tried to force his body deeper into a narrow crevice carved into an unyielding stone-and-mud hillside. His fingernails were already torn and the palms of his hands were bleeding as they clawed out another few centimetres of space. He pushed his shoulders and hips into the still-too-small hole, and wiped the tears from his cheeks with grubby fingers as he turned to look fearfully at the skies.

Above him, the Russian Mi-24 attack helicopters danced an elaborate tango across the skies as they manoeuvred into position for another bombing run. The armour on their hump-backed bodies glinted evilly in the morning sunlight.

Secure in his cockpit, the pilot of the leading Hind grinned in glee: he knew that he had caught this bunch of savages by complete and total surprise, slanting out from behind the hillside just after dawn while they slept next to their still smouldering fire. The village giving the mujahideen shelter had taken the brunt of the opening attack, as salvo after salvo of rocket fire brought houses and huts crumbling down and sent the inhabitants scurrying out into the open. That brought them straight into the path of the next wave of gunships, which, without mercy, used their machine guns at close range, the bullets hosing back and forth along the tiny pathways leading away from the village.

For Jalauddin, it was a sudden and brutal baptism by fire.

He had arrived in the village just a couple of days back from the neighbouring base at Zhawar, and he hadn't ever come close to any action. At fifteen, he was considered a full-grown man, and no mujahid would have dreamt of showing him any special consideration. But now, as he clung to his precarious perch and gazed in terror at the hunters in the sky, the tears in his eyes were those of a child, as was the churning in his bowels, which threatened to lead to the ultimate degradation.

It had gone on for several days, this latest Russian attack on mujahideen positions near Zhawar, a town to the south-east of the Afghan capital Kabul, which lay astride one of the main supply routes for arms from Pakistan. Ever since the Russian invasion of Afghanistan in 1980, the Pakistani intelligence agency, ISI, had been coordinating the operations of the Afghan resistance—the so called Soldiers of God, or mujahideen. Arms sent in by the Americans were routed through Pakistan to safe bases just across the border in Afghanistan, from where they were sent to mujahideen commanders all over the country.

Jalauddin's convoy had set off from Miram Shah in Pakistan a week before, each volunteer carrying on his back a thick sack filled with ammunition, in addition to a scattering of personal belongings and the AK-47 rifle which was for them like an extension of their bodies. They led a train of pack-mules, on whose backs were strapped disassembled mortars, rocket launchers and heavy machine guns. But most crucial of all was a small consignment of Blowpipe anti-aircraft missiles which, the CIA insisted, were the perfect counter to the overwhelming Soviet air power that was threatening to crush the mujahideen resistance.

It took them two days to reach Zhawar, the safe base centred around a series of tunnels dug deep into the mountainsides. The tunnels housed everything from a mosque to a small theatre for watching video films. One of the tunnels even held a generator, which ensured that operations being conducted in the first-aid tunnel would not be disturbed, and that visiting journalists in the guest tunnel wouldn't suddenly find themselves in darkness. The whole base was surrounded by Oerliken guns, SA-7 missiles, and minefields.

After they had toured the defences in some awe, Jalauddin and his fellow recruits were treated to their first glimpse of the man they had all come to follow—Haqqani, the fifty-year-old bearded commander of the region, a member of the fundamentalist Khalis faction and one of the founders of the fledgling Harkat-ul-Mujahideen.

Haqqani stood on an upturned ammunition crate and surveyed the recruits, most of them, like Jalauddin, barely in their teens, the fuzz of adolescence just about starting to stain their cheeks and upper lips.

'You are here not to fight, but to die,' intoned Haqqani. 'Through the grace of Allah, you have chosen to come here to crush the infidel, to take part in a *Jihad-al-dafaah* against the aggressors. As the Quran says, "*Wa qaatilul mushrikeena qaafatan kamaa uqaatilunakum kaafa waa'lamuu anallaha ma'al mutaqeen*—whosoever does any aggression against you, retaliate against them in the same manner but know that Allah is with those who restrain themselves." '

The recruits gazed at Haqqani in rapt attention, as his voice rose in messianic fervour. 'We are restrained in our revenge, but we will fight till the end against those who have entered the lands of Islam. And those of us who are truly blessed will meet martyrdom. For as the Prophet—peace be upon Him—has said, whoever dies defending his religion is a martyr, whoever dies defending his wealth is a martyr, whoever dies defending his homeland is a martyr.'

By now there was a shrill tone in Haqqani's voice, as he waved his arms about, his eyes glittering sightlessly as they focussed on some point way beyond the horizon. 'We in the Harkat-ul-Mujahideen actively seek that martyrdom, we want to die in the name of Allah. But before we give up our lives, we will take hundreds of the infidels with us, we will strike a blow against *kufr* that will never be forgotten.'

It was a message that the recruits had heard a thousand times before, a message that had driven them to leave their homes and families in Pakistan to seek a glorious death in the battlefields of Afghanistan. Yet as they heard the words again, ringing through the valley, the hair stood up on their necks, and more than a few of them had tears in their eyes.

Now, three days later, martyrdom hovered above Jalauddin's head, and suddenly death didn't seem all that attractive anymore.

The gunship banked slightly as its pilot spotted a young mujahid trying to scramble up the mountain a few hundred yards away. The pilot thumbed a button, and the four-barrelled 12.7 mm gun under him rotated and roared as it spat out a liquid stream of lead. The bullets severed the Afghan's legs as neatly as a surgeon's knife, sending him cartwheeling down the hill. There he scrabbled his way back towards the hillside, reaching out with crabbed fingers and dragging his torso along the ground, even as his life gushed out in great red fountains from whatever was left of his thighs.

Jalauddin tried to choke back his nausea but couldn't, and he retched down the side of his little niche, the vomit staining the sleeves of his woollen tunic. And then he tried to push himself even further into the shelter, painfully aware that his legs were still hanging out in the open.

Suddenly a boot thudded into his side and a voice bellowed, 'Get out of your hole, you little coward. We need to get those missiles working.'

With considerable reluctance, Jalauddin dragged himself out of his niche and ran after the lanky figure with a flowing white beard and traditional Afghan turban flying down the hill towards a small hut. Around him, the carnage was continuing. A couple of men were shooting at the gunships with their AK-47s, the few bullets which hit their targets bouncing off the thick armour like marbles against a brick wall. All that their defiance resulted in was the unwelcome attention of those dreadful machine guns, which soon hosed the rifles into silence.

Only the previous evening, the mujahideen had unpacked the first crate of the Blowpipes, and had clustered around to try and figure out how the new weapon worked. Now the lanky man was trying to pull out the missile launcher from the hut, screaming at Jalauddin to carry out the missiles.

Other mujahideen had reached the hut by now, and they helped carry the heavy and clumsy weapon to the narrow ravine which ran alongside the village. There they assembled the Blowpipe, with fingers that trembled in haste, before the man in the turban stood up to take aim at the nearest gunship.

Unfortunately for the mujahideen, the Blowpipe was already an obsolete weapon, and its dispatch to the Afghan battlefields was the subject of much controversy. Among its many weaknesses was a requirement that the man who fired the missile had to guide it onto the target with a thumb control. The mujahideen commander tried to do just that, even as a second gunship spotted the little group and flashed towards them with all weapons firing.

It was now that the mujahideen realized another charming characteristic of the Blowpipes: they rarely ever hit anything. And though the commander tried his best to steer the erratic missile, it sailed well past the target, even as bursts from the second helicopter churned up the ground all around them.

'Piece of shit,' screamed the commander, as he hurled the launcher away from him, grabbing Jalauddin by the sleeve of his robe as they both dived for the bottom of the ravine.

By now the approaching gunship was barely fifty yards away, swooping down like some giant vulture. With a blinding flash it released its rockets, which slammed into the lip of the ravine. Great clumps of earth flew into the air, half burying Jalauddin as he lay with his nose pressed to the ground. Spitting out mud and stray pebbles, he cautiously raised his head, and shuddered in disgust as he pushed away from near his face the disembodied hand of a mujahid who had been too slow to take cover. The man's blood coated Jalauddin's hair, and he could taste death at the back of his throat.

The mujahideen commander had leapt to his feet, and in a futile gesture of defiance, he was sending burst after burst from his AK-47 at the departing gunship. And then, as suddenly as it had begun, the air attack was over, the helicopter gunships flying out of the valley like so many satiated vampire bats, heading back for the base near Jalalabad. For the mujahideen, it was time to lick their wounds and take stock of one of the worst poundings in recent memory.

The commander leapt out of the ravine and turned to give a helping hand to Jalauddin. 'Next time, don't wait so long before firing back. It is your duty to kill the kaffirs, not to hide from them,' he said gruffly.

And then, unexpectedly, his face lit up in a wide smile and he squeezed Jalauddin's shoulder. 'Don't worry. It will be much better next time. What's your name? I'm called Nasrullah, Nasrullah Langryal.'

If real life was like a Bollywood blockbuster, there would have been a blare of trumpets and a clashing of cymbals in Jalauddin's ear. This was the man he would come to worship, as a guide, as a leader and as a father. Langryal was the Pakistan-born commander of the Harkat-ul-Jihad-Islami who had created havoc for the Russians in this part of Afghanistan. He was the man who would one day leave Afghanistan to set up the Harkat in Kashmir. The man who would become the most prized of catches for the Indian security forces. And the man who would inspire Jalauddin's own journey across the mountains to take up the reins of the jihad in Indian Kashmir.

But all that lay years in the future, and on that dusty morning in a valley in Afghanistan, surrounded by death on all sides, the boy merely muttered an inarticulate response to Langryal. But the commander's attention was already elsewhere, as he tried to restore some sort of order to the devastated camp.

More than fifty of the mujahideen had been killed in the attack; many others had been seriously wounded. All afternoon long, the local doctor struggled to try and help the injured, stitching up wounds with a blunt needle, and, in some cases, carrying out amputations with a large knife. Those who could be moved were packed onto the mules and sent back to Zhawar.

But it had been a long and painful day, and that evening, as the mujahideen gathered around a cooking fire under the shelter of a rock overhang, most of them were in an evil and bitter mood.

Langryal looked at his men, as they chewed on their naan

bread dipped in mugs of unsweetened tea, and smiled grimly to himself. He knew how to return his men to full fighting spirit.

After the meal, he turned to one of his lieutenants. 'Bring out the prisoner. Let's all speak to him for a while.' With a wide grin on his face, the man went off, and the mujahideen began to stir in anticipation.

A few minutes later a young Soviet soldier was pushed into the fire light. He was a boy, barely eighteen, his terrified face was covered in bruises and his nose had all too obviously been broken a little earlier. When his lips parted, a gap could be seen where his lower incisor should have been.

The Russian, like most of his compatriots in Afghanistan, was a conscript, drafted against his will and sent to fight a war he did not understand. Unable to take the systematic and savage bullying of his seniors at the army camp, he had thought of desertion and had crept out of the camp with a vague and woolly idea of somehow making his way home. Inevitably, he had run straight into the hands of a waiting mujahideen patrol, and they had forwarded him to Langryal as a special present.

'So, Ivan. What shall we do with you this evening?' Langryal got up unhurriedly from his seat and slowly strolled towards the captive, who was being held by the arms by two Afghans. He pulled out his pistol from its holster, and reached out with its barrel, tapping the Russian on the tip of his broken nose. The young man gasped with the pain, straining back against the restraining grip of his captors.

'We lost many good men today, Ivan. Men who are in Paradise right now, but men we are missing a lot. We are not very happy right now. How do you think we can be made to feel better?'

Langryal thudded a boot into the Russian's lower body, and then turned away, as a thought gripped him. He sought out Jalauddin sitting on the fringes of the group, his eyes wide as he stared at the prisoner, and his breath coming thick and fast.

'You there, what's your name . . . Jalauddin. Come here.'

And then he took out a dagger from deep within his tunic. 'Why don't you do the honours? Start with his legs, and take your time. We have all night, and all of tomorrow as well.'

Jalauddin moved forward towards the Russian, who had already urinated into his breeches. As he tested the sharpness of the knife on the back of his hand, a smile began to play around Jalauddin's lips, his first smile since he entered Afghanistan.

Chapter Five

US AND THEM

Soon it was time for Vijay to leave for Dehradun, for the Indian Military Academy. Habib dropped him off at the central bus station where he would catch a bus for Jammu. Because of the mountains surrounding the Kashmir valley from all sides, there were no direct train links between Srinagar and other parts of India. Those who wanted to travel to the plains had to go by road, across the Banihal pass, to Jammu.

'Look after Amma and Papa for me,' said Vijay, as he hoisted his bedroll and trunk onto the top of the bus. And then, with a grin, 'I don't have to tell you to keep on eye on Yasmin.'

'Don't worry. You look after yourself,' replied Habib, thumping him on the shoulder.

With Vijay gone, the days were just that much longer in Srinagar. In the afternoons, after college, Habib often found himself wandering by himself along the Boulevard and by the banks of the canals which wound through parts of downtown Srinagar. He met Yasmin whenever he could, but it wasn't all that easy for them to sneak off together now that their chaperone was missing.

Inevitably, Habib began to spend more time with Qasim. After several years in the madrassas, Qasim had abandoned education to help his father, a shopkeeper on Residency Road in the heart of Srinagar. But though he spent the day fitting shoes on customers in a dingy basement, surrounded by leather coats and half-finished suede loafers, his heart was in politics.

After the rigid Islamic indoctrination of the madrassa, where Maulana Lateef's cane had waved like a magic wand as it tried to instil just the right amount of piety in his charges, it was but natural that the first allegiance for Qasim was the Jamaat. But the right-wing group's Islamic exclusivity, its orthodox discipline, and its unquestioning avowal of all things Pakistani had begun to pall, and Qasim was looking for a new cause, and new heroes to follow.

Habib soon realized that there were depths to Qasim which he could not even begin to fathom. Sitting in the shop after the shutters had been pulled down one evening, he interrupted Qasim's flow of vituperation against the Central government in Delhi: 'I've heard you, Qasim. But what exactly is it that you want?'

'An armed struggle,' came the ready reply. 'We must get arms and ammunition, and then drive the Indians from Kashmir.'

Habib threw back his head and laughed, but fell silent as he realized that Qasim was perfectly serious.

'An armed struggle? Whatever for?'

'Because they stole our land in 1947. Because they will never give us equality. And because they are Hindus and we are Muslims.'

'Oh come off it. We could argue till we are blue in the face as to what really happened in 1947. After all, Kashmir did voluntarily accede to India . . . and the Indian army only came in to kick out the Pakistani invaders whom your friends in the Jamaat are so fond of. Yes, Delhi does periodically misbehave with Kashmir, and I get as angry about it as anyone else. But that happens with other states as well, doesn't it?'

'Those states don't have the history which Kashmir does. And those states are not Muslim-majority.'

'What does being Muslim have to do with anything?' asked Habib, beginning to get more than a little angry. 'Aren't there more than a hundred million Muslims in the rest of India

. . . more than in your precious Pakistan?'

'Your problem is that you have spent your entire life in your little upper-middle-class cocoon,' said Qasim quietly. 'Why don't you step out for a change and see what reality is all about? Come with me for the Friday prayers tomorrow—there is someone I want you to meet.'

*　*　*

Tucked away behind the densely crowded and narrow *galis* of downtown Srinagar is the 600-year-old Jamia Masjid mosque, the largest in all of Kashmir. Destroyed by fire three times in its history, this wooden structure, with its giant pine-wood pillars, has long been both a tourist attraction and the main centre of worship for the Muslims of Srinagar.

Habib and Qasim approached the mosque, weaving their way through a thick crowd of white gown- and skull cap-clad worshippers. As they walked, they swatted aside a buzzing swarm of stall-owners and little urchins waving clothes and amulets in their faces to try and lure them to the bustling bazaar which clogged the streets leading to the Masjid.

'Young Qasim,' squeaked a querulous voice just behind them. 'I'm glad you are teaching your friend the virtues of Friday namaaz.'

With a somewhat strained and sickly smile on his face, Qasim turned to confront his one-time teacher, Maulana Lateef. '*Wasalaam aleikum*, Maulana sahib. I have missed seeing you all these days.'

Maulana Lateef gave no indication of hearing him, as he turned to Habib, who was surveying the scene with just the faintest of grins.

'And as for you, young man, I am glad that you have finally given up hanging around with the kaffirs and are back where you belong.'

'We will see you after the namaaz, Maulana sahib,' said Qasim hastily, seeing Habib's face darken with anger, and pulling him away quickly.

Inside the Jamia Masjid, the rows of worshippers were

beginning to line up. Habib washed his hands in the customary fashion in a rectangular tank of water, and then took his position alongside Qasim.

After the namaaz, Habib turned to his friend. 'So, who is this great man whom you want me to meet?'

'We are to wait right next to that wall and we will be taken to meet him.'

A few minutes later a nondescript young man, barely in his twenties, sidled up to them. 'Qasim bhai? Qureshi is waiting to see you.'

They went out of the mosque and into a side road a couple of hundred metres away. Stepping across an open drain they reached a narrow and poorly-lit staircase. There, on the first floor, was a tiny little room, barely larger than a cubicle, housing three wooden chairs and a desk.

They waited for about ten minutes, and then a huge man came wheezing into the room, his grey kurta-pyjama straining to hold in the tyres of flesh that had accumulated around his midriff.

Mopping his forehead with a handkerchief, he extended his hand, 'Salaam aleikum, Qasim bhai. I'm glad to see you again. And who is this with you?'

'Waleikum salaam, Qureshi sahib. This is Habib Shah, my childhood friend. He's another man who follows causes strongly, once he believes in them.'

'Have you spoken to him about us?'

'No, not yet. I wanted you to talk to him, just as you spoke to me.'

Habib stirred a little uncomfortably in his chair, as the conversation about him swirled on, without directly involving him. And then he looked straight at Qureshi. 'Who are you, and where are you from?'

Qureshi chuckled delightedly, glancing across at Qasim, 'I see what you mean.' And then his face turned serious, and he leant forward towards Habib.

'You are a child of this Valley, a son of Kashmir, born of these mountains, these lakes and these rivers. And yet, have you never realized that you are a slave in your land, a subject living in chains under the rule of an alien people from across the mountains who rape and defile our motherland? We were promised the chance to select our destiny, to choose our future, but that promise, like so many others in the last few decades, was broken.'

As the words poured past Habib, crackling crisply as they bounced off the walls, he thought to himself, 'It's a good spiel, even if a bit clichéd in parts. I wonder how often he has used it.'

But despite himself he was drawn deeper and deeper into those mesmeric brown eyes half concealed under the layers of fat which thickly creased Qureshi's face. And it was with considerable effort that Habib brought out one word from deep within himself. 'How?'

'I beg your pardon?'

'How are we in chains? How is our motherland being raped and defiled? Doesn't much of the economy run on subsidies from the Central government? Aren't we free to elect our own leaders in most elections? Don't we have the freedom in India to worship our own God in our own fashion?' Habib began to warm up. 'Okay, I don't say that the politicians in Delhi are a great bunch, but surely we in Kashmir have been much better off in India than we would have been in a third-rate dictatorship like Pakistan.' He shot an accusing finger at Qureshi, who was sitting calmly, listening to him. 'And that's what you Jamaatis want us to become—puppets of the Pakistanis.'

'Habib . . .' began an agitated Qasim, but Qureshi waved a silencing hand at him.

'Whatever gave you the idea that I am with the Jamaat?' he asked Habib. 'Do I look like a fundamentalist to you? My full name is Zafar Qureshi, and I have been a close associate of Maqbool Butt.'

Then, seeing recognition flare in Habib's eyes, he added, 'Yes, Habib, I'm with the JKLF, back from exile in England to find the right men to lead the movement to its necessary conclusion: the full and complete independence of the Kashmiri people.'

From an almost nonexistent fringe group just a few years back, the Jammu and Kashmir Liberation Front had by the summer of 1986 begun to spread its tentacles throughout the Kashmir valley and beyond. Realizing that the fundamentalist agenda of the Jamaat was unpopular in Kashmir, the Pakistanis had thrown open their coffers to the leaders of the JKLF and offered them every possible help in building up their base in the Valley.

Habib grinned, a little wryly, at Qureshi. 'My apologies for equating you with the Jamaat. But if you are trying to recruit me to your cause, you are wasting your time. In the first place, India will never agree to let Kashmir go, and in the second place, I still don't believe that we would be better off as a tiny independent pawn than as part of one of the most important countries in the world.'

Qureshi leant forward to eagerly take up the debate, and for long hours the words and arguments cannoned back and forth. Qureshi was a highly skilled fisher of men and he recognized in Habib a prized catch, but for all his efforts he was unable to reel him in. But somewhere deep inside Habib a little hook had been planted, and when he left that dusty room well after dark, he carried that hook with him.

He returned to that room often in the empty weeks that lay ahead, chatting with Qureshi and Qasim, trying to understand what motivated them. For a man who had always been content with his comfortable upper-middle-class life, the dawning of radical beliefs would be a slow process, but Qureshi had plenty of time.

In the days that followed, the little barb sank deeper and deeper into Habib's soul. He tried to share his new-found confusion with Yasmin, but she looked at him as if he had come from another planet. That left no one for him to talk to but Qasim, and with each conversation another length of fishing-line was carefully pulled in and slapped onto the reel.

Habib began to read more about Kashmiriyat, that ill-defined essence of Kashmiri identity, a fusion of liberal Islam, Sufi beliefs, and vague nationalism. He read about the history of his people, and he burned with anger when he learnt about the discrimination they had often faced at the hands of the

Dogras who had ruled Kashmir for more than a century. Then he went with Qasim to Chrar-e-Sharief, the shrine that was the very symbol of Kashmiriyat, and he prayed at the *ziarat* of Nund Rishi. As he spent more and more time with Qasim, the thick books that he had bought to study for the IAS examination began to gather dust in a forgotten corner of his room.

Habib had just reached that age when rebellion comes naturally to most young men, when causes and great crusades call to both the mind and to the soul. In the elite colleges of India, even now thousands of bright young students read and reread the works of Marx and Lenin, taking into their hearts the message of total revolution, till admissions to business schools and fat salaries drive those notions far away. Others take to student politics and block traffic on the roads as they wave banners and shout slogans. But in a troubled region like Kashmir, anger against corruption, against bad roads, against useless phones, against government employees who don't work, and against unemployment is all too easily transformed into secessionism. It becomes Us and Them, and They are responsible for all of Our problems.

In the days that followed, Habib felt a familiar smouldering resentment when he was imperiously waved to the side of the road as a white Ambassador car bearing one of Delhi's top ministers hurtled down the road towards the Golf Course. He felt his temper rise as a cop tried to shake him down for a few extra rupees just because the licence plate on his bike was covered with mud. And he felt a sharp irritation when he was pushed off the pavement on Residency Road by a fat Punjabi woman bearing an armload of packages as she waddled determinedly towards a carpet store.

But where a few weeks earlier his reaction would have been, 'Goddamn politicians', 'Son-of-a-bitch policeman', and 'Fat cow', now a new all-purpose phrase began to come to his lips: 'Bloody Indians.'

Habib was still no militant. He wasn't even a committed secessionist. But Qureshi watched him, and smiled. From here to political activism would be a couple of short and simple steps.

Chapter Six

A RAID IN RUSSIA

Two years had passed since Jalauddin had first tasted action, and those years had changed him beyond recognition. He was now a man in every sense of the word, towering above most of his colleagues at six feet two inches in height, his sparse frame draped in the traditional shalwar-kameez. On his feet were thick leather boots, and on his head a fur cap, both taken from captured Russian prisoners before they were dispatched in Jalauddin's by now trademark style.

To guard against the wind which comes whistling down from the mountains on a cold Afghan winter morning, Jalauddin wore another trophy of war, a lightly quilted Russian parka, its pockets stuffed with loose rounds of ammunition and small cakes of the best Afghan hashish. On Jalauddin's face, the fuzz was gone, the years having replaced it with a thick curling beard which had never felt a barber's blade and which hung six inches from his chin. Every few minutes, and especially just before action, Jalauddin would reach up gently and tug at the beard, as if to reassure himself that it was for real. And there was one more change: a year ago a splinter fragment from an exploding Soviet rocket had laid open the side of Jalauddin's face, and despite the hurried patch up job in the tunnels of the Zhawar base, a small scar remained, twisting the corner of his mouth upwards in a perpetual sneer.

Sitting in front of a warm fire that March evening, his men around him finishing the last portions of their evening meal, Jalauddin was a contented man, as he delved in his pocket for tobacco with which to fashion a smoke for himself. His band of eight mujahideen had nearly completed a long and arduous trek across Afghanistan, to reach a position in the north-west of the country, just a few kilometres from the Amu river and the border with the Soviet Union.

A month ago, Nasrullah Langryal had approached Jalauddin as he prepared for bed, shaking out his blanket to get rid of insects and any passing scorpion. In the two years since they met, a close relationship had developed between the two men, Jalauddin's hero worship deepening into an adoration which he had never felt for another human being. Neither man, of course, would ever speak about it.

For Langryal, Jalauddin was the brightest of all his protegés; his skill with a gun and complete ruthlessness in battle complemented by a sharp intellect which had already set him apart as a leader of men.

Ritual greetings over, the two men sat down in front of the tent to share a smoke. Then Langryal came to the point. 'There is a call from Islamabad. Pakistani intelligence is taking the jihad directly into the lair of the Soviet bear; they are carrying out mujahideen raids across the border, inside the Soviet Union. These will be led by men from the Kunduz province, but some of us may also be given the chance to take part. Would you be interested?'

Jalauddin shivered with excitement. 'A chance to strike at the belly of the atheist is a call from Allah. How could I possibly refuse? How soon would I have to leave?'

'As soon as possible. Perhaps within two days. The ISI will give us the details tomorrow.'

There was silence for a few minutes. Both men were themselves Pakistanis, Langryal from the dominant Punjab province which controlled most aspects of Pakistani life, and Jalauddin from the Pakhtun areas of the North West Frontier province, the land of Kim and the Great Game, where the tribals saw themselves as the direct kin of the Afghans across an artificial international boundary.

But while they were Pakistanis by nationality, both

Langryal and Jalauddin were warriors of the Harkat-ul-Jihad-Islami, and as such they owed primary allegiance to a larger pan-Islamic cause. When that cause dovetailed with the interests of Pakistan itself, it was so much the better. And for years now, the Afghan war had been directed from Pakistan, under the command of the all-powerful ISI and its leaders General Akhtar and Brigadier Mohammad Yousuf.

The silence dragged on, as both men drew into their lungs the fragrant smoke, feeling the warmth entering their limbs. And then Langryal turned to Jalauddin. 'Somehow, I've never asked you. Why did you enter the jihad?'

Jalauddin shrugged his shoulders. 'My father has many sons, he wouldn't miss one. In my village, near Darra, we are brought up with guns. Peshawar is not far away, and most of the men in our area make weapons for a living. I first fired an automatic rifle when I was barely five, and my first rocket launcher when I was nine.'

He drew the blanket closer around himself and scratched angrily at a flea bite on the back of his neck. 'Our local mullah had links with the Jamaat-e-Islami, and he kept trying to talk the younger boys in the village into martyrdom. When my brothers took over the running of the family business, there was nothing to hold me in the village, and I decided to travel to Afghanistan.'

Langryal laughed in a not too unkind fashion. 'For one born with guns, you certainly burrowed deep into a hole the first time someone took a pot shot at you.'

Jalauddin scowled in the darkness; he hated to be reminded of his first day in action. Then he quickly changed the subject. 'Where do we have to go for this attack, and who is to command the operation?'

'You will command,' said Langryal quietly. 'For several months I have watched you become a man, and now it is time that you became one of the leaders of the jihad.'

The parting, when it came two days later, was short but painful. It was unthinkable that either of these men would express emotion to each other, so both Langryal and Jalauddin contented themselves with a quick hug, before the young man walked away down the mountain pathway without a backward glance. With him went the seven men who had been handpicked by Langryal for this operation, men with considerable combat experience between them but not old enough to challenge Jalauddin's authority.

Their journey took them first to the outskirts of Jalalabad, and then to Anawa at the mouth of the Panjsher valley, where the mujahideen leader Ahmed Shah Masood had successfully held off the Soviets ever since they invaded. Taking shelter with Masood's men, Jalauddin watched with unconcealed envy as they unpacked crates of the new Stinger missiles and deployed them on the hillsides to guard against a surprise helicopter attack. Once there was a fleeting glimpse of the great man himself, Ahmed Shah Masood, the Lion of Panjsher, dapper in his neat beard and stylish turban and chuckling like a little child as he raised the bulk of the missile launcher onto his shoulder.

And then it was time to move on again, heading north-west towards the Soviet border, flitting from camp to camp, with one eye perpetually cocked towards the sky just in case a roving gunship passed by.

Now the journey was almost over. Jalauddin and his men had reached the rendezvous point close to Sherkhan, a couple of hundred kilometres from the city of Mazar-e-Sharief.

Jalauddin lit his pipe and then passed it on to the first of his men. It had been a good meal, a goat bought from a passing shepherd and killed in the ritualistic *halal* fashion, its throat slit and a prayer uttered as it died. Then the mujahideen had dismembered the animal before cooking it with onions and plenty of chillies over a slow fire. Food was never particularly important for the mujahideen; they had learnt to survive on a staple diet of naan carried wrapped up in bundles and eaten even after it had gone putrid with age. But when the opportunity came, they all loved to gorge themselves as if there were no tomorrow.

One of Jalauddin's men belched, and looked hopefully into the pot to see if there were any scraps left. Then he turned to his commander. 'Now what happens?'

'Now we wait,' said Jalauddin. 'Wasim Beg knows that we are here, he will get in touch with us.'

They didn't have to wait for long. At dawn Wasim Beg's men entered the camp, after efficiently encircling it and keeping their weapons ready for any treachery. The fifty-year-old Wasim Beg walked up to greet Jalauddin, his face riven with the lines of great suffering and his flowing white beard adding decades to his appearance. Beg was a farmer who had lost his entire family to the Russians. Now he lived for just one reason—killing as many Russians as possible.

After the new arrivals had settled in, Beg explained the plan to them, scratching maps on the dust with a twig as he did so.

'This is where we are, near Sherkhan. The Amu—and the Soviet border—are barely twenty kilometres north of us. Across the border from us is the Russian city of Nizhniy Pyandzh, which we have often hit with rockets. Our target this time will be to the east, where there are a large number of Russian airfields and industrial towns, all of which are poorly defended.'

Beg sat back and looked straight at Jalauddin. 'I've been across the border five times over the past few years, but some of us need to go over once again tomorrow to look for the best target. I suppose all of you would be too tired after the long journey.'

It was both a question and a thinly veiled challenge, which Jalauddin was quick to answer. 'I would be honoured to accompany you on the reconnaissance mission. My men can stay here and get to know your followers.'

Wasim Beg inclined his head in assent. 'I am happy to say that we have been able to spread our word among Muslim shepherds on the other side of the river, and we can look forward to shelter and support. Rest now, my friend, we have a long journey ahead of us.'

*   *   *

There were three of them in the scouting party, and they moved stealthily past Afghan army positions near Imam Sahib towards the great river which separated the Soviet Union from Afghanistan. When they reached the river, Beg parted some reeds to reveal a tiny boat.

'We'll go across in this,' he said. 'Far more comfortable than how I went across the first time, using an inflated goatskin.'

'You crossed the Amu on a goatskin?' asked Jalauddin, his eyebrows rising in disbelief.

'Twice, actually. Once going there, and once returning. But I promised myself I would never do it again.' Beg glanced at the sky, where the sun was about to vanish for the night behind the hills on the horizon. 'Another couple of hours and it should be dark enough for us to attempt the crossing.'

The crossing was uneventful. Wasim confidently led the way towards a little hut a couple of kilometres away. The door was opened by Tahir, a clean-shaven man of indeterminate age who promptly took Wasim into his arms in a fond embrace, and then turned to repeat the process with Jalauddin. By and large the mujahideen had only a passing acquaintance with personal hygiene, but if Tahir was offended by the strong odours coming from his guests, he didn't show it.

In the morning, Wasim and Jalauddin set off with Tahir to search for a suitable target, leaving their colleague to look after the sheep.

Their guide led them in a punishing march up and down the hills in the region.

After several hours the hills suddenly came to an end, and before them lay a huge valley. The three men took shelter in a forest of pine trees and surveyed the area before them.

'That's the airbase at Voroshilovabad,' Tahir pointed. 'Beyond it you can see the main railway line, and then that spot right on the horizon is the city of Kolkhozabad.'

'The railway line is tempting, but out of range from here,' grunted Wasim, scanning the area with a pair of binoculars. 'It will have to be one of these buildings at Voroshilovabad. What's that huge grey structure just in front of the airbase?'

Jalauddin took the binoculars from him. 'Well, it's clearly a factory of some sort or the other. And it's certainly within the eight-kilometre range of the rockets.'

'That's it, then. Now let's mark this spot and get our bearings absolutely correct. We will be shooting by moonlight, and it would be ridiculous if we failed to hit anything.'

The operation went ahead in the middle of April. There were thirty-five men in the raiding party and four boats waiting for them in the reeds next to the Amu. The party was carrying two Chinese-built single-barrel rocket launchers, which had a calibre of 107mm and could do considerable damage. Each of the rocket launchers was carried by two men, while the remaining mujahideen had a rocket each.

The raiding party reached Tahir's hut just before dawn and was to spend the day hiding in the hills just behind the hut. It was a hot day, but Wasim kept an iron control over his men to ensure that they didn't finish their water too soon. With frequent Soviet border patrols in the area, the mujahideen had no choice but to hide under blankets behind some rocks, and going to fetch additional water would have been impossible.

The waiting was always the worst part, and Jalauddin spent the day under his blanket taking his AK-47 apart by touch, cleaning the pieces almost automatically and then putting them together again. Wasim Beg lay under his own cover a few yards away, burrowing deeper into the ground when the heat grew unbearable. And then, suddenly, it was dark, and the mujahideen struggled thankfully out from their hiding places.

Wasim addressed them in a low mutter, taking care to ensure that his voice would not carry to any passing patrol. 'We must walk fast now; we have a round trip of about twenty-five kilometres ahead of us and only eleven hours of darkness to make the journey in. All hell will break loose once the attack is over, and I don't need to tell you what the Russians will do if they catch us in their territory.'

Wasim had given an additional instruction separately to Jalauddin. 'There are clear directives from the ISI. No one is to be captured alive at any cost, this operation must not be traced back to Pakistan. If something happens to me, I leave it to you to ensure that no one surrenders or falls into their hands.'

They walked fast, in single file, the moonlight reflecting off the hills and clearly illuminating the narrow pathway at their feet. But by the time they reached the firing point, the stars in the sky were more than matched by the sprawling lights of Voroshilovabad, carpeting the valley before them like so many fireflies.

Jalauddin helped set up one of the rocket launchers, and pointed out the target to the operator. 'It's about eight kilometres away,' he reminded the man. 'Perhaps you should set a range of a little under that and the other rocket launcher will go for the exact range. That way we are sure that at least a couple of rockets will hit the factory.'

The time for silence was over, and the hills rang with traditional Afghan battle-cries as the rocket launchers crashed into action, the night suddenly lit up by long crimson streaks as the rockets headed for their target. There were fifteen rockets for each of the launchers, and they were all fired in less than four minutes.

There was no time to linger around to see how successful the attack had been, and the mujahideen set off at a fast trot back towards Tahir's hut. But as they approached the crest of the hill, Wasim allowed himself the luxury of a quick glance at the target and smiled as he saw huge tongues of flame licking at the night sky.

It was almost dawn by the time they reached the hut, and they had barely enough time to grab a quick bite before the inevitable Soviet response to their attack. 'Come on, let's return to that cursed gully. We'll have to hide till the evening,' said Wasim, picking up his gun and heading out of the door. As soon as they had taken shelter, the sun rose above the hills, and a swarm of planes and helicopters buzzed furiously towards the Amu river, like bees whose hive has been smashed.

All day long the Soviets pounded the hills and valleys just inside Afghanistan, on the far side of the Amu, while the mujahideen sweltered under their blankets. As night fell, they crept down to the river, and made their way across.

The next day was once again spent in hiding, in a valley not far from Imam Sahib. Wasim and Jalauddin took their positions near the top of a stony cliff which ran along one side of the valley, while most of their men lay down on the banks of a little stream further down the valley.

Shortly before noon, Jalauddin sat up, and quickly crawled

up to the top of the cliff. He sat there for a couple of minutes and then returned to Wasim. 'Afghan army,' he said tersely. 'There are about twenty-five of them, we will probably have to fight them off if they continue to head this way.'

The curl at the corner of Jalauddin's mouth was just a little more pronounced as he checked his AK-47 for the hundredth time that morning. Wasim looked at his face, and realized, with some surprise, that Jalauddin was enjoying himself immensely. 'He is a wild one,' he thought to himself. 'Some day he is going to be difficult to control.'

Jalauddin scrambled up the cliff once again, as Wasim signalled to the other men to take up ambush positions. The line of Afghan soldiers slowly approached their positions, the conscripts who made up the patrol dragging their feet as they walked, hoping, as always, that they wouldn't bump into a band of bloodthirsty mujahideen.

Jalauddin lined up his sights on the man who appeared to be the officer in charge, and was just about to squeeze the trigger when a corporal bearing an antique communication device came wheezing up to the target. After a few minutes of wild gesticulation into the handset at someone who clearly couldn't see the impassioned gestures, the Afghan officer turned away from the ravine, taking his men with him.

'I wonder why they went back,' said Wasim thoughtfully. And then, as that question was answered by a number of helicopters buzzing overhead, 'And I wonder what those sons of Satan are doing right now.'

The helicopters were flying back and forth in a rhythmic pattern a few kilometres from them. Jalauddin strained to get a closer look through the binoculars. 'Are they dropping paratroopers? Or are they just scanning the region looking for us?'

'Doesn't really matter,' grunted Wasim, as he settled back on a comfortable patch of mud. 'I suggest you catch a quick nap, we have a long march ahead of us tonight before we reach safety.'

They set off well past dusk, to ensure that they evaded any late patrols. It took them an hour and a half to reach the area that the helicopters had been patrolling.

'Keep an eye open,' said Wasim tensely and tightened his hold on his AK-47. 'They may just have dropped paratroopers who are waiting for us in ambush.'

The mujahideen moved from shadow to shadow in the darkness, a quarter of the men walking along the crests of the hills to guard against ambush, while the remainder took the easier route along the valley floor.

Unfortunately for Wasim, what the helicopters had sent drifting into the valley on tiny parachutes was something far more lethal than paratroopers. The night was lit up by a blinding flash of light as a butterfly mine went off under Wasim's foot.

All the mujahideen hit the ground, fearing ambush, but Jalauddin quickly began to crawl to where Wasim was lying muttering snatches of the Quran to keep himself from screaming aloud with the pain. The foot was almost completely severed at the ankle, hanging on by thin shreds of flesh and mangled bone. Sweat poured down Wasim's face, and his voice rose a little higher in prayer, as he stared down at the blood spurting from the stump.

'I must cut the foot,' said Jalauddin turning to the other mujahideen who were beginning to cluster around. 'Hold him firmly.'

'Don't take my foot,' pleaded Wasim, beginning to babble a little now. 'Take my life instead. I beg you, Jalauddin, kill me—give me *shahadat*—give me the death of a martyr.'

Jalauddin showed no signs of hearing him. 'Hold him,' he repeated, and five men moved quickly to obey, pinioning Wasim to the ground, while another man struck a light for Jalauddin to work with.

Wasim had become like an elder brother for Jalauddin, and the amputation of his foot would reduce him from a respected and admired leader of men to a cripple scrabbling for a living in the streets of Kabul. But as Jalauddin took out his knife to cut into Wasim's flesh, all he felt was the familiar thickening and swelling in his loins at the sight of someone in pain.

He tried to hide his growing excitement, but his breath was coming faster now, as he sliced into Wasim's ankle.

Chapter Seven

THE ELECTIONS

As the Indian Airlines plane rolled to a stop at Srinagar airport, Vijay quickly snapped off the restraining seat belt and stood up to reclaim his bag from the maws of the overhead luggage bin. He paused for a brief moment at the top of the flight staircase to look around and fill his lungs with the clean and crisp Kashmiri air. Then he hurried after the other passengers to the terminus building.

As he emerged from the building with all his luggage, his face lit up and he called out, 'Amma, Papa,' before rushing to embrace his parents and touch their feet. He glanced around once to note that they had come alone, and then as he struggled to fit the suitcases into his parents' ancient Fiat, he said, a touch too casually, 'Where's Habib? Wasn't he able to come?'

His father turned quickly, and slid into the driver's seat, and it was left to Amma to answer, 'No, beta. I guess he must be busy.'

A thin line of worry continued to crease Vijay's forehead as the car pulled out of the airport. He turned again to his mother. 'Amma, is everything okay with Habib? He hasn't replied to my letters for more than two months, and even earlier he had begun to send short messages on postcards. And I could gather from your letters that you hadn't really been in touch with him for a while.'

'Let's get home and then we will talk,' said Amma firmly, then changed the subject: 'I have to say that uniform looks really good on you. You've lost a little weight around the tummy and that suits you too.'

Vijay contented himself with looking out as Srinagar raced past the car windows. He noted the signs of growing prosperity, a number of concrete two-storied houses coming up in places where earlier there had only been shacks. Fifteen minutes later they reached home, where the staff lined up to greet Vijay baba, as they called him. Many of them had been with the family for years, especially the general handyman, Ghulam Razzaq, who had been the first person to put solid food into Vijay's mouth as he lay squalling in his cot. Now the wizened old man reached up to pat the cheek of the man who towered above him, 'A long life, baba. May Allah grant you a long life.'

A short while later a freshly scrubbed Vijay confronted his parents over a cup of kahwa in the lawn. 'What is it that you people are not telling me about Habib? When did he last come to see you?'

Papa glanced across at Amma, and then shrugged his shoulders. 'It's been about four months.'

Vijay almost dropped his cup in shock. 'Four months! He hasn't seen you in four months? Surely he must have come here when you had that attack of jaundice last month?'

Papa smiled wryly. 'No, it seems he wasn't able to come, but he did call once to make sure that I was alive.'

Vijay looked across at his mother, noting the hurt in her eyes. 'What about Yasmin, has she been in touch?'

'Yes, of course,' said Amma quickly. 'She comes over every week, and sat by your father's bedside for hours while he was unwell.'

'And what does she say about Habib? Are they still together?'

'She doesn't say anything at all about him, but yes, from what we hear, they are still very much together.'

As if on cue, a shy head poked around the hedge and a voice said politely, 'Hello, everyone. I heard that Vijay bhai was back.'

Vijay jumped out of his seat to hug Yasmin, and then said, with some surprise, 'My god, little sister, you have grown! I wouldn't have recognized you on the streets of Srinagar. Come to think of it, it probably isn't safe to allow you out on the streets of Srinagar any more—not alone anyway.'

Yasmin blushed prettily, but didn't bother to brush aside the compliment. She was now the picture of Kashmiri beauty: fair, smooth skin which had never experienced the trauma of teenage acne, a generous mouth with lips that curved elegantly at the corners, and, of course, those giant gray eyes outlined with kohl. The loose green phiran she wore couldn't really disguise what appeared to be a perfect figure.

She settled herself down on a cane stool and beamed happily at him. 'How long are you back for, Vijay bhai?'

'Just three weeks, unfortunately. And then I have to return to finish the course.' Vijay tried to restrain himself, but couldn't. 'Yasmin, how is Habib? Where is he? None of us have heard from him for a while.'

Yasmin reached out carefully to take a biscuit from the plate on the table and replied without looking at Vijay, 'Habib is fine, he's very caught up in some things he's doing. He . . . he said to apologize on his behalf for not being able to come right now.'

Later, as he walked Yasmin home, Vijay brought up the subject again, with all the doggedness of a pit bull terrier. 'All of you keep fobbing me off, but I insist on knowing what the matter is with Habib.' He turned to Yasmin, caught her arm and swung her around to face him. 'Out with it, Yasmin. Is Habib in some sort of trouble?'

Yasmin gazed at Vijay's face for a couple of minutes and then replied, 'No, Vijay bhai, Habib isn't in any trouble, but he has got very involved in politics.'

'Politics?' Vijay was incredulous. 'What sort of politics?'

Having begun to talk, Yasmin felt less nervous, and her eyes were steady as she looked back at Vijay. 'He's been spending all his time with Qasim, and with some other people whom I don't know very well. Vijay bhai, I think many of them are with the JKLF.'

'The JKLF!' Vijay's voice rose in outrage. 'That bunch of hijackers and woolly-headed fanatics? Has he gone completely insane? Have you tried to talk him out of this madness?'

'We've all spoken to him, Vijay bhai, but right now he's fully enthused by this new cause of his.' Sensing a faint hint of disloyalty in her own words, Yasmin rushed to qualify her remarks, 'I don't think Habib would ever do anything wrong, I just feel that he's been deeply influenced by Qasim and the others . . .'

Vijay held up a hand. 'You don't need to defend Habib to me, Yasmin. But I'd better meet him and kick some sense into him. My God, has he considered what this could do for his chances of getting into the IAS—they'll reject him out of hand.'

'That's what your father tried to tell him,' said Yasmin softly. 'There was the most terrible fight, Vijay bhai, and then your father ordered him to leave the house. He hasn't been back since.'

The row had sprung up over dinner at the Kaul household. Habib was full of his newly discovered grand plans for the conquest of the world, and had made the mistake of trying out some of Qureshi's jargon on Papa. He had got more than he had bargained for.

'Don't be more of a fool than you can help, Habib,' Papa had said crushingly. 'All young people dream, but this particular piece of nonsense could end up destroying your career and your life. If the police gets to know that you are hanging out with people like Qureshi, it will go into your record, and bang will go your chances of making it into the civil services.'

Habib had tried to defend himself. 'Papa, if our plans work out, then I could be one of the rulers right here in Kashmir. If our plans work out, then perhaps we could experience real power for the first time ever.'

Papa was scathing. 'So what do your wild friends think will happen? Are you expecting independence? Do you think India will get up one fine morning and walk out of Kashmir . . . or for that matter, do you think Pakistan will vacate its chunk of Kashmir?'

'Well, perhaps not,' Habib tried to hedge a little. 'Perhaps we could get some autonomy. But who knows, perhaps we will get full *azaadi*.'

'Oh, I see. So you think Kashmir will become independent. So tell me, son, what happens to the rest of India, where a hundred million Muslims will be looked at with suspicion and will be blamed by the Hindu right wing for a second partition of the country? What happens to us Hindu families who live in Kashmir? And finally, son, tell me what happens to a tiny independent Kashmir, with no resources of its own, no industry to speak of, and with insufficient grain to feed its people? Whose puppets will we be then?'

By this time Habib was starting to get angry himself, and he lashed out, 'That's not India's problem. And let me tell you, Papa, India will soon have to listen to us. There is already talk of guns entering the Valley, and if necessary the boys can drive the Indians out.'

A second mistake. And a big one.

'Guns? You are going to get guns into our Valley? You want to reduce my Kashmir to the level of an Assam or Sri Lanka? Have you truly gone mad, Habib, that you sit in my house and talk about guns? And whom are you going to drive out? Us? Will you come here with your guns and drive out Amma and me from Kashmir?' Papa rose from his chair, his hands shaking.

'Don't be ridiculous, Papa.' Habib was contrite now, as he tried to calm the elderly man. 'How could I ever do anything to hurt you?'

'You hurt me when you talk of bringing death into my Kashmir,' said Papa in a soft, tired voice. 'It's bad enough that the lunatic fringe talks like this, but when the madness enters our own homes, then it is time to worry for this land. Go away now, Habib, I would like to be alone.'

The food was congealing on the table, as Habib perfunctorily hugged Amma and stalked out of the room.

That was four months ago, and it was now left to Vijay to try and talk to Habib. That night Vijay lay for a long time under his quilt, unable to sleep. He reached out a hand towards the alarm clock which sat on the walnut side table. 'Shit. It's midnight already,' he said to himself, and gave up the struggle to fall asleep. He cautiously eased himself out from under the heavy bedclothes, gasping at the cold. Though a single-wire heater glowed in one corner of the room, it could do little to prevent the chill of the Kashmiri winter from filling the room.

'I must get Papa to fit a bukhari in my room,' Vijay thought, as he walked up to the windows of his room. The glass windows were open just a crack to allow some fresh air to come in, and the inner wire mesh was icy cold to the touch. His room was on the first floor, and he could see the lights on Shankaracharya Hill filtering through the leaves of the trees in the back garden. And then his eyes fell on a light shining in the window of a small one-room shack at the back of the garden.

'Ghulam Razzaq is still awake,' he thought to himself in delight. 'The old rascal hasn't yet given up his habit of staying awake till the wee hours.'

Vijay walked up to the foot of his bed and put on the heavy dressing gown which lay there, before sitting down to pull on a pair of thick woollen socks and leather slippers. In the garden the midnight wind hit him straight in the face and he half walked, half jogged across to the shack and rapped on the window sharply. There was an immediate answer; Ghulam Razzaq opened the door and smiled widely as he recognized his visitor.

'Vijay baba,' he beamed, unaware of the incongruity of using the diminutive for someone who towered fifteen inches above him. 'Come in quickly, you will freeze out there.'

Vijay plonked himself on Razzaq's bed, as the old man turned towards the little kerosene stove which was blazing away on a wooden table. 'Some tea, Vijay baba? I was going to make some for myself before going to sleep.'

Vijay nodded his assent, smiling fondly at the elderly man as he bustled around in his room. They had always been extremely close. Razzaq had functioned as Vijay's ayah, changing his nappies a dozen times a day. It was Razzaq who mashed the vegetables and cooked the *khichri* when the time came for Vijay to be weaned; Razzaq who dipped the fragile little body into a tub of hot water, soaping it under the armpits and down the back, smiling as the infant kicked his legs back and forth in the water, gurgling with delight at the splashing sounds.

On the nights when Amma was unwell, or if she had to go out, it was Razzaq who held Vijay against his shoulder, walking up and down the carpetted corridors, singing ancient Kashmiri love songs in a tuneless voice. Vijay made his first trip into the streets of Srinagar on the shoulders of Razzaq, clutching his hair firmly and drumming on his chest with two little feet to try and get him to go faster. Later, it was Razzaq who walked Vijay home after school, listening with great interest to his chatter.

Vijay accepted the cup of tea and grinned at the old man, 'Ghulam Razzaq, I've always told you not to have so much sugar. From what I can see, you don't have a single tooth left.'

Razzaq guffawed and shook his head, opening his mouth wide to point at a pair of yellowing fangs. 'Still got a couple.'

As they gossiped about the old days, Vijay jabbed Razzaq in the ribs. 'Do you remember the time you almost beat me to death?'

Razzaq looked hurt. 'It was only a couple of slaps. Besides, you deserved it.'

It had been a bitterly cold November, when Vijay and Habib were about eight years old. The lakes had begun to glisten with a veneer of ice, but the boys had been repeatedly warned that it was too thin and were forbidden from stepping on the ice.

That had done it. One Friday, while most of the elders of the neighbourhood had gone for namaaz, Vijay and Habib pulled out their cricketing gear and strolled out onto the surface of the small pond which lay just behind the house. Habib had the bat, and he met all deliveries sent down by Vijay right in the sweet spot, sending the ball crashing against the banks of the lake, hooting with delight and jeering at his friend's expression. An infuriated Vijay decided to take an extra long run up, and that was when it happened—a sharp cracking noise as the ice gave way under his feet, plunging him into the water.

'Through the grace of Allah, I hadn't gone to the masjid that day; for the first time in years, I had missed the Friday prayers,' remembered Razzaq.

He had heard the screams from the lake and had come running, dashing past the crying figure of Habib, who was crouched near the hole in the ice, trying to reach in to grab Vijay. Razzaq knew that the knife-sharp edges of the ice are often more dangerous than the cold, and he lay flat on the ice, reaching in gingerly to pull out the still figure bobbing in the frigid water.

And then he had gone running as fast as he could, clutching Vijay to his chest underneath his phiran, massaging the still body as he ran. He had gone straight to the house of a friend, where he knew that a *hammam*, or warm tub, was usually ready. Vijay was plunged into the hot water and his limbs were rubbed till he regained consciousness. Then he had tried to stand up, appearing little the worse for his experience. The disaster averted, Razzaq's concern had exploded into anger and he had given the boy the worst thrashing of his life. Habib had tried to escape, but Razzaq had caught him and given him some tight whacks as well.

Sipping his tea, Vijay squeezed Ghulam Razzaq's bony arm. 'Don't worry, old uncle, I forgive you.' Razzaq smacked his hand playfully, and then they were talking about the military academy, about Razzaq's only son, now working as a ward boy in Srinagar's main hospital, and about Habib.

'What is this new Islamic wave I'm hearing so much about?' asked Vijay.

Ghulam Razzaq spat eloquently on the floor of his hut. 'It's all these Bihari mullahs they got in some years ago, settling them here against all rules. They talk about the shariat, trying to tell us that Allah will be angry with us because of how we pray. They caught hold of me once, as I went to the *ziarat*, telling me that these shrines were un-Islamic.'

'What did you say?' asked Vijay.

Razzaq grinned wickedly. 'Look around you, I told them, look at the beauty of this Kashmir. Isn't this a place blessed by Allah? So how could He be unhappy with our methods of worship?'

Vijay laughed, and got up to return to his room. Impulsively, he pulled the elderly man into a tight embrace.

'It's good to see you again.'

The next morning Vijay went to Qasim's shop on Residency road. As he entered through the decrepit-looking doorway, Habib jumped up from where he had been sitting and rushed forward to hug him.

'Vijay, it's been too, too long. I'm so sorry that I couldn't come over yesterday, but I had to go to Sopore for some urgent work.' He dragged Vijay by the arm towards a pair of dusty cushions in the corner of the room. Vijay glanced across at the other occupant of the room, and they exchanged smiles devoid of any affection.

'Qasim. How are you?'

'Salaam aleikum, Vijay bhai. I hear that your uniform suits you well.'

Qasim fetched a couple of cups of tea and then addressed Habib. 'I'm off to Amirakadal for a while. Will you keep an eye on the shop?'

Without Qasim's baleful eye on his back, Vijay felt much more at ease and soon tried to bring up the subject which was eating him up. But Habib jumped in first, holding up a warning hand. 'Please, Vijay, spare me the lectures. I've already got an earful from Papa. Look, I know I have been a little out of line, and I am genuinely ashamed that I haven't been to see your parents in such a long time. But we are launching something new . . . something big . . .'

Vijay interrupted him in full flow. 'Habib, Yasmin tells me that you have contacts now with the JKLF loonies. For God's sake, tell me you aren't serious about this.'

'I'm not a member of the JKLF,' said Habib firmly, 'but Qasim is, and some of my other friends are. Vijay, you should meet some of these people . . .'

'All this talk of an armed struggle . . .'

Habib laughed, a little shamefacedly. 'I see you have heard all the stories. Look, all of that is a little over the top. I don't see any of us running around waving guns. But what we are doing—the big experiment I mentioned—is the formation of a rival political party. We will fight the assembly elections and, inshallah, win them. Then we can democratically rule in Kashmir and maintain our links with the rest of India.

So everyone will be happy, even Papa!'

'What new political party?' asked Vijay suspiciously.

'I have agreed to become a member of the Muslim United Front.'

Vijay half rose to his feet in dismay. 'The party of the mullahs! That's almost as bad as the JKLF—in fact it could well be worse. I can't believe that you have become a Jamaati.'

'No, Vijay,' said Habib quietly, 'I am not a Jamaati, you know my views on fundamentalism and on Pakistan. But there is no other way for us to express ourselves. Now that the National Conference has tied up with the Congress for the assembly elections, those of us who hate the Congress and all it stands for have nowhere else to go. And the MUF isn't just about the Jamaat; Lone sahib has joined us in Handwara, the Awami Action committee is supporting us in Srinagar, and thousands of secular people from the freedom . . . er . . . the secessionist movement are contributing what they can.'

'And you think this motley crowd can win elections? Put together I don't think all of them have won more than a handful of seats in the history of Kashmir.'

'True enough.' Habib nodded. 'The Jamaat itself has never got more than five per cent of the votes in any election. But this time could be different. Ever since you left the Valley, the call of Islam has been filtering down to the villages here; there is a new religious radicalism which is gripping many. You know that this isn't something that I would be happy about, but at least if people like me are in the MUF, we can try and steer the movement along secular lines.'

Vijay shrugged his shoulders. 'So tell me, how do you propose to win this election of yours?'

'Qasim has gone to an election meeting in Amirakadal— that is where I will be helping out. Why don't you come along and see what is happening?'

Vijay smiled wryly. 'With a name like Vijay Kaul I don't know how welcome I would be.'

'Don't be silly,' said Habib, leaping to his feet. 'If you want I can get you enrolled as a full member of the party.' He laughed at the expression on Vijay's face and thumped the big man on his back. And then they were laughing together; suddenly the years had faded away and they were once again the closest of friends with no barriers between them.

Habib signalled to the shop assistant to take over, and the two of them set off down Residency road towards Amirakadal. Vijay was surprised by the number of new shops which had sprung up along the road. And then he frowned just a little as he noted the growing number of women who were now in *burqas*; still a tiny minority but far more than just a couple of years before.

'All these girls in burqas,' he said in a stage whisper to Habib. 'That's a bit of a waste, isn't it—the scenery is certainly not as attractive as it was when I left!'

Habib shot a warning glance at him. 'For God's sake don't talk like that in Amirakadal. I'd hate to fish you out from the canal in this weather.'

It took them just a few minutes to reach Lal chowk. A short cut through a small side alley brought them to the banks of the canal, and a little further up was the bridge which gave Amirakadal its name. Habib walked confidently up to a shop festooned with the green colours and symbols of Islam and entered it, with Vijay just a couple of paces behind.

There were eleven men sitting inside, the candidate for Amirakadal and some of his key advisors. They were all slouched on a white sheet spread out on the floor, several ashtrays filled with cigarette butts scattered around them. The air was thick with blue smoke; clearly a long strategy session was in progress.

'Salaam aleikum, Yusuf sahib. I have brought my friend to meet you. This is Vijay Kaul.'

As Habib made the introductions, Vijay was conscious of a faint prickling at the back of his neck, tiny fragments of ESP doing a little dance under his collar.

In the years that followed, he would wish that he had a photograph of the gathering in that dingy room, even though the images of the men who sprawled there would always be vivid in his mind. He would tell himself a thousand times that if only he had known what would become of those men, he would have gladly donned a suit of dynamite and turned himself into a human bomb.

But all that Vijay felt that day was a vague unease. And with a smile on his face, he stepped forward to greet those who occupied the room.

Sitting in the centre of the group, his beetle brows raised in mild surprise at the intrusion, was a hefty figure with a thick nose and an even thicker beard. This was the candidate for Amirakadal, Mohammed Yusuf Shah. Four years later, he would rename himself Syed Salahuddin, before taking on the mantle of Supreme Commander of the Hizbul Mujahideen, the armed wing of the Jamaat and the top militant group in Kashmir. From a hideout in Pakistan-occupied Kashmir he would wage a relentless campaign of terror against the Indian security forces and against all those who opposed the diktats of the Hizbul Mujahideen. Later still, he would become the chief of the United Jihad council, the Pakistan-based confederation of leading militant groups.

To the right of Yusuf Shah, rising to his feet with traditional Kashmiri courtesy, was a frail young man. The two huge eyes on his thin, bearded face smiled at Vijay as Habib continued the introductions. 'This is Yasin Malik. Yusuf sahib wants him to be a counting agent.' Only a few years later, after training in Pakistan, Yasin Malik would be responsible for the first few acts of militant violence in Kashmir. Then, after several years in jail, he would become the supreme leader of the JKLF, receiving mass adulation from those who wanted complete independence. Later still, he would come to admire the methods of Mahatma Gandhi, and would set aside the gun for non-violent forms of protest.

'That's Javed Mir, he's the energetic one among us,' said Habib, pointing at a man with a three-day stubble, a pair of dark glasses dangling from his fingers as he leant against the wall looking out of the window at the busy crowds in the street outside. After Yasin Malik's arrest, Javed Mir would become the de facto head of the JKLF. At the height of the insurgency in 1990 he would be a Scarlet Pimpernel of sorts, eluding the security forces with ease and suddenly appearing at crowded rallies. Journalists would scramble in those years to try and interview him, travelling long distances in darkened cars or with blindfolds over their eyes.

Habib's voice went on. 'And that's Hamid Sheikh, sitting close to the bukhari as always—he's also helping us out.' The son of a simple cobbler, Hamid would become one of the movement's most charismatic leaders, before being killed in a shootout with the security forces.

There were other men in the room, very young, barely out of their teens. Several of them were friends of Yasin Malik, others were members of the Jamaat-e-Islami's youth wing. They all stepped forward to greet Vijay, and then the conversation turned smoothly back to the elections, which were now just weeks away.

Mohammed Yusuf Shah turned to Qasim who had perched himself on a sideboard. 'I want you to talk once again to Maulana Lateef. We must start using the mosques more effectively, it must become clear to all believers that a vote for the Muslim United Front is a vote for Islam and the Islamic way of life.' He then turned to another young man. 'You should take charge of mobilizing crowds for the Iqbal Park rally on the fourth. As all the MUF candidates are being presented before the people that day, it is very important that the crowds are large enough.'

As they returned home later that day, Vijay was in a thoughtful mood. 'How many seats do you actually hope to win?' he asked.

Habib shrugged his shoulders. 'Realistically? We are contesting forty-four of the sixty seats, we should win about twenty or twenty-five.'

'That few?'

'Well, it's a start. And it gives us a voice in the assembly.'

* * *

A couple of miles from Amirakadal, nestled at the foot of Shankaracharya hill in the high-security zone of Gupkar Road, was the residence of the National Conference leader, Farooq Abdullah, now back as chief minister after a settlement with Delhi. The mood here was far from sanguine. The latest intelligence reports indicated strong support for the Muslim

United Front in many areas as the traditional anti-incumbency sentiments of any Indian electorate found expression in support for the only effective opposition formation in the state. Till now voters always had a choice between the Congress and the National Conference. Now, with these two parties in alliance, the only other option was the MUF.

Farooq Abdullah's motorcade of well-polished white Ambassador cars screeched to a halt before the steel gates of the residence, which were quickly pulled open by two uniformed guards. Farooq Abdullah climbed out of his car, a dashing figure in his white kurta-pyjamas, tall and fair, with the hair beginning to disappear from the top of his head. He climbed up the flight of stairs which led from the driveway to the garden where other senior leaders of the National Conference were waiting for him.

He eased himself into a cane chair and pulled out a handkerchief to wipe his brow. It had been a dusty drive from his own constituency of Ganderbal, thirty kilometres to the north of Srinagar. Gratefully accepting a glass of water from a uniformed servant, he turned to one of his seniormost colleagues.

'So tell me, what is the latest feedback?'

Sheikh Nazeer, the party general secretary, answered, 'Well, it's almost certain that we will sweep the Jammu and Ladakh regions.'

Farooq Abdullah interrupted testily, 'Of course we will sweep Jammu and Ladakh. Tell me about the Valley.'

Nazeer shook his head mournfully as he spread a map of the state out on the table between them. 'We will certainly lose Sopore, Handwara, Idgah and Amirakadal. Brijbehara, Kulgam and Anantnag look dicey. And with three weeks still to go for polling, anything could happen.'

Another senior minister spoke up. 'I don't think we should panic. Even in the worst-case scenario they aren't going to get more than a dozen seats . . . and that's less than a fifth of the total seats in the assembly.'

'That's not good enough,' exploded Farooq Abdullah, 'we must step up our efforts, intensify our campaigning. We can't have a gang of fundamentalists in the Assembly. We can't have them preaching seccessionism and treason on the floor of the house, dressing up in their white robes and spouting pro-Pakistani garbage.'

Later that evening a group of young National Conference politicians gathered for dinner. A senior party leader walked up to two of them and put his arms around their shoulders. 'You know, we really must figure out how we can stop the MUF,' he said to them. 'There must be a way that you bright young men can think of,' he purred silkily. Nothing more was said. But the young men exchanged glances. Like the knights who killed Thomas Becket, they had received their cue.

*   *   *

The winter frosts lifted from the hills around Srinagar, the icy winds gave way to a soothing breeze tinged with the scent of far-off pine trees. The first leaves of spring began to show in the treetops, even as the cities and villages of Jammu and Kashmir came alive with the colour and noise of the election campaign.

Early in the morning, on election day, there was a knock at the front door of the Kaul residence, and a familiar stubbled figure entered the drawing room. 'Amma, are you there?'

Sunita entered the room, fresh from her morning prayers. 'Habib! Come in, beta, this is a pleasant surprise. Aren't you running off to the counting stations?'

'Polling stations, Amma,' Habib corrected her gently, as he bent to kiss her on the cheek. 'Yes, I'm on my way; voting begins in about an hour and a half. But I've never done anything major without taking your blessings, so here I am.'

Amma wisely refrained from commenting on what he was going to do, and contented herself with slicing an apple and thrusting it towards him. During Vijay's visit Habib had come over for dinner and there had been an awkward reconciliation between him and Papa. But plenty of unspoken words hovered in the air, and Papa had made it silently apparent that he still strongly disapproved of Habib's new political leanings. Since then Vijay had returned to Dehradun and Habib had only dropped in once, during lunch time when he could be sure that Papa was away at work.

Habib quickly drained the cup of tea that Razzaq had brought in and then rose hurriedly to his feet. Kissing Amma again, he muttered, 'I'd better be off. The others will be waiting for me.' Amma came to the door, and watched him disappear down the pathway leading to the road.

Amirakadal was full of flags, the red flag with a white plough of the National Conference, and the green flag of the Muslim United Front. Habib and the other volunteers sat behind a table near the polling booth, checking voters' names against a pile of dog-eared and scruffy typewritten sheets. Then they directed the voters where to go to cast their votes. Inside the polling station the voters had their fingers inked before being handed the ballot paper. There were several names on it, but only a couple really mattered.

By mid-morning, voting was proceeding smoothly in Amirakadal, but there were reports of trouble in other areas. An agitated young man came gasping up to Habib, 'We've just heard that Lone sahib's polling agents have been thrown out of booths in Handwara. There is massive rigging in many constituencies all over the Valley.'

Hamid Sheikh walked up to them, his face dark with anger. 'The bastards are trying to steal the elections. Well, they won't succeed here.'

But minor scuffles soon broke out, and disputes over who was a valid voter and who wasn't. The story was repeated in polling booths all over Kashmir, and that evening the whole of the Valley was tense as Muslim United Front activists huddled in small, agitated groups and analysed and re-analysed what the day's events could mean.

On counting day the tension flashed into open anger. As the counting exercise progressed, in what seemed to many a somewhat dubious fashion, a number of MUF candidates saw their hopes of victory disappear.

At the indoor counting centre where the votes for the Amirakadal constituency were being tallied, Habib and Hamid Sheikh were confronting the returning officer. 'You cannot allow this,' said Habib, his voice trembling with rage and frustration. 'This is cheating, and open cheating. You cannot allow those bogus votes to be counted.'

The returning officer looked at him firmly. 'Will you please allow me to do my work? If you persist in disrupting the counting I will be forced to expel all of you from the centre.'

Habib lost his temper in a spectacular fashion. 'Expel us? So that you can carry out your orders more easily?' His face was red, and his nose only millimetres away from that of the official, who responded by shoving him away. The next few minutes saw a confused scuffle and at the end of it Hamid Sheikh and Habib Shah found themselves in the tight grip of some sweaty policemen, being bundled off to the nearest police station.

They were thrown into separate cells and spent a considerable part of the next hour turning the air blue with abuse. Then they quietened down and slumped against the bars, watching other MUF activists being dragged in. It was a particularly filthy police station, the walls stained and unpainted, the floors caked with decades of accumulated dirt, and the smell of urine hanging thick in the air. A naked sixty-watt bulb hung from a frayed, crooked cord in the middle of the corridor, trying in vain to light up all the corners of their cells.

The shadows lengthened outside the tiny barred windows, and they knew that the verdict of the elections would have been announced by now.

'Here, take this. It's the last one,' said Hamid from his cell, as he rolled one half of a carefully divided unfiltered cigarette across the narrow pathway towards Habib's cell. Habib lit up and drew the smoke into his tobacco-starved lungs.

'How long are they going to keep us here?' he asked.

Hamid clenched his fists. 'They'd better keep us here forever, because if I get out . . .'

'Do you think any of our people have been allowed to win?'

'I don't know. Perhaps one or two.'

Habib finished his cigarette, drawing on it till the glowing tip began to scorch his fingertips, and then he stood up and rattled the bars. 'Bastards! Can we have some water? And some food?'

There was no response for several minutes. And then a door opened at the far end of the corridor and a couple of men walked down towards them, surrounded by a whole posse of policemen and security guards. Leading the group was the station house officer, the policeman in charge of the station. Just behind him was a short, dumpy man clad in a light blue kurta-pyjama, looking extraordinarily pleased with himself.

Habib hissed softly to himself as he recognized the senior National Conference leader. Across the corridor, Hamid Sheikh rose to his feet and gripped the bars tightly, his knuckles gleaming white in the dim light.

The politician stopped outside Habib's cell and turned to the SHO. 'Who are these specimens?'

The cop was standing at attention, as eager to please as a Labrador in the final obedience rounds of a dog show. If he could, he would have wagged his tail as he spoke. 'Sir, these are *goondas* from Amirakadal, sir. They were creating disturbance in the counting centre.'

The politician smiled slowly, as he turned to look at Habib in the eye. 'Ah, Yusuf Shah's *chamchas*. The Jamaat's flunkies. I see that they are finally where they belong.'

Habib said nothing, but continued to stare into the deep-set eyes in the plump face before him.

'I have good news for you boys. You have been soundly whipped—it's a landslide for us. A couple of seats, that's all you got. Now you know what the people really think of you . . . so why don't you run off home to Pakistan and leave all of us in peace?'

Habib spoke to the man for the first time, his voice low and thick with fury. 'You son of a whore. You may have robbed us this time, but we will be back. And we will bury you, and all those who are with you. You fucking arsehole, we will bury you.'

The politician's smile widened. 'Open the door,' he said to the SHO.

The SHO was visibly agitated. 'Sir, are you sure that is wise, sir?'

'Open the door, I said,' snapped the minister, and the intimidated SHO jumped as if he had been shot and scurried off to get the keys.

Surrounded by his gunmen, the minister entered the cell and walked right up to Habib.

'You'll bury us, will you?' His hand shot up and caught Habib squarely across the cheek, the rings on his fingers tearing open the skin in more than one place. Habib fell back, and then growled as he tried to hurl himself at the politician. But the security guards stepped in the way and caught Habib's arms, holding him in a tight grip.

'You will bury us, will you, you little piece of scum?' The other hand lashed out, striking Habib on the other cheek. 'You piece of shit, if we want we can have you cut into little pieces and thrown into the Dal.' The hands were now in constant motion, Habib's face snapping back and forth, while Hamid Sheikh shouted abuse from across the corridor. The guards forced Habib onto his knees, and the minister turned to the SHO, asking him to remove the belt from his trousers. Then the belt was flying through the air, hissing on its way down before wrapping itself around Habib's shoulders. 'Let this be a lesson, you turd, to you and your cohorts. Don't mess with us again.'

At a signal the security men let Habib fall forward onto his face, and the minister walked out of the cell. 'Where is his friend? I think he needs to learn some manners as well.'

Habib lay on the floor, his eyes filled with tears—not of pain, but of rage and humiliation. He struggled to get up, but gasped and fell forward again with a sudden stabbing pain in his side. Across the corridor he could hear the sound of the belt slapping into the body of Hamid Sheikh.

* * *

That evening there was an official dinner at the Centaur Hotel, nestled on a tiny promontory jutting out into the Dal Lake. While Habib and Hamid lay curled on the floor of their cells, Vijay's father, R.K. Kaul, struggled to get into a *bandgallah* coat which was now just a touch too tight around the neck, the years of easy living having endowed him with a couple of extra chins.

As a senior government servant in the state civil service, Papa was a pillar of the establishment. The election results should have pleased him, but as he finally won the battle to fasten the hook of the coat around his neck, his thoughts were sombre.

When news of the trouble during the counting had raced around Srinagar he had, at first, resolved to leave Habib to his own devices. But in the end he couldn't help himself and he had made a round of telephone calls to find out where Habib was. But there was no sign of the young man and no policeman seemed to know where he was being kept.

Papa slipped his feet into a comfortable pair of black shoes and walked downstairs, calling out to Amma as he did so, 'Come on, Sunita. We are really late, the chief secretary will be there before us if we are not careful.'

His wife emerged from her dressing room, stuffing a handkerchief and a tiny perfume bottle into a cloth handbag as she did so. 'Is the sari, okay?' she asked, checking her reflection in the mirror at the head of the staircase.

'Fine, fine, you look great,' said Papa with the automatic response of a man who has answered the same question every second day for thirty years. Then he bundled his wife into the waiting Ambassador car, before getting in himself. 'Centaur Hotel,' he told the driver and settled back in the seat, tugging at the collar of his coat, as if a few extra centimetres of cloth would miraculously appear if he tried hard enough.

Amma continued to rummage in her cloth bag, and then, without looking up, she asked softly, 'Is there any news of Habib?'

'No,' said Papa, abruptly and harshly. There were a few moments of silence before he went on. 'If that idiot wants to play with fire, if he wants to hang out with seccessionists and traitors, then there is nothing anyone can do.'

He gazed out of the car window at the lights of the Boulevard winking at the passing car, before repeating under his breath to himself, 'There is nothing I can do.'

At the dinner the mood was cheerful as National Conference ministers celebrated their sweeping victories. Papa kept to himself, sitting on a chair at one end of the room, periodically signalling to a waiter to replenish his glass and his plate of kababs.

A heavy figure dropped into the seat next to him. It was his minister, and though he didn't know it, the same man who had visited Habib and Hamid Sheikh in their cells a couple of hours earlier.

'So, Kaul, a great victory, *haan*? Now, inshallah, those Jamaati bastards know where they stand. They will never raise their heads again.'

'If you say so, sir,' replied Papa.

'If I say so?' the minister asked, raising his eyebrows. 'I'm a Muslim, you are a Hindu. Surely, you should be even happier than I am at what's happened to the MUF.'

There was silence for some time before the politician spoke again, impatiently. 'Well, tell me what you think. What's your problem?'

Kaul took a deep breath. 'My problem is that I think we sowed the seeds today for a very bitter harvest. The MUF would never have got more than a handful of seats. They would have got tiny crumbs of power, and in the end would have been seduced by the establishment as happens with political parties everywhere. The last remaining opposition to our accession to India would have faded away quietly. But now? I don't know.'

He paused and then stood up. 'Excuse me, sir, it's getting late. And it's cold outside.'

Chapter Eight

CROSSING THE BORDER

The summer of 1987 came to Kashmir like the fragrance of a million roses, as if the gods were intent on giving the residents of the Valley something to remember.

In the dark and dreadful decade that lay ahead, the people of Kashmir would look back on that summer often, holding the memory close to their hearts, waiting, hoping, longing for a change.

It was a summer painted by the sun in a hundred shades of gold. The soft light of dawn touched the treetops with a pale yellow gold, each leaf sparkling with its own highlights. In the mid-morning the brassy gold of the mustard fields waved at the farmers who rejoiced at the unexpectedly good harvest. And in the evenings the flaming red and gold of the sunset over the Dal brought lovers and honeymooners out in the shikaras for pleasure rides, and they sat back in their seats, trailing their hands in the water. It was the perfect experience in a perfect land.

The tourist rush was unprecedented; tourists came from all over the country and abroad. Every hotel room was booked, many times over; the houseboats were bursting at the seams; and the shopkeepers could not keep up with the demand.

And it wasn't just Srinagar that the holidaymakers thronged to. The streets of Pahalgam were crowded with trekkers heading up into the green valleys, on their way to places like Aru and Lidderwat. The rich Indian elite gathered in Gulmarg, staying in upmarket hotels and special government huts, sipping imported liquor before strolling out to the new golf course or walking up the mountain to Khilanmarg. For the more adventurous there were trips to Yusmarg, or, further out, to Sonamarg or even to Kargil, the gateway to India's little Tibet, Ladakh.

Habib had asked Yasmin to meet him at Pari Mahal, nestled high on a mountain overlooking Srinagar, just a few hundred metres away from the spot where they had first sat alone together. Yasmin had walked all the way up, and was just a little breathless when she entered the gates. 'I'm up here,' she heard Habib call, and she looked up to see him standing at the edge of the terrace just above her.

Yasmin huffed her way up the dilapidated steps and walked across to where Habib was standing right next to the parapet, gazing out at the city at his feet.

He heard her approach and turned to face her. 'Sorry, I'm late . . .' she began, but something in his eyes made her go silent, and she stepped back a pace. Then he spoke. 'Yasmin, I'm going across the Line of Control.'

Yasmin felt something turn in her gut. Then tears welled up in her eyes. 'No, Habib, no. I beg of you, don't do this.'

Habib reached out a hand, gentle and contrite. 'I'm sorry. Qasim has already left for Pakistan, another group is to follow soon and I have volunteered to be part of that group.'

By now she was sobbing freely. 'And what happens to me?'

Habib looked away. 'I don't know, Yasmin. I honestly don't know. I'm not sure that I have a future to offer you any more.' He paused, and looked straight at her. 'Maybe you should just try to find someone else.'

The slap left red and white imprints on his face, and his ears rang with the impact. Yasmin was trembling with rage. 'Find someone else? After I have spent the last four years of my life running around with you all over Srinagar? Who do you think will even look at me now?'

Habib reached out a hand, but she stepped back. 'Yasmin, try and understand what I'm trying to say . . .'

'Go to hell, you . . . you bastard.' The unfamiliar word tasted good on her tongue. Habib grabbed her by the arm. 'Listen to me,' he said but Yasmin turned her face away.

A couple of people had begun to stare at them with unconcealed interest, but neither Habib nor Yasmin could care less.

'Yasmin, you must know how much I love you—you are everything in the world to me. But what other option is there for us right now?'

'If your causes and friends mean so much more to you than I do, then I have nothing more to say. Just leave me alone . . . and . . . and . . .'

Habib tightened his grip on her arm, forcing her to look up at him.

'Yasmin, I *have* to go to Pakistan. You may not believe in the freedom movement the way I do, but at least try and understand what is driving me. I know that our nation . . . our people need me right now. What would you have me do?'

By now her anger had melted into desolation, and she was as vulnerable as a lost rabbit.

'I thought we were going to get married soon,' she said in a small voice.

Habib ran a hand through his hair. 'That's always been my dream too. You know that. I've wanted to marry you from the minute I saw you standing in that doorway, with that silly bag of shawls. But can't you see that I have nothing to offer you now? I don't know when I will be back, I don't know where the armed struggle will take us, I don't even know how long I have to live . . .'

Yasmin started sobbing again, and Habib pulled her to him, gently caressing the back of her head. 'Yasmin, I don't want you to spend your life waiting for me.'

Her voice was muffled against his chest. 'What other life do I have besides you?'

She pulled away and looked straight into his eyes. 'Tell me, Habib. What other life have I ever had? When have I ever known happiness except in these last few years?'

'Yasmin—' he tried to interrupt.

'No, you listen to me. All my life I have been alone. I managed, all by myself. Then you came, and I wasn't lonely any more. And now you tell me to be alone again? You say our people need you. What about me? Don't you think I need you too?'

There was nothing more to say, so Habib held her close to him. Groups of college girls walked by, tittering at the scandalous sight.

*   *   *

Habib's mind was made up, and three months later he slipped out of his house early one morning, a small knapsack on his shoulder and a bus ticket to Kupwara in his pocket. Yasmin came to the bus station to see him off, clutching a cheap dog-eared copy of a photograph they had once clicked together in a downtown studio.

'Take this with you,' she said, 'and look after yourself.'

Habib reached out his hand and gently touched her cheek. Then he turned and climbed into the filthy state roadways bus. It was a miserable vehicle, threadbare tyres supporting a suspension that had been knocked askew by a thousand potholes. The sides were dusty and stained in places with the vomit of young kids unused to high speed journeys through the hills. Habib found a place next to a window halfway down the bus, and settled into it, careful not to acknowledge Abbas, the second JKLF man who was making the journey, in the seat behind him. Then he heaved at the muddy window to open it, and, as the bus creaked out of the station, stuck his neck out to wave at the forlorn figure standing by the side of the road.

It was a long bus ride, punctuated by halts to refuel the bus and relieve full bladders. There was plenty of time to think, and to glance repeatedly at the photograph which he kept in his hand throughout the journey.

The highway from Srinagar to Baramulla was one of the best in the state, though that wasn't saying much. Just before reaching Baramulla the bus turned right to head for the border town of Kupwara, not far from the Line of Control, the de facto border between India and Pakistan. This was army territory, and they frequently got stuck behind long convoys of dark green one-tonne trucks ferrying men and equipment from one base to another. But at least the road, built by army engineers, was free of potholes.

It was late afternoon by the time the bus pulled into Kupwara. Habib and Abbas walked separately to another corner of the stand for the next leg, a minibus ride to the village of Trehgam, the main staging base for those who wished to cross the LoC.

Habib gazed in disbelief at the clattering and wheezing contraption which heaved itself tiredly upto the stand. With a wry smile at the driver, and a polite enquiry as to whether the bus would survive the mountain roads, he hurled his rucksack into the seat which had the least amount of stuffing pulled out of it by idle fingers. A few minutes later Abbas came and sat down next to him and pulled out the mandatory packet of cigarettes.

Outside their window the scenery changed by the minute. The sprawling mustard fields and languid chinar trees of the Valley were behind them, and they now passed through hillsides forested with pine, with cascading streams of water splashing alongside them or crossing the road to hurl themselves further down the mountainside.

Trehgam has often been called one of the most beautiful villages in Kashmir, and as they entered it in the early twilight of a mid-September evening, Habib and Abbas could see why. But their minds were on grimmer matters, such as looking for their host and guide, Asif Butt, a relative of Maqbool Butt, the Kashmiri secessionist who had been hanged by the government. Maqbool Butt was a man whom the separatists considered one of their earliest martyrs, and Trehgam was his home village.

Asif Butt was sitting on a ledge in front of a shop right next to where the bus came to a halt. He stood up as the two young men climbed out and ran a quick appraising look over them. No introductions seemed necessary. He led them down the street towards an unpaved mud track leading out of the village. They walked in silence through green paddy fields till they came to a two-storied stone house set amidst some trees. Two buffaloes grazed placidly in a straw enclosure right next to the house and three young girls were busy picking through a pile of grain which lay on a sack cloth in the courtyard. A small skeletal dog came yapping up to them and was quickly sent packing with a well-aimed kick. A couple of women came to the door of the house, but then retired in haste to the interiors.

The two men were led up the stairs to a huge room which took up most of the first floor. Thick rugs lay in one corner of the room, together with even thicker quilts. Then their host spoke for the first time. 'Rest here. You leave tomorrow morning for Pakistan and it is a long walk.'

He turned to leave the room, but stopped short and swung around again. 'If anything goes wrong, remember that you have never come to this house. And you do not know who I am.'

Asif Butt left Habib and Abbas to their quilts and their thoughts. A couple of hours later, dinner came up to the room, huge *thalis* of rice and mutton roganjosh. Asif Butt also joined them after a while.

'Which way will we go?' asked Abbas as he ate.

Butt glanced at him. 'Don't worry, your guide knows what to do.' Then he relented. 'But if you must know, you are going out through Athmuqam'

For one of the most troubled frontiers in the entire world, the Line of Control has always been remarkably porous. No matter what the Indian army tries, there always seems to be another pass through which militants sneak into India, another gap through which people can go across for training. And in 1987, the security forces weren't even paying too much attention.

The biggest problem that Habib and Abbas faced was the stiff climb up towards the mountain passes. Then they were through to Pakistani-controlled territory, and, after their guide had produced a coded slip of paper, to a warm welcome from the Rangers on the other side.

* * *

The next few days were a blur. Habib and Abbas were taken to Muzaffarabad in Pakistan-occupied Kashmir where they stayed at the Ayubi camp, run by the JKLF's Raja Muzaffar. Soon after arrival the newcomers were asked to take an oath of allegiance to the organization, swearing that they would gladly give their lives for the movement. Also present, smiling widely and trying to be as hospitable as possible, were a couple of Pakistani army officials.

For Pakistan, any hint of trouble on the Indian side of Kashmir was like manna from heaven. Since Partition, grabbing Kashmir had been the top priority of Pakistani foreign policy, the goal towards which all planning, all actions were geared. Kashmir was the one issue that could still unite all Pakistanis.

But so far, all efforts to get Kashmir had been thwarted. In 1947, and again in 1965, Pakistan sent in raiders and infiltrators backed by the army, hoping that the Muslims of the Valley would rise in support of the invaders and take their land into the welcoming arms of Islamic Pakistan. To their horror, on both occasions it was the local Muslims in Kashmir who had opposed the raiders, tipping off the Indian Army and helping it to counter the invasions.

The quest for Kashmir took on a new dimension after the 1971 Indo-Pak war. Months of brutal Pakistani repression of a separatist movement in what was then East Pakistan had come to a head when India intervened. The result was a brief war in which the Pakistani army was decisively defeated, and East Pakistan became an independent nation, Bangladesh. Ever since then, the determination to avenge the 1971 defeat was an article of faith in Pakistan. There could be no better way of doing that than by finally snatching Kashmir.

Four days after his arrival in Pakistan, Habib was taken to the capital, Islamabad, as a guest of the ISI. Then he and several others were transported to the adjoining city of Rawalpindi, where they were housed in a luxurious guest house complete with air-conditioners and TVs in every room. Abbas bounced on the fat mattress that graced their bed, 'Mashallah, these Pakistanis know how to treat their guests, don't they.'

Habib grunted. He had learnt to be a little more cynical. Soon enough, they had visitors, a well-built man in a green shalwar-kameez, who introduced himself as Brigadier Salim, accompanied by two others. They were all officers of the ISI.

The Brigadier clearly had decided that Habib was the more promising of the two men and directed all his remarks towards him. They exchanged pleasantries and notes on the popular mood in Kashmir. Then the Brigadier came to the point, after pulling out a packet of expensive imported cigarettes and offering one to Habib. 'I'm told that you are a member of the JKLF. A well-educated, articulate man like you? You could easily be heading your own group.' He smiled, then added, 'We can help you set it up if you like.'

Habib smiled back at the ISI officer, but the smile did not reach his eyes. 'You'll help me set up my own *tanzeem*? I assume you mean a pro-Pakistan group, not a pro-independence one like the JKLF?'

Brigadier Salim drew deeply on his cigarette, taken aback by the directness. 'Well, I think the point is loyalty to Islam. All the *Islampasand* groups do want to be with Pakistan, don't they? And isn't that what most of the Kashmiri people want, merger with Pakistan?'

The smile began to disappear from Habib's face. 'Brigadier Salim, what we are fighting for is self-determination. I have a quarrel with India right now, but that does not mean I am ready to be your slave.'

In later years, the Pakistanis would have little patience with groups like the JKLF which wanted independence from both India and Pakistan, but at that time they were ready to deal with anyone who could foment trouble in Kashmir. The Brigadier raised his hands in a gesture of peace, 'No, no, you misunderstood me. I have the greatest respect for the JKLF. We are your brothers, and we will help you no matter what your personal ideology is.'

But as he rose to his feet, he shot a brief venomous look at Habib, and then left the room. Two days later an ISI colonel arrived at the guest house to take the JKLF men to the training camp at Ilaqa-e-Gair, where they would learn all the basic tools of militancy.

As camps go, it was nothing much to look at, just three tents and a couple of instructors. But the Pakistani colonel who had driven them down assured them that the instructors were the best in the business. 'What Rashid can't teach you about an AK-47 doesn't deserve to be learnt,' he quipped.

At dawn the next morning, after namaaz, Habib and Abbas were led out towards a well-laid-out target range. On a rug in one corner was a small pile covered with a white cloth. With a dramatic gesture Rashid lifted the cloth to reveal a pair of AK-47s and spare clips of ammunition.

'These are yours, you can take them back to Occupied Kashmir with you. But first you must learn to look after them, as well as you would look after your own mothers.'

Habib gently hefted the rifle, caressing the smooth steel barrel glistening with a carefully applied coat of oil. It was the start of another love affair.

'They also come with wooden stocks, but we feel that these folding butts will be of more use in a place like Srinagar,' explained Rashid. 'Now watch while I take apart and clean the rifle. Neither of you will fire a single shot till you can do this with your eyes closed.'

The days passed quickly, hours spent firing shot after shot at the target—fifty rounds standing, fifty kneeling and fifty while lying down. Then the whole process was repeated with the selector set on burst fire, Rashid shouting from the side, 'Small bursts only. Get out three bullets at a time. You have to get a six-inch grouping.' Then the slow walk to the target to see exactly where the bullets were going and what they were doing wrong. And Rashid's voice saying, 'That's still not good enough. I think we will take another hundred shots.'

Then there were the other weapons. Examining grenades and throwing them with some accuracy was relatively easy. But mastering the revolvers proved surprisingly difficult. In ten seconds flat they had to snap open the chamber of a revolver, push in six rounds, and take a series of rapid shots at the cardboard cut-out of an Indian soldier impaled on a stake twenty feet away. Just when they seemed to be getting it right, Rashid would yell, 'Good, good. You are getting all your chest shots in. But what if the bastard has a bullet-proof jacket on? Try for head shots now. All six bullets in the head area.' And so it went on, day after day, week after week.

As the training came to an end, there was a brief trip to Darra, close to Peshawar in the North West Frontier Province. In that crowded chaotic town Habib and Abbas stared open-mouthed at the lavish spread of machine guns and rocket launchers scattered all over the arms bazaar as if these were nothing more unusual than rice and potatoes. Young boys tugged at their shirtsleeves, trying to lead them to their stalls, and shopkeepers thrust AK-47s into their hands, inviting them to test-fire the weapons into the air.

All around them other shoppers were doing just that and the barrage of gunshots almost deafened them. Habib ran a longing hand over a grenade launcher. 'How much?' he asked, and shook his head with some regret when the shopkeeper quoted a price of a lakh and a half rupees. For now, he would have to settle for the arms given to him by the ISI.

Two months later, as the first sprinkling of snow started to frost the mountain tops, a small group of men slipped into India through a mountain pass barely two hundred yards from a hut where a group of Indian army soldiers warmed their hands over a hissing kerosene stove.

Habib Shah, Pakistan-trained militant, was back in his homeland.

Chapter Nine

INTO FLAMES

They met in the cafeteria of Srinagar's leading hospital, a grim and murky room dotted with Formica tables and badly designed plastic chairs. The manager of the café, standing behind his chipped mosaic counter, all but bowed and scraped as they entered the room, and the solitary waiter rushed to mop the table, spreading the tomato ketchup stains evenly all over the table.

The men took their chairs, pulled off their dark glasses and began chatting comfortably. The tea, soft drinks and *pakoras* arrived quietly on the table; no one had to ask for them.

The men were all young, barely in their twenties, and they had the arrogance of unchallenged, easy authority stamped all over them. These men were the new rulers in all but name.

Can a land really change as much as Kashmir did in the two years between 1987 and 1989? While the government dithered and muddled along, power slowly and steadily shifted from the state to 'the boys'. No one quite knew who they were, and they rarely appeared in public. But their names were whispered excitedly at home, and legends were woven around their often apocryphal exploits.

Through carefully planned acts of terror and constant, clever propaganda the boys had weakened the resolve of the government to govern and the willingness of the Kashmiri people to be governed.

Habib Shah leant back in his chair and sipped his Limca.

Around him were the other members of the inner council of the Jammu and Kashmir Liberation Front, men often known by the collective acronym of their names as the HAJY group. Like Habib, they had trained in Pakistan and were now getting ready to reap the fruits of the years of preparation.

Then Habib looked across the table and his expression soured a little as he saw the unlovely and unshaven face of Shakeel Zaidi, who was, in his considered opinion, the biggest son of a bitch ever planted upon this earth. Zaidi was picking his nose. He twisted his finger further into his nostril and grinned insolently back at Habib. He couldn't care less what the JKLF man thought of him because he was there as a special guest, as the representative of the armed wing of the Jamaat—the Hizbul Mujahideen.

More pakoras were brought to the table, and then the waiter was imperiously waved away. Habib spoke up. 'Zaidi, were those acid attacks on the unveiled girls really necessary?'

Zaidi rolled his eyes and turned to Hamid Sheikh who was reaching out for yet another pakora. 'Not again. Can you once and for all explain to our so called secular friend here that the Islamization drive is a crucial and integral part of the movement? I'm sick of trying to convince this man that we will never be able to stir up our people enough if we don't use religious fervour.'

The JKLF commander-in-chief, Ashfaq Majeed Wani, held up his hand to silence Zaidi. 'Shakeel, we all agree with that. We've all backed the cleaning up of the video parlours and the liquor shops. But I have to agree with Habib; attacking young girls and throwing acid in their faces isn't going to do much for our image.'

'Bullshit. The whores must and will learn the words of the shariat. If we want Nizam-e-Mustapha in this land, it is never too early to show the people what that means. We will fight all perversions, and all those who oppose the laws of Islam.'

Habib's fingers were beginning to twitch. 'It's very easy to fight teenaged girls, isn't it?'

Zaidi smiled amiably across the table at him. 'I don't see you doing much fighting, Habib Shah. What's the matter, my secular friend? Is it the years of association with the kaffirs or is it something else?'

Ashfaq held back Habib with a restraining hand just before he leapt to his feet. 'There is no call for that, Shakeel. We will all need each other before the struggle is over. We are here to discuss the plans for August 15th, can we please stick to that?'

With one final sneer at Habib, Zaidi joined the JKLF leaders in planning the campaign for a total blackout in the Valley on the Indian independence day. But Habib remained aloof, sitting back in his seat silently, while his mind raced.

Ever since he returned from Pakistan, Habib's brain and organizational skills had taken him to the top of the JKLF hierarchy. The 1987 election campaign had shown the HAJY group that he was a man who could be trusted, and they gave him the responsibility of planning and controlling the inflow of arms from Pakistan. JKLF men inside Pakistani territory would get arms supplies from the ISI, or would buy them in the open market at Darra. Then they would hand the weapons over to Habib's special guides, who would ferry them across the Line of Control.

Habib had organized a network of sympathizers who would cache the weapons at locations close to the border and then distribute them all over the Valley. By now Habib had ensured that every major neighbourhood in the larger cities like Srinagar had its own cache of arms, most of them well hidden in lofts and attics.

Habib also planned the regular flow of young men to Pakistan for training, and helped with larger questions of strategy and policy.

What he had never done was take part in any actual violence, or in the bomb blasts that had begun to tear apart the veil of normalcy that still hung over the Valley. But Habib was an ambitious man, and his sights were already set on the leadership of the entire movement.

'I'll have to get my hands wet,' he thought to himself, waving for another soft drink. 'I'll never have the authority I need if I don't.' A picture of torn and bleeding bodies flashed

in his mind, and his stomach heaved and beads of sweat came
out on his forehead. Ashfaq glanced at him curiously, but then
turned his attention quickly back to the plans on the table.

Habib waited till the meeting was over and Zaidi had left
the cafeteria. Then he turned to his associates. 'It is time now
for the first of the killings. I think we should strike soon after
August 15th, and I would like to be the man who carries out
the operation.'

Ashfaq stared at Habib, and then smiled. 'Don't tell me
you have allowed Zaidi to rile you.'

'It's got nothing to do with Zaidi,' said Habib. 'I have to
get out into the streets too. The rest of you have done so, you
have all taken part in the operations. Now it is my turn.'

The others looked at each other and then nodded their
agreement. All that was left was to decide on the target and
on the method of the strike.

*   *   *

Habib sat in a little tea shop a few hundred feet away from
Khan ka Mohalla three weeks later, feeling decidedly unwell.
He had spent the night tossing and turning in a restless half-
sleep as strange, disturbing visions crowded his mind. He had
woken up with the taste of vomit at the back of his throat,
and had rushed to the toilet to try and throw up, but had only
been able to retch drily into the sink. Then the diarrhoea had
begun. The nervousness and tension turned his stomach to
water, and he had sat hunched up miserably on the pot for
what had seemed like hours.

The recollection made his stomach twitch again, and he
hastily forced himself to think of other things, as he reached
into his pocket for a cigarette. He had been chain-smoking
since morning, trying to calm himself down.

'Take it easy,' said the man sitting across him. 'You know
what they say, the waiting is the worst part.'

Habib forced a smile to his lips. 'No, don't worry. I'm
fine, it's just that I seem to have got some sort of a stomach
bug.'

'It's nervousness,' said his companion. 'Just before I bombed that bus, I thought I was going to shit myself into an early grave.'

Habib looked out of the tea shop at the crowds on the street. It was early afternoon. They had been waiting for the target for over two hours now. Shaukat Haldani was one of the National Conference's most senior leaders in Srinagar, a man of towering personality who had been one of the biggest thorns in the flesh for the fundamentalists and separatists. The JKLF had decided to kill him as the first in a series of assassinations aimed at frightening all opposition to the insurgency into silence and acquiescence. In those days politicians in Kashmir had hardly any security and most of them made easy targets. Habib's plan was to get Haldani as he went for his customary afternoon stroll, alone, through the market place which lay just outside his house.

As he reached out to stub his cigarette out in the ashtray, Habib could feel the comforting weight of the AK-47 which lay across his knees, under the phiran. The previous night he had knelt on the rug in his basement, cleaning and re-cleaning the weapon till it shone and sparkled in the candlelight. But he still felt a momentary flash of panic as he wondered whether he had remembered to fully reload the magazine.

The twitching in his stomach was getting worse, and he gave up the fight to control it.

'I'll just be back,' he said, standing up carefully, ensuring that his weapon wouldn't suddenly become visible. And then he hurried to the shopkeeper, asking him whether there was a toilet nearby. The portly gentleman manning the counter continued to count his cash as he gestured with a thumb towards the back entrance. Habib scuttled out, and found the tiny one-room shack which contained a stained white ceramic hole in the ground. He almost gagged at the stench, but then placed the rifle in a corner and squatted thankfully over the hole.

'I knew assassins are often full of shit, but this isn't what I had in mind,' he thought wryly to himself in a momentary flash of humour, as the water ran from his bowels.

There was a sudden rapping on the door. 'Habib, I think he's coming. Get out of there.'

Habib pulled up his trousers and grabbed the AK-47, all nervousness forgotten as the training came to the fore. The two of them eased out of the tea shop and positioned themselves in the street outside, waiting for their target to approach.

'I'll take him,' said Habib, and the other man glanced at him and nodded, before reaching under his phiran to take out a black handkerchief with which he covered the lower part of his face.

Habib noticed what he was doing and spoke sharply, 'Forget the mask. We have nothing to be afraid of.'

As Habib waited for Haldani to approach, time slowed down, but he felt no anxiety, and he marvelled at just how confident and calm he was suddenly feeling. The seconds ticked away, and Habib waited patiently till Haldani was just a few yards away before he stepped forward, pulling out the gun from underneath his phiran.

In the last moments of his life Shaukat Haldani did not flinch. He recognized death standing before him, and he looked straight into Habib's eyes as his fingers closed on the trigger. The bullets slammed into the politician's body, the impact lifting him off his feet and throwing him heavily on the pavement.

Lying spreadeagled on the concrete, his fingers twitching, the dying Haldani looked up at Habib and began to whisper something. Habib wasn't quite sure what he was saying, though he thought he could recognize stray phrases from the Quran. Then, as if he was very tired, Haldani closed his eyes and was still.

A splattering of blood had hit Habib's face, and he wiped it away angrily. The look in Haldani's eyes had burnt its way into his mind, and he knew he would carry the memory with him for the rest of his days.

He turned to look around him and realized with some surprise that only a few seconds had passed since he had whipped out the gun.

Pedestrians had begun to run for cover, trying to get as far away as they possibly could. A couple of shopkeepers, thinking fast on their feet, started hauling in the goods which normally lay spread out on the pavement, waiting to trip up unwary shoppers. As soon as they had brought all the merchandise in, they pulled down the corrugated steel shutters. They would swear the next day that they had been at home, ill with the flu.

Habib turned his back on the body and slowly, deliberately began to walk away. Everyone present on the road had seen his face clearly; that was good, it would add to the aura Habib wanted around himself. The other killer in the hit squad had already walked off in a completely different direction, and the JKLF lookouts posted all along the road had melted away quietly.

The action over, Habib's hands had begun to shake, and he tightened his grip on the AK-47 which was once again nestled against his belly, under the phiran. He suddenly became aware of a strange taste in his mouth and realized with disgust that while wiping his face he had deposited some blood between his lips. He gagged a little and spat repeatedly on the pavement, but kept walking unhurriedly till he reached the safehouse, a shop run by a JKLF sympathizer.

Qasim was waiting for him inside together with other JKLF activists and they embraced him before kneeling together to give thanks in prayer. Afterwards, they got for him a strong cup of tea, which Habib sipped gratefully. He was feeling just a little lightheaded, and the conversation was swirling around him without making too much sense.

The killing replayed itself perfectly before his eyes, again and again. Suddenly he started, as he realized what he should have done but hadn't.

'It's still not too late,' he said, almost to himself, turning to the shopkeeper to demand a pen.

Half an hour had passed since the killing, but no one had touched the body of Haldani as it lay on the pavement, the blood slowly trickling into the gutter. Most shutters were down by now, but in the street corners and side alleys the residents of the area had gathered to chatter excitedly about what had happened, flocking at a safe distance from the body like so many nervous vultures.

Conversation came to an abrupt end as the thin figure of Habib Shah returned to the street, accompanied by Qasim and two others. Habib walked with measured steps right up to the body and bent down to place a placard on it.

Then, without even looking at the stunned audience, he turned and walked away with the same measured gait. A local *paanwala* gathered enough courage to scurry up to the body, and to read what was written on the placard.

It said, in Urdu script, 'Traitor to Kashmir.'

The police arrived soon afterwards. So did the paramilitary forces and several leaders of the National Conference. They picked up the torn body and carried it away, before going to every house and every shop with questions about what had happened. But no one had seen anything. No one had heard anything.

* * *

For the JKLF, it was an evening for celebrations, and Habib was the hero of the hour. The HAJY group and other sympathizers gathered in the house of a prominent lawyer in Zainakadal. There was much rejoicing and talk of future exploits as succulent kababs were roasted over a coal fire. There was, of course, no alcohol of any sort.

Qasim took Habib aside. 'You cannot return to your own house now, perhaps not for several months. It was brave to spurn the masks but there is now the danger that someone at the market could betray you. Our lawyer friend has very kindly agreed to let you stay right here if you want. The other choice is to send you out of Srinagar—perhaps to Sopore or to Budgam.'

Habib shook his head. 'No, I would rather stay on here, if there is no inconvenience.'

The lawyer had joined them by now, and he smiled widely, 'No, no. It will be an honour.' He was one of the growing number of professionals who had begun to support the movement and were offering their services in any way possible. The top leadership already included doctors, engineers, and more than a few government servants.

After dinner Habib was ushered into a luxurious guest bedroom with walnut wood floors covered with exquisite silken carpets. Right next to the bedroom was a small glass-panelled sun room, the perfect place to soak in the sun on winter mornings.

After his hosts retired for the night, Habib sat in the sun room for a long while, alone with his thoughts. He thought of the movement, now slowly beginning to gather momentum towards triumph. He thought of the other obstacles that would have to be removed in the months to come—men in positions of power who would need to be killed. He thought of the possibility of being caught and the fate he would then suffer at the hands of the army. He recalled the expression in those eyes, the feel of the gun in his hand, and the taste of blood in his mouth.

As the endless night dragged on and the stubs piled up in the ashtray before him, his mind roamed uncontrollably into other areas, to memories that had been locked up deep inside his consciousness.

He thought of his life as it had once been, the carefree, relaxed life of one of the Kashmiri elite, a life of warm winter evenings in carpeted rooms and picnics in the summer at Pahalgam. He thought of the man who had once been his closest friend, and the family he had considered his own, now separated from him forever by what he had done that day.

But above all, his mind came back again and again to a young girl standing silently at a bus stop; to a pair of grey eyes, still and peaceful in moments of love as the deepest of lakes, or dancing with mischief and laughter like the snow-fed springs at the onset of summer. He remembered the way she would smile when they met after a few days, dimpling delightedly at him before looking away in momentary awkwardness. In his mind he caressed her hair, smoothing away the strand which always hung untidily over her left eye.

He remembered the thousands of little confidences, the talks about everything and nothing, the moments when he had laid himself bare as before no one else in his life. And as he raised the cigarette to his lips, he realized with some surprise that his cheeks were wet.

Habib hadn't spoken to Yasmin since the day he climbed onto the bus to go across the Line of Control. Occasionally he would watch her from afar when she left her home in the morning and headed for the new store she had opened, a small room on the Bund where she had on display shawls and some carpets. And he had asked Qasim to meet her once in a while to ensure that she was all right.

'I've tried to keep away,' he whispered to himself in the dark. 'But I can do so no more. I need her, I need her so much.'

*　*　*

In the heart of Srinagar there is a paan stall, strategically located close to the main colleges. In the days of peace this was a spot cherished by all students, the place where young men would sit together and talk, waiting for the girls to head home from their colleges. Then the separate groups of boys and girls would start walking close together, voices raised just a little higher than necessary, pitched to attract attention. This was the perfect spot for two young people to casually bump into each other, slipping notes to each other or whispering the time and location of the next secret rendezvous. Now, of course, all of that had changed; under the tyranny of the new hardline Islamic code few youngsters would dare to court openly.

Yasmin walked purposefully past the paan stall, barely noticing the man with large dark glasses sitting on the pavement. She didn't even notice when he got up and followed her, waiting for a thinning of the crowd before he spoke. And when he did she stopped in her tracks and forgot, for a minute, to breathe.

'Yasmin, it's me,' said the voice just behind her. 'Don't react now, keep walking.'

It took an almost superhuman effort for her not to swing

around and run into his arms. She walked on, and Habib followed a couple of yards behind.

'Can you return to the house in half an hour? I will meet you there.'

Yasmin nodded and kept walking. Soon she sensed that Habib was no longer following her, and the feeling of loss was almost physical in its intensity. She reached the shop and gabbled quick instructions to the salesman before pleading illness and heading home again.

She let herself in, and then checked to see that her grandmother, Hamida, was safely in her room. The old lady rarely left her room these days, spending hours praying and reading the Quran. Her only other major interest was in the kitchen; she was still fond of her food and usually prepared their meals.

Yasmin left the front door open a crack and waited for Habib to arrive. When she heard the creaking of the wooden steps leading into the house, she flew to the door, her heart thumping loudly. He was standing there, a little thinner than she remembered, with deep dark lines underneath his eyes. The beard was gone, though he had allowed his hair to grow a little and it curled over the tips of his ears. There was something else very different about him, but she couldn't quite put her finger on it. Something about the way he carried himself, the air of seriousness which surrounded him.

Yasmin took in all this in a couple of seconds, before gently reaching out a hand to lead him into the house and then through the central hall into her room. It was cluttered, as always, with stray cloth and shawl samples. And with all the vanities of a young woman: lipsticks and kohl pencils lying on the dressing table, and copies of *Stardust* piled up next to the bed.

Then she turned and looked up at him again. The dark circles were still there, but his eyes were softening and smiling at her, the tension which weighed on him lifting by the second. Not a word had been spoken yet, and there would be silence for a while, as they moved towards each other and hugged the years of separation away.

Behind them the curtain moved as Yasmin's grandmother peered into the room. Her lips parted in shock and she was about to say something sharply, but then she stopped herself. Hamida was seventy years old and had lived her life according to a very different, very strict code. But she adored her granddaughter, who had been her entire universe ever since the rest of the family passed away. They had never spoken about it, but she had been fully aware of Yasmin's pain over the past two years. And so she quietly let the curtain drop and slowly walked back to the Quran in her own room.

*　*　*

The killings increased throughout the autumn, blood splattered over more and more streets as the militants systematically tried to either eliminate or intimidate all who opposed them. But it still wasn't enough, and the militants knew it.

'One act, that's what we need. One act which will shatter the myth that freedom can never be ours. One act which proves to our people that India can be defeated,' fumed Habib as he paced back and forth in the hospital cafeteria, warming his hands on a cup of black coffee. The others looked up at him wearily. They had been through this a hundred times.

Habib pulled back his chair and sat down heavily, reaching moodily for some chips. 'Look at the pictures they are showing on television. Romania going free, boundaries collapsing all over Europe. It's a new world, and it will take very little for our people to believe in the possibility of azaadi. But we need that one act.'

Qasim was standing at the window, his hands thrust deep into the pockets of the down jacket he had on. It was a miserable December; the night seemed to come down ever earlier than usual, reaching malevolently through cracks under the doors to send little tendrils of cold stabbing at exposed skin. A solitary heater glowered dully in one corner of the room, as if aware that it couldn't really make much difference to the temperature in the room.

The door leading into the main hospital corridor swung

open and a tall distinguished-looking man entered. He was one of the city's best-known doctors, and a leading ideologue of the movement. Today he seemed both excited and alarmed at the same time.

'Have you all heard the news?' he asked, going on quickly as he registered the blank expressions of the men in the room. 'The new Indian cabinet has been announced—Mufti Mohammed Sayeed is the Home Minister.'

Qasim spat out an obscenity and thumped his fist against the wall. A Kashmiri Muslim had just become one of the most powerful men in India, in charge of all internal security. It was a symbolic gesture that could have an enormous impact on the people of the Valley.

'Bastards! This could be a masterstroke,' said Qasim, thumping the wall once again.

They were all speaking at once, waving their arms in agitation. Then Habib raised his hand and there was silence.

'I'm not so sure,' he said evenly. 'I think this could be what we have all been waiting for.'

Everyone turned to him for an explanation, and Habib leant forward and began to speak quickly and insistently. And the worried looks on those around him slowly fell away.

*   *   *

Six days later, at 3:25 pm on 8 December 1989, a young woman walked out of the Lal Ded Memorial Women's Hospital in the heart of Srinagar and crossed the road to wait for the minibus which would take her home. The bus was just a little late, and as she waited, she glanced at the watch on her wrist and tapped her foot impatiently.

From his position at the window, Habib saw the girl as soon as the bus took the corner and approached the bus stop. He turned to his companions and nodded his head, taking a deep breath to try and calm his stomach. The girl climbed in, as she did every single day, smiled at the driver, and found a vacant seat for herself.

The JKLF men had spread themselves throughout the bus, and two of them were in the front, blocking the exit. At a signal from Habib the guns were pulled out and the driver was told where to go.

Habib got up and walked up to the girl, whose face was beginning to show her terror as she understood what was happening. 'Dr Rubaiya Sayeed? Don't worry, you are now a guest of the JKLF. We will not harm you in any way, but we need you to come with us now.'

Soon the helpless and frightened twenty-three-year-old daughter of the new Home Minister of India was whisked from the minibus into a blue Maruti car. It was a long drive from Srinagar to the town of Sopore, a traditional militant stronghold where the JKLF planned to hold Rubaiya. But there were no roadblocks along the way and hardly any presence of the army or the police. Rubaiya was taken straight to the house of a government official who was a JKLF sympathizer. She would be kept here for a day and then shifted to another secure location.

Incredibly, it would be hours before anyone even realized that the Union Home Minister's daughter had been kidnapped. Dr Sayeed had earlier refused all security, and abductions were unheard of in Kashmir at that time. The first indication of what had happened came only after the kidnappers called a newspaper office.

Habib, Yasin Malik and Ashfaq Majeed Wani had stayed behind in Srinagar to coordinate the negotiations. Their list of demands was clear: freedom for five captured militants, including their old associate Hamid Sheikh.

In Delhi the white Ambassador cars of ministers and bureaucrats began to line up in front of the Akbar Road residence of Home minister Mufti Mohammed Sayeed, a man who was visibly shaken, and content for the moment to let the experts handle the job of getting back his daughter. There was panic and disbelief all around. If anyone had paused to think carefully they would have realized that there was no real danger to Rubaiya Sayeed. Many in Kashmir were unhappy with the kidnapping of a young girl and there had already been severe condemnation, notably from the Mirwaiz of Kashmir, Maulvi Farooq. There was little chance that the militants would have dared to actually harm her.

But the government in Delhi at that time was one of the most spectacularly incompetent that India has ever been blessed with, and the ministers dispatched to Srinagar to tackle the crisis were perfect representatives of that government.

One of those ministers, a man who would one day be Prime Minister of India, piped at the police chief in his gravelly voice, 'What is at stake here is the life of a young girl. How can you allow harm to come to her?'

The security experts at the special meeting that had been called at the Chashme-Shahi guest house wrung their hands in despair. 'Sir, with respect, nothing will happen to the girl. The kidnappers are already under pressure from those who consider the act unIslamic. We have already received feelers from the negotiators that the JKLF wants a face-saving way out of the crisis.'

'Nonsense. We have heard the JKLF repeating its threats to kill her, and that's not a chance we are willing to take.'

One of the special security advisors who had been flown in from Delhi to deal with the crisis leant forward and said patiently, 'Sir, if you bend before the terrorists even once, they will strike again and again. You will send a message to the people of Kashmir that terrorism does work—and I guarantee you that the terrorists will use any climb down by you to launch huge celebrations all over the Valley.'

It was like talking to a brick wall. 'The negotiators have told us that the militants have promised not to hold any celebrations. No one will even come to know that the prisoners have been released. You see, the life of a young girl . . .'

'And of course the fact that she is your Cabinet colleague's daughter has nothing to do with it,' thought the advisor bitterly, but wisely kept his thoughts to himself. The minister was not someone who took kindly to dissent, no matter how sensible it was.

The meeting broke up for lunch, and the ministers spoke at length to the chief minister, Farooq Abdullah, who reluctantly accepted the decision of the Central government.

On 13 December 1989, Hamid Sheikh walked free from the Shoura hospital where he was being treated, together with four other top militants. Two hours later, after some highly tense moments for the government, Rubaiyya Sayeed was also freed.

* * *

Habib gazed in awe at the scene at Bohrikadal in front of him. It was as if a dam had been broken, and pent-up emotions were flowing freely down the streets.

It was barely two hours since the news of the release of the militants had come in, and half the population of Srinagar seemed to have come out into the streets to celebrate. The great Indian government had been defeated. The boys had won. Now Romania would be repeated in the Valley; independence was around the corner. So the people danced in the streets, and shouted all the separatist slogans, because now they knew that this was the winning side.

Habib turned to grin at Hamid Sheikh as he blinked in a somewhat bemused fashion at the crowds. 'I think they want you out there. Go on, here's your five minutes of glory, and then we better get you out of here to safety before they try to arrest you again.'

They gunned the scooters they were sitting on and headed into the crowd. Ashfaq pulled out a pistol and fired a few shots into the air. Those standing around them jumped, but then the cheering grew even louder. One semi-hysterical man jumped onto the top of a parked bus and shrieked at the top of his voice, '*Nara-e-takbir.*'

'*Allah-o-Akbar*,' came the response from tens of thousands, the mob pulsing back and forth like some giant amoeba, no longer seeming as if it was composed of individual human beings.

Another man took up the chant, dancing like a dervish as he pulled at the front of his phiran as if he meant to tear it into shreds. Then he screamed a new slogan: 'Indian dogs go home.' And the amoeba changed voice, shouting along with him.

Hamid Sheikh stood up on the seat of the scooter. If the bullet injury which had put him into hospital still bothered him, there was no sign of it right now. He held up his hand and made the 'V' sign which had come to symbolize the movement, and the crowd went wild. By now four or five slogans were being simultaneously shouted, and the net result was wave after wave of incoherent noise.

Their job done, the ministers from Delhi were heading towards the airport to catch the plane which would take them home. As their motorcade sped through the streets of Srinagar, they must have noticed the celebrations, but they said nothing to each other. Some of the cars escorting them were caught up in the crowds and the drivers were forced to contribute towards the victory party.

Habib tapped Hamid Sheikh on the shoulder and gestured to him to head towards the safe house. The scooters began to weave their way out of the Bohrikadal square, but it was quite a task, with hundreds of excited men trying simultaneously to pat them on the back or just touch them.

They roared down the street and pulled up after a few minutes next to a car that would take them to a safe house. As he sank back in the upholstered seat, Habib smiled happily, 'I still don't believe it. Look at all those people!'

Qasim grunted darkly from the front seat. 'Yes, its great. But we will have to keep at it now every day. We can't allow this momentum to slip, every single day we must get thousands out on the roads.'

'I know. But it won't be difficult now. The people believe now that they can take on India and win. And that's all we needed.' Habib leant forward and tapped the driver on his shoulder. 'I'll get off here.'

Then he turned to Qasim, 'I'll head back to my room at the hospital. I'll meet up with the others later in the evening. You take Hamid to the hiding place.' Qasim nodded and Habib embraced Hamid Sheikh one more time and then slid out of the car. Within minutes he melted into the crowds that continued to throng the roads and walked towards the hospital, listening with a singing heart to what the voices were saying all around him.

Before long he reached the hospital compound and slipped along the boundary wall towards his room. The hospital had long been a meeting ground for the separatists and a junior doctor had offered Habib the use of his hostel room as a hiding place. The other inhabitants of the floor had learnt to ignore his presence, but this time many of those who passed him on the staircase flashed him a quick smile. One or two made as if to speak, but then thought better of it and carried on down the steps.

Habib turned the key in the wooden door and entered the room, switching on the white fluorescent tubelight as he did so. He had taken pains to ensure that the room looked like that of any hostel resident, thick medical tomes piled on a dusty writing table, pens and pencils clustered in a wooden glass next to a yellow table lamp. The only other items of furniture in the room were a cane chair and a bed heaped high with a double quilt. The toilets were down the open corridor, making a midnight leak quite a painful ordeal.

Facing the door was a wooden cupboard set inside the wall, its white doors fastened with a strong Harrison lock. Habib double locked the main door behind him and walked upto the cupboard, selecting the appropriate key from his keychain. The cupboard was essentially full of clothes, but the bottom shelf was crammed with stacks of old magazines. Habib knelt on the floor and eased them out. The plank on which the magazines lay had been carefully loosened earlier, and now came away easily in his hand. Underneath lay Habib's personal weapons: the ubiquitous AK-47 and a Kalakov pistol which he had taken a fancy to in Pakistan. There were also six grenades which, after some thought, Habib decided to leave in place.

He thrust the pistol into the band of his trousers and put the AK-47 under the mattress of the bed. He had just begun to lift the magazines back into the cupboard when a soft knock on the door made him start. He crouched motionless for a few seconds. There was another knock. Thrusting the remaining magazines into the cupboard haphazardly, Habib glanced quickly at the mattress where the rifle was, and then with one hand on the pistol under his shirt, walked up to the door.

'Who is it?'

'Habib sir, it is me, Ahmed.'

Habib cautiously opened the locks, pulled the door open, still tense, and relaxed when he recognized Ahmed Razzaq, the son of the man who had worked for so long at the Kaul residence. He was a few years younger than Habib and Vijay, but they had all often played cricket together as boys. Ahmed had a remarkably effective bouncer which had more than once threatened to knock their teeth out.

'What are you doing here? And how did you know that I live in this room?'

'Sir, I am a ward boy in this hospital. We all know what you do now, sir, and we all talk a lot about you.'

Habib waved Ahmed to the chair next to the writing table. 'And?'

'Sir, I also want to join now. I want to be a *mujahid* and train in Pakistan. Sir, thousands have decided only today to go across. We all feel we can win azaadi now, and I want to be part of the movement.'

Habib smiled wryly at the enthusiasm. 'Does Ghulam Razzaq know about this?'

A faint frown creased Ahmed's forehead. 'No, he doesn't know, and you know he wouldn't approve. But I want to do what all my friends are doing.'

It was as if the release of the militants had set off a deluge. According to some estimates, more than 5000 young men decided to cross the Line of Control for training that night itself. For some, like Ahmed, the 'movement' offered glamorous liberation from the routine of bedpans and puking patients. For others, it was to become a crusade for whatever was left of their lives.

Ahmed was Ghulam Razzaq's only son, born when he had already entered middle age, and the image of the old man waiting patiently for his son to visit him in his hut briefly crossed Habib's mind like a dark shadow. Then he shrugged his shoulders and reached under the mattress for the AK-47, which he slung under his phiran as Ahmed smiled in excitement.

'Come with me,' Habib said, leading him out of the room.

Chapter Ten

MASS MOVEMENT

In the winter of 1989-90, the Kashmir uprising was a mass movement. It was a heady time for the militants, a time that would never come again. One call and tens of thousands would be out in the streets. Every major demonstration brought together mothers and grandmothers, doctors and lawyers, policemen and ex-convicts. The call for azaadi drifted urgently with the winter winds from town to town, village to village.

The Indian government didn't quite know what to do. In fact, Indian control hardly existed any more in the Valley. Most of the bureaucrats and local functionaries seemed to be taking their orders from the militants. By now there were thousands of them, young boys with guns and attitude strutting openly on the roads.

But Habib was worried. 'The scum is starting to get into the movement,' he confided to Qasim late one evening. They were heading for yet another supreme council meeting, this one on a houseboat moored at the floating gardens in the heart of Srinagar. Both of them were dressed in jeans and pullovers and were ready to masquerade as tourists from Jammu in case they were stopped by the security forces.

'Time could soon be against us. We must strike for independence now, while the Indians don't quite know what to do and the people are on our side.'

The shikara was easing its way along the golden red reflection of the sun on the waters of the Dal, and Qasim wasn't really in the mood for pessimism.

'Can't you see the fire in their eyes every day? The people won't be quietened again.'

Habib shook his head. 'You are wrong. I know our people, most of them are too soft for a prolonged fight. They are with us right now because they think we are the winners. If it gets ugly, and if the Indians dig in their heels and refuse to leave, the mood will change. It won't take long for us to change from being the heroes who are bringing freedom to the bastards who brought ruin to the Valley.'

The shikara was now passing through a narrow channel of clear water, houseboats moored on one side and the floating garden on the other. Raised on a patch of accumulated silt right in the centre of the Dal lake, the floating garden now accommodated a couple of crops a year for enterprising farmers. One or two of them could be seen braving the icy conditions to pull at weeds from paddleboats. The Dal hadn't frozen over, but the water was cold enough to be lethal to anyone unlucky enough to fall in.

The shikara approached a houseboat moored just a little away from the others. Faded paint declared the name of the boat as 'The Pride of India', and Qasim smirked a little at the irony. Long before they reached their destination, Habib approvingly noticed the JKLF guards on the roofs of the houseboats they were passing. In the summer, all these boats were crowded with tourists, but now they were at the disposal of the movement. Habib had himself worked out the security system for the meetings, the guards on the rooftops of the houseboats would give more than enough notice of any approaching police motorboat; and it would be almost impossible for the security forces to take the land route to the meeting spot, as it meandered through countless tiny footpaths crossing the backwaters of the Dal over narrow bridges. A couple of JKLF lookouts could hold off an entire company of soldiers while their leaders made their getaway.

As the shikara reached the wooden steps of The Pride of India, the boatman back-paddled furiously to prevent a sharp jolt. Habib clambered out of the boat onto the steps and turned to give a hand to Qasim, who was carrying both their guns. They walked through the small wooden veranda into the main drawing room of the houseboat, where they were greeted with some exasperation by the rest of the JKLF high command, all of whom had been waiting there for a while.

Qasim grinned cheekily and held up his little finger as he walked through the room towards the toilets further back in the boat. This was a luxury houseboat, and the bedrooms were tastefully decorated and panelled in exquisitely carved walnut wood. The bathrooms had all the amenities a homesick foreign tourist could want, down to running hot water in the showers and Western-style toilets with working flushes. All the waste poured into the waters of the Dal, but that was something those who swam in the lake during summer tried not to think about.

Qasim zipped up his jeans and returned to the drawing room, where he grabbed some walnuts from the table at the centre of the room. Then he jabbed a finger at Habib and said, 'He thinks we should move fast before the people lose interest.'

Hamid Sheikh grunted. 'We have been talking about it. We've decided on the date.'

Qasim raised an inquiring eyebrow. Hamid went on. 'The 26th of January, the day the Indians celebrate their republic day. That's the day we will formally pull down their flag, hoist our own, and declare independence. The Pakistanis will quickly recognize us as the legitimate government and many other countries will follow. The Indians will have no choice, it will be a fait accompli.'

Habib took it from there. 'We must maintain the tempo, though. The people must continue to come out into the streets in their hundreds of thousands. And we must get our sympathizers in the bureaucracy and in the police to cripple the government as much as possible. By that date there must be no authority in the state but ours. Then even the fence-sitters will have no choice but to toe our line.'

The plans were prepared to the smallest detail, and they almost worked. But what the militants hadn't bargained for was the sheer cussedness with which India dug in its heels.

Sent in to take over as the governor of the state was a hardliner, a man who was often accused of having strong anti-Muslim sentiments. The chief minister, Farooq Abdullah, promptly resigned, and the reins of the state were now entirely in the hands of the governor. What followed was something the Kashmiris soon came to refer to as 'crackdown', the reimposition of state authority through often brutal means. Curfew was imposed for days on end and people remained shut up in their homes, unable to go to the market or to work. The first incidents of human rights abuse by the security forces came to light, the first major incident itself being one of the worst—scores of people were shot down near the Gawakadal bridge as they approached a BSF patrol. It was the first such massacre that modern Kashmir had seen.

The bitterness of those days would result in years of hostility between the average Kashmiri and what he saw as a repressive government. But at the same time the tough measures slowly led to the fizzling out of the mass movement.

On 26 January there was gloom in the JKLF camp. The day had turned out to be a disaster. Though they were even more popular now than they had been just a couple of weeks earlier, the chances of their riding to power on the shoulders of a triumphant mass of people like in East Europe appeared dim. The army would have found it difficult to control huge mobs without the use of heavy force, leading to more Gawakadal-style massacres; but the total imposition of curfew even in the smallest neighbourhood had prevented the JKLF from getting the crowds together in the first place. 'Block all the tributaries and the river won't flow,' said the army chief in satisfaction.

Qasim had promised to try and get to the hospital by the middle of the afternoon, but it was proving almost impossible. Srinagar was completely deserted, not even a stray dog barking in the streets. The sides of the roads were a collage of steel shutters, all the shops were closed and their owners huddled at home. The only humans on the streets were the soldiers, wearing camouflage outfits and thick helmets and clutching their guns nervously. At every street corner impressive roadblocks had been erected, and the security forces were making certain that no civilian vehicle was out on the road.

Qasim emerged from the side alley leading out from his house in Maisuma and walked across triangular piece of concrete land to the main road. A huge roadblock was in place there with more than twenty-five soldiers guarding it. As he walked towards the soldiers, Qasim was uncomfortably aware of at least a dozen barrels pointed straight at him, together with the machine gun that was mounted on an idling army truck. For all he knew, he was the only civilian out in the open in the whole of the Valley at that moment, and he cursed the impulse that had prompted him to try to make the rendezvous with Habib. It wasn't going to serve any useful purpose, and could lead to his getting arrested. But he was out in the open now and trying to retreat would only make matters worse.

Within minutes he felt his arms being grabbed by two jawans, even as the captain walked up to him. 'Where the hell do you think you are going? There is a fucking curfew in place. Get back into the alley.'

Qasim contorted his face into a pitiful expression and whined at the officer, 'Sir, I have the most terrible pain in my stomach. I think it is appendicitis. It's agony. I have to get myself to the hospital.'

The captain shoved him on the chest. 'Didn't you hear me? Get back into the fucking alley.'

Qasim had turned to go when a small convoy came racing up to the road block and the captain jumped back and saluted smartly as he recognized the brigadier in charge of his unit.

'What's the problem here?'

'Sir, this civilian wants to break the curfew. He says he wants to go to the hospital.'

The brigadier looked closely at Qasim, who was by now beginning to sweat in fright. He knew that he'd been incredibly foolish drawing attention towards himself like this. Rubbing his stomach with one hand, he kept his head hanging down, looking at the ground just in front of his feet.

Fortunately for him, the brigadier misinterpreted his

agitation as a sign of great physical distress. Turning to the captain and pointing to the other vehicles in the convoy, he said, 'Tell him to jump into the back of the two-tonner. We'll drop him off at the hospital, it's on our way.'

Qasim could hardly believe his luck as the soldiers frisked him quickly and then hustled him into the two-tonner, where he joined the waiting detachment of soldiers squatting on the floor. The tailboard was slammed up and they were off, screeching at full speed through the deserted roads.

His courage returning slowly, Qasim raised his head to glance at the army personnel around him. Most of them seemed to be from South India, and Qasim figured that they wouldn't be able to speak too much Urdu. A young jawan sitting right next to him grinned and held out a bundle of beedis. Qasim took one, nodded his thanks and looked over the tailboard at the motley convoy which was following them. The brigadier had obviously been picking up other stranded citizens. In the car just behind was a family he recognized— a leading theatre personality whose mother had died the previous evening sat huddled with his relatives. This was the only way they could take the body to the cremation ground during the curfew.

A few minutes later they were at the front gate of the hospital, and the convoy stopped long enough for Qasim to jump out. As the army unit moved on, Qasim chuckled in relief and hurried inside. The hospital compound appeared as deserted as the streets outside and he only felt safe after he had reached Habib's room.

The room was dark, and he could barely make out Habib as he walked back to the bed and flung himself down. Qasim flicked on the lights and was stunned to see Habib looking more desolate and miserable than he could have ever imagined.

'What's happened?' he asked with deep concern.

'It's all over, Qasim. The movement is over.'

'Oh don't be ridiculous. It's just a minor setback. Okay, we missed the 26th deadline, but by calling for our own civil curfew today we've retrieved the situation. Now no one will know whether the empty streets today were because of us or because of the soldiers.'

'You don't understand, Qasim. It's over. For a few more weeks, or even months, we will be able to get the people out. And then one day they will stay in their homes and it will be just us out there.'

Habib ran a hand through his hair and Qasim felt growing disquiet as he noticed the tears welling up in his friend's eyes.

'The armed struggle will continue,' he said lamely.

'Yes,' said Habib quietly, 'the armed struggle will continue. But without the mass mobilization of our people an armed struggle will end up being just another insurgency, and the Indians will crush it, like they always have.'

In the weeks that followed, Habib's gloom seemed ridiculously misplaced. As they rode on top of a bus to Chrar-e-Sharief a fortnight later during the biggest demonstration yet, surrounded by what seemed to be the entire population of northern Kashmir, Qasim laughed at Habib and jabbed him in the ribs. 'Look at the people! There must be half a million out there. And you thought they were going to abandon us.'

Habib smiled a little shamefacedly as he brushed the snowflakes from his hair, but his inner doubts remained. And over the next few months, as the curfew continued to wear down the people of the Valley, slowly, very slowly, the crowds began to thin. There was still anger. There were still the demands for azaadi, the slogans daubed on every wall. Whenever foreign media crews came to the Valley, a large crowd would miraculously materialize and chant the usual slogans, asking the Indian dogs to go home. But the regular flood of people in the streets of the towns and villages of Kashmir gradually ebbed away.

The mass movement was over. The war of attrition had begun.

Chapter Eleven

TERROR

Zaidi stepped back from the grave where he had just spread a green flag over the freshly turned earth. The man who lay inside the grave was now a *shaheed*, a martyr for the cause, shot down by the security forces as he attempted to throw a grenade into a crowded market place.

Zaidi turned around to look at his band of men, all members of a new group that had broken away from the Hizbul Mujahideen, their faces sombre as they remembered moments shared with the dead man. He raised his Kalashnikov to the sky and fired a quick burst, snapping his men out of their gloom.

'Nizam-e-Mustapha!' he shouted, firing another burst, and his slogan was taken up by the other militants. Now they were all firing into the sky, their disregard for wasted ammunition and for the possibility that an army patrol could pass by showing just how strong these militants had become in a few weeks.

The trickle of blood that had been flowing through the valley was now a raging torrent. Both the militants and the security forces had lost several men, but the greatest number of casualties were among ordinary civilians.

Zaidi faced his men, standing straight and tall amidst all the graves. They called this the martyr's graveyard, all those who died while fighting the security forces were carried here and buried draped in the green flags of independent Kashmir. Zaidi would have preferred Pakistani flags, or the banners of his new group, but for now he was ready to go along with the consensus among all militant groups that their men should be buried draped in a common flag.

He raised his Kalashnikov again, and the gunfire stuttered into silence.

'They killed Hanif, and they killed Altaf. I say to you, enough of our softness. Let the blood of all who oppose us flow like water in the gutters. We will kill ten for every one of us who is martyred. And now we won't spare anyone who isn't with the movement. You have seen what the SLF and the Allah Tigers have been doing. You have seen the green terror they have spread among all the renegades, the traitors to Kashmir, and among the kaffirs. Now it will be our turn.'

That night Zaidi's men followed him like a pack of silent wolves as he approached the whitewashed house standing alone in a Srinagar suburb. It was surrounded by a well-maintained though tiny garden and was separated from the other houses in the neighbourhood by a thin fence. It was past midnight, and most of the lights were out, although the militants could see candlelight filtering through a chink in the curtains on the first floor. This was the house of K.L. Raina, a retired engineer who had spent thirty-five years of his life attempting to fix the water problems of Srinagar and who now devoted himself to writing short stories for children; none were published yet but that didn't stop him from trying.

Raina was a Hindu, a Kashmiri Pandit, a man who had never dreamt that he could be unsafe in his own homeland, but who was starting to feel twinges of fear as he heard about attacks on other Hindus across the Valley.

Zaidi pounded on the door with the butt of his rifle. There were a few minutes of silence, and the militants could see that the light in the first floor had been put out. Zaidi pounded on the door again, and called out loudly, 'Mr Raina, sir, we know you are there. Don't worry, we won't harm you in any way. We merely want to ask you a couple of questions.'

Long minutes passed, and then the door was slowly opened. Raina, seventy-one years old, with an incredibly wrinkled face and a white moustache, looked out at the waiting men.

Even in the dim light of the moon Zaidi could see the fear in Raina's eyes and he smiled and said with exaggerated civility, 'Don't worry, sir. I am sorry to disturb you so late at night, but there were one or two questions we had to ask you.'

Raina pulled together the shawl that was covering his thin shoulders and tried to muster some dignity. 'At this time? Can't it wait till the morning?'

'I'm afraid not, sir,' replied Zaidi amiably. 'It really is most urgent.'

The old man stepped out of the house. 'Okay, go ahead.'

'No, not here. I'm afraid you will have to accompany us. And could you please tell your son to join us too?'

Fear flickered in Raina's eyes once again. 'He isn't here. He had to go away for a relative's wedding.'

'No, he didn't, we saw him eating dinner with all of you just a couple of hours ago,' said Zaidi courteously. 'Will you ask him to come out of the basement, or must we come in and search for him? That could disturb the women—your wife and daughter.'

The voices carried inside the house, and Ajay Raina soon appeared. As a thirty-five-year-old, he was more at risk than his father, which was why he had remained in hiding.

'Thank you for joining us. Now let's move on.'

The militants had been at the house for more than fifteen minutes already, and some of the neighbours had noticed the commotion. A couple of middle-aged men now approached the house.

'Salaam aleikum, *bhaijaan*,' said one of them, extremely politely. 'I'm Rasheed Sheikh, from the road department. Is there some trouble? We know these people, they are good Kashmiris.'

Irritation flared in Zaidi's eyes. There was nothing he despised more than Muslims pleading for their Hindu friends and neighbours. But he kept his voice cordial.

'Don't worry, my friend. We just have one or two questions to ask. They will be back at home within fifteen-twenty minutes.'

'Can't you talk to them here?' asked Rasheed timidly.

Zaidi's deputy, Tariq, stirred a little, easing the strap of the Kalashnikov on his shoulder, as if the gun had suddenly grown heavy. It was a small movement, but it had the desired effect. The neighbours shrunk back and moved closer together.

Zaidi smiled again. 'No, I'm afraid we must really be on our way now. We'll return Raina sahib to his house in a few minutes.'

There was no further opposition and the band of militants walked off, leading Raina and his son.

The night dragged on. For the women of the family there was nothing to do but to huddle before the bukhari and wait. Mrs Raina was praying, reading out aloud from the big red Ramayana which she kept permanently perched on a wooden stand. Sushma Raina, her daughter, kept weeping, her eyes straying to the door every few seconds. Rasheed's wife, Salma, had volunteered to stay on with them, and she wandered in and out of the kitchen at periodic intervals, brewing strong cups of kahwa.

It was at 4:30 in the morning that there was finally some noise in the garden outside. Sushma jumped to her feet and was about to walk to the door when there was a loud crash as a body came through the window, shattering the glass into a million pieces, and showering the room with wooden splinters.

Sushma screamed in fright, and then looked at the body. Then she screamed again, and again. It was Ajay. His face was puffy and caked with dried blood. The nose had obviously been broken. His lips were torn and most of his teeth were missing. A shawl had been loosely draped around him, but beneath that his body was naked, and the bare flesh that was visible was speckled with the circular black marks of cigarette burns.

Sushma took a couple of steps towards her brother and then turned and retched on the floor. She was still screaming, almost hysterically. She had seen Ajay's face closely now, had seen the empty sockets where his eyes used to be, and the one eye hanging obscenely down his cheek, still attached to the optic nerve.

The door crashed open. Zaidi walked in, with two of his

men half dragging, half carrying Raina between them. They hurled him onto the ground in front of his wife, who was still sitting paralyzed before the bukhari, the Ramayana clutched in her hands as if it was some sort a shield. Unlike his son, Raina was still alive, and he scrabbled at the floor as he tried to get up. But both his arms had been repeatedly broken, as had all his fingers, and he soon collapsed face down again.

Salma Sheikh appeared at the door of the kitchen. Her hands were clutching a cup of kahwa, and were shaking uncontrollably, sending the liquid splattering onto the floor. Zaidi glanced at her and his face tightened in anger. 'Get out of here. Leave.'

Salma stood frozen where she was, her eyes wide in horror as she stared at Ajay's lifeless body. Zaidi strode up to her in a few quick steps, grabbed her arm, and pulled her towards the door. 'Get out of here right now, and tell your men not to interfere, otherwise you will get the same treatment as these kaffirs.'

With a final horrified glance at the body, Salma fled down the garden. Tariq hissed to his leader, 'She may get the authorities. They all seem to be Hindu-lovers in this neighbourhood.'

Zaidi shook his head as he walked back towards where Raina was lying on the ground, 'They won't dare do anything. We have enough time.'

He reached Raina and thrust his boot into his side, turning him over. Raina whimpered softly as Zaidi nudged him in his broken elbow with his foot. Then Zaidi spoke to Mrs Raina. 'Your husband is a traitor, and a police informer. He is also very foolish. Despite considerable persuasion neither he nor your equally foolish son admitted to being informers.'

The old man whispered softly, his voice barely audible as it bubbled through the blood in his mouth, 'I've told you a hundred times. We have nothing to do with the police. You've killed my son, don't you think I would have admitted it by now?'

He raised his head dully. 'But you know this already, don't you? You know we are completely innocent of any wrongdoing. And you are doing all this despite that.'

Zaidi knelt on the floor next to Raina. His voice was soft and low, almost soothing.

'We took your son's eyes. Do you know why we left yours?' He smiled, and went on without waiting for an answer. 'Because we want you to see what we do to your wife and your daughter.'

Zaidi stood up abruptly and turned to where Tariq was holding Sushma firmly by her arms. 'Bring her here, right in front of her father so that he can get a good view.'

* * *

The cremations were at noon, four piles of firewood stacked around the bodies of the Rainas. A distant relative lit the pyres. Not too many people had come for the funeral; many Hindus were too scared to leave their homes, others had already fled the Valley for Jammu and other regions. But the Rainas' neighbours were there, Salma's eyes puffed with weeping, and Rasheed's stomach knotted with guilt as he repeatedly wondered what he could have done.

Vijay stood with his parents among the mourners. He had left the military uniform at home and was wearing a simple white kurta-pyjama with a thick shawl draped across his shoulders. The Kauls had known the murdered family for years. Papa had worked with K.L. Raina while he was in the government; Vijay had laughed and played with Sushma a hundred times when they were children, and Ajay had been like an indulgent elder brother.

The phone call had come early in the morning, and Vijay had rushed to the Raina residence. It had been left to him to try and clean up the bodies as best as he could and arrange for transport to the cremation ground. Now he watched quietly as the flames leapt towards the sky.

After the funeral, few of those who had gathered spoke to each other. As Vijay led his parents to the car, he voiced the concern that was eating him up, 'Amma, Papa, my leave finishes in three days' time. I think both of you should think about coming to Delhi with me for a few days, just till things stabilize a little.'

Papa had recently retired from the government and now lived a simple life in his own house, a red building in Karan Nagar which he had bought with the accumulated savings of a lifetime. The government pension, even for someone who had been a senior civil servant, was nothing to write home about, but he managed a reasonably comfortable existence.

Both he and Amma were beginning to feel insecure because of what was happening around them, with the militants repeatedly singling out Hindu families as targets. In addition, there were the provocative slogans shouted at demonstration after demonstration, and the subtle hostility of many they had considered lifelong friends.

But Papa was a stubborn man, and arrogant to boot: 'I'll be damned if I'll allow a bunch of thuggish kids to chase me out of my house,' was his only response. In the end they agreed that Vijay would return to Delhi alone and that they would join him if things became any worse.

Papa had bought new locks for the doors and would make rounds of all the rooms before turning in, to ensure that every door was shut and every window bolted. But sleep came slowly and was always fitful: at the slightest noise in the garden Papa would come wide awake and sit listening for footsteps on the path.

* * *

They came early, just before dinner, at around eight one evening. There were eleven of them, young men clad in phirans, all armed with Kalashnikovs. They split up neatly, four of them moving to cover the back exits and the windows while two stayed as lookouts on the main road.

Papa had been half expecting the knock on the door for so long that it was almost a relief that it had finally happened. He gestured to Amma to stay where she was and then slowly walked towards the entrance of the house. He had often debated whether the best course of action would be to ignore the knocks and pretend that there was no one home, but in the end had decided that it would be a futile gesture, and one which could annoy the militants further.

He lifted one corner of the lace curtain at the window which overlooked the driveway. Then he clenched his teeth as he saw all the Kalashnikovs. The knocking on the door had become more impatient, and someone was calling out in Kashmiri.

With unsteady hands the fifty-nine-year-old man unlocked the three bolts he had painstakingly fixed on the doors, and then he stepped back as the militants streamed in, shoving him back roughly. They were all wearing masks, folded handkerchiefs covering the nose and mouth.

'We know that your son has left, old man, but call your wife into the drawing room,' said a man in a red mask who appeared to be the leader of the militants. Amma emerged from the dining room, and the two of them were propelled towards a sofa, where they sat close to each other, Papa reaching for his wife's hand and holding it tight to try and give her strength and courage. She squeezed his fingers back, and even in the middle of his desperate concern and fear, he felt proud of her.

'We have been watching you for some time,' said Red Mask. 'You are traitors to Kashmir.'

Papa replied cautiously, feeling for every word in his mind before he uttered it. 'No, we are not. I am a retired civil servant, and I have no time for politics. All we want is a chance to lead a comfortable and normal life.'

'Normal life? When thousands of our boys are being butchered? Our women dishonoured? That is why we call you a traitor. Your son is with the army and you are an informer.'

'My son has joined the army but I carry no information to the security forces; I know nothing which is worth mentioning.' Papa heard the pleading note in his own voice and changed tack. 'Look, can I request you to please contact someone high up in the movement? My wife and I are known to him, and I believe he will vouch for us. Please get a message to him for us.'

'Whom are you referring to?' asked Red Mask.

'Habib Shah. I understand he is now one of the top commanders of the JKLF. Please ask him about us, take a message to him from us.'

'There's no need for that,' came a voice from the corner of the room, where a tall and thin militant had been standing quietly, holding an AK-47 loosely in his hand. Red Mask stepped back deferentially as the man who had spoken walked forward, taking the cloth off his face as he did so. 'I'm right here.'

Papa winced as if in sudden physical pain, and Amma gasped as she recognized Habib. She started to rise to her feet but he held up his hand and snapped, 'Please remain seated.'

Habib came right up to Papa and looked at him straight in the eye. 'What he said is correct. You have no loyalty to Kashmir, and therefore no right to be here any more.'

Papa's face had crumpled and he looked incredibly old and defeated. Tears were welling up in Amma's eyes as she stared in disbelief at Habib looming over them, one hand on his hip and the other holding his Kalashnikov. There was no trace of emotion on his face, which looked cold and hard, as if carved from ice.

'You know what happened to the Rainas. To the Ganjus, and to so many others. You must leave now. Leave Kashmir before the same happens to you. There is no place here for those who serve the government.'

Papa looked up at Habib. 'You know perfectly well that I am retired. I live in this little house on my pension. I have no savings, no place to go . . .'

'Go to your son,' Habib interrupted. 'Go to Delhi. Just leave this place.'

A small flash of spirit returned to Papa. 'So, Habib, you have come with your guns to drive us out of our home after all, just as I had once said you would.'

Habib turned to go. 'I don't want to banter words with you. You have been warned. Leave before it is too late.'

Through the entire exchange Habib hadn't once glanced at Amma. Now she abruptly rose to her feet and walked towards him, shaking off Papa's restraining hand. The tears were streaming down her cheeks now, but she appeared not to notice them. In four quick steps she reached the JKLF leader and grabbed his arm, forcing him to turn around and look at her.

No words were said, but he saw it all in her eyes, all that they had gone through together. The bouts of malaria, through which she had nursed him; the childhood cuts and bruises touched with mercurochrome and bandaged efficiently; the little confidences about what was happening in school; the special chocolate cakes she baked for birthdays. He looked deep into her eyes, and then coldly removed her hand from his arm.

A small gesture with his head and the JKLF men melted away towards the door. Habib Shah followed them out, leaving the old couple alone in what had till then been their home.

*　*　*

The plane tickets to Delhi had been booked for the following Tuesday. Amma sat quietly on the floor, trying to pack the memories of a lifetime into cardboard cartons. There was only so much that they could carry with them on the aircraft, but Papa's former colleagues in the government had promised to try and send some cartons and trunks in some vehicle going by road to Jammu.

The Kauls had been promised protection by the government; they had been asked to shift into a safe house. But Papa had refused, saying that he wouldn't be willing to live as a prisoner in his own homeland.

Amma carefully lifted dinner plates wrapped thickly in old newspapers into the open carton in front of her, and stuffed scrunched up paper into the carton for some additional protection. Then she turned, with a small smile, to Yasmin who sat next to her holding a roll of sticky tape in her hands.

Yasmin hadn't left the Kaul residence for the past three days, trying to soothe the guilt that was corroding her insides by busying herself with the packing. She peeled off a strip of tape, and bit it off with her teeth.

'I think we are almost all done. But Amma, I don't see these plates surviving the journey to Delhi in a truck.'

'I know,' said Amma ruefully. 'But I can't bring myself to leave them behind. Are you sure you can't use them?'

'Quite sure. And you have already forced me to take so many of your clothes and other knick-knacks.'

They both skirted the issue that they really wanted to talk about. They had been avoiding it for the past three days as if it were a minefield that lay between them.

Amma finally brought it up on Tuesday morning, barely an hour and a half before they were to leave for the airport. 'Yasmin, what has happened between us and Habib shouldn't affect your relationship with him.' Yasmin began to cry, and Amma hugged her. 'We'll see you again soon. And you know that you'll always have a home with us.'

Habib had come to Yasmin's house the previous evening, whistling softly to lure her to the window. She had initially not wanted to respond, but had finally decided to stalk out and tell Habib what she thought of him. But he had pre-empted her with a burst of words: 'I know what you are thinking, Yasmin, but it's not like that. I had to be firm, I had to be harsh. They have to go away, you don't know how bad the situation here has become for the Hindus. Amma and Papa would never have anything to fear from me or my men, but what about the other groups? You know what some of them are like . . .'

He had gone on, urging her to understand, till he was sure he had prevented her outburst. There was so much that Yasmin still wanted to say, but she was suddenly very tired, and sadder than she had ever been.

Now, as she looked at the suitcases being carried out, a vivid image returned to Yasmin's mind: a small girl, dazed by what life had done to her, sitting quietly outside a store in Gulmarg. And then a car had drawn up to the kerb, and a lady draped in a sari had climbed out to change everything. It was an image that had never really left Yasmin.

The suitcases were put into the boot of the car, and the house was locked. The luggage which was to go by road had already been sent to Papa's friends in the government. It seemed that the entire population of Zafar Bagh had come to see the Kauls off. They had been immensely popular and their one-time neighbours were deeply distressed to see them go.

Yasmin leant against the wall of the house and watched the Kauls climb into the blue Ambassador in which a neighbour was driving them to the airport. She would never see Amma again.

Chapter Twelve

VARUN

The loud and cheerful voice of the Oxford radio announcer filled the room, and Varun Mathur stretched out a sleepy hand to hit the snooze button on the radio alarm in a well-practiced gesture. The volume was set to maximum to ensure that he would eventually wake up, although the process could take up to half an hour.

Varun tapped the snooze button thrice before he finally emerged from under the duvet and looked with horror at the time on the clock. 'Shit!' he muttered as he leaped out of bed with all the speed the after-effects of an evening well-spent at the New College bar would permit. He'd made the mistake of trying to match an Irish friend pint for pint, and though he'd bailed out soon enough, there was still a sharp throbbing in his temples.

'That was clever of me,' he thought, as he furiously brushed his teeth in the sink that had been thoughtfully provided in one corner of the room. 'And just before Professor Jeffries toasts me for my tutorial.'

Half an hour later, Varun felt only a little more human. He desperately needed a strong cup of coffee and glared unhappily at his coffee machine, which had never quite worked satisfactorily in the three weeks since he had bought it. Then he brightened suddenly as he realized that this was Wednesday, and that his favourite coffee maker didn't have any classes in the morning.

He staggered out of his room, and walked down the

corridor towards a room three doors away. He banged on the door with his fist. 'Wakey, wakey, Sarah. Time to surface— unless you've got someone in there you don't want the world to know about.'

He heard a low grumbling noise from inside the room, then the door creaked open, and Sarah stood there trying to force her eyes open. 'Good morning!' shouted Varun with breezy cheerfulness. 'You look wonderful! And I need coffee.'

As Sarah tried to explain eloquently what she thought of people who woke her up at 11:30 on Wednesday mornings, Varun brushed past her and headed for her espresso machine. 'That's no language for a lady to use. Do you want a mug or no?'

Two thirds of a mug of thick espresso later, Sarah was inclined to look at him a little more charitably. 'Why are you bleating around my room at the crack of dawn anyway? Don't you have this great big tutorial today?'

Varun rummaged in her shelf for a shortbread cookie. 'Yup. In half an hour. And Professor Jeffries is going to hit the roof. Thanks to you and your boyfriend I have the worst headache of my life, and I'm going to have to defend what Jeffries will consider shockingly reactionary.'

Having found the cookies, he turned back to her. 'Where is John anyway? When I left you guys he was already on his sixth pint of Guinness. The man's amazing.'

Sarah laughed. 'After you wimped out and went home, we hung around for an hour or so more. John had an early morning seminar, I guess he must be there right now.'

Varun shuddered theatrically. 'Theoretical physics on a hangover? I told you he's nuts.'

The three of them had met during the Oxford University Fresher's week, and had soon become inseparable. John and Sarah had taken just a couple of weeks to fall violently in love with each other, and it was soon left to Varun to mediate their various tiffs and spats. In return they threatened, with parental consideration, that they would do all they could to keep him out of trouble.

'Got to go,' said Varun, snatching another cookie from

the box. 'If I'm not back in a couple of hours, come and look for me at Balliol. The professor may have formally crucified me on the college gates, and there could be a bunch of tourists taking photographs. And while the former is acceptable, the latter definitely isn't!'

He ran back to his room to pick up his essay and then rushed to his tutor's building.

Professor Jeffries was a brilliant man, one of the best International Relations tutors at Oxford, but he was fixed in his views and quite dogmatic about what he called the rights of the individual; rights that he felt should be defended with quasi-religious zeal.

Varun tapped on the half ajar door leading into the tutor's apartment, and then walked in to be greeted by a blast of warmth from the double radiator in the room. The room was untidy in the extreme, and a rich aroma of Monte Cristo cheroots hung thick in it. Varun smiled at the Professor, who waved him amiably towards an overstuffed sofa with the smouldering butt of a cheroot. The other two students who were part of the tutorial group were already sitting there, a young American girl from Somerville College, and a South African who had just graduated from the University of Cape Town.

Professor Jeffries opened another little carton of Monte Cristos with his fingernail. He was as untidy as his room, a thick shock of white hair hanging down to his collar, and his brown tweed coat not quite matching the grey Marks and Spencer's sweater he had on underneath. 'So what were we to discuss this week? Ah yes, self-determination and freedom. And the young Mr Mathur had seemed quite excited about the subject—so why doesn't he read out his essay?'

Varun took another deep breath and shook out the A4 sheets covered in his sloping handwriting. He began to read and could see the Professor frown at the line he was taking. But as he ploughed on, the tutor also began to look quite interested. And as he approached the lengthy conclusion of the essay, Varun began to feel confident and quite pleased with himself.

'In conclusion, I would argue that self-determination as a concept was extremely valuable in the post-colonial period, as nation after nation began to demand independence and freedom from its colonial masters. The colonial powers were European nations, and the rulers were detached from the people they governed. Self-determination then was both just and inevitable.

'The problem comes when we try to extend that concept to the self-determination of all minority groups in the modern world, and the problem is particularly acute in countries like Yugoslavia and India which are "patchwork quilts" of a large number of ethnic, linguistic and religious groups.

'Political self-determination, or independence, for each of these groups is, in the long run, bound to prove disastrous. The partition of India showed that when you slice a nation along religious lines the net result is often increased hostility, not peace and permanent security.

'The more you break up a "patchwork" nation, the greater the scope for internecine warfare between the communities who once lived together but who now represent separate nation states. In my opinion this is precisely what we are going to see in Yugoslavia, a nation that is now being splintered along ethnic lines. I think the coming years are going to see hostilities between the Serbs and the Croats or the Serbs and the Bosnians increase, not decrease, because of the break-up of Yugoslavia. The same could be the pattern in the constituents of the former Soviet Union, Muslims and Christians who had lived together peacefully for decades suddenly turning on each other in their quest for self-determination.

'How then can the rights of minority ethnic or regional groups be guaranteed? The answer, in my opinion, will lie in economic, not political self-determination. Economic power and decision-making will have to be decentralized and transferred directly to the people. With economic power and local self-government in their hands, their desire for political self-rule will automatically disappear.'

Varun put the paper down and braced himself for assault. To his surprise, Professor Jeffries was fairly muted, as he puffed deep at his cheroot and turned to the American girl. 'Cynthia, your comments on all that.'

Cynthia smiled apologetically at Varun. 'Well, I agree about the economic self-governance, but doesn't the collapse of the Soviet Union show that when people want independence, they are bound to eventually get it?'

Varun was quick to retort. 'Go back another couple of years to Tiananmen square. Why has the Soviet Union collapsed and not China? After all, there was a great deal of disquiet in both countries. In the Soviet Union Gorbachev tried to give political freedom without first providing economic liberties. The Chinese did the exact opposite, they maintained the status quo politically while liberalizing the economy. The results are there before us.'

'Sounds like you don't believe in democracy,' said Cynthia.

'Oh, I do. And in true democracy, which would mean proper choices, and proper self-government at the grass roots level as well. All I'm saying is that you can't give independence to every small group which parrots the cry of self-determination, because all you'll get is prolonged civil war.'

The sparring continued for a while, till Professor Jeffries looked at his watch and announced a truce. All three students left their essays on his table, and walked out. Paul, the South African, punched Varun on his arm as they filed down the stairs, 'I thought I was going to choke when you started to beard the lion in his own den with your attack on all he holds dear.'

Varun grinned back, 'I think I got away with it.'

'Wait till he marks the paper,' said Cynthia darkly, to which Varun shrugged his shoulders, '*Que sera sera.*'

It was autumn, and the gardens were no longer painted with the warmth of the English summer sun. But as Varun led the way into the huge main garden of New College with the thickly wooded mound at its centre, he looked around in contentment at the beauty of the college he had come to love so much. There was a small patch of sunlight in one corner of the garden, and the three of them settled down on the crisp grass.

It was their final year at Oxford, and conversation turned inevitably to the exams, which were only a few months away.

'I can't possibly put in five to six hours a day like you guys do,' said Varun gloomily. 'I have too many other commitments, *Cherwell* takes up all my time on Tuesdays and Wednesdays.'

'Its your own fault,' said Paul unsympathetically. 'Why on earth did you decide to become news editor for the paper in the second last term before the finals?'

'I can't help it; I didn't know till a month ago that I would turn down all those juicy Goldman Sachs offers to become a journalist. And now if I am to be a journalist I need the experience on my CV.'

'Bloody Indian inefficiency, as always. No wonder none of your trains ever work,' grinned Paul, rolling onto his back on the grass.

Varun punched him playfully in the stomach and said, 'Indians are going to be running South Africa soon, so you had better get used to it.'

'Have you decided yet where you would like to work?' Cynthia asked.

Varun shrugged his shoulders. 'Wherever I get a job. Personally, I would like to try my hand at TV journalism, that's something that is yet to take off in India. Those who enter now are bound to ride the wave when it comes.'

Paul laughed. 'So we are going to see your mug plastered on CNN, getting your nuts shot off by Kashmiri terrorists, now that we know where you stand on self-determination.'

'Where do you think the inspiration for that essay came from? I may be about to get a B minus, but it was worth it.'

'I'd love to go to Kashmir someday,' Cynthia said.

Varun glanced at her. 'So would I. I hear it's the most beautiful place on earth. I went once, for a family vacation, but I was only three at the time so I don't remember a thing. And I have a horrible feeling I may not get the chance to go there again.'

Chapter Thirteen

CORDON-AND-SEARCH

In the nights, Srinagar was a ghost town. Shops shut down well before dusk, and cars scurried to get off the roads. People headed straight for home and safety after work, anxious to be indoors before dark.

And as the deep orange glow of the sunset on the Dal gave way to a brooding blackness, a veil of fear would descend over the valley. Nothing moved to disturb the darkness, except for an occasional army patrol speeding through the streets, nervous soldiers keeping their eyes open for the flash of a rocket. The silence was almost total, broken only by the stray barking of dogs in the distance. And sometimes by the sound of gunfire.

In the spring of 1992, it was two years since the insurgency had blown up. Though the people's involvement in the movement had dwindled, there seemed to be more militants than ever before, and they were better armed, better trained and better equipped. Though the security forces held their own during the day, they were forced to pull back into the safety of the barracks once it was dark, leaving only a few men outside, holed up in heavily protected bunkers.

And so the nights belonged to the shadowy men of darkness slipping through the side streets from one house to another, planning their moves for the coming day, and wreaking retribution on anyone who was thought to have assisted the army in any way.

It was about nine at night, and Yasmin had just finished

having dinner with her grandmother when there was a muffled knock on the door.

The two women jumped in alarm and looked at each other with frightened expressions. Then Yasmin went up to the tightly bolted door. 'Who is it?' she asked in a tremulous voice.

'It's me,' came the reply.

'Habib,' she cried in joy and flung the door open. And there he stood, thinner than when she had last seen him. He had stopped shaving, and the stubble on his face had thickened into a full beard. Habib turned to the men standing behind him.

'It's okay, Qasim. Go to the carpenter's house, I'll join you in a couple of hours.'

And then she was in his arms, holding him as if she would never let him go, barely conscious of the disapproving look her grandmother gave her. But these were unusual times, and muttering to herself the old lady went into the inner room, leaving the couple alone.

There was time then—barely enough—for all the little things that lovers do, small murmurs of contentment, fingers exploring each other's faces.

'How have you been?' he asked at last.

'I've been okay,' she said, her head on his shoulder, 'just a little tired sometimes. I had another run-in with Ayesha—having lost the battle to get me to wear a burqa, she is now pressurizing me not to work.'

Ayesha was the local head of the Dukhtaran-e-Millat, the Daughters of the Nation, a hardline organization of women. They fully subscribed to the fundamentalist view that women should be veiled and should stay at home. Free-thinking and outgoing women like Yasmin were anathema to them.

Habib sat back angrily. 'Did she threaten you again? If she did, I'll . . .'

'No. She knows about my relationship with you and restricts herself to the usual taunts about scarlet women. But my friends are scared. There was another acid attack on an unveiled woman not far from here. I had warned you, Habib,

I had warned you that there would be a clash some day with the fundamentalists.'

'Tell me about it,' said Habib bitterly. 'The Pakis have clearly decided that those of us who want complete independence cannot be trusted. All the money, all the new arms are being sent to HM.'

HM, or the Hizbul Mujahideen, was the armed wing of the Jamaat, and it stood firmly for accession to Pakistan. Its strict Islamic doctrine and opposition to complete independence for Kashmir had limited appeal for the people of the Valley, but in military terms there was no questioning its complete dominance among the militant outfits.

Habib walked over to the window. He parted the thick curtains just enough to peer out without making himself visible to anyone outside. On a rooftop a couple of hundred feet away he could make out the thickly swaddled figure of the JKLF lookout. At the height of the mass movement in 1990, there were entire neighbourhoods in the heart of Srinagar which the militants could claim as their own 'liberated zones'; but now Habib and his men were forced to keep shifting from house to house, locality to locality, worried about betrayal, constantly looking for that one elusive night of peaceful sleep.

'I think we are safe here tonight,' he said, turning back to Yasmin. 'There are only six of us here, the other boys have gone downtown. That will prevent any leaks to that bastard Zaidi.'

'You know,' he said, as he nuzzled into her neck, 'I am absolutely convinced that Zaidi and his cohorts are giving direct information about the JKLF to the Indian Army. It isn't a coincidence that we have lost thirty-five boys in the last two months, ever since we started direct cooperation at the neighbourhood level with Zaidi's group. But that's it, I'm calling a halt to sharing information with them—let them get it from their masters in Islamabad if they want.'

'Do you know what I want?' demanded Yasmin softly.

'What?' he asked, crinkling his face as he gently traced the outline of her face with his finger.

And for some time there was soft laughter in that little

corner of what was once Paradise. There was love and comfort, there was joy in living.

* * *

About four kilometres from where Yasmin and Habib held each other, in the heart of the army cantonment at Badami Bagh, grim-faced men belonging to the 7 Garwhal Rifles were filing into position. The only light came from a tiny lantern kept in the corner of the veranda from where their commanding officer was about to address them.

They were used to this pre-dawn ritual; the preparations for what the army called 'cordon-and-search', and what the local population called 'crackdown'. This was something the army did almost every night in those terrible years, and it led to tremendous alienation among the people of the valley.

Accompanying the soldiers into the square was a bleary-eyed Varun Mathur. His dreams of becoming a TV journalist had come true after he returned to India triumphantly bearing much better results than he had expected. And now he had been sent to cover Kashmir for the first time. He and his crew had landed at the airport the previous afternoon, and because they were army guests, they had been taken in an escorted convoy to Badami Bagh. In 1992 Kashmir was still a war zone, and for a new arrival there was plenty to gawk at: soldiers with bullet-proof jackets manning the intersections; the odd burnt-out and deserted building that was once home to a Kashmiri Pandit family that had been forced out of the Valley; and the convoy itself—a two-tonne army truck with a machine gun mounted on it leading the way, another truck bringing up the rear, and in the middle, a row of jeeps. Crouched in one of those jeeps were the would-be intrepid journalists peering out at the world through bullet-proof glass.

Soon after his arrival, Varun had been ushered into the office of the Brigadier General Staff, Arun Roy, and had promptly demanded to be allowed to film 'some action.' And this was the result, Varun's first ever cordon-and-search operation.

On the veranda, the commanding officer was beginning to speak. 'Our target this morning, gentlemen, is Zafar Bagh. We have no specific information, so we will be using the "cats" to flush out any terrorists who could be hiding there. The usual pattern will be followed, Company Alpha will be deployed down the left side canal, Company Bravo will take positions behind the main road to block off any possible escapes . . .'

As his voice droned on, Varun glanced at the reassuring presence of his cameraman, T. Raju, who was by now a Kashmir veteran for whom all of this was old hat. The third member of the team, the sound recordist, Ravi, puffed unconcerned at his cigarette and checked his equipment one more time.

And then it was time to leave. The soldiers clambered into the waiting trucks and the TV crew was bundled into the back of the nearest vehicle. A side gate of the cantonment was opened and the convoy eased cautiously out into the silent streets of Srinagar.

All headlights were switched off, each vehicle navigating by the dimmed sidelights of the truck in front. This was both to avoid alerting the militants' well-established information network, and to ensure that the convoy wouldn't become an easy target for a militant rocket.

*   *   *

Dawn was still an hour away, and the city continued to sleep in uneasy darkness.

Ten minutes later, the Garhwal Rifles had reached their destination. Four trucks stopped at the main road leading into Zafar Bagh and the soldiers scrambled out quickly; the other vehicles picked up speed as they fanned out to encircle the neighbourhood. Within minutes Zafar Bagh had been completely sealed off by the army cordon, a thin line of soldiers in camouflaged outfits manning every road and intersection, nursing their rifles nervously and scanning the rooftops, for that was where any militant breakout was most likely to occur.

The surprise was total. By the time the JKLF lookout on the roof in front of Yasmin's house had realized what was happening, the escape routes had been blocked.

Habib was snapped into immediate wakefulness by the insistent pounding on the door. He sprang to the window as Qasim shouted at him in a muted voice, 'Habib. We are fucked . . . it's a crackdown . . . the bastards are all around us.'

As Yasmin looked at him with naked terror in her eyes, Habib grabbed his AK-47 and told her, 'Whatever happens, you haven't seen me, you don't know me, I wasn't here. Khuda hafiz, my darling.'

And then the six men were running down the side of the street towards the canal from where they had planned to get away. They were still well inside Zafar Bagh, and the soldiers were on the periphery.

'We'll go down Teesri gali,' gasped Habib, 'from there we'll be able to slip into the canal and swim across into Habbakadal. The army won't have reached there yet.'

Darkness at this point was a friend and an ally, as they flitted along the narrow side streets. They slowed as they reached the end of Teesri gali, and while five of them waited, flattened against a shop shutter, Qasim edged his way forward to peer at the canal road. He turned around almost immediately, his face crumpled in shock and panic. The security forces had plugged every bolt-hole—waiting by the banks of the canal was a Border Security Force patrol, together with an armoured vehicle complete with a mounted machine gun.

'It's a fucking joint operation,' he whispered as he rejoined Habib. 'The goddamned BSF has already reached the canal—we are trapped.'

One of the younger militants, a sixteen-year-old whose face was yet to show its first stubble, looked ready to burst into tears. 'Habib bhai, should we shoot our way out? We can surprise them, and be in the canal within seconds.'

'Don't be a fool,' said Qasim savagely, 'they have one of those black vehicles of Satan out there, the machine gun would cut us into shreds before we moved ten steps.'

Habib was quiet, as his mind raced at the speed of light. 'There is only one option,' he said finally. 'I don't believe the army knows we are here—I think it is just our bad luck to have been caught in a random crackdown. We'll just have to bluff it out.'

Qasim stared at him. 'Are you mad! You must be the most wanted man in the entire Valley—what makes you think they won't spot you?'

Habib shrugged. 'If they do—it's bad luck. But no one in the army has seen either of us for years; we don't look the same as we did when their intelligence last filmed us in 1990. Besides, what choice do we have?'

There were several tense moments of silence, and then Qasim nodded slowly. Turning to the other men, he said, 'So be it. Let's hide the guns in this drain and hope that they don't find them till later. We cannot go into anyone's house at this stage, so let's wait for the call from the mosque and then join the crowds as they gather.'

The AK-47s were gathered and pushed deep into a ditch at the point where it went under the road. And then six desperately worried—and frightened—men sat in the shadows to wait for the call to prayer.

They didn't have to wait long. As the first rays of sunshine painted the sky with thin strands of orange, a polite major from the army walked up to the doors of the neighbourhood mosque. 'Imam sahib,' he said to the wizened old man who answered the knock, 'would you be so kind as to make the call from the mosque loudspeakers? Please ask all the men in Zafar Bagh to gather at the central square. They should carry nothing with them, and should leave the women and children at home. We promise that no one who is innocent will be harmed in any way and that no one will be mistreated.'

It was a familiar speech, the Imam knew the drill. Soon lights were appearing in the windows of Zafar Bagh and the first few men were stepping out into the cold morning air.

Varun and his crew had been unceremoniously dumped out of their truck and then left to their own devices. They latched onto a patrol being led by a cheerful Sikh captain waving a none-too-lethal swagger stick.

'So what happens now?' asked Varun.

'All these men will gather in the square, where they will paraded before a group of army informers. If any of them turn out to be terrorists, then that's it for them. Meanwhile, patrols like this will search the entire neighbourhood for any militants who hope to escape by hiding in cellars or attics.'

'But isn't it humiliating for all of these people to be turfed out into the cold like this? Wouldn't it be better if you only searched once you had definite information?'

The captain glanced at Varun. 'Off the record, let me say that I agree with you. And I believe we are now planning to phase out the entire system of cordon-and-search—but till we get definite orders, this is the way it has to be.'

The square in the heart of Zafar Bagh was starting to fill up with men, young and old, all clad in their phirans, and most of them clutching tiny *kangris*—the pots filled with burning coal which helped warm icy fingertips. And on all the faces was a mixture of resignation, bitterness, and just a touch of trepidation.

As a group of residents filed past the alley where Habib and his men hid in the shadows, the militants casually stepped out and joined the procession towards the square. Without a backward glance at each other, they split up and moved to different parts of the open area.

The soldiers were all around the square, asking those who entered to sit down on the ground. Habib walked as calmly as he could to where the crowd was the thickest, and squatted on the ground. The cold radiated up from the earth which was still speckled with traces of the night's frost, but when Habib looked down at his hands, the palms were moist with sweat, and there was a barely perceptible tremor in his fingertips. He quickly thrust his hands into the pockets of his phiran. From the corner of his eye he spotted Qasim a couple of hundred feet away, filching a cigarette from a distinguished-looking man with silver hair, and his lungs suddenly ached for a comforting puff or two.

'I knew I should have bought another packet yesterday,'

he muttered to himself, as he waited for the next act in the drama.

All over Zafar Bagh soldiers were entering houses, searching lofts, and looking for any hidden basements. This was a highly disciplined unit of the army, and most of the soldiers were unfailingly courteous and polite to the women and children who remained behind in the homes. Both the Indian and the foreign press had made much of incidents in smaller villages where security personnel had savaged local residents in operations like this, and now the army was at pains to try and seem correct in every way—especially with a TV crew filming every step.

Varun watched as his cameraman zoomed in on the captain knocking on the green door of a small house. 'Come right in,' said Yasmin, surprisingly calm. 'It's a tiny house, there is only me and my grandmother.' She waited till the cursory search was over and the captain had thanked her and left the house, before throwing herself onto the bed and breaking down.

A row of BSF vehicles entered the Zafar Bagh square and lined up along the wall of a school building. Each carried a 'cat', or informer, a former militant who had renounced the cause, either voluntarily or under the threat of further beatings. The cats had their faces covered with hoods in which little openings had been cut for the eyes. They sat in the back of the Maruti Gypsies, peering out through the windshields, with their minders sitting close beside them.

The soldiers swung into action like so many uniform-clad shepherds, making the sitting men of Zafar Bagh get up in small groups and file in front of the Gypsies. Each man was asked to stop before every vehicle and turn around a couple of times so that the cats could get a good look.

From where he was sitting, Habib saw Qasim being waved into the line and he stopped breathing. Agonizing minutes passed, as Qasim was displayed like some prized slave in an ancient Roman auction, and then Habib let out his breath with a rush as the last army jawan in the line jovially pounded Qasim on the back and waved him away.

And then it was Habib's turn. As the soldiers took hold of him, he forced himself to relax, trying to get his breathing to slow down. He stared into the dark windscreen of the first Gypsy. The informer inside shook his head and he was led to the second vehicle. Habib was paraded before three more vehicles, and in each case the hooded informer shook his head.

As Habib approached the fifth Gypsy, the cat inside stiffened. 'It's him . . . it's him . . . it's Habib Shah.'

The soldier sitting next to him shot forward and peered out through the windscreen. 'Are you sure?'

'Of course I'm sure, you idiot. Before I crossed over to the army I was with the Hizbul Mujahideen, and Habib and his men once questioned me with a pointed stick up my arse. That man is Habib Shah.'

And then all hell broke loose. As the soldier blew an insistent whistle, an entire squad of men wrestled Habib to the ground. His phiran was pulled over his head so that his arms were pinioned, and a number of gun barrels were pointed at his chest.

'Drag him into the school compound,' shouted the commanding officer. 'And double check the identity of every single man in the square—there must be other terrorists hiding in this crowd.'

Varun had arrived back in the square just in time, and he glanced to his right to ensure that Raju was capturing the footage of what could prove to be the scoop of the year. As Habib was dragged into the compound, he caught a brief glimpse of the camera and tried to shout a message for the millions who would watch this scene over and over again. But his voice was muffled by those who held him, and within seconds he had disappeared into a forest of uniforms and waving guns.

Qasim watched the scene from where he stood, almost 400 metres away. He knew that he was safe, but in his eyes there was a terrible emptiness.

Behind the green door, inside her small house, a young woman sat on her bed, tears trickling down her cheeks. She had heard the commotion coming from the Zafar Bagh square, and she knew there could only be one explanation.

Chapter Fourteen

A NEW JIHAD

Jalauddin stamped out the embers of the small fire on which he had been warming his hands for the past few hours. Dawn was just a few minutes away, soon the light would be good enough to shoot by. He loosened the woollen blanket which he had wrapped around himself; it was cold, but the parka he had brought with him from Afghanistan was quite adequate.

He examined the weapon that lay in his lap. He had bought it in the arms bazaar at Peshawar just a couple of months back, after trading in his old AK-47. His fingers delicately traced the carving on the metal trigger guard, and then ran back to caress the wooden stock, slippery and fragrant with the gun oil he had spent hours rubbing into every crack and crevice.

He raised the weapon to his shoulder, marvelling once again at the incredible balance the English gunsmith had built into it, and then glanced around. The horizon stood out clearly now, and the bushes at the edges of the fields could be seen distinctly. It was time to get into position.

He reached out and shook Karim, who had dozed off in a sitting position right next to the fire. Karim snapped awake instantly, and sat up ram-rod straight. Then they both turned to look at the brooding figure sitting on a rock some distance away.

It had been a couple of years since Jalauddin had last seen Langryal. As the Soviets pulled out of Afghanistan, Jalauddin had returned to his village near Peshawar, trying to get back into the routine of crop cultivation and family politics. When it all became unbearably dull, he would help out the local drug smugglers get their opium in from Afghanistan, providing some arms and muscle to their operations. The jihad had begun to fade from his memory.

Then Langryal arrived in his village unannounced. Jalauddin had greeted Langryal with all the affection and respect he still felt for the man he considered his mentor, and had then quickly summoned Karim, another of Langryal's proteges, from his village just a few kilometres away.

Now as the sun swept away the last remaining shadows of darkness, Jalauddin walked up to Langryal, 'Khan sahib, are you all set? We should get into position soon if we really want good sport.'

Langryal looked at him unblinkingly for a couple of seconds, and then flashed a quick smile. 'So this is what you call sport now, is it? A few birds kicked out from their bushes?'

Jalauddin smiled back. 'I'm sorry, Khan sahib, we have no Mi-24s for you to hunt here in Peshawar; you will have to make do with some of our local partridges. Although let me tell you, these birds can often be as hard to hit as the gunships.'

Langryal reached out his hand for Jalauddin's weapon. 'This looks like a woman's gun.'

Jalauddin was visibly affronted. 'It's a twelve bore, Khan sahib. A twenty-five-inch Churchill, double barrel. I use it every week for some shikar.' Hunting was a new passion acquired from the local landlord, a man with whom Jalauddin had spent several happy hours chasing antelopes and partridges all over his farm. He'd brought Langryal to the farm early this morning, certain he would enjoy the shikar too, and now he was just a little miffed at his mentor's lack of interest.

Langryal examined the gun carefully, snapping open the barrel and looking inside. Then he held it out to Jalauddin and rose to his feet. 'Let's get started. What do I shoot with?'

'You use the Churchill. I'll help beat the birds from the bushes.'

Langryal nodded, and they set off for a nearby patch of sugarcane. Jalauddin positioned Langryal and Karim at one end of the fifty metre-long field of cane, and then walked to the far end with a couple of young boys from the village whom he had promised a few rupees in return for their help.

They shook out a long length of rope and each of the lads took one end and walked to opposing sides of the field. At a signal from Jalauddin, they began to walk down the sides of the field, sawing the rope across the tops of the sugarcane. This resulted in a tremendous cacophony, to which Jalauddin added his own contribution by hurling stones and clapping his hands. As the beaters approached, Karim opened his own shotgun and stuffed in a pair of no. 6 shells. Then he glanced across to his right where Langryal was standing in a relaxed posture, the Churchill thrown over his shoulder as he gazed unconcerned at the beaters.

The first bird broke back over Jalauddin's head, and he glared at it as it sailed over him, well out of range for the waiting shotguns. Then a fat black partridge fluttered out of the side of the cane, flying fast and level towards the right, not trying to gain any height. In an unhurried movement, Langryal brought the Churchill to his shoulder, tracking the bird for a split second, before pressing the trigger. There was a puff of feathers and the partridge somersaulted in mid-air.

At the sound of the shot, another partridge took to the air from inside the cane, this one heading straight for Langryal. This would be the most difficult shot of all. Langryal waited till the bird was just a few yards over his head, and then hit it with a direct blast of lead. At that range the pellets had no time to spread, and the shot disintegrated the bird, feathers landing on Langryal's head as if in benediction.

As he opened the shotgun to reload, a pair of brown partridges erupted from the very edge of the field, flying directly between Karim and Langryal. Karim got one, but then swore to himself as his second shot went too high. The bird had almost reached safety when Langryal snapped shut his reloaded gun, swivelled around and fired without seeming to take aim, bringing down the partridge inches away from the extreme range of the shotgun.

It was brilliant shooting, and as Jalauddin reached them, he muttered his approbation with what appeared to be a measure of filial pride. Langryal smiled, and handed the Churchill over to him.

Then he said, 'Enough of this now, let us sit somewhere and talk for a while.' Jalauddin looked disappointed. 'But, Khan sahib, there are plenty of other fields left. I thought you may want to enjoy the sport for a little longer.'

Langryal shook his head firmly, but smiled to take the edge off his refusal. 'When the jihad is on, such small sport cannot interest me for long.'

Jalauddin squatted on his haunches with ill grace, shaking out some tobacco from a little pouch into his palm as he did so. 'I thought the jihad was over. The Russians have left, and now our brothers are killing each other.'

Langryal looked straight at him. 'This is a new jihad, against a new enemy. I'm going to Kashmir.'

That surprised Jalauddin. 'I thought the Kashmiri movement was to be left to the locals. That's what the ISI man had told me when I returned from Afghanistan.'

'The plans have changed. The Kashmiri fighters can't take on the Indians.' Langryal's lips curled just a little in disdain. 'They fire their guns while hiding behind parapets, throw grenades while crawling for cover. It has been decided that some of us from the Afghan war will go to strengthen their backbones. We are also to lead them towards the correct path of Islam, show them how their true goal should be oneness with the Ummah.'

For three years the Pakistanis had backed the insurgency in Kashmir. At first they had tapped into the popular mood by backing the pro-independence JKLF. Then, slowly, they began to shift their support to the far more pliant Hizbul Mujahideen, and to other groups that wanted Kashmir to be part of Pakistan. Now it was time to send in men whom India would term as foreign mercenaries, and whom the insurgents would call guest militants: Pakistanis or Afghans who were battle-hardened in the war against the Soviets.

'We met a couple of months ago. Our amir, Maulvi

Shadatullah Khan, was there, as was your old commander Haqqani. We were joined there by one of the top leaders of the Harkat-ul-Mujahideen, Maulana Masood Azhar, I don't know if you have ever heard of him. There was talk of merging our organizations to form a new group, the Harkat-ul-Ansar, a group which will be the hammer of Islam.'

Jalauddin shifted a little on his haunches in excitement. Langryal went on, without seeming to notice: 'The new group will take time to set up. But I am leading a group into Kashmir. Some locals, others from here. I leave in a few days.'

Jalauddin looked across at Karim, who was also sitting rivetted, before asking quietly, 'Why didn't you consider us for the mission? It wouldn't have taken me all that long to wrap up my work here.'

'I know, and I thought of calling you. But then I felt it is best if I go across myself and see what the situation is before taking all of you there. Besides, it's good to have loyal friends waiting at home, it will be up to you to help me if things go wrong.'

Karim spat extravagantly into the mud. 'We beat the Soviets. How much trouble can a bunch of *banias* be?' Langryal smiled, but shook his head. 'Don't underestimate them. The Soviets we beat in Afghanistan were a ragtag bunch of conscripts, forced against their will to fight in an alien land. The Indian soldiers believe they are fighting in and for their motherland. There's a big difference.'

'I guess so,' agreed Jalauddin, 'they did beat the Pakistani army in all the wars so far. But they have never been up against the mujahideen.'

Langryal stretched out on the embankment that fringed the meadow, reaching out for a couple of sprigs of green chickpeas from the adjoining field. 'What do we have to lose anyway? If we return safely from the jihad, we are heroes. And if we die, we will go straight to heaven as martyrs.'

*   *   *

There was a third possibility—capture, imprisonment and a life spent in a dark cell behind iron bars.

Nasrullah Langryal entered Indian territory with fourteen men, and moved along the mountain heights to a virgin part of Jammu and Kashmir, till now untouched by militancy and violence. This was a region some distance away from the Valley, a remote, thickly forested and hilly province called Doda. Here Langryal planned and executed a series of raids and ambushes, spreading the message that the 'guest militants' had come to Kashmir.

In Pakistan, Maulana Masood Azhar was busy organizing the merger of the HUM and the HUJI into the new Harkat-ul-Ansar. He sent his deputy, Sajjad Afghani, into Kashmir, and began making preparations to cross into India himself, taking the safe route via Nepal.

But by 11 February 1994 all three were in jail. Langryal was picked up after a raid by the Indian army near his base in Kapran; Sajjad Afghani and Masood Azhar were arrested while travelling in an autorickshaw in the town of Anantnag. It was a blow that the Harkat-ul-Ansar never fully recovered from. The outfit would launch a whole series of kidnappings and hijackings to get back its jailed leaders, but not till the dawn of the new millennium would any of them walk free again.

Chapter Fifteen

VARUN IN SRINAGAR

The green taxi sped down Residency Road as if it was being chased by an armoured car, and Varun took a tighter hold of the strap that was dangling from the door frame to his right, turning to smile ruefully at the cameraman Raju, who sat slouched comfortably, as if he hadn't a care in the world.

Minutes later the car swerved dangerously off the road into a side street and screeched to a halt in front of a huge iron gate ten metres inside the alley. The gate was opened, and the driver nodded his thanks to the boy who had swung it open. Beyond the gate was a tiny courtyard, about twenty yards square, crammed with a number of taxis, all of them vintage Ambassador cars.

Varun clambered thankfully out of the car and headed for the front entrance of the hotel. He loved Mansoor, the taxi driver, dearly, but often wondered if he wasn't a far greater threat to life and limb than the JKLF and the Hizbul Mujahideen put together.

He pushed open the glass door with a feeling of homecoming. Ahdoos had been the only functioning hotel for the past three years, and was the main shelter for the stream of journalists who had come cascading into the Valley ever since the troubles began. The furnishings were eccentric, the fittings more than a little frayed around the edges, and phones and electricity were both available only occasionally. But the hotel normally had hot water on tap, and divine food when the chef was able to turn up.

Besides, by now the hotel had become like a second home and the staff were like family. Varun pounded on the counter and bellowed for Shakeel, the receptionist, who emerged from behind a curtain with a big smile on his face. 'There you are at last,' he said, clasping Varun to his chest. 'I had begun to wonder if you had abandoned us completely.'

'No such luck,' grinned Varun. 'There were some big stories breaking down in the plains. Besides, things seem more under control here.'

Shakeel shook his head dolefully. 'Far from it. The killings continue, grenade attacks by the militants happen all the time, and innocent young men are still picked up by the security forces and are never heard of again. We civilians are caught in the middle and we pay the price.'

Varun nodded his head grimly. It was a familiar story, one that he had heard all over Kashmir during his last visit a couple of months before. It was obvious that popular support for militancy had begun to wane, and dramatically so, although no one had the nerve to say a word against 'the boys' on camera. But at the same time, anger and bitterness against the security forces still ran high, fuelled every week by the heavy-handedness of those who made the mistake of treating every Kashmiri as an active or potential militant.

'Salaam aleikum, Shakeel bhai,' said Raju, as he toted some of his equipment into the reception area.

'Waleikum salaam, Raju sahib. Please leave your bag, I'll send it up to your room.'

'Trust my camera to your hooligans? Fat chance. Do we have our usual room?'

'Yes, of course. I'll send the suitcases up.'

As Raju headed off down the dark passageway towards the staircase, Varun leant on the reception counter for a few minutes more, chatting about life in the Valley. 'Tell me, how active are all of these "guest militants"?'

Shakeel shrugged. 'We are hearing a lot about them. They are good fighters and have lifted the morale of some of the tanzeems. But others are unhappy that outsiders have come into the movement. Is that the story you have come to do?'

'Well, I mentioned their presence in my last story as well, but now I plan a more in-depth piece, trying to analyse what they stand for and what they actually want.'

'One word of advice, Varun bhai. Don't put yourself into their hands hoping for an interview. They aren't like our local Kashmiri militants with whom you go off so happily. These are different men, journalists aren't necessarily safe with them. Be particularly careful of the Harkat-ul-Ansar.'

So far there had been an unwritten covenant of peace between the militants and the reporters who came from other parts of India and from abroad to cover the insurgency. Journalists like Varun had felt perfectly safe getting into unknown cars right in the courtyard of Ahdoos hotel and being whisked away blindfolded into the hideouts of the top leaders of the militancy.

There were codes to follow, which were soon picked up by Kashmir hands in the press, and so far no journalist had been hurt. But times were changing, and Varun nodded his agreement to Shakeel. 'No, I wasn't planning on seeking an interview with anyone in the Harkat-ul-Ansar. In any case, the organization must be a shambles right now with the arrest of Masood Azhar, Sajjad Afghani and Langryal—all within a couple of months.'

'It's in trouble, but still dangerous.'

'Don't worry. I wouldn't even know whom to contact in the Harkat.' Varun pushed himself away from the reception desk. 'Not like the JKLF, where I'm sure you can still arrange for me to interview Javed Mir over a plate of kababs right here in the hotel.'

He started off towards the staircase, but then paused and turned back. 'Do me a favour. Please book a call to my Delhi office. If your exchange hasn't improved, it will probably be day after tomorrow by the time the call is put through.'

Trotting up the stairs, Varun turned down the corridor towards Room 104, faintly dismayed to see it looking even more shabby than the last time. He was even more dismayed to find Raju in deep conversation with Gopalkrishnan, the cameraperson for KTV, the only other major TV organization in the country. Though Varun was by now used to KTV crews dogging his steps as he tried to chase exclusive stories, he had hoped that this time he would have Srinagar to himself. Besides, he didn't like Gopalkrishnan too much. There had been a couple of run-ins in the past; Gopalkrishnan had refused to lend Varun's team a spare tape just before a vital unscheduled press conference, and on another occasion he had deliberately misled them over the whereabouts of a politician whose comments were needed for a breaking story.

But Varun perked up a little when he learnt that Gopalkrishnan was here with Sanjiv Deshpande, KTV's principal correspondent, and the man who often handled Kashmir for them. Not only was Sanjiv a much nicer person than his cameraman, he invariably carried tucked away in his suitcase the odd bottle of vodka and, if you were lucky, Scotch, specially arranged by his pet bootlegger. With the militants imposing the Islamic code, liquor was not available in the Valley, and few journalists had the nerve to defy the ban on booze by carrying their own supplies. Somehow Sanjiv had always got away with it.

Promising to drop in for a snifter after dinner, Varun escorted Sanjiv and Gopalkrishnan to the door, and then slumped in a chair, only to jump up as the phone rang. 'Sonofabitch. The call is through in twenty minutes, that must be some sort of a record.'

Waving to Raju to lower the volume of the TV set, Varun picked up the receiver. It was Shakeel, sounding a little bemused. 'A call for you. From the army exchange.'

Now it was Varun's turn to sound bemused. 'Army exchange? How do they know that I'm here?'

Shakeel shrugged at the other end of the line and put the call through. It wasn't a very clear connection, and Varun pressed the receiver hard against his ear. 'Yes, this is Varun Mathur here.'

'Good afternoon, Mr Mathur. This is Colonel Brar, calling from the Badami Bagh cantonment. I was sitting behind you in the Indian Airlines flight to Srinagar and recognized you instantly. You are the man who did that report on the foreign mercenaries, aren't you?'

Varun's mind was racing as he tried to figure out all the possible angles. In a war zone like Srinagar it was always sensible to be extremely careful while talking to strangers, especially to someone who had called up out of the blue and who may or may not be the person he claimed to be.

'Yes, I am,' he answered cautiously, sitting down on the bed and taking out his notepad and pen, just in case.

'Mr Mathur, why don't you come to Badami Bagh tomorrow morning? We have someone with us whom you might want to meet.'

'Who?'

There was a low laugh. 'You won't be disappointed. We liked your last few stories. This will be quite a scoop for you.'

'Okay, where should I come, and how do I get there? Should I come to the main Batwara gate?'

'No, come to the side gate, near the helipad. Do you know where that is?'

'Yes, I've been there before.'

'Roger. I'll have Lt Shastri meet you at the gate and take you in. Is eleven all right?'

'Yes, that's absolutely fine.'

'Could I have the names of those who will be accompanying you?'

'Just my cameraperson. His name is T. Raju, and we'll be in a green taxi, JKT 3984.'

As the phone was disconnected, Varun sat there staring dumbly at the instrument for a couple of seconds, as Raju walked up to him with a lit cigarette. 'You look as if you need this. What's the deal?'

Varun explained, and Raju stared out of the window thoughtfully. 'I don't suppose it is a trap of some sort.'

Varun shook his head. 'No, it sounded like a call routed through the army exchange. Besides, if one of the militant groups wanted to get us, they would hardly try to lure us to one of the highest security zones in the whole of Srinagar. They would pretend to be Javed Mir or someone like that and try and get us to go downtown.'

'They wouldn't even have to do that,' grunted Raju. 'They

could just walk into this dump and whisk us away ... Um ... the other problem, of course, is that this jaunt means crossing the line.'

There was silence for a minute or two. In those days there were few rules that were more firmly hammered into the head of any journalist wanting to cover Kashmir than the need to avoid 'crossing the line'. A journalist could either come to the Valley as a guest of the army, stay behind walls in heavy security and travel in fortified convoys. Or he could stay out in the open, with absolutely no security, relying on his press card to keep him out of trouble with the militants. You couldn't do both. Living 'in the open', in a hotel like Ahdoos, and zipping in and out of army bases was the surest way to arouse the suspicions—and perhaps the wrath—of some militant group or the other. Some journalists took the rule to extremes; if they were 'in the open', they wouldn't greet the commander of a passing army patrol, even if he were their own brother, just in case someone was watching.

'I don't think we have a choice,' said Varun eventually. 'This sounds like a big story, there is no way we can miss it. We'll use Mansoor, he won't tell anyone where we are going.'

Mansoor came early to get them the next morning; they knew that the security checks could take a long time. They drove down Residency Road and turned right, skirting the high-security zone of Gupkar Road, to approach the sprawling Badami Bagh cantonment. Always a mini city, the years of militancy had made it even more self-sufficient; those who lived in it found it impossible to move outside without security, especially during the hours of darkness. Mansoor drove past the main Batwara gate and slowed down a few hundred yards further as he approached the side gate. The nervous-looking sentry manning the outer barricade looked a bit tense, and then relaxed a little as he compared the number on the licence plate with a slip of paper in his hand.

A young army officer walked out of the sentry hut and approached their car. Varun climbed out and walked slowly up to him. 'Good morning, I'm Varun Mathur from Vision TV.'

'Yes, Mr Mathur, I recognize you. But can I please see your press card? I'm Lt Shastri, by the way. You'll have to leave your taxi outside, of course.'

'Of course. That's my cameraperson Raju, he's already taking out the stuff.'

Raju was busy piling up the equipment on the side of the road—a tripod, a case containing the Portalights, a bag with spare tapes and batteries. In early 1994 the equipment for a TV crew was far bulkier than it is now; Varun went back to help Raju, and they both groaned under the weight as they staggered up to the inner barricade for the mandatory security checks.

The sentry opened up everything, poking suspiciously at the mess of cables inside the bags even as Lt Shastri muttered at him impatiently. Then they were through, piling into the jeep that was waiting for them on the other side. Seconds later they were at a large hut on the edge of a gigantic field that essentially functioned as a helipad, but which could also be used as a driving range by the odd golf-minded general.

Waiting for them at the entrance of the hut was a large Sikh colonel. 'Mr Mathur? Brar here.'

'Hello, sir,' said Varun politely, shaking the proffered hand. And then he couldn't restrain his curiosity any more. 'Sorry to be blunt, but can I ask whom you have for us to interview?' In his mind he thought, 'If they've done all this to produce some retired general who wants to air his views on tactical warfare, I'll murder someone.'

Colonel Brar laughed. 'Come in, Mr Mathur, come in. We have a room here where your cameraman can set up. Whom do we have? Have you heard of a man called Nasrullah Langryal?'

Varun went pale, as little voices began to scream 'scoop, scoop, scoop' inside his ear.

'Nasrullah Langryal? The HUJI and Harkat-ul-Ansar commander?'

'I see you have done your homework,' smiled Colonel Brar. 'Set up your equipment. We'll get him in shortly.'

'Any ground rules?' asked Varun warily.

'No, none at all,' Colonel Brar sounded shocked. 'Ask him what you want. As you know, we've had him with us for some weeks now; I think you will be as fascinated by his psyche as we were.'

Raju had by now arranged the setting for the interview, two chairs facing each other in the gloomy, completely bare room. He looked ruefully at the blank white wall which would be in the background during the interview, and decided that there was nothing that could be done about it; trying to drag in flowerpots or repositioning curtains would make the whole thing look artificial. He unravelled two long microphone wires and stretched them across the concrete floor, one for Varun and the other for Langryal. Meanwhile Varun unpacked the Portalights and set them up on their stands.

A few minutes later they were all set, and Varun turned to Colonel Brar. 'We are all set for the interview, but we'd like to get some cutaways . . . I mean, some footage of Langryal being led in.'

Brar nodded. 'Fine. Come here to the door and you can get some shots.'

The room they were in led out to another, much larger room which was a kind of hall, and a short while later a group of four men appeared at the far end of the hall, escorting the chained figure of Langryal.

At first glance Varun wasn't terribly impressed. Langryal seemed a small, shrunken man, clad in a faded phiran and with his head covered by a woollen bonnet. He'd been under sustained interrogation for more than a month now and that seemed to have aggravated the limp which was a legacy of the Afghan war. He was led to his chair, where he sat quietly, his head down as he refused to make eye contact.

Varun began with his questions softly, trying to establish some sort of a rapport, some connection before reaching the tougher questions. Langryal answered in monosyllables to begin with, and then, slowly, he opened out. After twenty minutes of patient prodding, Varun began getting the answers he wanted.

'Why are you here? What is your objective?'

'We want a united Islamic Ummah, from Africa and Europe to India. Inshallah, we will achieve that goal.'

'So it has nothing to do with Kashmir and the Kashmiri people?'

'What is good for Islam is good for the Kashmiri people as well.'

'You are saying that your main goal is not Kashmir and Kashmiri azaadi but a pan-Islamic confederation?'

'That is correct. All Muslims should be freed.'

'But Muslims are perfectly free to practise their religion in a country like India . . .'

Langryal raised his head for the first time, and looked straight at Varun. 'And the martyrdom of the Babri Masjid? What of that?'

'That was something bitterly condemned by millions of non-Muslims as well all over India. State governments were dismissed and inquiries set up.'

Langryal continued to stare straight at Varun, his eyes glittering under the glare of the TV lights. 'We would prefer direct action to unite all Muslims under one rule.'

Varun changed tack a little. 'How many of you foreign fighters are there in Kashmir right now?'

'Enough. And their number will grow and grow. They are coming to us in their thousands, from Pakistan, from Afghanistan, from Sudan, Somalia, Palestine . . .'

'Aren't most of the fighters Pakistanis, like you?'

'Yes, but the others will follow.'

'Tell me, what do you think will be your future, your fate?'

It was perhaps a low blow, and the glitter faded from Langryal's eyes as his head dropped again. 'I will probably spend my entire life in jail. But I don't mind. I had a mission and I carried it out.'

'Your men recently kidnapped and killed Major Bhupinder Singh to seek your release. Do you think that was correct?'

'No. I think kidnapping isn't Islamic.'

A clicking noise from behind Varun's left shoulder told him that Raju had finished another tape, the third so far. He turned and shook his head as Raju held up a blank tape enquiringly. 'No, I think we are all done.'

Langryal continued to sit there, staring at the floor, as the soldiers entered the room once again and helped him to his feet. Then the chains were refastened around his wrists, and the back collar of his phiran was pulled over his head, a simple way to both immobilize him and to ensure that he couldn't survey his surroundings. Raju quickly pulled his camera off the tripod and followed the soldiers out of the building as they shepherded the bundled-up figure down the stairs and into a waiting army truck.

Varun watched the truck drive away, and then gratefully accepted a cigarette from Raju. Colonel Brar had come out to join them on the veranda. He smiled broadly at the journalists, 'Nice interview, I thought. And I am glad that the man was so candid about his long-term goals.'

'How important are these foreign militants now?'

'I'll arrange an interview with the BGS if you like, he can give you all the details. But the short answer to your question is that many of them are coming in and they are giving a tough fight to our boys. Many of the locals used to hide behind a wall and fire a short burst before running for cover. These guys fight to the death. But if you ask me, the Pakis are making a big mistake. These guys have no sympathies with the Kashmiris, and the Kashmiris have no great affection for them. The more the movement is taken over by the foreigners, the wider the rift between the Kashmiri people and the militants. And that's good news for us.'

Varun didn't dare to trust the tapes to the usual route out of Srinagar—a stout brown paper packet taped up tightly and sent via the afternoon flight back to Delhi. He decided that he would keep the tapes with himself and edit the interview after returning to Delhi.

But he couldn't help the smug expression that sat on his face that evening as Sanjiv and Gopalakrishnan came to their room for dinner. Sanjiv raised an eyebrow, curious and half envious, as he poured generous helpings of vodka into the thick tumblers they had taken from the bathrooms. 'Big story, huh?'

'Not bad. Wait and see what it is. What did you do today?'

Sanjiv grimaced. 'Human rights violation. We went to check out the Hassan Khan story.'

Varun knew the case. 'Young guy, not much older than sixteen, picked up by the BSF in a routine sweep and his body delivered back to the parents the next morning. Is that the one?'

'That's the one. I'm convinced that the local commandant is corrupt—he's the sort of man who picks up innocents to see if he can extort some money out of the relatives. Though in this case the boy wasn't with them long enough for there to be any blackmail attempts—besides he was from an extremely poor background. So this was probably just bad intel; privately the forces admit that the kid was no militant.'

The brooding figure of Gopalkrishnan suddenly spoke up from behind his glass of vodka. 'All these army types are bastards. Look at the way they talk to the locals. Look at the way they harass ordinary citizens. When you drive to the fucking airport, they harass you. Treat you like some fucking animal.'

There was sudden silence in the room. Varun was a little surprised by the vehemence of the outburst. Then Sanjiv broke the silence, 'Come on, Gopal, all of them aren't bad. Some exceed their brief and some just don't know how to deal with the absolute power which they seem to have been given . . .'

'Fuck it,' exploded Gopalkrishnan. 'That's easy for you to say, you don't have to live here under their thumb all the goddamn time.'

Varun intervened smoothly. 'I agree that the rougher elements in the forces have to be reined back. You can't expect a solution here while waving a stick at the population. But you know, the militants often behave even worse with the civilians than the security forces do. And I'm not sure . . .'

'Give the locals azaadi and forget about this hellhole,' pronounced Gopalkrishnan, pouring himself another slug.

'Come on, get real!' Varun was starting to get angry. 'I'm not even sure any more that the majority of Kashmiris really

want to be left alone under the rule of the foreign militants
and the fundamentalists.'

He was warming to his theme when he caught Sanjiv's
eye, and noticed the warning hand that he had casually raised
just below the edge of the table. Just then there was a knock
on the door and Raju changed the subject with some alacrity.

'Food! About time that Shahid came to take our order.'

Their waiter entered the room, grinning widely from ear
to ear. He had served them the very first time Varun came to
the Valley, and they had forged a strong bond over the years.
There were times when the whole city had been under curfew
but Shahid had crept out of the hotel to get some chicken to
make the *yakhni* that Varun adored. On another occasion,
Varun and his taxi driver had driven across riot-scarred
Srinagar in the middle of vicious stone throwing from angry
mobs to get Shahid home.

Now Varun rose to his feet and hugged Shahid fondly.
'How have you been, you rogue? And what do you have for
us this evening? Wazwan?'

'Varun sahib at the hotel and no wazwan to eat? I value
my life. We can get you goshtaba and we can get you yakhni.'

Varun smiled broadly at Sanjiv. 'Well, my day is made.
I'm convinced that the main reason I have chosen Kashmir as
my beat is the food here.'

'I'll go for the goshtaba too,' said Sanjiv, and Raju
concurred. 'Gopal? How about you?'

Gopalkrishnan seemed to have retired into deep
contemplation of the colourless liquid in his glass. But he
silently nodded his head, and then said gruffly, 'And I'd like
some seekh kababs.'

Sanjiv turned back to Shahid. 'Two plates goshtaba, one
chicken yakhni, some naan, and a plate of seekh kababs. And
some Coke or Pepsi if you have some.'

'Will do. Anything else? The room okay? TV tuned all
right? Shower working?'

'Everything is fine,' smiled Varun. 'Incidentally, how is
your brother? I haven't seen him since he went off to open
that dhaba at Pahalgam.'

'He's not making too much money right now; there are hardly any tourists around. Only some foreigners come, and they are mainly students on a tight budget.' Shahid picked up a couple of used glasses and started to move towards the door. 'Inshallah, peace will soon return, and with it the tourists.'

There was a snort from Gopalkrishnan, 'Fucking dreamworld all you bastards live in. You Kashmiris are too soft . . .'

Sanjiv cut in quickly. 'Where are you guys going tomorrow? Will you be in Srinagar or are you heading out somewhere?'

'No, we are travelling to Sopore. I believe it has quietened down considerably in the last few months, but it's still a hotbed of militancy. How about you?'

'Back to Delhi, I'm afraid. It will be nice to be warm once again, but the prospect of spending some quality time with my far-from-beloved news editor doesn't exactly fill me with joy.'

Varun laughed and rose to his feet. 'That reminds me, I'd better call up the office and tell everyone at home that I'm still in one piece. It'll be faster to call from the reception. I'll be back in a few minutes.'

Sanjiv stood up as well. 'I'll come with you, I have to call my wife.'

They walked down the corridor, and Sanjiv said, 'Don't allow Gopal to rattle you. He's basically a good sort, just a little highly strung.'

Varun nodded. 'He doesn't seem the most stable of people to come to the Valley with, though.'

'No, he's quite okay most of the time,' said Sanjiv defensively. 'He's worse after he's had a peg or two.'

Varun shrugged. It really wasn't any of his business. Personally, he wouldn't have dreamt of coming to Kashmir without a reliable cameraperson; someone like Raju, who was quick with his reflexes and experienced enough to be a perfect sounding board on the direction a story should take. Plus Raju was level-headed enough to have a fine instinct for the dividing line between an acceptable risk and one that was too dangerous. Varun never took any decision on their shoots without consulting him.

They reached the reception and handed Shakeel the numbers to dial before stepping out into the courtyard for a quick smoke. The steel gate leading into Ahdoos had been closed and locked, and Srinagar had retreated into its nightly shell of complete silence and inaction. The only disturbance would be the barking of the street dogs and, occasionally, the sound of gunfire as militants fired on the army and BSF bunkers dotted across the city.

Now the silence was broken by a loud bang, followed by hysterical firing. Both Sanjiv and Varun leapt back. 'I think they've hit the Lal Chowk bunker with a grenade,' said Varun, peering over the gate at the small stretch of road that was visible.

'Could be, though I think it sounded further away,' said Sanjiv. 'It may even be the Dal gate bunker. Poor buggers, it must be a nightmare spending the night in one of those bunkers, surrounded by sandbags, darkness and a thousand people plotting to kill you.'

'I was once foolish enough to spend Republic Day eve in a bunker in downtown Srinagar,' replied Varun, pulling open the door to return to the warmth of the reception. 'It sounded like Diwali night to me. They hit the bunker with everything from pistol fire to a couple of grenades. I think I aged ten years in those eight hours.'

A few minutes later Shakeel finally got through to Delhi, and Varun was on the line to his news editor. 'I've got a big story here,' he whispered, keeping one eye on the door through which he could still see Sanjiv puffing at the butt of his cigarette. 'Can't talk about it now, but keep space for my story once I return. I plan to take the flight on Saturday.'

'Can't you return earlier?' asked the harried editor, running a despairing eye over the rosters before him.

'Well, let's see. There are rumours that the government might be planning some initiatives, like releasing some of the jailed militant leaders. If that isn't happening, then I can fly out earlier.'

Chapter Sixteen

A LONG HOT SUMMER

Waves of heat shimmered across Delhi, the sun scorching the ground mercilessly as it reached with fingers of fire into every corner to banish all hope of respite in the shade. It was already 43° C in Delhi, and it was still only the middle of April.

Vijay Kaul unlocked the door of his Maruti 800 and winced as the blast of superheated air leapt out of the interiors to singe his face. Parking the car for even half an hour in the sun meant that the interiors were perfect for baking a pizza or two, and he waited for the worst of the hot air to disperse a little. Then he eased himself into the car and hastily switched on the air conditioner, which hissed in muted protest at the enormity of the task he was thrusting on it. He winced again as he tried to touch the steering wheel, and reminded himself to get a cover for it as soon as possible.

He pulled away from the parking lot in front of the Defence Ministry and started down Raisina Hill towards the majestic but deserted expanse of Rajpath. There was hardly anyone to be seen outdoors, except for some gardeners lying under trees at the edge of the boulevard's lawns. They had stripped down to their vests and shorts, and looked as if they would like to hang their tongues out and pant like dogs. Beyond them, there was some water in the canal which ran alongside Rajpath, and some street urchins had found the perfect way to beat the heat by taking off all their clothes and jumping straight in.

Vijay stepped on the accelerator as he headed towards India Gate. In front of him the road shimmied and wobbled in a mirage, giving the illusion of puddles of water spread all along its surface. Vijay drove even faster, easing his damp shirt front away from his soaking skin as he raced for the shelter of his residence. Five minutes later he was home, standing in front of the desert cooler.

He groaned in relief as the blast played over his face, and then turned to grin at his mother as she walked into the room. 'My God, Amma, you have no idea what it is like out there.'

She smiled at him. 'Rooh Afza?'

'I'd love some, thanks.'

Amma pottered off, and then returned bearing a glass of the sweet red liquid. Vijay accepted it gratefully, and then asked, 'Where is Papa?'

'It's time for his afternoon nap. He'll be up in half an hour or so.'

Retirement and exile did not suit Papa. He had put on too much weight. He had also become impatient and somewhat cantankerous, and keeping him in good humour was now a full-time occupation for Amma.

She sat down on the sofa and gestured to Vijay to take a seat. 'What did they want? Why did you have to go to the ministry?'

'Remember Captain Rajiv Sahni, my coursemate at the IMA? He's working at the ministry these days, and he wanted to see me. He had some news he wanted to give me before it was officially announced.' He paused, uncertain about how she was going to take it.

'And?'

'And our unit is being shifted from the cantonment here. We are being posted to Badami Bagh.'

There was silence for several minutes. They had all expected it, they knew that some day Vijay would be called to serve in the Valley. But for a while Amma's mind churned with fear at this, the first posting for Vijay in a danger spot.

Then she smiled bravely, 'At least you will be away from this heat.'

'Plus I'll get a chance to see Srinagar again. It's been almost four years.'

Amma nodded and then she was lost as half-forgotten memories came rushing back. The stream running behind the house, its waters, crisp and sweet, gurgling happily over flat round stones; the willows bent over like gnarled old men, their leaves caressing the surface of the water with a lover's touch; the fragrant fields of saffron at the small farm which Papa had purchased in Pampore.

She remembered the market behind the Jamia Masjid, the bargains spread out on cots, and heavily veiled ladies jostling for little sweaters for their grandchildren; the reflection of the Hazratbal mosque glistening in the Dal Lake like a mini Taj Mahal, as the muezzin called the faithful for their evening prayers; and the weekends at Gulmarg, where in summer the carpet of thick snow was removed for spring cleaning by nature and replaced with exquisitely woven rugs of the most colourful of flowers.

She thought of her valley and the memories were suddenly so fresh that she could taste them at the back of her throat; and the longing to be back was so sharp that it was like a knife turning in her chest.

'Perhaps we could come with you,' she said hesitantly. 'Badami Bagh will be safe enough, and I'm sure there will be enough room in your accommodation for us.'

'We will not go to Badami Bagh,' Papa's harsh voice rang out from the doorway. There was no mistaking the determination in his eyes. 'We will not be caged up inside an army fortress as if we are some sort of wild animals. We will return to Srinagar when we can be free, when we can be at liberty to roam about in our own streets. Till then, we will not set foot in the city.'

'Papa, you both will find it difficult living here on your own,' said Vijay carefully, trying to avoid angering the old man. 'And I'll be lonely there without you. I think I'm getting decent accommodation, so why shouldn't we all be together?'

'Vijay, I've made my position clear. I will not go to Srinagar and hide behind a wall of security. Your mother and

I will be fine here.' Suddenly he smiled. 'We aren't yet too old to look after ourselves. Mary is here to do the cooking and the cleaning, and when my fixed deposits mature, we should have enough money to afford a driver as well. Don't worry about us.'

There was nothing more to say.

Later, when Amma was helping Vijay with his last-minute packing, she thrust into his suitcase a large packet containing a shalwar suit and a smaller packet with a pair of earrings and a necklace. 'Give this to Yasmin when you meet her. And give her a hug from me.'

There hadn't been a single month in all those years when Yasmin hadn't written to them. On the seventh of every month or thereabouts, the blue inland envelope would drop through the slot in their front door, the neat handwriting inside full of the latest news from Srinagar. The Kauls had repeatedly urged Yasmin to fly down to Delhi, Papa saying that he would arrange the tickets, and that he would try to get her any job she wanted in the safety of Delhi.

But Yasmin had always refused. They all knew what it was that bound her to Srinagar, but it was never mentioned. Not in her letters. And not by any of the Kauls.

'Tell that girl that she should make at least one trip to Delhi. Let her see all that there is on offer here, and then she can make up her mind for herself,' Amma said, stuffing some jars of pickle into the side of Vijay's suitcase, even as he rolled his eyes heavenwards in mock despair.

'Yes, Amma, I'll tell her. Now please leave that suitcase alone. I don't think it can take any more without bursting at the seams.'

* * *

It was several weeks after he arrived in Srinagar that Vijay could finally meet Yasmin. He knew there was no way he could go marching up to her house in an army uniform; it was unsafe for him, and it would be unsafe for her after he left. So he put on civilian clothes—a pair of kurta-pyjamas and a phiran—and then hitched a ride with some friends in a mini-convoy that was passing close to Zafar Bagh. As the convoy slowed at a roundabout, he slipped out from the back of the two-tonne truck, and quickly walked away into a side alley. A few minutes later he was at the well-remembered door, which he tapped on sharply.

Yasmin opened the door warily, but then squealed with delight as she recognized Vijay. Then she glanced around, almost guiltily, and gestured to Vijay to step in quickly.

As he did so, she flung herself into his arms. A couple of minutes later, he gently pushed her back, and studied the tears that were pouring down her cheeks.

'If you are this unhappy to see me, I can always leave.'

She smiled a watery smile. 'Silly! It's been so long.' Then she led him towards a sofa, clutching his arm tightly. 'How are Amma and Papa? I got a letter a few days back, but there was no mention of the fact that you would be in Srinagar.'

'I know. Security concerns—just in case someone was opening and reading your mail. One sec, before I sit down, can I go and say hello to your grandmother?'

'Yes, of course. But I'm afraid she may not recognize you. She's getting on now, there are days when she doesn't even seem to know who I am.'

Vijay knocked once on the half-open door, and then stuck his head around the curtain. Yasmin's grandmother was sitting on her bed, the Quran open on a wooden stand in front of her. She smiled in response to Vijay's greeting but looked completely blank, as if she had never seen him before. So he reached down and touched her feet, and then backed out of the room slowly.

Yasmin had disappeared into the kitchen to make some tea. 'What will you have to eat?' she called out to Vijay. 'Have you had lunch, or should I quickly heat up something?'

'No thanks, I've eaten. Just get the tea and come back here.'

She returned carrying a tray with the tea, and a couple of jars of dry fruit. 'I'm sure you still live on raisins and almonds, so I got some for you,' she grinned, even as Vijay shook his head in injured innocence and grabbed the jars.

Yasmin curled up on the sofa, drawing up her legs beneath her, and he took a close look at her for the first time in more than three years. She wasn't a girl anymore. Her body had filled out, and there were faint lines of worry etched at the corners of her eyes.

He reached out gently and ruffled her hair. 'How have you been? I've been getting your letters, and the birthday cards. You never forgot.'

'How many brothers do I have?' she asked, smiling.

'True. Now tell me what you never wrote in those letters. What has it been like here for you?'

'There are ups and downs,' she said sadly. 'More downs than ups, actually. It's a constant tussle between the militants and the security forces. Then there is the Hurriyat, which thinks it can take the movement forward by calling for a strike every second day. It's probably all okay for them, but it is we who suffer, with no food, no classes.'

The major secessionist leaders had recently come together to form the All Party Hurriyat Conference, a body that saw itself as the 'true representative' of the Kashmiri people. The JKLF had also joined the Hurriyat, after formally renouncing the gun, but most of the Hurriyat leaders were pro-Pakistan.

'Are you still going to the shop?'

'No, I finally had to close it last month. There are just no tourists anymore, not even the foreigners, and I had begun to lose money. So now I teach at a small school not far from here.'

She laughed suddenly, 'It's a girls' school, so I have a new set of headaches, with some of the Jamaatis wanting to check and monitor what we teach and what sort of a uniform we allow the girls to wear. A couple of major tussles with my good friend Ayesha . . . but eventually things got sorted out.'

A few minutes passed in companionable silence, as Vijay cracked shells with his teeth to get at the almonds inside. Then, without looking up, he said, 'Have you heard from him recently?'

'No.' The reply was a whisper. 'Not one word since he

was taken. Perhaps he doesn't want to write to this address because he thinks that I might be harassed by the security forces.'

'A sensible precaution,' nodded Vijay. 'Actually, I find it quite incredible that no one in the security forces seems to know at all about your existence—except for me, that is, and I'm not telling anyone.'

Yasmin reached out and touched his arm, a look of desperate worry on her face. 'Vijaybhai, do you know how Habib is? I only hear rumours from time to time and get scraps of information from Qasim and the others when they drop by.' She suddenly put a hand over her mouth as she realized the indiscretion.

Vijay wrinkled his face in distaste. 'Qasim comes here, does he? Don't look so worried, even though I'd love to arrest that son of a bitch I can hardly stake out your house, can I? I'll just have to look for other methods. Now, Habib. I can tell you that as of Monday, when I last got some information, he seemed quite okay. They are keeping him in high security at Kot Kindri outside Jammu, but apparently conditions aren't too bad there.'

'Vijay bhai, I hear that they beat up those whom they capture, that they torture them for information.'

'Don't worry,' he reassured her. 'Habib is not small fry, he's seen as one of the topmost JKLF men. They will treat him carefully. After all, the government knows it has to start talking to men like him at some point.'

'Do you think they will release him soon?' The hope was so desperate, so transparent on her face that it broke his heart, and he hesitated before replying truthfully. 'I really don't know, Yasmin. I have heard that the government would like to be lenient towards the JKLF because it is at least a counter to the Pakistanis and to the Pak-lovers in outfits like the Hizbul. But releasing a man like Habib would have to be a decision taken at the highest level.'

'So I have no option but to keep waiting, and praying, and hoping,' she said with just a touch of bitterness.

Vijay was silent. 'I know it hasn't been easy for you,' he said finally.

'No one knows what it has been like for me,' she said softly. 'You men chase your dreams, and do what you think you have to do. And it is the people who care for you who end up paying the price.'

'We all tried, Yasmin. We tried to warn Habib that he was making a mistake.'

There was silence again, and this time it continued for a long time. Vijay glanced at Yasmin, and saw the emotions chase each other across her expressive face. They had been bottled up for too long inside her, and now they came pouring out, the words tumbling and jostling against each other.

'I get up in the morning, I go to the school. Then I come back, cook some food for my grandmother and make sure that she is all right. If I have some shopping to do, I go to the market, making sure that I am back before sunset. And then I sit here, in my room, alone. There is normally no electricity, so I light a candle and stick it on the table. The hours go by, so slowly that every minute seems to last a lifetime. And I sit here, watching the candle burn down into a stump, gazing at the flame as it flickers, staring at the wax as it trickles onto the table. I sit here for hours, Vijay bhai, looking at a burning candle. That's my life . . . Do you know what is the very worst thing in the world, Vijay bhai?'

He shook his head helplessly.

'Loneliness.' The word came from deep inside her, as if it was tearing something on its way out.

'Loneliness. Not having anyone to talk to. No one to share your life with. No one to show you any affection, no one to sympathize if you are feeling bad about something. I've been lonely for so long, Vijay bhai, and I still can't understand what I have done to deserve it.'

Vijay reached out a hand for her shoulder, but she didn't seem to notice.

'You know the story of my life. I still miss my father. I thought that over the years I had built up an immunity to loneliness. But obviously I hadn't. Then I found all of you, and that makes it so much more difficult for me to accept being lonely all over again.'

Vijay pulled her close to him, and she smiled a little sheepishly through her tears. 'Here you are at last, and all I can do is complain.'

'Why don't you come to Delhi, you stubborn girl?' Vijay asked her gently. 'You and your grandmother? We'll find a place for you to stay, or you could even stay with Papa and Amma, they have more than enough room. And you know they would be delighted to have you with them. Why are you staying on here? For what?'

'How can I impose like that?' she said hesitantly.

'Impose? Do you want to be slapped? You'll be company for them as much as they will be for you. And you'll have no trouble finding a job in Delhi.'

She pulled herself back and wiped her eyes. 'Vijay bhai, you know why I have been waiting here. But I will think about what you've said.'

There was silence for a few minutes, broken only by the cracking of almond shells. Then Yasmin spoke again, 'Vijay bhai, I've never been too interested in politics, but there is something I want to know. Do you think Habib and the others will ever get what they want? Will India ever agree to let Kashmir go?'

Vijay didn't even have to think for a second. 'No,' he answered decisively. 'That is something that will never happen.' He searched for the words in his mind, and then began to explain it to her gently, 'You see, Yasmin, what is at stake here is not just the Valley and the people who live in it. It's the future of India itself. The government will never allow Kashmir to secede, because of the implications for the rest of the country.'

He spoke on slowly, and Yasmin listened in silence, understanding for the first time why the rebellion in Kashmir was perhaps doomed right from the outset.

India is, and always has been, a patchwork quilt of nationalities and races, a giant sprawling continental mass which contains a billion people who practise just about every religion known to man, and who speak more languages than the whole of Europe put together. The Mizo from the North

East has very little in common with a Tamilian from the South; they almost certainly wouldn't be able to communicate with each other if left alone in a room.

Holding the patchwork together is the thin thread of a vaguely defined Indianness—loyalty to the flag and to the Indian cricket team, a pride in the democratic traditions of the country, a love for Bollywood movies, and a loose sense of shared culture and identity.

But in the far-flung border regions of the country, where this identity is most easily under threat, one factor that helps to rein in the inevitable separatist tendencies is the awareness that India will never, ever, let go of any part of its territory. In Assam, in Mizoram, in Punjab, the Indian state fought out prolonged insurgencies, and made it clear that come what may, independence from India would never be considered, even if the insurgency lasted a hundred years. Eventually, in region after region, the insurgents blinked first, came overground, contested state elections under the Indian constitution, and soon became ministers in their states, proudly carrying the Indian flag on their official cars.

But it just needed one exception, one snip of the thread and the separation of one panel from the quilt, and suddenly the Balkanization of India would become a very real possibility—the frightening prospect of a hundred Yugoslavias.

Vijay finally ran out of words, and Yasmin nodded slowly. 'Do you think Habib and the others realize this?'

'I don't know,' shrugged Vijay. 'Perhaps they feel that there is still hope somewhere. Or it could be that they have climbed onto the back of a tiger and don't know how to get off.'

Vijay suddenly looked out of the window in alarm. It had got dark, and he realized that he had to return to Badami Bagh, and in civilian clothes at that. He hugged Yasmin one more time and said with mock severity, 'I'll be back soon to discuss your air tickets. I'm not going to allow you to live here by yourself much longer.'

Yasmin smiled, but said nothing, and Vijay eased himself out of the door to begin the somewhat perilous journey back to safety.

Chapter Seventeen

HABIB'S RELEASE

Qasim rushed into the house, flapping his hands in excitement. 'Yasmin, he's out. They have released him.'

Yasmin went very still. 'When?'

'An hour ago. They released him, along with four or five top JKLF leaders. I just heard . . . apparently all of them are being brought home in a huge procession.'

Yasmin threw down the cloth she was holding and started for the door.

'Your slippers,' grinned Qasim. 'Where's the fire?'

The girl skittered to a halt and ran back into the house, pausing to fling her arms around her grandmother and kiss her soundly on both cheeks before bundling up against the biting November wind.

Then she emerged from inside the house and smiled a tremulous ,smile at Qasim. 'Take me to him. Quickly.'

In the centre of Srinagar, just before you reach Maisuma, there is a bridge that crosses one of the many canals which run through the city. Just before the bridge the army had erected one of its bunkers, a semi-permanent structure consisting of sandbags piled on top of each other and topped off by a corrugated iron sheet. The whole bunker was covered by netting, to prevent militants from throwing grenades through the narrow slit that separated the sandbags from the roof. In this bunker crouched five soldiers, one of them manning a light machine gun which poked out through the netting. Outside, another handful of soldiers stood with their backs to the shops that stood on either side of the road. Each wore a bullet-proof vest and a helmet, and a wary expression on his face.

Though by the winter of 1994 tempers had cooled considerably in the Valley, death was still never very far away: a grenade dropped casually by a passing cyclist; a sniper on a rooftop; or even, in some cases, a bomb concealed cleverly in an abandoned car or a suitcase. The authorities could not afford to be complacent. Especially not on a day when JKLF leaders had been released from jail and large numbers of people would be out in the streets.

A small convoy came hurtling down the road, and came to a halt next to the bridge. Vijay Kaul climbed out of his jeep and told the drivers of the two trucks accompanying him to position themselves on the side of the road.

This was JKLF territory, the spot where there would be trouble, if any. But the mood of today's demonstration didn't seem ugly—it was more of a victory procession, the people of Maisuma welcoming home their leader after two years in jail.

Vijay's thoughts went, as they often did, to the man who was at the centre of the festivities. 'Habib, have you really changed so much? Or are you still there, the Habib I knew, hidden away somewhere under a mask, carried away by the role you are playing?' He grimaced, and turned away. 'Or maybe you have just become a lousy little bastard.'

The noise of the approaching crowd grew louder, and then it appeared at the end of the road. Someone had found a drum and was pounding on it enthusiastically. A couple of young men draped in JKLF flags were dancing and shouting slogans which were being echoed by those who followed. And borne on the shoulders of his supporters was the thin but heroic figure of Habib Shah.

As the mob reached the thin line of soldiers, Vijay stepped forward. 'That's enough. You can't cross the bridge, prohibitory orders are in place.' Behind him, a group of policemen got ready with the tear gas launcher.

From his perch Habib looked down at the man he had once called a brother, and his lips curled sardonically. Then he twisted around a little and held up his arms, and the mob hushed.

'For two years they held me, but they could not break my spirit. And they cannot silence my voice, and the voice of all of Kashmir. *Hum kya chahte?*'

'Azaadi,' bellowed a thousand voices. 'We want freedom!'

'Indian dogs,' prompted Habib. 'Go home!' screamed the mob.

But even as the sound of the slogans eddied around him, Vijay relaxed a little. A dozen such encounters had left him with a finely tuned instinct for the mood of the mob, and he sensed that this crowd was not really looking for trouble. After registering its presence it would probably break up, and Habib would be taken home for further festivities.

As the mob shouted and throbbed to a rhythm of its own, Habib turned back to face Vijay, and there was a hint of a defiant smile on his lips. And then he looked up beyond where Vijay was standing, and his expression changed suddenly.

A man and a woman had appeared near the banks of the canal, and were approaching rapidly. The woman was in a green phiran, her hair tied up in the traditional Kashmiri veil. Her large grey eyes were full of unshed tears, but on her face was a look of unutterable and complete delight.

'Yasmin,' whispered Habib, his voice thick with yearning and the pain of the long separation. He slipped from his perch and began to move towards her. The crowd seemed to have disappeared, and he could no longer hear the slogans and chanting. The enemy stood not far away, but he couldn't care less. The universe had suddenly shrunk, and there was just him and Yasmin.

Fifty yards away, two men began to drift from the centre of the crowd towards the army bunker. They were clad in the ubiquitous dark grey phirans which are worn by just about everyone in the Kashmir Valley, the thick woollen cloth providing protection against the biting cold wind, and the loose cut of the garment enabling the wearers to carry kangris to keep themselves warm. Though phirans have sleeves, many prefer to wear them more like ponchos, with the sleeves hanging emptily, so they can huddle the kangris close to their bodies.

But these days there were other ways in which the phirans

were useful, and the two men approaching the bunker carried AK-47s beneath the loose folds. They waited for the right moment, when the crowd was pressing thickly against the three soldiers standing outside the shops next to the bunker, the soldiers' attention fixed on the men shouting slogans.

And then, in a smooth practiced movement, the men whipped up the fronts of their phirans, brought their guns up to bear, and fired at point-blank range into the unprotected faces of the armymen. The soldiers never had a chance, the bullets slamming through flesh and bone and splattering red and grey against the whitewashed wall behind them.

The phirans were whipped back down as the militants vanished into the crowd. But from a balcony across the road, the third member of the hit squad began to fire at Vijay and his men near the bridge.

Time was moving very slowly. It was only a couple of seconds since the first shot had been fired. The bodies of the soldiers began to crumple, their legs kicking wildly as blood spilled onto the road. Inside the bunker, the man holding the LMG bellowed an inarticulate, frightened cry as his fingers tightened spasmodically on the trigger, and the sharp, whipping cracks of AK-47 gunfire were suddenly matched by a heavier ripping sound. It was echoed by shots from near the bridge, as a young jawan standing near the trucks began to shoot back at the militant in the balcony. And suddenly many soldiers were shooting, and some of them wildly.

The crowd turned to flee, but bodies had begun to drop. The militants melted away as smoothly as they came, and others paid the price. Crumpled forms dotted the road, and Vijay was screaming as loud as he could: 'Ceasefire! Don't shoot!'

The guns stuttered into silence.

*   *   *

Habib had almost reached Yasmin when the first shots were fired. Their eyes were locked, their hands stretching out for each other. As the gunfire began, Habib glanced back in shock and then began to run so that he could knock her down onto the ground and shield her.

And then it happened. He saw something change in her eyes, a bewildered, almost quizzical expression entered them. She looked down at the spreading stain on the front of her dress, and then stood very still.

'Habib,' she whispered as he reached her. And he gazed at her as the light slowly faded from those beautiful, luminous eyes.

Vijay stood in the middle of the road, surveying the scene around him, where death had waved a scythe across the road, and the blood of soldier and civilian mingled and flowed through the gutters.

And then he noticed the tableau by the side of the bridge, and he began to run.

Habib Shah sat on the road, Yasmin's body draped over his lap. There was no expression on his face, but his fingers moved gently, caressing Yasmin's face.

Vijay came to a halt a few feet away, the tears freely streaming down his face. 'Yasmin. My little sister.'

And then to the man holding her: 'Habib, let me help you. We need to rush her to the hospital.'

Habib slowly raised his head. There was still no expression on his face, but his eyes were haunted and dark with agony. He gave no sign of recognizing the man standing above him, and then he spoke, slowly and painfully. 'Go away. Get away from here.'

Vijay reached out an imploring arm, but then let it drop to his side. And then he turned, and slowly walked away.

The sirens of the ambulances were echoing down the road, and an army convoy was screeching to a halt. The crowd had all disappeared, except for those who had been left lying on the road and those who were assisting the wounded.

By the side of the bridge, Habib Shah continued to hold the girl who would have been his bride. He held her long after everyone else had left, he held her as night came down like a shroud over the road.

Chapter Eighteen

JALAUDDIN IN INDIA

It had been four months since they entered India, and Jalauddin and his men had begun to feel at home in the hills near Kupwara where they had made their camps. It was heavily wooded mountainous country, with sparse pockets of population scattered thinly in tiny villages nestled against the hillsides. The nearest road was scores of miles away and, more importantly, so was the nearest BSF picket.

For Jalauddin this was a mission of revenge. Langryal had been in jail for a year now, and sometimes Jalauddin feared that he would never see his former commander again. All he could do was take some steps to try and force the hated kaffirs to free Langryal, and if that failed, then to exact as high a price as he could.

The band had waited in the Pakistani town of Kel for several months for the right moment to cross the Line of Control into Indian territory. They were in a queue; there were more than 300 foreign militants in the Kel camp with them. Though the inactivity had galled Jalauddin and his men, their turn had finally come, and they had crossed the frontier under the cover of heavy firing from Pakistani artillery guns which forced the soldiers in the Indian border posts to remain underground in their bunkers.

After a couple of days of hard marching, the group had reached their destination. And by now Jalauddin's band had established three or four main hideouts in the forests, shifting from one location to another just in case some alert BSF patrol happened to pass by. For provisions—and entertainment—there were always the villages to go to.

It was well past midnight when Jalauddin's group entered Sirikot. There was no electricity in this remote area, and in the absence of moonlight the village lay in pitch darkness. Sirikot was among the larger villages in the area, but had a population of barely a thousand. The villagers were simple farmers. Most were Muslims, though there were several Sikh families as well. There had rarely been any discord between the communities.

All but two of the men with Jalauddin were Pakistanis. One was an Afghan, and one, Mohammed Kar, was a local Kashmiri. His main job was to act as a guide and interpreter. None of Jalauddin's men could speak any Kashmiri, and not all the villagers understood Urdu. Kar belonged to a village about thirty kilometres away, but he was familiar with the entire region.

Sirikot was built on a hillside, and the path leading up to it rose steeply for the last 200 yards. But the militants were used to tramping up and down mountains all day long, and none of them were even slightly out of breath as they walked past the thorny bushes that marked the outer periphery of the village.

Mohammed Kar had been here before, and had noted the best hut to take shelter in. It belonged to a farmer who obviously wasn't very well off. His hut, a simple structure of two rooms, one set on top of the other, needed repairing, and the big courtyard in front of it was a sea of mud. But it was set a slight distance away from the rest of the village and had a superb view overlooking the valley; one lookout was all they would need to get advance warning of any BSF patrol. And right behind the hut was the escape route, a trail heading uphill and back into the forests,

The militants carefully skirted the village as they approached their destination. They knew that even if they were spotted, the villagers would almost certainly be too scared to tip off the security forces about their presence, but there was no point in taking any unnecessary chances.

As they reached the hut, Jalauddin waved a hand at

Karim and Muzaffar, and they smoothly took up flanking positions on either side of the wooden door leading into the courtyard. Kar walked up to the door and banged on it smartly. He waited for a few minutes, and then rapped on the door again.

A few more minutes passed, and then a visibly scared man of about forty slowly pulled open the door. Kar immediately pushed him aside and stepped into the courtyard, followed by all the other militants.

Jalauddin now took charge. 'Do you speak Urdu?' he enquired.

There was a terrified nod, and a furtive glance at the arsenal of guns that Jalauddin's men were carrying.

'What is your name?'

'Abdul Bhatt, sir.'

'Don't look so frightened, Abdul, we aren't here to harm you. All we need is shelter for a couple of days. We will take one of the rooms in your hut, you won't even know we are here.'

Abdul looked even more terrified. 'Sir, you are always welcome. But if the army comes to know, they will take me away . . .'

Jalauddin frowned and growled in what he correctly guessed would be an intimidating voice, 'Are you refusing to give shelter to the mujahideen who are fighting for your freedom?'

The wretched Abdul looked around at the men surrounding him, each nursing an AK-47 and a couple of them casually caressing the triggers with their forefingers. Then his head dropped, together with his voice, 'No, sir. Who am I to deny you anything.'

Jalauddin nodded. 'Good. Other than you, who else lives in this house?'

'Just my wife and my daughter. I have a son, he is working in Baramulla.'

'Fine. I see that your hut has two rooms; you can remain in the ground floor room with your family, we will take the room on the first floor. We will not disturb you, and have no requirements, except for food three times a day.'

He walked right up to Abdul Bhatt and looked at him at point-blank range. 'Just one little warning. You breathe one word about our presence here, and you will die painfully.'

Abdul shook his head. 'I won't say anything.'

Jalauddin took hold of his arm, forcing him to look up. 'Let me make myself clear. Do you know what happened at Malangaon last month? What happened to Akbar Rashid there?'

'Yes,' whispered Abdul.

There was a smile now on Jalauddin's face. 'He took a cycle ride past a BSF camp and dropped a note saying that we were in the village. The BSF came, but we had left by then. But we came back, in the night, one week later. I did it myself, while his entire family watched. I peeled his skin like that of an orange.'

The sweat on Abdul's face was glistening in the lantern light. 'I swear in the name of Allah I won't say anything.'

'Good.' Jalauddin released his arm and thumped him on the back. 'Then you have nothing to worry about.' He glanced at the window of the ground-floor room, where he could see, silhouetted in candlelight, Abdul's wife and daughter. 'Tell them also to keep silent, and not to budge from this house. In the morning you will work in the fields, but they should remain here.'

Abdul nodded again, and Jalauddin waved his men up the rickety staircase which led to the room on the first floor.

There was no furniture in the room, just a plain sheet spread on top of a carpet. Hung on a row of pegs along one wall were some shabby-looking clothes. A couple of trunks piled in a corner of the room presumably held the family's other possessions. A huge calendar dominated one of the walls; it showed the black cube at the Qa'aba in Mecca and thousands of pilgrims clustered around it at the time of Haj.

Those who entered the room were supposed to take off their shoes and keep them in a small rack just outside the door, but Jalauddin didn't bother and he left a trail of mud on the sheet as he entered the room.

Kar looked at him disapprovingly. 'Why must you dirty all the rooms where we stay?'

Jalauddin stared back at him. 'What is it to you? Besides, if we have to make a quick getaway, who is going to have the time to tie laces?'

Karim changed the subject quickly, 'How long do you really plan to spend in this dump?'

'Not more than a day,' Jalauddin replied, making himself comfortable with a pair of bolsters. 'We have to make good time now if we are to make the rendezvous with the others. We are supposed to join them by the end of the month and I would guess we still have several days' march ahead of us.'

He turned to Mohammad Kar for confirmation, and he nodded. 'Yes, it will take us at least a fortnight or so.'

Muzaffar said, 'What is this town we are going to?'

'It's called Chrar-e-Sharief. It houses one of Kashmir's most venerated shrines, and the army rarely enters the town. We will be quite safe there, it will be a good place to rest for a couple of months till Ramzan is over. Many mujahideen groups are already in the town.'

* * *

The morning passed slowly. Mohammed Kar and two of the younger militants had been sent out of the hut on lookout duty; they would be replaced later in the afternoon. The other militants lay sprawled on the threadbare carpet that lined the floor of the hut, the windows of the room securely shut. By noon, Karim was bored, and he looked across at Jalauddin and gestured beseechingly towards the window

Jalauddin nodded and Karim stood up in relief and threw the window open. It overlooked the courtyard that lay in front of the hut. Beyond that was a panoramic view of the valley and the snow-capped hills. This was the season for paddy cultivation, and in the distance they could see the farmers toiling in ankle-deep water.

Then Karim looked down at the courtyard. Abdul Bhatt's wife was sitting on a stone platform right in front of the hut, making thread on a spinning wheel. The courtyard was about thirty square metres, and a huge hole in the ground at one corner evidently functioned as some sort of a well. Bhatt's daughter was leaning over the hole, drawing mud-coloured water in a steel bucket.

Jalauddin walked up to join Karim at the window as he watched the girl pour water from the bucket into a tub, where she had stacked some dirty utensils. She looked about fourteen years old, and was pretty, with sharp features and pink, dimpled cheeks.

Karim and Jalauddin looked at each other, and then out at the courtyard again. Several minutes passed. Then Jalauddin stretched languorously and walked out of the room and down the stairs. The girl skittered into her room at the approach of the giant stranger, and Abdul Bhatt's wife looked up nervously from behind her spinning wheel.

'Salaam aleikum,' said Jalauddin, averting his eyes respectfully. 'I am sorry to disturb you, madam, but we feel we made a mistake by telling your husband to go to the fields. Could you go and call him, please?'

'It's about fifteen-twenty minutes away,' she demurred.

'I know, he told me. But we need to talk to him urgently.'

She rose to her feet slowly, and called out to the girl in Kashmiri. 'Shaheen, get ready.'

'No, leave her here,' said Jalauddin casually. 'We would like some lunch, and will then leave this village after talking to your husband. Could you ask her to prepare some food for us?'

Bhatt's wife clearly appeared reluctant to leave, but she sensed she couldn't argue with this man. And so she slipped on her shoes and left the house, after muttering some quick instructions to her daughter.

Shaheen lit the stove and put some water on to boil. She was about to reach for the jar of rice when she sensed some movement behind her. She whirled around to find that the stranger had walked into the room and that he was smiling at her from a few feet away. Behind him was Karim, and the thickly bearded Afghan. She caught a quick whiff of heavy body odour and saw the Afghan shut and bolt the door. Then there was no time to notice anything else.

Chapter Nineteen

CHRAR-E-SHARIEF

'There it is, just beyond those hills,' said their guide, pointing a finger.

'I can't see anything yet,' grumbled Jalauddin.

'Can you see those satellite transmission dishes on that mountain? It's a couple of kilometres from there. I suggest we camp for the night here, so that we can enter Chrar early in the morning.'

Rations were starting to run a little low as they hadn't stopped at any village for the past two days. They were all looking forward to some rest at Chrar-e-Sharief. They knew that eighteen Harkat-ul-Ansar militants under Zubair were already in the town, as was a large band commanded by the maverick Pakistani, Major Mast Gul.

They entered Chrar by the soft light of the winter dawn, as gentle streamers of sunlight filtered through the leaves of the trees and played on the wooden facade of the *dargah* that had made the town famous.

It was the *ziarat* of Nund Rishi, the patron saint of Kashmir and a symbol of the tolerant, Sufi version of Islam that had always been practised in Kashmir. The shrine at Chrar-e-Sharief was more than just a major centre of pilgrimage, it was a symbol of Kashmiriyat itself.

From their vantage positions the guards on lookout at Chrar had alerted their companions inside the town of the approaching band of armed men. As Jalauddin and his group entered the town, they found themselves confronted by the business end of several AK-47s. But once the introductions had been made, the guns were put away and warm embraces exchanged.

An imposing bearded man stepped out from the front door of a house. 'Salaam aleikum. I'm Zafar, and I welcome you on behalf of all the mujahideen who are present here. All arrangements have been made for your stay.'

As he stepped back after hugging Jalauddin, Zafar looked a little puzzled. 'Where is Mohammed Kar? I thought he was going to guide you here.'

Jalauddin bent down to lift his pack back onto his shoulder, as he answered in a detached fashion, 'He wasn't feeling very well, I think he ate something really bad. He couldn't walk such a long distance so we left him behind and got a new guide.'

As he settled the pack comfortably on his shoulder, Jalauddin caught the smirk on Karim's face, and he quickly flashed him a warning look. It wouldn't do for these Kashmiris to find out what had really happened to Kar.

'Come on,' said Zafar, leading the way, 'let me take you to where the others are.' As they walked, Zafar pointed out the various lookouts which the militants had posted. Though the army had already received some information that foreign militants were taking shelter at Chrar, no action had been taken yet, and no army patrols had entered the town in weeks. The presence of the dargah was an obvious restraining factor; any damage to it would never be forgotten by the people of Kashmir.

'Which are the tanzeems that are present?' asked Jalauddin.

'The majority of the fighters here are guest mujahids, from Pakistan and Afghanistan, though there are a few of us Kashmiris as well. The mujahids are mainly from your group, the Harkat-ul-Ansar, and some men from the Hizbul Mujahideen. But we also have some mujahids from other tanzeems, and some fighters from the Lashkar-e-Taiba.'

'The Lashkar? What is that?'

Zafar smiled. 'They are married to the jihad, and are backed by the Markaz-ul-Dawa-wal-Irshad. I'm surprised you haven't heard of them. They make some of you Harkat mujahids seem like real softies.' He smiled wider to take away any sting, and looked around with a searching eye before pointing to a grim-looking man walking on the periphery of the group, a light machine gun casually draped over his shoulder. 'That's Abu Talha. He's from the Lashkar, and he has already butchered dozens of Indian soldiers.'

Jalauddin looked at the man with some curiousity, taking in his black shalwar-kameez, the pyjamas ending well above the ankles. Later in the evening he sought the man out over a campfire, and introduced himself.

'What exactly does the Laskhar stand for?'

'We are the real army of Allah. We believe in the jihad, and in the need to die fighting in the jihad. You must have heard about our parent organization, the Markaz-ul-Dawa.'

Jalauddin shook his head, and Abu Talha looked a little displeased. 'It's the fountain of Islamic revival, the centre for preaching, based in Muridke, near Lahore, and gives direction to the millions who believe in the jihad as a way of life. You should come to Muridke sometime, especially during the Ijtima in November when hundreds of thousands gather every year to hear the call to jihad.'

Jalauddin nodded thoughtfully, tugging at his beard once again. 'Yes. I think I would like that.'

*   *   *

In the heart of the Badami Bagh cantonment is a looping road leading up a hill to a cluster of buildings. When you get past the security guards, and walk up a well-carpeted wooden staircase, you come to a tiny room just a little bigger than a broom closet. A stack of telephones are kept on a revolving carousel, and underneath the pane of clear glass which tops the desk is a detailed map of the entire Kashmir valley.

Two wooden plaques mounted on the wall list the names of those who have occupied the swivel chair behind the desk; the names of the men who have been Brigadier General Staff in Srinagar. Though the BGS reports to the general who commands the army corps in Srinagar, he is arguably the single most important man in the operational chain of command, and that tiny little room is the effective nerve centre from where the war against the militants is conducted.

There are, of course, imposing control rooms located near by, complete with giant maps and sophisticated communication systems, and it was in one of these rooms that the top security officers in Kashmir met to take stock of the reports coming from Chrar-e-Sharief. Present were the BGS, the director-general of police, the local head of the Border Security Force, and the representatives of the intelligence agencies. Also present, as a representative of the government, was the advisor to the governor, Lt Gen Zaki.

The tone at the meeting was worried. They had met before to discuss the reports of militants entering Chrar, and had hoped that the problem would quietly go away. The army and the BSF had been instructed to conduct operations near Chrar, but so far there had been no confrontation with the militants. Now the militants were becoming increasingly brazen about their occupation of the town, and the first whiffs of the story were starting to appear in the local newspapers. The arguments raged back and forth.

'Look, it is a wooden mosque and in a tightly built-up area. I think we need to be careful about moving in, the danger of the terrorists harming the shrine is just too great.'

'That's true, but we have to do something fast. The media is already getting hold of this, and you don't want the terrorists to be proclaiming Chrar a so called liberated zone the way they did in Sopore. Remember how much hassle we had there.'

'I think we should stay in the distance, send feelers that we are about to move in, and allow them to slink away.'

In the end, a decision was taken. A loose army cordon would be established around the town, with army units taking control of the hills but refraining from actually entering Chrar-e-Sharief.

The siege had begun.

* * *

Habib Shah looked much older than his years. There were strands of grey in his hair, and dark bands of sorrow under his eyes. Some had arrived during his years in prison, but most had come in the months after the death of Yasmin.

Habib's house was by now a centre of political pilgrimage for those who still believed in the movement. Every day dozens of men would arrive at the little flat in the back alleys of Maisuma to talk, to plan and to strategize. For all their outward bravado, there was below the surface an undercurrent of despair. They knew the movement was dying.

It was being killed by the daily successes of the security forces, who gorged on the flood of information that was suddenly available to them, enabling them to target the active militants, reducing their effective lifespan in the field to just a couple of months. It was being poisoned by the activities of some of the foreign militants, many of whom clearly had little sympathy or affection for the locals. Above all, the movement was atrophying because of the growing apathy of the people in whose name it was being carried out.

But those who rode the tiger couldn't climb off. And every day the men would gather in Habib's front room, to puff at endless cigarettes, and to sip at their teacups, nodding sagely at each other as they muttered words about the inevitable achievement of azaadi, inshallah.

Then, in the evening, they would all get up and go scurrying to reach home before the hours of darkness. And Habib would be left in peace to mourn.

Dinner would be a quiet affair at a table set for one. After that, as Habib lay down on his bed, the memories would tiptoe into his room to wave away the prospect of sleep. He had missed Yasmin during the years in prison, but he had known that she was out there waiting for him. Now the one word that haunted him was 'never'. I'll never see her again. I'll never hold her in my arms again.

He tried to channel his emotions into hate for the soldier who had pressed the trigger, but he couldn't escape the taste of guilt that lay thick and slimy at the back of his throat. He had always known that Yasmin didn't share his passion for the movement, but he had believed that it would be he who would have to pay the price for his involvement, not those around him.

Now he had lost everything. And all for a dream that would never come true.

In the morning Habib was once again the perfect revolutionary, sitting in dignified command as he granted audience to his people, waving away the mumbled words of those who would seek to commiserate, as if his personal loss was of no great significance. The only man who knew what he was going through was Qasim, and he sat close to Habib, with shadows of worry and sympathy tucked away under his eyelids.

Habib forced his wandering mind to pay attention to what the senior Hurriyat leader was saying. 'Habib bhai, we must raise this issue before the world. The siege of our holy shrines cannot be allowed, and we think that we should call for an indefinite strike till the Indian Army moves away from Chrar-e-Sharief.'

'Maulvi sahib, I share your outrage, but I'm not sure that our people are really all that enthusiastic about all these frequent hartals,' Habib replied courteously. 'It does make life very difficult for the average Kashmiri.'

'Sacrifices have to be made, no one will die if they don't eat for a couple of days,' replied the man in front of him, surreptitiously trying to draw in his ample paunch.

'Quite,' said Habib drily. 'But if I may make a suggestion, I think it would be more effective if some of us were to make a trip to Chrar-e-Sharief to try and break the siege as a gesture of solidarity with the mujahids who are stuck inside. Qasim and I were discussing it earlier, and we think the journey to Chrar could be made the day after tomorrow.'

It took the car a little over an hour and a half to get from Srinagar to Chrar-e-Sharief, and they then faced the task of trying to get through the army cordon. At first the captain manning the checkpoint had no intention of letting them through, but after an hour of shouting and arguing, punctuated with lengthy walkie-talkie conversations that the captain had with his superiors, the officer shrugged his shoulders and allowed them to pass.

Half an hour later, Habib and the others were being led to the shrine by Mast Gul and his men. Qasim hadn't made the journey, nor had any other Hurriyat leader. Habib had travelled with three JKLF men, who also doubled as his bodyguards. A small smile came to Habib's face as he turned the corner and saw the dargah standing proudly there. But the smile soon disappeared as he spotted the telltale signs of digging in the gardens adjoining the shrine and saw the huge banners plastered all over the adjacent *khankah*, or mosque, blaring the virtues of the Hizbul Mujahideen. He turned politely to Mast Gul as the Pakistani strode along next to him.

'I see signs of digging right next to the walls of the shrine. You haven't mined the shrine, have you?'

Mast Gul never missed a step. 'A purely defensive move. I want the army to think that the shrine could be in genuine danger if they decide to move in.'

Walking a few steps behind the guests from Srinagar was Jalauddin and his lips curled in contempt. These Kashmiris and their obsession with saints and dargahs! It was, in his opinion, downright un-Islamic. But then, what did you expect from these JKLF turds? They even wanted the Hindus to come back to the Valley. With some effort, he restrained himself from making any sarcastic comments, but later, as they sat in the mosque and Habib once again raised the subject of the safety of the shrine, Jalauddin's patience snapped.

'No pile of wood and mortar is worth more than the divine work which we are here for. And people like you should be grateful that we are here to help in your liberation.'

Habib stared at the big man who sat before him tugging at his beard. The dislike was mutual and crackled like electricity in the room.

'I don't believe we have been introduced,' he said politely.

'This is Jalauddin, from the Harkat-ul-Ansar. He came into the valley about six months ago,' Mast Gul intervened smoothly, appearing completely unperturbed by the sudden tension in the room.

Habib's lips tightened in anger. He recognized the name, and had heard the rumours from Sirikot. 'Yes, of course. I have heard of you, and of some of your activities since you entered my land.' There was just a slight emphasis on the last two words. 'Let me tell you that this shrine is more than just a pile of wood and mortar to us Kashmiris. It is a symbol of our ethos and our nationhood. It matters as much to us as anything else we are fighting for.'

'A little less time spent running to shrines and a little more attention to learning how to fight, and all of you would be much closer to independence,' sneered Jalauddin.

Now it was Habib's turn to lose patience. 'We fought all right for several years before all of you came here. And we certainly didn't pick on fourteen-year-old girls to prove our manhood.'

Jalauddin smiled in genuine delight as he realized that Habib must have learnt about Sirikot. He slowly scratched himself under his kurta, as he savoured the words he was about to speak.

'The kaffirs killed your woman, didn't they? Pity. A couple of nights with some of us and we might have been able to protect her.'

For a moment Habib couldn't believe his ears. Then a mist came over his eyes, and he started to leap to his feet to get at the man sitting in front of him. A JKLF man quickly flung his arms around Habib and dragged him back down, holding him tightly. He was painfully aware of the rows of Pakistani and Afghan guns in the room all around them.

Habib was almost incoherent as he mouthed abuse at Jalauddin. The words bounced off Jalauddin, who calmly withdrew some tobacco from his pocket and started to fashion a smoke, turning away from Habib to chatter softly with Karim.

Mast Gul stepped in again. He was annoyed with the unnecessary conflict that Jalauddin had sparked off; he knew that the support of men like Habib could be crucial in the weeks to come. 'Jalauddin and Karim, why don't you both go and check that the lookouts are in place?' Then, after Jalauddin had stalked out of the room, Mast Gul stretched out an appeasing hand. 'My apologies, Habib bhai. That man is a little wild, and his remarks are unforgivable.'

Habib was trembling in anger, his eyes moist with the tears of frustration. He reached for a smoke with shaking hands, and tried to force himself to regain control. He nodded curtly at Mast Gul, who then began to explain his strategy for the defence of the town.

A few minutes later Habib was in full control of himself again, and he patiently began to debate with the other man the virtues of quietly leaving the town for another area.

Half an hour passed, and then, after tea, Habib and his colleagues from Srinagar stood up to go. Mast Gul embraced them at the entrance to the khankah.

'Khuda hafiz, Habib bhai. Mushtaq here will see you till where your car is parked. He is from your town, his father runs a bakery in Srinagar.'

Habib smiled and raised his hand in farewell. Then they started walking back down the winding road leading to the outskirts of the town, where the car was parked.

Walking back with them, like a ceremonial guard of honour, were about a dozen of the foreign militants, their weapons ready in their hands like natural extensions of their bodies.

Habib noticed that Mushtaq was looking just a little nervous, and he wasn't surprised when the little man subtly manoeuvred him out of earshot of the others.

'I respect you a lot, Habib bhai. I know that you are with the JKLF, and not with my group, the Hizbul, but I need advice, and I have no one to turn to but you. I want you to meet a very special man who has come into Chrar-e-Sharief. Only two of us know his real identity, the others think he is just an ordinary guest militant. But I want you to talk to him.'

Habib's curiosity was piqued. 'Who is he?'

'His name is Major Irfan. He's a major in the ISI who came across from Pakistan just a few days back with some special instructions for a couple of us. He must have just taken over sentry duty not far from your car. Please, you must meet him.'

Habib sighed. He had had enough of Pakistanis for one day, but an ISI major was clearly someone worth meeting. However, the cloak and dagger surprised him; surely a man from the ISI would be more than welcome here, so why was this Major Irfan slinking around pretending to be someone else?

He turned to Mushtaq. 'What instructions has he given you? And why hasn't he gone straight to Mast Gul?'

Mushtaq was about to speak, but then he snapped his mouth shut and drifted a couple of yards away from Habib as one of the Afghans came up to join them.

They walked on in silence for a few more minutes till they came to where the car was standing, in the middle of a concrete rectangle at the edge of the town. At one end of the rectangle was a stone ramp leading up to the garage of a house, from where any lookout had a good view of the valley which led to Chrar-e-Sharief. A man was squatting on the ramp, gazing out at the valley, an AK-47 nestled in his lap. He didn't seem aware of the group approaching him from behind.

'That's Major Irfan,' whispered Mushtaq. 'I'll lead you to him, while pretending to show you the approach roads to the town.'

Habib nodded as he and Mushtaq reached the ramp. The other militants were some distance away, clustered near the parked car, sharing a smoke.

As Habib walked up the ramp, the ISI man heard the footsteps, and began to rise to his feet. Habib's attention was momentarily diverted by the spectacular view over the valley, which fell away sharply in a cliff just a few feet away.

Mushtaq began making the introductions, 'Major Irfan, this is Habib Shah, you must have heard of him. And Habib bhai, this is Major Irfan, from the ISI.'

Habib turned towards the ISI man, a smile on his face. And then the smile vanished as he looked straight into the horrified eyes of Vijay Kaul.

Chapter Twenty

INSIDE CHRAR

It had all begun a few months before, when the BGS had summoned Vijay to his room. Also present were a senior police official and a civilian in a fawn safari suit.

The BGS smiled broadly at Vijay as he waved him to a seat, 'Sit down, Captain, and be at ease, please. Can we get you some coffee, or some kahwa?'

Vijay was sitting bolt upright at the very edge of the chair, wondering why the hell he had been summoned for this ordeal.

After prolonging Vijay's agony by chatting aimlessly about this and that, the BGS finally came to the point. 'Captain Kaul, we know that you are a local, born and brought up right here in Srinagar. Tell me, your Kashmiri is still completely fluent, isn't it?'

'Of course, sir,' replied a mystified Vijay. 'It's my mother tongue, and we usually speak it at home.'

The BGS spun a glass paperweight on the top of his table, as he weighed his options. Then he looked up abruptly, 'Captain Kaul, would you like to leave your unit for a few months and work on special ops for a while? I have to warn you that it could be dangerous.'

Vijay didn't hesitate. 'It would be an honour, sir. But what exactly are we talking about here?'

'You know of our Psy Ops cell, don't you, where we try to demoralize the enemy through media and propaganda management? Well, we are now thinking of expanding the concept. To be more precise, the police is going to be running some special operations against the terrorists, and we all thought it would be a good idea if a couple of armymen were also involved in the exercise. You will work closely with the police in this, and the ops could involve undercover work, mingling with the civilians and things like that. And another thing—you'll be given the acting rank of a major.'

Vijay's eyes were shining by now. 'Sir, it sounds wonderful. Thank you, sir.'

'Good show, Major Kaul.' The BGS rose to his feet and extended his hand. 'You've had some bad luck recently—that bridge incident near Maisuma. But this will give you a chance to bounce back.'

The pain shone through in Vijay's eyes at the mention of that terrible day, but he stepped back and saluted smartly.

'Go with these men. You are in their hands now,' said the BGS, sitting down again and twirling the carousel to find the phone he needed.

Four weeks later, Vijay casually walked out of a tea shop in a small village near Badgam. He was filthy, his hair and fingernails thick with dirt, and his cheeks looking as if they had never been touched by a decent blade. He had on a shabby and patched phiran, and on his feet were a pair of plastic shoes, which he dragged along the ground as if he could hardly support their weight. He had settled the two-rupee bill he had run up for a couple of cups of tea after whining long and loud to the proprietor about the ravages of inflation on a daily-wage worker like him. As he shambled back to the site where a gang of other workers were disconsolately shovelling gravel and tar into the potholes on the main road, the hangdog expression remained firmly plastered on his face, but inside he was feeling a sense of deep satisfaction.

A tip from a captured Hizbul Mujahideen militant had brought him to this village, and after long hours working with the road gang as a casual labourer, he had slowly edged closer to his quarry, Altaf Dar, the divisional commander of the Hizbul Mujahideen in this region. They had known that he lived in this area, but somehow no informer had ever been able to reveal his exact location, and several raids had yielded absolutely nothing. Vijay had seen Altaf's photo a thousand times, and now he had seen the man himself, huddled with his associates in the back room of the tea shop.

Vijay reached the road gang but walked on past them without slowing down, as some of his co-workers looked up at him in mild surprise. He contorted his face as if in extreme agony, massaging his stomach in a pointed gesture, and the foreman nodded in a resigned fashion. When Vijay was thirty yards beyond the crew, at a bend in the road as it led out of the village, he slowed down and looked imperceptibly to the right where he knew the BSF man was hiding in the thick undergrowth, radio ready in his hand. A small nod of his head, and then Vijay sank down on his haunches on the side of the road, clutching his stomach and looking the very picture of misery.

Barely five minutes later the green BSF Gypsies came barrelling down the road; the lead vehicle slowing for a fraction to allow Vijay to hurl himself in. 'The bastard is at the tea shop. Make sure that your men cut off the escape route through the back door,' he barked

'Don't worry, they'll be in position,' grunted the moustached BSF commandant sitting next to him, as the four vehicles sped past the gaping men on the road gang and zeroed in on the tea shop. Seconds later, two Gypsies were screeching to a halt near the front door, while the men from the other two raced down a side alley to cover the rear. The door was knocked open and the BSF men grabbed a shell-shocked Altaf Dar, cup of tea still in his hand. The sheer speed of the smash-and-grab raid had taken him by complete surprise, leaving him with no time to think of escape or a fightback

'Pull out, all units. Pull out immediately,' snapped the BSF commandant into his walkie-talkie as they ran back to their vehicles, half dragging and half carrying Altaf Dar with them. This was the most dangerous moment, as Dar's associates could launch a sudden counter attack. They threw the militant into the back of one of the Gypsies, and then engines were revving as they headed back down the road.

Vijay looked at his watch in satisfaction. Less than a minute since the Gypsies had entered the village, and they had with them the local head of the Hizbul Mujahideen. So much neater and more efficient than those goddamned cordon-and-searches.

He looked over his shoulder at where a stunned Altaf was lying bundled on the floor, as a burly trooper knelt on him and tied his hands behind his back.

'Papa II?' asked the commandant, and Vijay nodded his assent.

As you drive down Gupkar road in Srinagar, past the residence of the chief minister, and the rear entrance of the Badami Bagh cantonment, you come to a little white house set about forty yards off the main road, overlooking the Dal Lake as it peeps from behind Shankaracharya Hill. Today the charming little house is the residence of Jammu and Kashmir's senior-most bureaucrat, tastefully decorated and well maintained. But at the height of the insurgency the house was simply called Papa II. It was the main interrogation centre for the BSF and its name could bring a sweat to the brow of even the most innocent of civilians.

The convoy zoomed up the hillside from the main road and up to the house. Altaf was dragged out of the Gypsy, his eyes flickering as he recognized where he was. Then three hefty BSF men led him towards a tent in the back garden of the building, even as Vijay walked into the main office of the commandant, a room which was usually as hot as a sauna because of a huge and remarkably effective bukhari standing in one corner.

Vijay didn't have the inclination to attend the initial interrogation; though he knew that it was necessary to break the militant as quickly as possible before his associates got the news of his arrest, watching the process always made him uncomfortable. Besides, he knew the BSF men would call him as soon as Altaf Dar began to talk.

He sat down, with an exhausted sigh of relief, in one of the overstuffed sofas in the room, reaching out briefly to warm his hands against the bukhari. Then he looked down at himself in disgust, noting, as if for the first time, the layer of filth that coated him like a second skin. A trooper walked in with a tray of kahwa and some biscuits which the commandant waved in Vijay's direction. 'Kahwa? We make the best kahwa in the entire country.'

'I know,' smiled Vijay, 'I've had it before. But I had better get myself cleaned up a little first, before I leave muddy fingerprints all over your china.'

He hauled himself up once again and headed out towards the little bathroom that lay at the end of a wooden corridor. There he scrubbed his face with Lifebuoy soap, deciding with regret that the rest of his body would have to wait for a shower back at Badami Bagh.

The sound of a faint yell came from the tent behind Papa II, and Vijay wrinkled his nostrils in some distaste. Back in the commandant's office, he asked, 'How long do you think it will take?'

'Not long at all. Most of the locals don't take more than a few minutes, unlike the foreign mercenaries whom we have to work on for days together. I've had dozens of men leading me to where their guns are hidden without our laying a finger on them; they were shitting in their pants just being here in Papa II.'

Vijay nodded and leant back in the sofa, shutting his eyes briefly. He didn't have to wait long. A big man in a BSF uniform entered the room fifteen minutes later and saluted smartly. 'Sir, he's talking.'

'So soon?' exclaimed a surprised Vijay, glancing at his watch. The man smiled, 'I just slapped him a couple of times, sir, and that was enough.'

'Come on,' said the commandant, 'let's go and see what he has to say.'

It was a dark room, and Altaf was squatting on his haunches with his back to the wall, looking just about as miserable as a man can look. There was no need for any further violence, as he poured out the answers to all their questions—where the guns belonging to his unit were hidden, and what their planned targets were. Then he became a little less willing to provide information as they asked him the names and addresses of the other men in his unit, and the commandant had to repeatedly step back and nod to the troopers who were waiting silently at the back of the room.

After an hour of questioning, Vijay spoke for the first time. 'One last question, Altaf. Do you know any of the men who are inside Chrar-e-Sharief?'

Altaf shook his head, but after a tiny pause, and Vijay was quick to pounce. 'You hesitated, you bastard. So you do know some of those men. Who are they?'

'I swear on my family I don't know,' whined Altaf, shaking his head violently from side to side. 'I only know what I read in the papers.'

'There are HM militants inside Chrar. Don't tell me you don't know where they are from.'

'I swear on my parents . . .' began Altaf again, and Vijay turned to the commandant.

The questioning continued for another twenty minutes, and then Vijay had the information he desperately needed. 'I don't know most of the men inside the town,' said Altaf dully. 'But I know that Mushtaq Malik has joined them. He was a HM commander in Srinagar when I was last there.'

'Mushtaq Malik from Srinagar,' repeated Vijay scribbling quickly. 'Where did he live, and who were his close associates?'

Back in his room that night, Vijay stared at the notations in his diary, his mind working overtime. He knew that he'd just been given a great opportunity to put into effect some of the plans that he had been dreaming about ever since the special operations began. But he wasn't quite sure what the best way forward was.

He put the diary back on the table and switched off the light. He'd have to meet some of his friends in the police for lunch to see if they had any bright ideas.

By two the next afternoon he had all the answers. The superintendent of police had laughed in glee as Vijay mentioned Mushtaq. Then he thumped Vijay on the back and said, 'You are going to owe me a bottle of Scotch for this. Mushtaq

Malik, you said, belonging to the HM, and living in the Zainakadal area?'

'That's right,' said Vijay, glancing down at his diary once more.

The SP laughed again. 'Well, guess what? We have our own man inside that group, a man called Khan. Mushtaq takes orders from him. He thinks that Khan is a committed Jamaati, but in fact he's now one of us. A lot of our recent successes in the downtown area have been because of him.'

A slow smile spread over Vijay's face. 'Is that a fact?' he said softly.

* * *

One week later, Mushtaq Malik walked into a small house near Badgam. He had left Chrar-e-Sharief as soon as he got the message from his commander, taking one of the secret routes that the army didn't know about. He was just a little mystified at what the urgency was, and a little put out at being forced to make the dangerous journey out of Chrar. With him was Rafiq, a resident of Chrar-e-Sharief who had joined the Hizbul Mujahideen a few months after him and in whose home Mushtaq had been living all these days.

The steel door of the house had been left ajar, and Mushtaq pushed it open, before cautiously sticking his head in. He smiled as he recognized his commander and then he stepped across the threshold, together with Rafiq. 'Salaam aleikum, Khan sahib. I have been hearing the bad news from Srinagar; so many of our boys being killed.'

Khan nodded his head sadly as he got up to greet them, and then quickly came to the point.

'I'm sorry I had to force you to come out of Chrar-e-Sharief. But there is a very important mission that only you can do.' He paused, as if noticing Rafiq for the first time. Mushtaq reassured him, 'Don't worry, Khan sahib, Rafiq is like my brother, we can speak before him.'

Khan nodded again. 'A man has come from Pakistan. A major in the Pakistani ISI. He has a message straight from the top Pakistani leadership and it is a message meant for you. I want you to listen to him carefully.'

Mushtaq sat down, as if his legs couldn't take his weight. His heart was suddenly thudding deep inside him. Soon a well-built man emerged from an inside room.

Vijay Kaul was dressed in a shalwar-kurta, a cap on his head, and he wore the arrogant expression of one who is used to being in command. He nodded curtly at Mushtaq and Rafiq, and then spoke in colloquial Urdu. 'My name is Major Irfan. We have been watching you, Mushtaq Malik, for quite some time. The reports have been excellent, and we know that you are loyal to Pakistan and to the movement.'

Mushtaq smiled shyly. If he was surprised that the ISI would be keeping track of a low-level militant, he didn't show it.

Vijay went on. 'I have been sent to Kashmir on a special mission. But I will need your help.' He looked up once at Mushtaq and then continued, 'What are your relations like with Mast Gul?'

Mushtaq looked bewildered. It was the last question he had expected. He thought for a minute, and then replied, extremely cautiously, 'Okay, I guess. I really haven't interacted too much with him.'

'He is a fool,' snapped Vijay, causing Mushtaq to rock back on his heels. 'A self-glorifying fool who is too busy posing for photographs and hamming it up for the TV cameras. The jihad doesn't need those who think that they are above the movement. He is ruining the reputation of the jihad and he must go.'

There was stunned silence for quite some time, before Mushtaq glanced across at Rafiq and then said, 'I don't fully understand. What is it that you would like us to do?'

Vijay cheered inwardly. The cover story had been bought, hook, line and sinker. He leant forward seriously, 'I want you to take me into Chrar with you. Pretend that I am an old colleague of yours from Srinagar, a guest militant who is on the run from the security forces and who wants to take shelter in Chrar.'

Rafiq spoke for the first time since they had entered the room. 'And what happens then? What happens after we take you into Chrar?'

Vijay paused for a few seconds. 'What happens? We will kill him. I will kill him, with your help.'

And Vijay sat back and watched the acceptance slowly dawn on their face.

They had re-entered Chrar without trouble, and Vijay had been taken into the fold without much question. Slowly he had worked out how he was going to kill Mast Gul and the other militant commanders. With Mushtaq's help, he had manoeuvred a gas cylinder into place at a shop next to the road where Mast Gul walked every day, a cylinder that would go off like a bomb when triggered. All that was left to do was to wait for the appropriate moment.

Mushtaq and Rafiq had kept their secret well, though the doubts and worries occasionally returned to plague them, especially at night. Now, on seeing Habib Shah walking through the town, Mushtaq had taken the impulsive decision to share the burden with one of Kashmir's greatest leaders.

* * *

The seconds ticked away slowly. Vijay's mind was racing as he gazed at Habib. He thought of trying to run, but knew that there was no way he could escape.

Habib kept staring at Vijay, thinking, irrelevantly, that he had kept himself well. He knew that Vijay must have crept into the town on a crucial mission, and that it was vitally important to find out what it was. He opened his mouth to speak, but then a mental picture flashed through his mind, of Vijay at the mercy of Jalauddin and his men, strapped naked to a table as they worked on him. Slowly, he shut his mouth again.

Beads of sweat were beginning to pop out all over Vijay's forehead, and next to him Mushtaq stirred uncomfortably. Habib spoke at last. 'You are Major Irfan from the ISI, I gather.'

'Yes, I have been sent here from Islamabad,' replied Vijay, his voice surprising him with its steadiness.

Habib turned to look at the foreign militants who were still clustered near the car. There were five of them, men with the traditional Afghan headgear on top of their shalwar-kameezes, guns and ammunition belts draped casually all around their bodies. The three JKLF men who had accompanied him into the town were leaning against the car, gossiping idly with the driver.

Then he looked back at Vijay, 'Well, we can't really talk here. Why don't you accompany us as we leave the town? We can talk in the vehicle.'

'As you wish,' replied Vijay, inclining his head in assent.

They walked towards the car, Mushtaq looking more than a little bemused. Habib gestured to the front seat, 'Try and squeeze in, Major Irfan. It will be a bit of a tight fit, but we don't have far to go.'

Vijay clambered in, as did the other JKLF men. Then, just before he climbed in himself, Habib caught hold of Mushtaq's arm and whispered to him softly in Kashmiri, so that the foreigners wouldn't understand and the JKLF men wouldn't overhear. 'Let me find out more about the mission. But till you hear from me, do not act on any instructions that he has given you. Do you follow me? Wait for my orders, and those of no one else.'

Mushtaq nodded. He realized that something was wrong, and was glad that the decision was out of his hands now. He watched as the car pulled away, and then turned to grin reassuringly at the foreign militants who hadn't budged from where they squatted disinterestedly.

There was silence in the car as it moved out of Chrar into the no-man's land before the army checkposts. Then Habib tapped the driver on his shoulder. 'Stop for a minute. I think our guide can leave us now to go back.'

Vijay got out of the car, and Habib opened his own door and stepped out as well. Then he moved close to Vijay, so that those inside couldn't hear him. 'I don't know what you were doing there, and I know that you will not tell me. But do I have your promise that you will not take it any further?'

Vijay looked at him steadily. 'You have my word. You know that I cannot go in again now.'

'If you do, then you will die. And it will not be a death that will come easily. Go away now.'

As Habib started to turn back towards the car, Vijay spoke softly, 'Why didn't you hand me over to your colleagues?'

Habib's eyes were flat, and emotionless. 'I don't know. I'll ask myself that question tonight, as I try to sleep.'

Then he was back in the car, ignoring the curious looks the other JKLF men were giving him. And as the car sped on again, Vijay began to walk towards the nearest army post. The mission had been blown, but he was aware that he was lucky to be alive.

* * *

Varun wheeled his squeaky metal trolley out of the airport building, Raju following close behind. A metal fence kept the taxi drivers and touts at bay, and as he walked towards the opening in the fence, Varun's eyes scanned the faces on the far side, looking for Mansoor, the elderly taxi driver. He smiled as he saw the stubbled and jowled face peering over the fence, topped neatly by a thick fur cap.

It was early March, and reports about the siege at Chrar-e-Sharief had begun to trickle out to the national press. Varun had bullied his news editor into giving him permission for a trip to see what the ground situation really was.

He yielded the trolley to Mansoor's waiting hands, and submitted with good grace to the bone-crushing hug which signified friendly affection for the taxi driver. And as Varun gingerly counted his ribs to ensure that they had all survived, a grinning Raju stepped forward for a dose of the same treatment. Then they piled the tripod onto the top of the Ambassador and the suitcases into the boot.

'Where to? Should we go straight to Ahdoos or are you booked somewhere else?'

Varun leant over the back of the front seat. 'We'll go

quickly to dump our stuff at Ahdoos, but then we have to go to Chrar-e-Sharief. We only have a day here this time, we have to fly back tomorrow. Can we make it there and back before sunset?'

Mansoor glanced at his huge HMT wristwatch. 'It's already 2 p.m., but it's only an hour and a half to Chrar if we go via Badgam and avoid going into the city right now. So why don't we forget about the hotel for the moment and go straight to Chrar?'

Varun settled back in his seat. 'Fine. You are the boss. Now tell me, how are things, and how are your sons?'

As Mansoor accelerated past the rows of army trucks lining the road to the airport, he spat expressively out of the window. 'What is there to say? Same old nonsense. Army with guns on one side and militants with guns on the other. We in the middle with the damned Hurriyat sitting on our heads.'

Varun raised his eyebrows in mild surprise. Mansoor had always been a strong supporter of the militant movement, and Varun had gathered that one of his sons was active with the Hizbul Mujahideen. It was normally difficult to get a word against the militants or the Hurriyat out of Mansoor.

'You seem to have changed your attitude, old uncle,' he teased.

'Who hasn't changed?' replied Mansoor bitterly. 'The Hurriyat calls for hartals and for strikes. We suffer. The militants threaten tourists. It is our stomach that goes empty. I'll show you some of the houses which these so-called leaders have built. Huge structures, two-three floors, all built by those who didn't have two coins to call their own till all this madness started. They get money by the bagfuls, and it is our sons who must die for them.'

'But your sons are okay, aren't they?' asked Raju, looking concerned.

Mansoor raised his hands expressively and the car wobbled dangerously. 'Inshallah. I haven't met Rehmet in eight months. But I believe he is all right.'

As they spoke, the taxi began to groan its way into the hills, the road winding a silvery-grey path through thick pine forests. After a while two huge satellite dishes became visible on a distant hill-top, and Mansoor pointed them out. 'Chrar lies just beyond those dishes. That's where the army has built one of its camps.'

Half an hour later, the taxi was driving past the camp which housed the dishes, the profusion of army trucks and jeeps testifying to the seriousness with which the security forces were taking the siege. A couple of kilometres further they hit the army checkpoint, a steel barrier dragged across the road and guarded by a pair of surly-looking jawans. They refused to even listen to Varun, and waved him in the direction of a hut fifty metres up the hill on the right-hand side of the road. 'Go talk to the captain. We cannot decide anything.'

The captain was sitting in a chair in the centre of the lawn in front of the hut, and Varun walked up to him confidently. As he introduced himself, a man wearing the uniform of a major in the Indian army stepped out of the hut.

Varun turned to him as well, and began to repeat the introduction. The man smiled, 'I know who you are, I have often seen you on television. My name is Vijay Kaul, and I am temporarily keeping an eye on things here. So tell me, what can we do for you?'

'We want to go into Chrar-e-Sharief and see what the situation is like.'

Vijay sighed, and then gestured to Varun to follow him towards the edge of the garden, to the wall that overlooked the road leading to Chrar.

'Do you see the check-point? That's where our authority ends. If you cross that point you are entirely at the mercy of the militants, and most of them are foreigners. There is nothing that we can do to protect you, no way we can save you if they decide to kidnap a juicy TV crew fresh out of Delhi.'

Varun looked back at him steadily. 'I am aware of the dangers, they aren't unusual for us. We frequently put ourselves into the hands of the militants, and so far they have never harmed us. I take full responsibility for our safety.'

'And what happens if they grab you?'

Varun shrugged. 'That's our problem. We know that there is nothing that you will be able to do.'

The captain had walked up to join them, and Vijay looked to him for his opinion. 'What do you think, Sanjay? It's really your call.'

'Sir, we have orders to allow any journalist to enter if they want to, as long as they accept full responsibility for their own actions,' the younger man replied.

Vijay sighed again. 'Okay. Go through. But for heaven's sake be careful. Some of the men in there are real nuts, and they don't care all that much for journalists.'

'Don't worry,' smiled Varun, squeezing Vijay's arm. 'We'll be fine.'

Despite his bravado, there was a tightness in Varun's stomach as the barrier was pulled aside and the car moved into the deserted section of the road which lay ahead. There wasn't a soul in sight, and the only sound was that of the straining Ambassador engine. They were moving downhill now, and in the far distance they could make out the buildings of Chrar-e-Sharief. As his heart pounded, Varun glanced yet again at the windshield of the car, to reassure himself that the huge paper sign with PRESS written on it was still scotch-taped securely to the glass.

Without warning, two men appeared on the side of the hill about fifty yards ahead of them and began to clamber down towards the road. Varun tapped Mansoor on the shoulder. 'I think you should slow down.'

Mansoor lifted his foot from the accelerator, as they watched the men reach the side of the road. Both appeared to be unarmed and looked like Kashmiris. As the car drew up to them, one of the men raised his hand to stop it, and then, without a word, they opened the doors and climbed inside. 'Drive on,' said the older of the two men in Kashmiri to Mansoor, settling back in his seat.

'How far to Chrar?' asked Varun chattily. In response the man put a finger to his pursed lips in an unmistakable gesture, and Varun subsided. Ten minutes later they drew up at the concrete square that marked the entrance to the town of Chrar-e-Sharief.

There were small buildings around the square; all had their shutters pulled down. Some men, who looked like civilians, were sitting in front of one of the buildings, sharing a smoke and going through an old copy of a Srinagar newspaper. They looked up as the car reached the square, then got up quickly and disappeared down a side alley. Through the gaps between the buildings that lined the square, the rest of the town could be seen sprawled across the valley, and in the distance the spire of the dargah itself rose elegantly from the cluttered structures all around it.

'Wait here,' said their new guide, and Mansoor quickly cut the engine of the car. 'Go and call them,' the man said to his younger colleague, who scampered off down the main road. Varun and Raju climbed out of the car, the cameraman holding his Betacam cradled against his body. Varun looked around the now deserted square, and then casually let his eyes slide around the tops of the buildings. That was where the lookouts and guards would be posted.

He quickly spotted three militants, perched behind makeshift bunkers on a roof that commanded the approach road, aiming their AK-47s straight at them. And he thought he saw at least two others on top of a water tank a little higher up the hill.

Raju made as if to hoist the camera to his shoulder to begin taking some shots, but their guide stepped forward quickly, and Varun shook his head in a silent signal. Raju lowered the camera, and perched himself on the bonnet of the car.

They didn't have to wait long. A group of eight militants appeared at the bend of the main road where it turned right to head into the town centre. Varun ran a practiced eye over them as they approached. Most of them looked like foreigners, Afghans or Pakistanis, though one or two may have been local Kashmiris as well.

The group reached them, AK-47s in their hands, and no trace of a smile on any of their faces. Varun had often met militants before and he was struck by just how unfriendly these men seemed: Still, he stepped forward confidently, his press card clutched securely in his hand.

Jalauddin walked the final few steps towards the taxi, taking in the young man in his jeans and casual shirt approaching him, and the cameraman beginning to get off the bonnet of the car. To his right, Zafar was the first to reach Varun. 'Yes?' he asked in Urdu. 'Who are you, and what do you want?'

Varun had a wide smile plastered on his face, and he extended the press card, taking care to avoid any sudden movements and keeping his hands well away from his body. 'Salaam aleikum. We are from the press, from a private TV company. We have come to film the situation in Chrar-e-Sharief.'

Zafar took the press card from him and Jalauddin craned his neck to examine it over the Kashmiri's shoulder. Then, without a further word, Zafar looked at Raju, who also extended his card.

Jalauddin looked up from the cards, his expression bleak. 'It says here that you are from New Delhi.'

'Yes, of course,' agreed Varun readily. 'We are from Delhi, from a private TV company.' The emphasis was on the last three words. Throughout the insurgency, the militants had expressed little animosity towards journalists from other parts of India. The only exception were those who worked for the state-run television network, Doordarshan, which was targeted by several militant groups because they felt it carried nothing but government propaganda. Unlike other reporters, Doordarshan employees in the early 1990s could only move about under heavy security, and several of them had been killed.

Zafar scanned the press card suspiciously, 'You don't have anything to do with Doordarshan?'

Varun shook his head vehemently. 'No, no. Nothing at all. We are from Vision TV, a private TV company, making programmes for private TV channels.'

Jalauddin had been staring fixedly at Varun's face, and he suddenly snapped, 'He's lying. I recognize him. He was on TV a couple of days ago, doing some programme on Doordarshan.'

Varun's stomach turned, and he bitterly regretted the impulse that had led him to agree to anchor a one-off current affairs programme on Doordarshan days before returning to the Kashmir valley. But he kept his voice rock steady, looking at Jalauddin straight in the eye.

'You are mistaken. I am with a private TV company. Please look at the press card. I also have a letter from my editor in my pocket. Why don't you take a look at it?'

'Get your hands up, you bastard,' barked Jalauddin, and both Varun and Raju scrambled to comply. The AK-47s were now levelled straight at their stomachs, and Jalauddin stepped forward to yank the letter from Varun's pocket. He glanced at it, and then threw it onto the road.

'That means nothing. Anyone can write a letter. Tell me who you really are, and what you want. Quickly, before I lose my temper.'

Two Afghans had closed in from the sides, and they pushed Raju against the side of the taxi. The barrels of their guns were inches away from his chest, and their fingers were uncomfortably close to the triggers. Mansoor had been pulled out of the taxi and forced to squat a few metres away.

Jalauddin stepped close to Varun, so close that Varun was almost overpowered by the strong odour of unwashed body and woodsmoke. The barrel of the AK-47 came up and touched Varun under his chin.

Varun was breathing in shallow gasps, and he could clearly hear the thumping of his heart. The sweat was pouring freely down his back, but the reporter in him noted in a detached fashion that he wasn't really feeling frightened; he was too busy trying to convince the militants. His eyes flashed from Jalauddin to Zafar and back again.

'Will you please believe me? We are from a private TV company. We make programmes and sell them all over the world. You can call up any of your associates in Srinagar and give them my name. They will tell you that I am to be trusted. Call Yasin Malik, call Geelani sahib. They all know who I am.'

Zafar stepped forward carefully, and laid a hand on Jalauddin's arm, but the big man shrugged it off. 'I know who you are. You are a fucking spy.'

There was a snicking noise, as Jalauddin cocked the gun with a deliberate motion. Varun could hear himself go on talking, though at another level his mind was becoming increasingly detached, watching the scene as if it was a spectator. Funny, he thought, your life doesn't flash before your eyes. I don't know who thought that one up.

Then another voice intruded. Zafar spoke firmly, 'Wait, Jalauddin. Let's first find out what the truth is. We can't hurt a genuine journalist, it could seriously damage the movement.'

Jalauddin hesitated. 'I could take him to one of these huts and question him.'

Varun's stomach turned again. The bullet would probably be better, the voice inside his head said.

But Zafar shook his head. 'No, let's just take the taxi driver aside. He'll know the truth.' With some reluctance Jalauddin took the barrel of his AK-47 away from Varun's face and joined Zafar as he pulled Mansoor to his feet and dragged him out of earshot.

Zafar spoke to the elderly taxi driver. 'Tell me, uncle, who are they? Don't worry, nothing will happen to you. I just want to know the truth about them.'

Mansoor looked across the twenty metres that separated him from Varun and Raju, looked at the guns that were trained on them, and a shadow flickered briefly across his grizzled face. Then he met Zafar's eyes, 'The boy is telling the truth. They are from a private TV company. I have often worked with them in the past. They are sympathetic to us.'

Jalauddin growled and stepped forward, but Zafar restrained him with a raised hand. 'Sympathetic to the movement?'

'Sympathetic to the people of Kashmir,' replied Mansoor. 'You can trust what I say. I have given a son to you already.'

Zafar studied Mansoor's face intently. Then he nodded his head, and began to move back towards the journalists.

'This old man is probably in league with the Indian bastards,' protested Jalauddin weakly as he followed. 'I say we should shoot them all.'

But Zafar wasn't listening, and he approached Varun,

who was watching him apprehensively. 'Our apologies. You are welcome in Chrar-e-Sharief. We will lead you into the town.'

Varun felt his legs sag in relief. He nodded to Raju, who quickly pulled out the bag containing cables and microphones from the car. Varun hoisted the tripod onto his shoulder and began to follow Zafar as he headed back down the main road, speaking urgently into a walkie-talkie he had in his hand. Then Zafar stopped and walked back to the journalists. 'Can you wait for a few minutes? We want to get the people of the town out onto the roads as well.'

'Of course,' said Varun, a weak smile plastered on his face. 'We will take some shots here in the mean time.'

Raju raised his Betacam as Varun pointed out some of the footage that he wanted. The militants gathered around them, looking curiously at the TV equipment they were carrying, and Varun began to chat with them casually. The ice had been well and truly broken, and one of the big Pakistanis chuckled as he unslung his AK-47 and handed it to Varun, who ran his fingers over the sequins which the man had pasted all along the stock.

'Why the sequins?' he asked.

'They look pretty,' replied the Pakistani, taking the gun back again.

'Which tanzeem are you from,' inquired Varun, 'the Harkat-ul-Ansar?'

'No,' said the man proudly, 'I am from the Lashkar-e-Taiba.'

It was the first time that Varun had heard the name, and he scribbled it down in his notebook. Then he grinned at the big man, to ensure that he took no offence. 'I haven't heard of the Laskhar before.'

'Don't worry,' replied the other man. 'You'll hear a lot more about us in the years that lie ahead.'

A faint noise could now be heard from inside the town, a susurration like the sound of waves over a coral reef. Zafar gestured to Varun and Raju to move on, and they crossed the bend in the road to be greeted by a sea of humanity. The men with guns had moved like shepherds through Chrar-e-Sharief, ensuring that all civilians turned out for an impromptu demonstration, and now men, women and children were clustered on the main road, shouting slogans praising Pakistan and calling for azaadi.

Jalauddin suddenly appeared again at Varun's elbow, and the journalist flinched visibly. The gun still dangled in Jalauddin's hand and he tapped Raju on the chest. 'You bastards better film what the people are saying.'

Raju nodded and got to work. They filmed the crowds as they moved through the streets towards the dargah. They filmed the slogan-shouters, zeroing in on the young boys who were jumping up and down as they mouthed the words, jostling each other to ensure a prime location in front of the camera. When possible, they filmed the gunmen moving like silent sharks through the mob, nudging the residents of Chrar to greater vocal efforts.

As they reached the dargah, Varun drew in a deep breath at the simple beauty of the walnut wood structure. Then Raju was filming again, balancing the camera on the tripod that he had hastily erected on a platform which stood at the centre of the courtyard in front of the shrine. The crowd still clustered around, shouting itself hoarse, warily watching the militants who had taken up positions all around the courtyard.

'Get the banners on the adjoining building,' whispered Varun while pretending to help Raju adjust the tripod. The cameraman casually panned from the crowd to the khankah, and to the huge cloth banners which proclaimed that Kashmir would become part of Pakistan. Another giant sign simply read 'Hizbul Mujahideen', underlining the affiliation of many of the militants present in the town.

Then they sought permission to enter the shrine itself, and they took off their shoes and tiptoed inside to take shots of the intricate carvings that covered the marble tomb of the saint. Some civilians were praying inside the shrine, and Varun took the opportunity to record his piece-to-camera, standing with his back to the tomb as he looked intently into the camera lens, ending with the stock phrase, '. . . from inside the shrine at Chrar-e-Sharief, this is Varun Mathur for Vision TV.'

They emerged to be greeted by Mast Gul himself. The flamboyant man with the long locks and bushy beard loved being filmed, and though he refused to give an interview, he gladly posed for them, marshalling his troops and crouching behind his machine gun as he fired mock bursts towards the army camps in the distant hills.

It was getting dark by the time they finally left the town, waving goodbye to the militants who walked them back to the concrete square where the car was parked. As the town disappeared into the gloom of an early dusk behind them, Varun and Raju looked at each and began to smile. The smiles soon turned to chuckles, and then into huge whooping gusts of relieved laughter. Mansoor also joined in, and Varun leant over the front seat to hug the elderly man.

Raju began to rewind the tape in the camera, looking into the viewfinder to ensure that he had been able to capture everything properly. He smiled again in satisfaction and waved to Varun to have a look. Then he began to laugh again, 'My God. Can't we think of a safer profession? Like testing bungee-jumping equipment?'

'Don't laugh too much right now,' said Varun seriously. 'We have to come back again tommorow morning. I want more shots of the outer defences that they have erected.'

It was completely dark by the time they reached the army checkpoint, and from a distance they could see Vijay pacing around at the side of the road. He smiled in relief as he saw the taxi. 'I've aged a dozen years,' he said through their window. 'I thought they had decided to keep you there. Any problems?'

'Umm, no, not really. It was okay,' said Varun with a straight face. 'In fact they have invited us back tomorrow.'

'I'm afraid not. New orders have just come from the army headquarters. They think all this media coverage is glorifying Mast Gul and the others, and have now said that no journalist is to be allowed in.'

'That's ridiculous,' protested Varun in exasperation. 'Haven't they learnt yet that the presence of the media is one of the best ways to restrain the militants? There is no way that Mast Gul will burn down the shrine if he has a TV camera pointed at him.'

Vijay looked apologetic. 'Look, I agree with you, but there is nothing I can do. So guard those tapes carefully, they could be the last record of the situation inside Chrar for quite some time.'

*   *   *

Two months later, Varun was fast asleep, nuzzling his pillow contentedly, when the phone rang. He burrowed deeper into the pillow hoping against hope that the caller would just go away, before reaching out a resigned hand towards the receiver. Then he sat up with a jerk. It was his editor on the other end of the phone line.

'Wake up, Varun, and get your skates on. They've burnt down the shrine.'

'Shrine, what shrine?' babbled Varun as his brain yawned sleepily and tried to catch up with his tongue. 'You mean Chrar-e-Sharief?'

'I don't mean the Vatican, you twit. Of course, Chrar-e-Sharief.'

'Who did it?'

'No idea. The army and the militants are blaming each other. But if you are going to find out what happened, you better get a move on. The plane leaves in an hour and a half, and the car will be at your doorstep in about twenty-five minutes. And for heaven's sake, be careful. We have already heard that there is a lot of tension all over the Valley and rioting in many areas. Ravinder will be going with you as your cameraman, Raju can't be located.'

Seven hours later Varun stood on a hillside overlooking Chrar-e-Sharief and gazed in horror and grief at the smouldering remains of the town. He could make out a blackened emptiness filled with rubble at the spot where the shrine had stood so proudly, and all across the town the dark trail left by the fire as it had raged across Chrar, devouring the wooden structures that lay in its path. Gunshots could still be heard from inside the town, together with frequent landmine explosions.

Varun turned away, a sick feeling inside him, accompanied

by bone-deep tiredness. It had been quite a journey; he had begged and threatened his way onto the flight to Srinagar after being told that there was no space on board. Then a hitched ride in a police Gypsy across the riot-scarred face of Srinagar, and more hitched rides on army vehicles till Chrar-e-Sharief.

Next to him, Ravinder lowered the camera from his shoulder. 'We'll have to call it Charred Sharief now,' he quipped, biting off the words as he saw Varun's expression. 'Sorry, poor joke.'

Varun ignored him and walked up to the burly army officer who had escorted them till the hillside, a man wearing the uniform of a brigadier. 'Can you give us any details of how it happened?'

'You'll have to get the on-record interview from someone else, but I can brief you off the record if you like,' replied the officer, and Varun smiled in assent.

'As you know, there was a fire here two days ago. We believed that Mast Gul was trying to escape through the Traj Bal Nala using that fire as a cover. But we couldn't move in because of heavy shooting. Then, last night, another fire broke out close to the shrine. We have no idea how it started, though we believe that one of the militants began it as a diversion, to help the others escape. We tried to send in the fire engines, but they kept firing with machine guns and the fire engines had to stop some distance away. By the time we reached the shrine, there was nothing left.'

'And you couldn't capture anyone?' asked Varun, raising an eyebrow.

'No, but we hope to soon. We did kill some of the militants; those are their weapons that you can see piled up next to the table.'

Varun walked up to the weapons and stopped suddenly as he saw a familiar AK-47, its stock decorated with a splattering of sequins.

'Something wrong?' inquired Ravinder.

'No, not really. I knew the owner of that gun.'

'Well, the smoke coming from the shrine will give us a

good backdrop from here. You better do the piece-to-camera now.'

'Okay. Just give me a couple of minutes to gather my thoughts.' Varun walked ahead a little and sat down to look at the ruins of the town. He couldn't quite explain the deep melancholy that had gripped him, but he could see what might have happened the previous night as if it were playing in front of his eyes. The army inching in towards the town, nervous after the previous night's fire. Gun shots and tracer bullets coming from the centre of the town, sending the soldiers scurrying back towards cover. Mast Gul leading his men towards a gully, determined to get out while the going was good. And there, standing close to the dargah, a man fiddling with explosives, sending a malicious look towards the shrine which he had despised. He looked familiar. Was it Jalauddin? Or was it someone else? And did it really matter?

Varun sighed and rose to his feet. There was work to be done. 'Stupid bastards,' he muttered to himself. Ravinder raised an enquiring eyebrow. 'The army. I warned them not to shut out the media. If only there had been TV cameras here last night, the shrine would still be safe.'

They returned to Srinagar well before dusk, and were delighted to find a taxi standing outside the hotel. Curfew had been imposed all across the city and angry young men were fighting pitched battles with the security forces at street corners. 'Can you get us to Hazratbal?' Varun asked the taxi driver, Abdul Wani, a man he'd never used before.

Wani crinkled his brow in doubt. 'With this curfew and all the trouble? Unlikely, but we won't know till we try.'

Varun smiled. Here was a man after his own heart. 'Let's go then.'

'Why Hazratbal?' asked Ravinder. This was only his second trip to Srinagar, and it all seemed quite strange to him.

'Habib Shah is bound to be holed up in there. We must get his reaction to what happened at Chrar.'

Wani proved to be a master at finding his way through the security checkpoints which had been erected all across Srinagar, and Varun rode shotgun in the front seat, jabbing at the PRESS sticker on the windscreen and getting out every kilometre or so to wave his press card at a sceptical army officer.

There was a tangible aura of grief and anger hovering over the entire city, as the people of Srinagar mourned the destruction of the shrine they all loved so much. They weren't quite sure whom to blame, but the security forces seemed the most convenient target for them to vent their anger on, and mobs of young men banded together to hurl stones at anyone in uniform. The acrid stench of tear gas hung like a cloud over many neighbourhoods.

The taxi drew up at the square in front of Hazratbal, and Varun smiled at Ravinder, somewhat surprised that they had been able to reach their destination. Two armoured BSF vehicles stood in the square, stones pattering onto their hides from time to time as young boys popped out from the mosque to show their defiance before scurrying in again. The rest of the square was completely deserted; the shutters of all the shops in the area hadn't been raised all day long. The BSF commander and two of his men were standing out in the open, scorning the odd stone that came close to them.

Wani reversed the taxi a little to ensure that he was out of range, and Varun drew in a deep breath as he nodded to Ravinder, 'Come on, let's go. Leave everything else, let's just carry the camera.'

They hurried along the sides of the square towards one of the alleys which opened onto the square, about twenty-five yards from the Hazratbal gate. A small squad of BSF men were trying to chase stone-throwing young men down the alley, pausing every dozen steps to fire tear gas shells. The boys had set some tyres on fire and the thick smoke from the burning rubber added to the fumes of tear gas.

'Let's get some shots of this,' said Varun, and Ravinder rolled the camera as they manoeuvred for position between the stone-throwers and the BSF men. The presence of the camera began to stir up the young men and they started punctuating the hurling of bricks with the usual anti-government slogans.

'Come on, let's go and find Habib,' said Varun after a few minutes, and they backed away carefully towards the Hazratbal gate. The BSF commander saw where they were headed and made as if to send someone to stop them, but then thought better of it.

Varun helped Ravinder as they climbed over the fence which surrounded the Hazratbal complex. The mosque itself loomed about thirty yards ahead of them, its white majesty contrasting beautifully with the darkening skies. There were only a few minutes of daylight left, and Varun could sense the BSF troops behind him pulling back towards their vehicles, preparing to leave the area.

They kept to the left of the Hazratbal compound as they inched forward towards the mosque, staying out of the direct line of fire of the boys who were throwing stones. After a few dozen steps, Varun began to wave his hands frantically to attract their attention. 'Call Habib Shah. Tell him that Varun Mathur is here, from Vision TV.' The stone-throwing thinned down, and a couple of young men in their late teens waved their hands in acknowledgement as they scampered off to find Habib. 'Wait there,' shouted another young man, and both Varun and Ravinder froze where they were. Ravinder still had his camera on his shoulder, and his hands were busy trying to extract the last few seconds of footage before the light gave way completely.

Varun didn't see the stone coming. A young boy, barely eleven, stepped forward to heave one last rock at the BSF vehicles before they disappeared. His aim wasn't as strong as his determination, and the stone flew wildly to the right, to crash against Varun's left temple.

He slumped to his knees, waves of pain and nausea running through him. He raised one hand to his forehead and felt the blood pouring from the cut, then he smiled feebly at Ravinder who was trying to prop him up. 'I'm not having a very good time in Kashmir these days,' he tried to quip. He could hear footsteps pounding on the marble courtyard as some of the young men rushed to their aid, even as the boy who had thrown the stone stood aghast, his hands clapped to his mouth. Then Varun blacked out.

'Now what do we do with him?' Habib Shah gestured towards the still unconscious body of Varun half an hour later. They had taken him into the mosque, and had cleaned the wound as best as they could, dabbing it with some bright red antiseptic lotion.

Ravinder spoke from the chair where he was sitting. 'I think our taxi should still be waiting in the square. We'll just try and get back to the hotel right now.'

Habib peered closely at Varun's forehead. 'Yes, but he needs stitches, and I have a feeling he'll have a scar that will last him the rest of his life. I also hope he doesn't have concussion. You need to take him to a doctor.'

Ravinder looked helpless. 'Where on earth will I find one at this hour in the middle of a curfew? The army is perhaps the only option, but how will I get him to an army doctor . . .' he broke off, suddenly aware of where he was.

To his surprise, Habib nodded reasonably. 'Yes, that is what you should do. But you should speak to someone in the army first, to warn them that you are coming. They are extremely jumpy today. Come with me, there is a phone in this complex which you can use.'

A few minutes later, Ravinder looked a lot more cheerful. An extremely cooperative army PRO had promised to divert an incoming convoy to the main road which ran close to Hazratbal, so that their taxi could be escorted straight to the Badami Bagh cantonment. 'You'll have to spend the night here, though,' the PRO had said, and Ravinder had agreed in some relief.

Habib stood near the gate of the Hazratbal complex and watched the taxi pull away. Then he jumped a little, as a figure in a dark gray phiran materialized out of the darkness right next to him. 'Do you have a couple of minutes?' the figure asked, and Habib stared at him in disbelief.

'Vijay Kaul. Do you have a death wish that you walk around like this?'

'I was in the convoy and couldn't resist the opportunity to speak to you.'

Habib paused for several minutes before replying. 'All right. Come with me.'

Habib waved away his JKLF guards and led Vijay towards the side of the mosque where the waters of the Dal Lake lapped against the steps leading up to Hazratbal. The lights of the mosque reflected softly in the water, and clouds of giant mosquitoes rose up to welcome the two men. They sat down on the steps, and Vijay offered Habib a cigarette, which he accepted after a while.

'You know that he did it, don't you?' asked Vijay softly. 'Jalauddin. He burnt down the shrine in a deliberate act of vandalism.'

'That's what you claim,' replied Habib evenly, glad that the darkness prevented Vijay from reading the acquiescence in his eyes.

'That's what I know,' said Vijay. 'He's escaped now, and presumably will soon be back in Pakistan, where he will be hailed as a hero.'

There was no reply. The cigarettes slowly burnt down to their butts, the smoke drifting upwards and keeping the mosquitoes at bay.

Vijay crushed his cigarette carefully under his sole. 'I have wanted to meet you all these months, just to say how sorry I am about Yasmin . . .'

'I don't want to hear it,' cut in Habib harshly, and this time the silence continued even longer. The electricity went off suddenly, taking with it the reflected points of light in the water that had been keeping them company. The night was oppressive. The curfew had ensured that there was no movement on the roads, and everyone seemed to have gone to bed early.

'How long will this continue?' asked Vijay at last.

'Just what are you referring to?'

'Militancy. What you call the movement. How long will the killings and the destruction continue?'

'Till your people give mine their independence. Till we get what we want,' came the quick and standard response.

Vijay waved his hands impatiently. 'You know that will never happen, not till this land turns to ashes. And in the meantime it is men like Jalauddin who will rule here.'

'So be it,' replied Habib, rising to his feet. 'Go home now, Major Vijay Kaul. You are wasting your time.'

Part Two

Chapter Twenty-one

THE REPUBLIC DAY MISSION

Varun leant forward in excitement. He knew the precise moment when the plane would cross the snowy slopes of the Pir Panjal and emerge over the Kashmir valley. It was always a sight worth waiting for: the land stretched out below like a tapestry of green and brown, with the towns speckled across it like silver sequins.

It was January 2000. It had been several months since Varun had last visited Kashmir. To his horror, at the age of thirty he was already a senior citizen in the world of TV journalism, and that condemned him to a life behind a desk, getting young kids fresh out of college to sally forth into the field. It had taken a prolonged tantrum before he was allowed to escape to the Valley for a series of special stories.

His smile of anticipation widened as the plane touched down, and he began to look for familiar faces among the airport crew. Raju looked at him in amusement; he'd been to the Valley just a few weeks ago.

'When was the last time you were here?' Raju asked, as they piled their luggage onto the trolleys and began to look for a familiar taxi driver.

'During the Kargil war, of course, but not since then,' replied Varun. 'Damn, I don't see anyone we know . . . let's just grab the first cab that comes along. Is this new hotel any good?'

Raju grimaced. 'Well, better than Ahdoos now. That one has become more than a little rundown.'

Varun looked around him as they headed for the hotel. It never failed to amaze him just how much Kashmir seemed to have changed in the past four years. There was an air of lightness all around, and an absence of the fear that used to hang over the city like a dark cloud. Evidence of how much the situation had improved slid past their car windows.

Varun smiled as he stared at an army soldier sitting by himself inside a PCO booth, his INSAS gun casually leaning against the wall in a corner. Four years ago, that man wouldn't have dared to enter the market, not without an accompanying posse of at least a dozen soldiers.

All around them the roads were almost free of security patrols, and unarmed local policemen in khaki casually loitered in the street corners where machine guns had once been mounted.

Varun suddenly grabbed Raju's arm and pointed to a small shop, protected by wire mesh, with a sign declaring that 'Wine and Beer' were available there. 'Look! That's one for the books. If that isn't a sign that the power of the HM is finished, I don't know what is.'

Raju grinned. 'You are out of touch. This is the year two thousand, boss. Now they serve you booze in the hotel bars, even in your room if you want. And no one seems to mind.'

Three hours later they were sipping from cans of beer in the wood-panelled bar on the ground floor of the hotel. They called for a couple of bowls of peanuts and plates of mutton tikkas, and then Varun turned to survey the rest of the bar. There weren't too many people there. In a dimly-lit corner a large Sikh gentleman was huddled next to a tiny man wearing a fur cap, talking earnestly as he tried to convince him to source all his carpet exports via Honey Singh Enterprises Inc, Srinagar, India.

On another table a young Muslim man, barely in his twenties, sat by himself and downed one Scotch after another. He was well dressed, in what appeared to be clothes stitched in the West, and Varun surmised that he was an expatriate who was back in Kashmir to visit friends and family, and had sneaked out to enjoy a couple of forbidden pegs.

And sitting right next to them at the bar was a bemused-looking foreigner, staring at his can of beer with an air of bewilderment. 'A journalist, fresh in from the US or the UK,' guessed Varun, as he raised his own can to toast the other man in a friendly gesture. 'Hi. I'm Varun Mathur, from Vision TV in Delhi. Have you been here a while?'

The other man jumped as if he had heard a gunshot and then smiled sheepishly. 'Hi. Bob Gilman, from the Broadcast Network. Just in today, actually, and it is my first time in Kashmir. In fact, I was just posted to South Asia.'

Raju slid the mutton tikkas in Bob's direction, and he accepted one. 'Are you here on your own?'

'I'm using one of the local cameramen, Humzar Ali. He's upstairs in the room getting ready.'

Varun and Raju looked at each other quizzically. They knew almost all the local journalists extremely well, and had forged deep friendships with many of them. But they had never heard of any Humzar Ali.

Varun shrugged. 'Must be a new guy, I've never met him. So how do you like Kashmir? Isn't it the most beautiful place on earth?'

'I guess so,' said Bob doubtfully. 'It's just that I've never been to a war zone before, and it's a bit intimidating—all the soldiers and security checks.'

'War zone?' trumpeted Varun incredulously. 'What war zone? This place is almost back to normal—you should have seen what it was like four or five years ago.'

'Well, Humzar took me somewhere today, and we were surrounded by dozens of men shouting about how they want their freedom . . .'

'Maisuma,' said Varun, rolling his eyes. 'A place on the main road next to a bridge, with a triangular stretch of concrete heading in towards two alleys?'

'Yes,' nodded Bob.

'It's the oldest trick in Kashmir. They get gullible TV crews coming to the valley for the first time to go to Maisuma and there is always a demonstration just waiting to happen. TV crews get footage, the separatists get mileage. Everyone is happy. If you really want to know what the people think you have to get out of the journalist-trap areas of downtown Srinagar. Go to the other cities, go to the rural areas. And above all, talk to people individually, and off camera. Otherwise they will invariably give you the standard line which will save them from the wrath of any militants lurking nearby.'

A fresh round of drinks was placed before them, and Varun glanced at his watch. Raju and he had accepted a dinner invitation at the residence of an old friend, and they needed to leave the hotel soon.

'I don't know,' said Bob, sipping his beer. 'The people seem very fed up.'

'The people *are* fed up,' said Varun vehemently. 'They have been screwed for too long by everybody. They still don't like the security forces. They don't like the Pakistanis and Afghans who are about seventy per cent of the militants today. They don't like the Hurriyat. And they have no leaders to call their own. There, were so many hopes from the state government after it was elected in 1996, but it has done nothing for the people. No development, no welfare schemes. Nothing.'

'Well, I did get the impression that the locals are sick of the gun, even if they aren't backing India,' said Bob, reaching out for another tikka.

'Of course they are sick of the gun. Unlike in 1990 when the JKLF was strong, these aren't *their* militants. Anyway, militancy isn't what it was. Though thousands of the foreigners came in during the Kargil war, you don't have militants lurking in every neighbourhood like you did earlier. There aren't that many militants any more, and those who are active are almost all foreigners.'

'Varun, the time,' Raju stepped in smoothly. He knew that once Varun got going on the subject of Kashmiri militancy, it would require another nuclear test to slow him down. 'We'd better get cracking.'

'Oh shit, it's 8:30 already,' muttered Varun, gulping from his can, and rising to his feet. 'See you around, Bob. I assume you're staying on for the Republic Day celebrations day after tomorrow?'

'Yes, of course. I'm trying to arrange for the passes.'

Varun and Raju headed for the door, and out into the frigid January air. Their taxi driver was waiting patiently for them, and he handed them the kangri on which he had been toasting his fingers. Raju grabbed it with some glee and cuddled its warmth against his chest. Though both of them were well bundled up, the freezing wind growled and nipped at their ears as they huddled in the unheated car.

There was still plenty of activity on the streets; many shops were open, and several cars were zipping busily back and forth down Residency Road. And as their taxi turned right onto the Dal Lake Boulevard, Varun stared in amazement at the scores of people who were gathered on the banks of the lake: young men chatting in small groups, elderly men sitting on their haunches by the side of the road puffing contentedly at their beedis, and mothers clutching their children by the hand and turning down their insistent, shrill demands for another packet of peanuts.

'Just look at them,' Varun said softly. 'And in this cold. Remember this place three years ago? There wouldn't be a soul on the streets after six—even we used to hesitate before venturing out after dark. And now, it's almost nine, and they are all happily wandering around.'

'This is nothing,' replied Raju. 'You didn't come here in the month just before the Kargil war, did you? You had to see Srinagar then. There were more than a hundred thousand tourists, and all of them domestic, from South India, Gujarat, Mumbai. The locals went wild; they made more money in that one month than in the past decade.'

Half an hour later, their host Imtiaz Ahmed elaborated, as they sat on a thick carpet in his bedroom, sipping at their glasses of Royal Challenge. 'Yes, last summer we caught a glimpse of what life can be like if normalcy returns. We saw how much money the Indian middle class now has, and how ready they are to spend it on their vacations. You know that I have three houseboats? Well, in early April I charged five hundred bucks a night and I had to turn away a dozen tourists a day. So the next week I charged a thousand bucks. I still had to turn away a dozen tourists. Then I charged two thousand rupees a night. And I was still turning them away.'

He shook his head sorrowfully, pouring himself another lethal-looking peg of whisky. 'And then those Pakistani bastards across the border fucked it all up for us. The sons of bitches are bankrupt themselves, so they want to take all of us down with them. Of course, the government helped them screw us up by closing the airport for those three days at the height of the conflict.'

Varun grinned, 'So, Imtiaz, no more sympathies with Pakistan? I thought you used to keep a Paki flag in your bedroom closet.'

Imtiaz held his ears in mock apology. 'Burnt it years ago. Just after the militants first extorted money from me.'

Raju helped himself to some peanuts from the bowl in front of him, even as Imtiaz signalled to the young boy he had hired as a domestic help to bring in the dinner. 'I haven't heard that story,' Raju said.

'They picked me up from the house and took me downtown. Some strange group called the Freedom Force, or something like that. Big Pakistani flags all over the room where they kept me. Then their chief walked up to me and said that he wanted two lakh rupees as a donation for the cause. I laughed in his face and said that I couldn't raise that much even if I were to sell everything I own. So he pulled out his pistol and cocked it.'

Raju's hand stopped midway between the peanut bowl and his mouth. 'Then?'

'Then we haggled like village women in the *mandi*, even as he kept raising his pistol and jabbing it into my ear. We finally agreed that five thousand rupees was acceptable value for my hide, and I returned home.'

Varun laughed. 'When was this?'

'Oh, I don't know . . . 1996, I think, just before the assembly elections. Ah, food is here.'

They heaped their plates with rice and mutton roganjosh, sitting cross-legged on the carpet, and eating with their fingers in the true Kashmiri style. After a few minutes of dedicated chomping, Varun broke the silence. 'What news of Habib Shah? How is he managing now?'

Imtiaz shrugged. 'Habib is still in Maisuma. No one pays too much attention to him any more, everyone is too busy trying to survive. The security forces are still running wild, often picking up innocent people and killing them. A great way to win over the people of the state. I don't know why the government doesn't just send all the soldiers to the Line of Control. Let them plug the LoC to prevent all these foreign militants from coming through and leave all of us civilians alone.'

Varun reached out for some more rogan josh, spooning the thick fragrant gravy onto the rice on his plate. 'We must go and see Habib. Perhaps day after tomorrow, on Republic Day.'

Raju spoke through a mouthful of rice, 'I assume security will be very tight if Farooq Abdullah is coming for the parade.'

'Well, security is always tight on Republic Day. And these new suicide bombers that the Lashkar-e-Taiba has started to send in are making everyone nervous,' replied Imtiaz.

They called themselves the *fedayee* squads. Groups of two or three men, sworn to die for the jihad, who would break into army camps and fight till death. They were one of the main reasons why Varun and Raju had come to Kashmir this time. As had many others. When they returned to their hotel just before midnight, Varun grimaced as he spotted Gopalkrishnan skulking around the reception area. He had on his usual surly expression, and nodded curtly at them.

'Fucking telephones aren't working again in this goddamn hotel. I have to make a call urgently—you don't happen to have a satellite phone on you, do you?'

Raju replied evenly, 'Actually, we do. But it is still in the case, I need to take it out and set it up. I'll do that tomorrow.'

'No, please do it now. I really must make a call.'

'Gopal, I'm afraid it's just not possible. Even if I were to take it out, it will take a couple of hours for the battery to charge.'

'Why don't you try?'

Raju was starting to get irritated. 'I said it isn't possible right now. It's already twelve—why can't you wait for the morning?'

Gopal stared back at Raju. There was a look of something that approached desperation on his face, and Varun thought he could make out a sheen of sweat on his forehead. 'No, I have to talk right now—I need to speak to my wife. Fuck it. I'll see if one of the PCO booths is open.'

He turned towards the door as Varun gazed at him in amazement. 'Gopal, don't be an ass. It's midnight in the middle of January, two days before Republic Day. Who is going to be there at a PCO booth?'

But Gopal had stepped out into the cold, and soon disappeared down the driveway. Varun looked across at Raju. 'What on earth was that all about?'

'God knows. That man is nuts.'

*   *   *

The cameraman woke up early on Republic Day, feeling the familiar heaviness of dread deep inside his stomach. He lay awake for some time, staring at the ceiling above him. The correspondent was still huddled deep inside his quilt, letting out soft snores of contentment every few minutes.

The previous day had proved that the Semtex plan could work. To test the concept, he had taken a fresh camera battery and had carefully inserted a few tiny slivers of Semtex into its crevices. If caught, he would pretend that the bits of Semtex must have got deposited accidentally on the battery when he was filming the captured weapons depot a few weeks earlier.

He had then taken the battery into the heart of the Badami Bagh cantonment. They had been stopped at the gate like always, and had been taken to the metal detectors that scanned their bags and their bodies. His heart had almost stopped beating when the soldier pulled out a new gizmo that was meant to detect plastic explosives. But, as always, the soldier only aimed it at the bags. The Anton Bauer battery mounted on the back of the camera was ignored.

Now it was Republic Day in Srinagar. Time for the final act.

* * *

Varun stood with Bob Gilman right outside the Bakshi stadium. It was 10 a.m., and the parade was due to start in just a few minutes. Raju and Humzar Ali were both busy taking shots of heavily armed soldiers frisking some sad-looking government employees as they queued up to enter the stadium.

The roads outside the stadium were completely deserted: the Hurriyat Conference had given its customary call for a strike on Republic Day, and in any case most residents felt that it wasn't worth the effort trying to negotiate their way through the thick maze of security cordons that had been thrown up all over the city.

'Everything should be fine by the afternoon,' Varun reassured Bob, even as their cameramen returned to their sides. Varun shot a quick glance at Humzar, who looked extremely young, barely in his late teens. He was a tiny man, dwarfed by the Betacam that was balanced on his shoulder. A thick mop of curly hair framed his face, and he met Varun's scrutiny with some nervousness, baring his teeth ingratiatingly.

Varun fished out a packet of cigarettes and held it out towards Bob. 'What did you guys do yesterday?'

Bob declined the proffered cigarette. 'We roamed around the city, and then went to meet the BGS at Badami Bagh. We wanted to ask him about the security arrangements for today.'

Varun laughed, 'I think we all went to meet the BGS yesterday. It must have been like an assembly line of interviews for the poor man.'

Bob glanced impatiently at his watch. 'What's the delay? Why can't we go into the stadium now?'

'I think the superintendent of police in charge of security will take us in personally. There are also other journalists and TV crews who are being escorted from the Tourist Reception Centre to the stadium, not everyone came directly here like we did.'

Fifteen minutes later all the other journalists straggled in. It had been an exhausting journey of repeated security checks for them at each of the cordons that the army and the police had erected around the stadium. Varun waved a cheery greeting at Sanjiv Deshpande who was there with Gopalkrishnan. 'Hi, boss. We are meeting in Srinagar after years.'

Sanjiv punched his arm. 'Well, I never see you in Delhi, except on the tube. So I guess Srinagar has to be the rendezvous.'

A harried-looking policeman walked up to the milling journalists. 'Gentlemen, let's head into the stadium, shall we? Can you please join the queue near the gate so that the guards can check your bags?'

*　*　*

The cameraman steeled himself as the queue edged forward. He had mounted the battery stuffed with Semtex onto the back of his camera. This was the real thing now, and if the guards detected the explosives, there could be no escape, and no explanations.

His head was light, as if floating a little above his neck, and the pumping adrenaline was making him feel nauseous. But there was nowhere to run to. The wall of the Bakshi stadium was to his left, and a fence to his immediate right. In front of him, he could hear a couple of reporters guffawing at an off-colour joke. Just seven more men were between him and the security guards.

His correspondent turned around, and frowned a little as he saw the expression on his face. 'Is everything all right? You aren't looking too well.'

He forced a slight smile and spoke with surprising calmness, 'I'm not feeling very well. I think it's the water in the hotel.'

'That's strange. I feel perfectly fine. And you should be more used to the water here than I am. Anyway, we'll soon be in.'

'Don't worry. I will be fine.'

Two more men to go. He watched his correspondent yield himself to the searching hands of the armymen, and then he stepped forward in his turn. He held out his press card, that magical badge that would ensure that the scrutiny wasn't too detailed. The army havildar ran an expert hand all over his body, and then gestured to the camera.

'Will you switch that on, please?'

'Of course,' the cameraman replied, flicking a small switch and then swivelling the viewfinder so that the soldier could peer into it. The havildar saw the flickering image on the tiny screen, and then nodded, waving the cameraman on.

He began to move forward, before another voice stopped him in his tracks. 'One minute, please.' A second soldier approached him with a flat metal detector in his hand. The cameraman held out his arms, with the camera held at full distance from his body. The metal detector was waved up and down his body, but not over the camera.

He had been banking on that, and it was with a huge sigh of relief that he moved past the gates of Bakshi stadium, straight into the arms of more soldiers, for further frisking.

Five minutes later he joined his correspondent on the steps leading into the stadium. The journalists walked past the empty chairs that lined the VIP enclosure and onto the turf inside the stadium, where there were only the security officials, top government officers, and the bored-looking contingents which would take part in the parade.

The TV crews set up their tripods on the grass, a few metres away from the podium where the chief guest would give his speech, and began to film the pole from where the Indian flag would be unfurled.

Suddenly the cameraman overheard a fragment of conversation between a couple of journalists behind him that caused him to abandon his camera in a hurry.

'Ali Mohammed Sagar should be here soon. We should try and get sound bites from him after his speech.'

'Sagar?' asked the cameraman, almost stuttering in his agitation. 'I thought that Farooq Abdullah was going to take the salute. That's what we'd been told, wasn't it?'

'Yeah, wrong information,' replied his correspondent. 'That bloody cop yesterday was obviously winding us up, he probably thought that we would be more likely to film the parade if we believed that Farooq was coming. But we've just been told that he is still in Jammu.'

'Well, that is the main parade these days,' added another of the journalists standing around. 'It would have been quite a surprise if Farooq had in fact come to the Valley, although it would have been a nice gesture.'

The cameraman slowly nodded, and then walked back to the tripod. In a casual move, he took off the Semtex-filled battery from the camera and replaced it with an ordinary battery from the bag. He also changed the tape, to make it seem as if these were routine precautions before a long stretch of uninterrupted filming.

The tension slowly started to ease out of his body. And the dominant emotion in his mind was huge, soaring relief. He wouldn't have to die just yet.

Chapter Twenty-two

THE CABINET MEETS

The red signal turned to green, and the white Ambassador accelerated as it sped past the Delhi race course. Vijay Kaul sat uncomfortably on the edge of his seat. This was the first time that he was ever meeting the Prime Minister of the country.

Without bothering to signal the turn, the driver of the car braked and swung right into Race Course Road. Twenty yards ahead, a huge steel barricade barred the way forward, and the car screeched to a halt. Vijay Kaul climbed out of the car, and the unsmiling Special Protection Guards man who had been sent to escort him led him towards the hut that had been erected on the left-hand side of the road. It took several minutes for the formalities to be completed, and then Vijay was led through the maze of gates towards the Prime Minister's residence.

Behind him other cars were pulling up before the barricade, as India's top ministers arrived for the special meeting. The barricade was repeatedly swung open to allow the cars through to the VIP parking area. But eventually, all of the ministers had to complete the last stretch on foot.

Vijay sat in the air-conditioned waiting room for quite some time. There were two other men present, one of whom he recognized as the cabinet secretary of India. These men were led into the Prime Minister's room after a few minutes, while Vijay sat on patiently. Then the door opened, and the joint secretary in the Prime Minister's Office gestured to him.

In a reflex gesture, Vijay checked his boots to ensure that they were still shining, and then walked through the door.

There were eight men inside the room, sitting comfortably on well-upholstered sofas. The Prime Minister, dressed casually in a kurta and dhoti; the Home Minister, toying with his spectacle case which was placed on the table before him; and the Defence Minister, slumped in his chair and wearing his trademark khadi kurta-pyjama. Then there was the director of IB, the Intelligence Bureau, and the secretary, RAW, the Research and Analysis Wing, India's main external intelligence agency. Completing the row of inquisitors were the cabinet secretary, the home secretary and the principal secretary to the Prime Minister, a man who was also the national security advisor.

Vijay snapped to attention and saluted smartly. The Prime Minister smiled and waved him towards a chair. Then he drawled slowly, 'So, Major Kaul. What is all this?'

Vijay knew that all the details were there in the files kept before each of the men, but he quickly began to race through the salient facts once again.

The Prime Minister raised his hand to stop him in full flow. 'One minute. This man who came to you, how reliable do you think he is?'

'Sir, his name is Haider Ali. He says he has been with the Lashkar-e-Taiba for several years, and that he is a close associate of Jalauddin. He says he was with Jalauddin inside Chrar-e-Sharief, and that he has accompanied him on several missions. He was able to describe Jalauddin and his activities very accurately.'

The Home Minister glanced at the director of the IB, who nodded. 'Sir, we've gone over Haider Ali's statement with a toothcomb, and it seems to tally completely. All the incidents he mentioned did take place exactly when he said they did.'

'You have met this Jalauddin, haven't you?' the Defence Minister asked Vijay.

'Yes sir, I had entered Chrar-e-Sharief in March 1995, and I spent some time with him.'

'And?'

'He was a fanatic, and extremely dangerous. He always made me feel uncomfortable. In my opinion he's capable of pulling off something like this.'

The Home Minister stirred in his chair. 'Do you know why this Haider Ali approached you? I mean, why you? Why not someone else?'

Vijay shook his head. 'I'm afraid I have no idea, sir. I asked him that question. All he said was that he had heard of me.'

'And what does he want? Money? A pardon?'

'Actually, sir, he didn't mention any price at all, nor did he lay down any conditions. He just seemed angry with Jalauddin.'

The Home Minister settled back unhappily and looked at the Prime Minister, who was resting his chin on his hand, appearing to be fast asleep. Then he suddenly snapped out of his reverie. 'Thank you, Major Kaul. Will you wait outside?'

Vijay leapt to his feet and clicked his heels, before leaving the room. Then the Prime Minister looked around him. 'What about this plot? How feasible is it?'

The DIB opened the file before him, 'Let's take it one step at a time, sir. Haider Ali claims that Jalauddin has come into India. Fair enough, there are thousands of infiltrators here. Then he says that the terrorist has been able to smuggle in a Stinger missile, with which he plans to shoot down an aeroplane. I suppose that's feasible as well.'

The RAW chief spoke up, 'Oh yes, it's feasible. Our organization has often commented on the free availability of Afghan war surplus Stingers which could fall into terrorist hands.'

The Stingers had been sent to the Afghan mujahideen by the Americans, after earlier SAMs like the Blowpipe had proved to be completely inadequate. Within months, the Stingers had tilted the balance of power in the Afghan war; the helicopter gunships, which the mujahideen feared so much, could no longer operate with impunity. By the time the Russians pulled out of Afghanistan, more than 250 aircraft had been shot down by Stingers.

234 THE SRINAGAR CONSPIRACY

But there was a sting in the tail. The remaining Stingers were still in the possession of the mujahideen, and eventually became part of the arsenals held by the Taliban and by its rivals in the Northern Alliance. Other Stingers had been carefully siphoned off by the Pakistanis, and to the horror of the Americans, many of the lethal missiles began to show up in the arms bazaars outside Peshawar. The CIA offered large sums of money to try and get back the Stingers, but few were returned.

'Now is when the story gets tricky,' continued the DIB. 'This Haider Ali doesn't seem to have been privy to the real details of the so-called plot. All he knows is that the terrorists are planning to shoot down an aeroplane being used by a very important dignitary. This is the exact fragment of conversation that Haider Ali overheard; Jalauddin tells his lieutenant Karim, "When the bastards are running around chasing their own tails, that is when we will use the Stinger on the plane. Then the people will take to the streets again, and azaadi, inshallah, will follow." '

There was a gesture of disbelief from one of the men at the other end of the room. 'It sounds a bit improbable to me.'

'I don't know,' said the Defence Minister thoughtfully. 'Who would have believed all these *fedayee* attacks we are seeing, two or three men breaking into an armed camp and fighting to the death? For that matter, who would have believed the Kargil intrusions last year, even as we were talking peace with the Pakistanis? I think it's sensible to be prepared for the worst.'

The Home Minister spoke, in his careful and precise manner. 'I'm sure all you gentlemen must have realized the possibilities of who the target could be.'

The RAW chief nodded unhappily, 'President Clinton arrives on 20th March, just about a month from now. That doesn't leave us with much time.'

'We will have to warn the American Secret Service about the threat. And in the meantime, we have to find this man Jalauddin. Tell the J&K government, and get them to move fast on this. I also think we should set up a special operation squad here in Delhi. Call the DGP in Srinagar and tell him to send his best men to join the group. Perhaps that young man, Kaul, can be used on the squad; he seems to know all the people involved in this mess.'

The Prime Minister looked around him. 'Is that all, then?'

The national security advisor spoke for the first time: 'I hope all of this isn't an elaborate charade, aimed at distracting our attention. I hope there is nothing we are missing in all of this excitement over the Stinger.'

The Prime Minister shrugged. 'How can we tell? I think we might have to try and get some more information out of this Haider Ali. Or ask him to try and get some information for us.'

Chapter Twenty-three

SAD AND DEFEATED

Habib had aged. Time had sketched fine lines near his mouth,
darkened the skin under his eyes and dabbed small streaks of
silver into his hair.

But the slump of his shoulders didn't come from age. Nor
did the gap in his teeth where a carelessly swished police
baton had knocked out one of his incisors during a protest
demonstration. The fire had slowly, very slowly, faded from
his eyes, and he looked like a sad, defeated man.

And that was what Habib was, a sad and defeated man,
as he sat silently on the carpeted floor of his Maisuma home,
wearing around him a thick cloak of tragedy which he
clutched ever closer to himself with every passing month.

Varun was led into the room by Qasim, and he almost
failed to recognize Habib at first glance. Then he approached
him with his arms outstretched, and was rewarded by a warm
smile as Habib rose to his feet.

'*Waray choo*, Varun bhai,' he said as he hugged the
journalist. 'So you too have forgotten me now like the rest of
the world?'

Varun looked a little ashamed. He hadn't had the time to
meet any of the JKLF leaders during his last three visits to the
Valley; they had become increasingly unimportant in the new
fight between the security forces and the foreign militants. 'I
am sorry, Habib. I really did want to meet you last time, but
I ran out of time, and had to rush back to Delhi. And on the
previous trip it wasn't my fault—who asked you to get

yourself arrested again?'

Habib led him towards the comfortable-looking cushions that were stacked on the carpet next to the wall. 'Sit here, I know how you hate sitting cross-legged. You will have lunch with us this afternoon, won't you?'

It was more of a command than a request, and Varun knew that it was futile to even think of protesting.

He settled himself down on the cushions, as did Raju, who was busy catching up on old times with Qasim. Then Varun turned back to Habib, who was gazing at him with disconcertingly frank eyes.

'So, why are you here today? Is there a story you are chasing?'

'No. I've already done what I had to, and have sent it to Delhi. I've just dropped in for a chat.'

Habib looked both surprised and a little sceptical. Then he glanced at Varun's forehead and smiled. 'I see that your scar is still there. It must be reminding you of Kashmir every morning as you shave.'

Varun fingered the scar ruefully. 'Not that I need much reminding. I never did get around to thanking you for all you did that day.'

'Don't be silly,' Habib waved his hand dismissively and changed the subject. 'How is Delhi? And how is the government doing?'

'Remarkably stable actually, the most stable government in a decade. And I think they are serious about looking for a solution here in Kashmir.'

'Oh no, here it comes,' Habib held up his arms in mock surrender, as he pretended to hide his face. 'You are going to try and convert me once again.'

Varun was forced to smile. 'No, I'm not. But you know, Habib, the Centre is looking for other alternatives here in Kashmir. They know that the state government isn't delivering effective administration, and they would be only too happy to get a viable alternative. Someone like you.'

'So you want me to betray the others in the movement? Forget about 70,000 graves across the Valley?'

'At least ensure that no more graves have to be dug. And come on, I know what you really feel about the "others". What do you have in common with the Jamaat? Or with the Pakistani militants who are coming across the border these days?'

The mock cheerfulness that Habib had plastered on his face faded a little, and he didn't reply. Varun knew better than to press the point, and the conversation drifted to other areas.

'Are you still with Vision TV?' inquired Habib. 'We don't get the channel that easily here in Srinagar.'

'Yes, I'm still with them. The atmosphere there is great, and they treat me well.'

'Not thinking of a transfer to NDTV, are you?' teased Habib. 'Isn't that supposed to be the best news organization to work for?'

Varun laughed. 'No such luck right now. But maybe I should send them my bio-data.'

'Well, lots of people here want to join the media now. Everyone wants to work for TV,' said Qasim.

'Yes, we keep seeing new people. There was this cameraman we met a couple of days ago, Humzar Ali. We've never met him before,' replied Varun.

'Who?' Habib looked puzzled.

'Humzar Ali. He's a local, from Srinagar, now working as a freelancer with Bob Gilman of the Broadcast Network. Small man, with curly hair.'

Habib glanced at Qasim. 'Have you met this man? I thought I knew all the local journalists.'

'Never heard of him. And I don't think he's ever come to any of our press conferences.'

'Well, you aren't going to see him now,' Raju said. 'I got chatting with him the other day, and he's apparently shifting to Delhi—he's got a job with some TV company there.'

'Hmmm,' said Habib as the food was brought in, and then they all dismissed Humzar Ali from their minds.

After lunch the journalists rose to go, and Habib got up too. 'Must you go so early? Come, I'll accompany you outside, it's time for my walk in any case.'

They stepped out into the narrow back alleys of Maisuma. Not far from them stood the JKLF office, looking more than a little derelict. A group of young boys had set up a wooden crate as a makeshift wicket and were busy playing cricket with a tennis ball. A little kid, barely in his teens, was taking guard, and he smashed the next delivery over the bowler's head, before scampering down the pitch for a couple of runs.

Varun ruffled a curly head as they passed the cricketers, stepping onto the ledges that ran in front of the houses to avoid disturbing the game. 'So who are their idols now? Still the Pakistani cricketers like Shahid Afridi?'

'No,' Habib shook his head. 'Now they have no idols, they play for themselves.'

'I don't know,' disagreed Qasim, as he skipped nimbly aside to avoid being decapitated by a crashing cover drive, 'some like Akram and Younis. But I've also met many who worship Sachin Tendulkar and Ganguly.'

They reached a T-junction in the alley, from where the main road was clearly visible. In the distance, they could see their taxi parked by the side of the road, the driver sunning himself on an upturned wooden carton next to it. Habib stopped and turned around to say goodbye to the journalists, but Varun paused for a moment. 'Um . . . is it okay if we keep walking with you? We aren't in any hurry.'

Habib hesitated momentarily and then recovered smoothly. 'Of course, it's a pleasure.' They turned left and then moved further into the back alleys, which grew narrower and filthier. There were just the six of them, Habib, Qasim, Varun, Raju, and two other young men whose job was presumably to guard the JKLF leader.

'Just look at this,' Habib gestured towards the drains that were overflowing onto the roads. 'The government couldn't give a shit about how the people are having to live.'

Varun nodded absent-mindedly. He was busy looking all around him; he'd never been into this area before. The houses all around them clustered ever closer together, before suddenly opening out into a clearing, and Varun gasped audibly at the sudden beauty of the spot that was revealed to them. A wide canal intersected their path, green with algae but still flowing reasonably swiftly. Thick willow trees lined its banks, and a couple of shikaras were moored in front of them. They belonged to flower-sellers, who would follow the water to the tourist traps on the Dal Lake.

They crossed the canal on a rickety wooden bridge, and Habib turned right. A hundred yards ahead he stopped and gestured to the others to wait where they were. Then he walked on alone for a dozen yards, before turning left into a thick grove of trees. Varun stared after him curiously, before realizing that the trees sheltered one of the smallest graveyards he had ever seen.

Habib came to a stop beside a tiny marble headstone, barely a foot high. He squatted next to it, and then was still.

Raju raised an enquiring eyebrow at Qasim, who whispered, 'Yasmin. The girl he would have married. He comes here every single day.'

The minutes stretched out slowly, and still Habib squatted where he was. Varun stirred uncomfortably, he suddenly felt as if he was an intruder, in a place where he did not belong.

'I think we will head back,' he said quietly to Qasim, who nodded understandingly. 'Tell Habib that I will soon see him again.'

The journalists began to walk back, and as they crossed the bridge, Varun paused and looked back one last time to where Habib sat silently. A strong emotion was threatening to cause a lump in his throat, but he wasn't sure whether it was sympathy or pity.

Chapter Twenty-four

THE MURIDKE PLOT

Vijay Kaul pulled up a chair to his computer and bent down to switch on the UPS. The power supply to his home had begun to fluctuate wildly in the past few months, with the sixty-watt bulbs moving from mood lighting to TV-spotlight intensity in a matter of seconds, and then back again. In self-defence he had been forced to wire all of his electronic gizmos to a series of voltage stabilizers.

He pushed the power button on the front of his computer, and then strolled off to fix some snacks while the machine booted. He padded barefoot into the dining room and pulled open the fridge to examine its contents. 'Cheese, fine. Some mayo. No ham, but there is some salami,' he muttered to himself and pulled out a bottle of Coke to go with the food. After the dextrous slapping together of a quick sandwich, he returned to the computer room and clicked on the icon that would connect him to the Internet.

'Please, oh please let the lines work today,' he prayed silently, and then rejoiced as the modem sang its screechy sound of welcome, as it mated with the VSNL server.

Vijay bit a chunk out of his sandwich and then glanced at a scrap of paper kept on the table. 'Now, what was that URL? . . . Here it is, www.dawacenter.com.'

He typed it in carefully, and then swigged at his bottle of Coke as he was taken to the 'Official web site of the Lashkar-e-Taiba and the Markaz-ul-Dawa-wal-Irshad'. It had changed since he had last seen it, though the home page still had its characteristic image of an open Quran, with an AK-47 emerging from it. The banners which promised the destruction of the 'terrorist states' of India, the US and Israel had been replaced by sophisticated-looking links which lured the surfer to the history of the jihad, and to the latest news from the holy war. There was even an account number at the Faisal Bank in Karachi, Pakistan, to which donations could be sent.

But the pages that contained the history of the Markaz were still the same, and Vijay went through them again.

The text came up on a bold blue background, and Vijay scrolled through it casually.

'During the Afghan jihad, the youth of a rather battered Muslim Ummah took part to please Allah (SWT). In 1986, Markaz-ul-Dawa-wal-Irshad was established to organize the Pakistanis participating in the Afghan jihad on one platform.

'In 1987, a training centre was established at Jaji in the Paktia province of Afghanistan to train the members of this organization. Soon, another training centre, namely, "Mo'askar Taiba" or "Taiba training center", was established in the Kunnar province. The Mujahideen trained at these centres and performed outstanding operations. As the activities of the Markaz expanded, its educational and jihadic sections were separated.'

Vijay took another sip of his Coke, and then glanced at his watch. It was well past midnight, but the sound of heavy trucks passing by on the main road outside continued to rattle his windows. He tapped on his mouse and scrolled further down on the page.

'Consequently, in 1993, the jihadic and warfare wing of Markaz-ul-Dawa-wal-Irshad was established with the name of "Lashkar-e-Taiba". Later this organization emerged as a powerful force in the occupied J&K. Thousands of Mujahideen were trained to fight in Afghan, Kashmir, Bosnia, Chechnya, Kosovo, the Philippines and in other areas where Muslims are fighting for freedom.

'May Allah (SWT) give success to Mujahideen worldwide and give freedom to all the occupied Muslim lands.'

Vijay surfed idly to other pages, marvelling as always at the sheer force of ideological determination that flickered through onto his monitor. Checking the Markaz website was something he tried to do every couple of months; in the past few years the Markaz-ul-Dawa-wal-Irshad had emerged as the leading propagator of jihad in southern Asia.

In the schools and seminaries it ran in Pakistan, thousands of young boys were taught to believe that salvation lay in the holy war, and that the greatest honour was to die for the jihad. Once they believed that completely, they were automatic recruits for the Lashkar-e-Taiba, the armed wing of the Markaz, which would send the boys to fight in Kashmir and in other parts of the world. The new Lashkar recruits would hitch their pyjamas above their ankles as a sign of ideological purity, and would journey home to smash their TV sets. Then they would be ready to die.

A host of dialogue boxes suddenly sprang up on Vijay's computer screen informing him that he had been disconnected from the net. He groaned to himself, mentally cursing the frayed telephone lines that ran into his apartment. He didn't really have the energy to log on again, so he went into his hard disk, pulling out some old pages from the Markaz site that he had saved.

Almost automatically, he went to the pages from the last Ijtima, the annual conference of the Lashkar-e-Taiba every November, a gathering that Vijay had labelled as the largest congregation of terrorists in the world. Past conferences had seen thousands listen to speakers extolling the virtues of the jihad, and giving graphic and often gory details of their exploits in Kashmir. This time many of the speeches had been broadcast in Real Audio over the net, and Vijay had promptly saved all of them.

Now he clicked on one of the audio files, and the impassioned voice of the Lashkar chief, Hafeez Mohammed Saeed, began to play out scratchily over the computer speakers, boasting triumphantly about the latest attack on an Indian army camp.

Vijay leant back in his chair and closed his eyes. He had

heard this speech so often that he almost knew it by heart. *'Junagarh lena hai, Hyderabad lena hai. Pakistan ke mussalman, tumhe apna haq Clinton nahin dega, haq Jihad se milega,'* bellowed the disembodied voice, as Hafeez Saeed prophesized the imminent break-up of India and the absorption of its fragments into Pakistan.

The voice was suddenly silenced as the audio file came to an end, and Vijay opened his eyes and reached out to close the folder. Then he switched off the computer and walked to the window. The huge halogen lights poured yellow illumination onto the main road outside, and Vijay lit a cigarette as he stared at the Tata trucks that were trundling along on their post-midnight journey through the nation's capital. In his mind's eye he visualized the tiny band of fanatics that were out there somewhere, and he thought of the slim chance of getting to them in time.

He looked at his watch again. Two in the morning. Time for bed. He was tired, and quite depressed.

*   *   *

Jalauddin had watched Saeed in rapt attention, with stars in his eyes.

For hours he and thousands of others had squatted on the assembly ground at Muridke listening to theological justifications for the jihad, and to the experiences of those who claimed that they had just returned from the battlefields of Kashmir.

This was Jalauddin's third Ijtima; he had first attended the annual Lashkar congregation in 1996, at a time when he had been deeply dissatisfied with what he considered the Harkat-ul-Ansar's far too casual attitude towards the plight of Langryal and the others who were rotting in Indian jails.

The Lashkar-e-Taiba's call to jihad had struck a chord inside him that was just waiting to be struck; and before the 1996 congregation was over, Jalauddin had formally transferred his allegiance to the organization. As an experienced fighter, he was more than welcome, and the commander of the

Lashkar had personally administered the oath to him and had given him a new Arabized name or *kuniat*. Then he was sent to the Moas'kar-e-Taiba in Afghanistan for the basic twenty-one-day course, training that he found almost humiliatingly elementary. Sensibly, his commanders spared him the more extensive ninety-day course, and allowed him full leeway to plan and carry out his own actions inside Kashmir. They also didn't protest too loudly when Jalauddin insisted on using his own name instead of the kuniat he had been given.

The speeches had come to an end, and the next namaaz was due in a short while. Jalauddin's bladder was bursting, and he rose slowly from his position, wincing a little as the circulation returned to his calves. Then he made his way through the packed hordes squatting all around him. He got a number of curious glances; the word was out that he was an extremely successful mujahid who had killed many of the hated Indian soldiers. Many of the first-timers wondered why he wasn't going to address them—the answer was that Jalauddin would have sooner faced an entire mountain division on his own than addressed a huge gathering. There are some things that even a mujahid can be scared of.

Jalauddin walked towards the public toilets, grinning to himself as he spotted the huge banner that he and Karim had put up, showing the dagger of the Lashkar-e-Taiba piercing the flags of India, the US, the UK, Russia and Israel. It had taken them some time to paint it, and he was quite proud of the artistic achievement. Some distance away, another banner asked for donations, claiming that even ten rupees could lead to the end of an Indian soldier's life.

He relieved himself, groaning softly with contentment, and emerged from the shed. Then he became aware that he was being watched, and he came to attention, his hackles rising invisibly like those of a tiger that has suddenly sensed the hunter hiding in his machan. There were three men standing there, a few yards away, with long beards and Afghan headgear. The man in the centre had the silver hair of age and authority in his beard, and the soft light of complete power glimmering in his eyes.

He stepped forward and approached the wary Jalauddin, his arms half held out in an unmistakable gesture of comradeship. 'Asalaam aleikum. We have been watching you, and we have heard a lot about you. My name is Abu Hanif Ibrahim.'

Respect lit up Jalauddin's eyes, and there was genuine admiration in his response. 'Waleikum salaam. You need no introduction, sir, and I apologize for not recognizing you immediately. I am honoured that you have found me worthy of your attention.'

Ibrahim inclined his head, accepting the compliment as nothing more than his due. Then he took Jalauddin's arm and steered him away from the crowds. 'Come with me, young man. There is one who wishes to talk to you. And I think it will be worth your while.'

'My men are still with the congregation . . .'

'They will wait. You can rejoin them after the namaaz.'

Jalauddin said no more, and Ibrahim volunteered no further information, as they moved towards the outskirts of the Muridke complex. All signs of habitation fell away behind them; just one small house could be seen ahead, tucked away in the shelter of a few huge trees.

As they reached the door of the house, Ibrahim patted Jalauddin on his back. 'Go on inside now, I will return to the congregation. There is a truly great man who is waiting for you, and he will lead you to your destiny.'

It was with curiosity, and with more than a touch of trepidation that Jalauddin swung open the wooden door, after pausing to take off his footwear. It was dark inside, and his eyes took some time to adjust. All he could make out was a figure sitting inside, a white turban coiled above his forehead and an AK-47 balanced on his lap.

Then his vision cleared, and he recoiled in stunned surprise, 'I know you! You are . . .'

The figure held up a warning hand. 'Here I am nothing but a humble servant of Allah. Abu Fateh is my name.'

Jalauddin was on his knees, and he wasn't quite sure how he had reached there. He was gazing at the man with what was almost devotional fervour. 'You are anything but that. You have put fear into the hearts of the infidels like no one else has; they search for you everywhere and have tried to kill you so often... But we all thought that you were in Afghanistan...'

Abu Fateh smiled gently. 'Yes, I know. Everyone thinks that I am in Afghanistan, including most of the Taliban. But I have found some new hosts, and they are generous indeed.'

He waved Jalauddin to a more comfortable seat, and asked him if he wanted something to drink. The big man shook his head, feeling as overcome with awe as he had been that day when he had first met Langryal.

Abu Fateh talked of other matters for a while, and slowly Jalauddin began to feel at ease. Then the figure in white came to the point.

'I have heard of you, Jalauddin. I have heard that you are a man who is totally devoted to the jihad. Are you ready to make any sacrifice?'

Jalauddin did not hesitate. 'I would consider it an honour to die in the holy war.'

Abu Fateh nodded. He had expected no other answer. 'How long have you been with the Lashkar-e-Taiba?'

'For about three years now. Before that I used to be with the Harkat-ul-Ansar.'

'Would you have any objections to quitting the Lashkar-e-Taiba?'

There was a brief pause before Jalauddin replied. 'Not if there is a good reason for it, Abu Fateh.'

'There is good reason. I have a plan. Something that will shake the world. But we don't want to embarrass our hosts, and we don't want to involve the organizations that have accommodated us here. This is something that will be ours. Yours and mine. And that of the men whom I will place under your command. But time is short. You must be prepared to leave within weeks for India.' He spoke on, explaining the plan. Jalauddin listened to him in silence, nodding his head often and smiling to himself.

Then, an hour later, Jalauddin rose to go, but the other

man stayed him by raising his hand. 'One more thing. It is possible that you will soon hear about actions by other mujahids. Don't allow yourself to be distracted. They have their tasks, and you have yours.'

*　*　*

It was still in the last millennium that Jalauddin and his men set off from Lahore, chugging northwards in an ancient train, even as the cold mid-December air wheezed mistily past their grimy glass windows. The Punjab countryside rolled green and fertile past them; the odd village looming up through the fog.

There was still over an hour to go before the train reached Chak Amru, and Jalauddin decided that he wanted to stretch his legs. He was suddenly tired of the cramped second-class compartment, and of his companions huddled next to him. He rose from the wooden bench and stepped over the outstretched legs of a sleeping Karim, walking to the open door at the end of the corridor.

Fishing out a cigarette from his kurta pocket, he gazed out at the farmland. There weren't too many villagers to be seen, and that was quite unusual for this part of the subcontinent. He sensed a movement behind him, and knew, without turning around, that Karim had come to join him.

He extended the cigarette packet behind him. 'We should be there soon. Are the others ready?'

Karim nodded. 'Muzaffer is all set to go, and Salim is as ready as he ever will be. I worry about that man, he's just too feeble-minded for comfort.'

'Don't. He'll be okay once we've crossed into India. Call them here, we should leave the station as soon as possible, just in case the Indians have an agent or two waiting to see if someone gets off the train with guns.'

Chak Amru is an unlovely town, important only because it is situated a couple of kilometres away from the border with India. Jalauddin and his men were greeted at the station by a low-level ISI agent, who whisked them away in a battered jeep, shouting instructions over the engine noise as he drove.

'You will spend the night in Sukumal, it's a village right across the border from India. You'll cross the border tomorrow night, after a day's rest.'

Jalauddin grunted his assent, and then slumped low in his seat, pulling the cap lower over his forehead to get some protection from the wind. They were housed in a small green house on the outskirts of the village overlooking the wide, nearly empty river bed that marked the boundary with India. From their room they could get a clear panoramic view of the terrain before them, and Jalauddin stood by the window with a pair of powerful binoculars, planning the route they would follow.

The ISI officer entered the room. 'Your guide is waiting in the back garden, he sneaked across from the other side last night and knows all of the BSF's ambush points.'

Jalauddin didn't lower the binoculars. 'Where exactly is the BSF camp?'

'You see that knoll across the river, to the side of the rice fields? The camp is just behind that, and there are about thirty to forty men in it. There is thick jungle on either side of the camp, and the paths through it are often monitored through the night. We lost a few men in an ambush just a couple of months ago. I think the best thing for you to do . . .'

'Get that guide in here,' interrupted Jalauddin, and the ISI man scurried out to comply.

The guide was a weaselly little man from a band of Gujjars, nomads who lived with their cattle on the Indian side of the border. The Pakistanis would pay him 25,000 rupees for a night's work, more than he would have earned in a year selling milk.

Jalauddin glanced at him, and then turned back to the window. 'Which way will you take us in?' The guide walked up to him and pointed. 'Sir, we will follow the river bed to the left-hand side, walking through those patches of elephant grass. We won't leave the river bed for a kilometre or so, because the BSF has lots of men waiting in ambush in this area. Then we will enter the broken ground you can see in the distance, making our way through the ravines till we come to my camp—which is about five or six kilometres from here. From there, the main highway is just a few minutes' walk, and you can catch your bus from there.'

'Why can't we go across from the right? It seems to me that the cover is much better there.'

'No sir, they have put up barbed wire in that region and also have solar-powered lights. You will see them coming on later tonight, after dark.'

Jalauddin nodded in agreement and then put down the binoculars before walking up to the cot standing at one side of the room and flinging himself onto it, still fully clothed, boots and all. 'Wake me up in a couple of hours.'

The next morning, Jalauddin dressed himself in the borrowed clothes of a Gujjar milkman and accompanied a herd of buffaloes as they walked from the village towards the river. He was well wrapped up in a blanket, and had, of course, left his weapons in the house. On reaching the river he glanced once or twice across the border, noting the pillbox which was manned by a couple of helmeted BSF soldiers. And as he swished twigs to keep the cattle moving, he casually ran a practiced eye along the route they would take.

It never failed to amaze him how porous the border really was. Though the Indians had realized a long time back that infiltration from Pakistan was the main reason why the insurgency in Kashmir still survived, they hadn't yet been able to figure out a way to systematically plug the frontier. In the higher mountainous stretches near Kupwara or Baramulla, the problem was the altitude and terrain that didn't allow any fences to be erected. But even here, in the plains, there was little barbed wire, no trenches, no landmines, just a vague imaginary line running along a river bed.

And that night there were few problems for Jalauddin and his men as they crept through the river and along the thick patches of elephant grass into Indian territory. There was no moon, but the guide was good and knew exactly where he had to go. By six o'clock the next morning the band of men had reached the town of Harinagar, which straddled National Highway 1A, the main arterial road connecting Jammu to

Delhi, hundreds of kilometres to the south.

The guide left them at the door of a sympathizer in the town, another local who would be well paid for the hospitality. His main function was to regulate the inflow of both men and armaments from Pakistan, and he relieved his new visitors of the bags of explosives that they had carried across the border. They also left their guns with him. They had a long bus journey before them, and there was no way weapons could escape scrutiny. Besides, arrangements had already been made for them to get all the arms they needed at their eventual destination.

Also waiting for them would be the case with the Stinger missile. It had been sent by ship and then smuggled into a Gujarati port with the help of a corrupt customs officer. Then the case had been sent in a truck filled with other goods to Faridabad, an industrial township on the outskirts of New Delhi. Jalauddin and his men had waited patiently in Pakistan till they received news of the crate's arrival, before starting on their own journey.

By eleven in the morning, the five men had walked up to the main bus station in Harinagar. Jalauddin went up to the booth selling tickets and smiled engagingly at the man sitting inside. 'Five tickets, please.'

'Where to?' came the irritated reply.

'Delhi.'

Chapter Twenty-five

PAHARGANJ

That was almost three months earlier. Since then Jalauddin and his associates had made themselves at home in a small guest house at Paharganj, not far from the New Delhi railway station. There were only nine rooms in the guest house, and Jalauddin signed a long-term agreement with the owner, promising to occupy an entire floor for six months. They only visited the farmhouse at Nangal Deri once, for the test of the Stinger, after which they hid the missile safely behind a false wall in the basement.

In response to the inevitable curious questions from neighbours, they had a simple cover story: they were refugees from Afghanistan, men owing allegiance to the Northern Alliance which was holding out against the Taliban, and had fled their war-torn country to try and eke out a living in India. The story was accepted without a murmur; the alleys of Old Delhi were home to any number of Tibetans, Bangladeshis, Afghans and others, all trying to make a new life for themselves.

Most of their time was spent watching TV, and it was on the flickering twenty-one-inch screen in one corner of his room that Jalauddin had watched the drama of the hijacking of the Indian Airlines plane from Kathmandu to Delhi, which was taken to Kandahar in Afghanistan. This was less than a week after they'd arrived in Delhi, and then there were a few days of hope for him, as he realized that Nasrullah Langryal's name was on the list of militants that the hijackers wanted released. But in the end there was nothing but bitter disappointment, as the hijackers accepted Masood Azhar and two others in exchange for the hostages, leaving Langryal in jail and Sajjad Afghani's body in the graveyard where he had been buried after his death in an abortive jailbreak.

For several hours then Jalauddin had stormed about his room, mouthing invective and thumping at the walls. Then he had remembered the words of Abu Fateh, and was silent once again. And soon the new inhabitants of Sarfarosh Guest House, Paharganj had fallen into a comfortable routine.

Close to their guest house was the magnificent Jama Masjid, where they went every Friday for namaaz. But Jalauddin had drilled words of warning into all his men: 'The men you meet here are Muslims. But never forget that these are Indians, and that their loyalty is to their country. Never let anyone get even a whiff of what our true plans are.'

On 6 March, two and a half months into their stay at the guest house, Jalauddin left his men in their rooms and walked down the crowded street to look for an autorickshaw. It was time to meet the cameraman.

He climbed into the three-wheeler and asked the driver to take him to Karim's, the almost legendary dhaba that did roaring business serving authentic North Indian Muslim cuisine in a back alley close to the Jama Masjid. The autorickshaw driver was obviously a deeply religious man, and Jalauddin surveyed the pictures of the Qa'aba and the quotations from the Quran that were liberally pasted all over the inside of the vehicle.

'Are you a visitor to Delhi?' enquired the driver chattily. 'Myself Salim, and I can take you for a special guided tour of the Red Fort if you like.'

Jalauddin shook his head and stared out at the chaotic traffic on the road, rebuffing any attempt to draw him into a conversation. The driver looked a little hurt, but then contented himself with trying to break the hurtling-through-Delhi's-streets-in-a-fragile-vehicle record.

The autorickshaw zoomed past the butchers' shops that lined the route to the Jama Masjid and screeched to a halt near a densely packed alley that led off from the road in front of the mosque. As Jalauddin stepped out and reached for his wallet, Salim made one last effort to make friendly conversation, 'At Karim's you must have mutton isstew, and the mutton korma. Best food in the world.'

Jalauddin smiled, and paid the driver. 'I'll do that. Khuda hafiz.'

Then he went down the alley and turned left into the courtyard of Karim's. The cameraman was waiting for him there, looking nervous and ill at ease. The rendezvous had been fixed the previous evening on the phone; for the cameraman it was the first contact since early February.

They walked up the stairs and found an empty table. The waiter came for their order, and they both demanded the stew and the korma, together with plenty of tandoori rotis. Then the cameraman leant across the table and whispered savagely, 'What is the matter with you people? I haven't heard anything from all of you for several weeks, and then you suddenly call and summon me to this place. It's not that easy for me to get away like this. And what happened on Republic Day? You had told me that Farooq would definitely be there. I took the most appalling of risks, and it was all for nothing.'

Jalauddin looked at the other man levelly. The cameraman wasn't to know that Republic Day had been nothing more than a test. The hit squad from Muridke had known that Farooq wouldn't go to Srinagar for the parade, but they had wanted to see whether the cameraman would have the guts to go through with the operation, or whether he would chicken out—or worse, blow the whistle just before the event. But he had proved himself, and it was time to let him know what was really expected of him.

Jalauddin bared his yellowish teeth in what he imagined was an apologetic grin. 'I am so sorry about Republic Day. He changed his plans at the last minute. But never mind, it has all worked out for the best. There is a new plan now, and you are the key.'

They had deliberately chosen a late afternoon time to meet, and the normally bustling restaurant was fairly deserted. There was no one to overhear them as Jalauddin carefully explained what the cameraman would have to do, although there were a few moments of silence after the waiter banged down the divine-smelling plates of food before them.

There was an even longer period of silence when Jalauddin finished his well-prepared speech. The cameraman was gazing at him with disbelief and shock in his eyes. He opened his mouth to speak, but his lips were quivering. Then he looked around the room, like a trapped animal, and tried again. 'You have to be joking. There is no way that I can do what you ask. It just isn't feasible . . . I will not do this.'

Jalauddin had expected this response, and his expression was hard and merciless. He broke off a piece of roti and swirled it in the gravy before transferring the morsel to his mouth. 'Actually, you *will* do it. You know that you don't have a choice. Especially now, after all that you have already done for us.'

The fight seemed to go out of the man sitting in front of him, and he sagged visibly, like a wax doll that has been kept for too long in the summer sun. He ran a hand through his thick mop of curly hair and whispered, 'Bhai, please listen to me. This is not possible. We cannot get away with it. Do you know the security measures they have? We won't even get close to him with the Semtex.'

'You managed in Srinagar, on Republic Day, didn't you?' said Jalauddin mildly. 'With all of that security? You will manage again. Either that, or you will die in the attempt.'

Jalauddin looked at the broken man across the table, and he knew that he had won; the cameraman would do whatever he was told to do.

They paid the bill and left, the cameraman stumbling slightly on the uneven surface of the alley as if he had forgotten how to walk. Just before they parted ways, Jalauddin caught his arm for a final whispered remark. 'One last thing. You have a couple of weeks to make all your arrangements, and to make certain of your success. And pull yourself together. Remember, our deal only stands if we succeed in our aim. If not, then . . .'

The cameraman nodded blindly, and briefly looked up at

the implacable face of the big Pakistani. Jalauddin read the
fear and the hatred in the other man's eyes as clearly as a neon
sign; but he was used to confronting those emotions, and there
was a soft smile on his face as he moved away smoothly to
mingle with the crowd.

Chapter Twenty-six

CLINTON ARRIVES

A special room had been set up at the ministry of defence to deal with what had been labelled 'the Stinger crisis'. A task force had been detailed to investigate the so-called plot, headed by a special secretary in the home ministry and consisting of men taken from the Intelligence Bureau, the National Security Guards and the army. In a complete breach of protocol, Vijay Kaul had been asked to lead the operational wing of the S-squad.

Vijay drove up Raisina Hill and looked for parking on his left, in front of the imposing fawn-coloured expanse of South Block. In front of him, nestled in the middle of its huge gardens, was Rashtrapati Bhavan, the home of the President of India, and to his right was North Block, where bureaucrats in the finance ministry were sitting till late at night that week, trying to come to terms with the sharp criticism their latest Union budget had evoked.

Vijay locked his Maruti and walked across the road into the ministry of home affairs at North Block, where he flashed his ID card at the grim-looking security guard. Then he walked down the dimly lit corridors, the sound of his boots echoing off the high-domed ceilings, before turning into the plywood-partitioned shoebox which passed off as his new office.

It was only eight in the morning, and North Block was almost completely deserted. But Vijay's colleagues in the S-squad were at their desks, patiently ploughing their way through stacks of Intelligence Bureau reports on just about every ISI cell and every known fundamentalist Islamic group in the country. They were looking for any scrap of information about any contact with a group of Afghans, and in particular for any lead on a man who looked like Jalauddin. But so far there wasn't even a scrap of vague cover-your-ass information from some sub-inspector in a distant mofussil to chew on.

'Nothing?' asked Vijay despondently, and slumped into his chair without waiting for an answer. A peon entered the room carrying a cup of tea, sweetened to the point where it could give you instant diabetes. Vijay took the cup and sipped at it gratefully.

'I have to go before the boss in an hour—and he will be briefing the PM later in the day. I think we are now coming to the point where we need to take some urgent decisions. We have informed the DGPs of most states about the possibility of a terrorist strike, but have asked them to keep quiet. Do we now go public and flash the bastard's picture on TV or not?'

'I think not,' replied Sheetal Jain, a young IB operative who was one of the country's top experts on terrorism in Kashmir. 'You run the danger of panicking him into premature action. Plus you could create general panic. Can you imagine what news of a rogue Stinger would do to airline bookings?'

'True,' muttered Vijay. 'Next question. Is the son of a bitch in Kashmir, or is he elsewhere in the country?'

'Back to square one,' replied Sheetal. 'It all boils down to the implications we can draw from what your friend Haider Ali said. You said that he was of the opinion that Jalauddin was not planning to strike in Kashmir.'

Vijay looked helpless. 'That was his guess, nothing more than that. Look, let's go over it again, step by step. Haider Ali was not part of this new group that Jalauddin is leading. He's an old associate of Jalauddin's, from the Chrar-e-Sharief days, who says he happened to bump into him right here in Delhi. Jalauddin tried to talk him into joining the group, and they all spent a couple of days together. None of them were willing to speak about their target, but late one night he overheard that scrap of conversation on which all our information is based.

Haider Ali then left Delhi and returned to Srinagar, where he contacted me.'

'Do you know what I think?' snorted Arun Batra, an officer from Military Intelligence. 'I think there is something dodgy about this entire story. Overheard a conversation? Doesn't happen outside the movies. And why travel to Srinagar? Why not talk to someone right here? With respect, sir, he didn't have to go all that way looking for you, he could have spilled the beans to anyone.'

'So what do you suggest? We sit on our hands and pretend that none of this ever happened?' snapped Vijay.

'I still feel we should get this Haider Ali down here and put him through the wringer. Find out all that he really knows.'

'Oh, for heaven's sake, we've been through this a million fucking times. I'm convinced that Haider told us all that he knows. Shoving electrodes up his butt isn't going to change anything; remember, he didn't have to volunteer any information in the first place. Besides, we've now asked him to try and scout around for more dope; if he gets anything, it would be invaluable.'

'That's all very well,' replied Batra coolly, 'but, sir, it's already the 14th of March. Clinton gets here in six days. If he is the target, then we don't have much time.'

*   *   *

With less than a week for Bill Clinton to arrive in India, the American Secret Service seemed to have taken complete possession of the luxurious Maurya Sheraton Hotel on Sardar Patel Road, not far from the American Embassy. An entire floor had been reserved for the men in black, who strode back and forth busily, trademark dark glasses fixed firmly on the bridge of the nose.

Though they were working closely with the Indian security agencies, visiting Indian sleuths were left in no doubt that this was American territory, and many a cop was left salivating enviously at some of the high-tech gizmos they could glimpse tantalizingly through half-open doors.

Vijay had arrived for yet another meeting with his American counterpart, John Cassell, and they were kneeling around a large-scale contour map of the Indira Gandhi International Airport and its surrounding areas.

'Secure, secure, secure,' said the American, slashing at the plastic that covered the map with a fibre-tipped pen, drawing large crosses and circles in red ink. 'It's from just these two or three areas that someone can potentially hit Air Force One with a Stinger, and you guys will have to ensure that a fucking fly cannot move on the ground in these locations.'

'Blanket security coverage, that's what I've been told,' replied Vijay. 'We will have more men on the ground there than you can count. I assume you are still coming with me tomorrow for a complete survey of the entire area.'

'Yes, of course.'

They straightened up, and John padded to one corner of the room to pour them both cups of coffee. He returned and handed a cup to Vijay. 'Somehow, I don't see it. We have war-gamed the Stinger scenario a million times, ever since those fuckers at the Agency started handing them out like chocolates during the Afghan war. For various reasons, a successful and fatal strike is unlikely, especially if we are forewarned. Besides, your systems here in Delhi seem quite okay, and we've had the same reports from Mumbai, Jaipur and Hyderabad.'

'What about Bangladesh and Pakistan?' asked Vijay quietly. 'The President is going there too, and who knows where this bastard Jalauddin is by now.'

The Secret Service man sank into a well-upholstered sofa and sighed heavily. 'Yeah, I know. It's a problem. Dhaka should be okay, but the President wants to make some big flight by helicopter to meet some Bangladeshi children—the path is over a thick forest.' He caught the look of alarm on Vijay's face and sighed again. 'Yeah, I know, I know. We'll just have to get him to cancel that. Too bloody dangerous. And Pakistan . . . well, we are working on something there, it should be okay.'

Vijay got up to go, stretching himself as he did so. It had

been a long morning. 'I hope you are right. I'd better go; see you tomorrow.'

John rose as well, 'I'll see you out. You know, I wonder if this Jalauddin character is really planning something. The bastard has screwed up what could have been a wonderful holiday for us as well.'

'Believe me, he exists. As to his plans, who knows?'

It was almost lunchtime the next day, and Vijay stretched luxuriously in the unmarked limousine that was taking them around the areas close to the airport. They had stopped at a red light, and there was heavy traffic on the road; scooters, cars, trucks and cyclists clustered thickly all around them.

John Cassell looked out of the window, 'Where exactly are we right now?'

'That's the National Highway 8 ahead, we've already checked it out thoroughly. Mahipalpur is to our right, and if we turn left we will come to the new Radisson hotel, and then if we keep going straight down the highway, we'll eventually reach Jaipur. I think we are almost done now.'

'Yeah,' nodded John. 'If that bastard has a Stinger, it will be the basic variant, not the POST, or the Reprogrammable Microchip missiles. Effective range is unlikely to be more than six-seven kilometres.'

Vijay was about to ask the driver to head back to the hotel, when he suddenly changed his mind. 'Tell you what, let's just go one last time down the road straight ahead of us, the one which leads to the Airports Authority residences.'

'Sure,' said John, yawning again. 'I haven't got too much to do this morning.'

They drove down the heavily potholed road, passing a couple of workshops where mechanics were hammering at ancient Contessas and clambering over vintage Fiats with oil cans in their hands.

After a kilometre or so they came to a crossroad, from where they could see the outer boundary of the airport looming up towards their right. 'That side is okay,' muttered Vijay, half to himself, as he asked the driver to turn left, towards the Centaur hotel.

There was wilderness on both sides of them, interspersed with huge warehouses where cargo containers were stored. Vijay suddenly sat up straight, as he spotted a dirt track leading off the road towards the left. He leant over to the front seat where a Delhi police inspector was sitting. 'Where does that track lead?'

'It goes towards some ancient stone quarries,' came the reply. 'There's nothing much there—a couple of deserted pottery units, I think.'

'You think?' asked Vijay, sceptically. Then, turning to John, 'Should we have a look?'

'Why not?'

The big car turned onto the track, which tested its suspension to the full. As the inspector had said, there was nothing but wasteland on either side, though they passed a small village as they drove. They could see the ugly buildings of Mahipalpur less than a kilometre away, and the occasional derelict pottery factory tucked away behind brick walls or barbed-wire fencing. All these units had been shut down after the Supreme Court had ruled that they added to Delhi's pollution.

The car came to a halt, and they climbed out, using their binoculars to scan the terrain. Vijay was busy explaining to the inspector where he should post some of his men. Eventually, of course, a detailed roster would be drawn up, and cleared by the highest authorities in the land; but it never hurt to talk directly to those who would have to implement the plans.

'Come on, let's go,' said Vijay, tapping John on his shoulder, as he swung the car door open.

'Hang on a second,' said John, who had a pair of binoculars to his eyes. 'What's that building there, surrounded by trees?'

Vijay looked at the inspector, who quickly scanned the papers he had attached to a clipboard. 'It's a deserted farmhouse, sir, attached to one of the pottery units that have been closed down. The owners are in Dubai and haven't visited it for months. I think there is a chowkidar at the farm.'

John glanced at Vijay, who nodded, 'Yes, let's check it out.'

They bumped their way to the iron gate that was set in the six-foot-high brick wall that surrounded the farm, raising a huge plume of dust behind them. The gate was locked with a thick iron chain wound around the handles held together by a gigantic brass padlock that defied burglars to crack it open. Vijay hoisted himself up on the wall, taking care not to cut himself on the barbed wire that topped it.

'A small building—one, maybe two rooms. Trees covering most of the property,' he reported. 'Where is that chowkidar?'

'Sir, if the owners don't come here for months, the chowkidar could be taking it easy at his own home. It doesn't look as if he stays on these premises,' said the inspector.

Vijay lowered himself to the ground and dusted his hands against his trousers. 'Hmm. Owners in Dubai.' He looked around him, and spotted a hillock a couple of hundred metres away, the by-product of quarrying in some distant era. 'Do one thing. Post a couple of men on that hill, let's say from the eighteenth onwards. They will be able to cover this entire area. Tell them to reach the spot quietly and to see if there is any movement at this farm.'

* * *

Sunday, 19 March 2000. India had been preening like a new bride, awaiting the arrival of Bill Clinton, for this was supposed to be a new start, the long-overdue reordering of American priorities on the subcontinent. For decades the US had tried to equate India and Pakistan, talking of the two countries as though they were Siamese twins. Not any more. The State Department, and the countless hordes of foreign policy experts who pitched their tents in TV studios, were at pains to point out that from now on American policy would recognize and reflect India's strength as a potential Asian superpower.

Air Force One lowered its landing gears for the final approach into Delhi. Vijay watched it coming, unaware that he was holding his breath. Then the touchdown, and soon the American President stepped onto Indian soil, beaming at the waiting TV cameras.

Reports came in from all the security men. Nothing unusual had happened. No suspicious movement was seen.

At the farm near Nangal Deri, the iron chain continued to rust around the handles of the big gate. No one had visited the farm. No one had approached the area.

The 20th was the festival of Holi, the day when normally sane Indians tend to go beserk, smearing colour on each other and generally letting their hair down. President Clinton wisely left for a day's visit to Bangladesh, where his flight to a village had been cancelled by the Secret Service. He returned to India that evening.

Nangal Deri slumbered softly. It couldn't care less.

On the morning of the 21st, Bill Clinton left Maurya Sheraton to address Parliament. Varun Mathur sat in a South Delhi studio, surrounded by cameras and foreign policy experts. Varun was anchoring the President's speech for a TV news channel, and the experts were already predicting what would be said in Parliament House.

'You see,' remarked the Delhi correspondent of a leading American newspaper, 'the US has realized that it may have to take sides in South Asia, and that so far it has been backing the wrong horse. A tiny, bankrupt, fundamentalist dictatorship like Pakistan on the one hand, and the world's largest democracy on the other. Look at India's strengths. The fourth largest economy in the world in PPP terms. A budding infotech superpower. And, let's face it, a potential counterweight to China, with which the US is bound to have trouble in the years to come.'

A red light flashed up on camera no. 6, warning Varun that his reaction to that statement was being beamed into millions of homes, and he quickly composed his face into an expression of complete attentiveness. But surreptitiously his eyes were scanning the bank of monitors that lay just behind his guests, which were carrying the various live feeds that were coming in. The monitors told him that Clinton had just left the hotel, and that the reception committee at Parliament wouldn't be able to swing into action for another ten minutes or so.

A voice squawked confirmation in his earpiece. 'Keep the discussion going for another five minutes, then we will cut across to Parliament House. Hand over to our correspondent there.'

The red light on camera 6 was on again, and Varun turned to his next guest. 'Professor, if Timothy is right, and there is a shift in US policy, what would you expect to hear from Bill Clinton on this trip?'

The elegant-looking professor straightened his Cambridge tie and then spoke. 'Well, I think he will take a stand against violence in Kashmir; he will denounce the massacre of the Sikhs by militants last night, and he may slam cross-border terrorism—although he will only do that indirectly. If we are lucky, he may tell Pakistan that he is not going to mediate in Kashmir.'

'You see,' continued the professor, moving into top gear, 'everyone talks so much about the danger of a war in the subcontinent. But why is there tension? Because Pakistan frequently tries to raise the temperature in this part of the world. And why does it do that? Because it feels that a world concerned about a nuclear flashpoint could be tempted to intervene. Pakistan hopes it will get something in Kashmir if that happens. So the best thing for the American President to do would be to tell the Pakistanis that even if they raise the ante by encouraging further acts of violence, the world will still not intervene. Bang goes the rationale for any further provocation.'

Varun was only paying attention with half his mind; the other half was focussed on the feed coming from Parliament House. He suddenly started, as he spotted Sanjiv Deshpande from KTV standing on prime real estate, not far from where Bill Clinton would walk. Standing close to him was his cameraman, Gopalkrishnan, sweating profusely in the mild heat of a mid-March morning.

'How the hell did he get there?' Varun raged inwardly. 'I thought no cameras were to be allowed into that area. The bugger is going to get a prime scoop, and we will look like idiots.'

There were just a few minutes more to go before Bill Clinton arrived at Parliament House. The top Indian politicians who would receive him were moving into position, and there was little possibility that the Vision TV correspondent would be able to move to where the KTV team had reached.

Varun tore his eyes away from the monitor and moved on to his third guest, a member of a top international think tank on Kashmir.

'Dr Robertson, we are going to hear a lot on Kashmir on this trip. What, to your mind, is the solution? And how can the international community help?'

'Only one solution comes to my mind—the conversion of the existing Line of Control into the permanent international boundary between India and Pakistan. There will be initial howls of protest from both the countries, but I think the Indians will gladly come to terms with this. The Pakistanis will have to be persuaded to play along somehow. That's one part of the solution. The other part is that India must win over the Kashmiris on its side of the border; give them something that will allow them to feel that the sacrifices haven't been in vain. Some sort of autonomy within the Indian union, for example. And then, of course, ensure that the security forces are reined in, and that development gets to the people.'

They went into a break and Varun was about to call out to the director, asking her to try and organize a quick relocation of their correspondent, when he spotted the security guards moving in, forcing Sanjiv and Gopalkrishnan to leave the area. Gopalkrishnan was arguing bitterly, but it was to no avail. When Clinton arrived at Parliament House, there was no cameraman within a hundred yards.

Clinton delivered his speech, which was greeted by applause inside Parliament and by some self-congratulatory smiles inside the Vision TV studio. The MPs at Parliament house mobbed Clinton, but he left the building unscathed.

The next few days were a blur. Bill Clinton travelled to the Taj Mahal, to Rajasthan, to the cyber city of Hyderabad, and to Mumbai. Every journey was agony for Vijay Kaul and for the combined security staff of both countries. Every day the S-squad sat and reviewed each microsecond of Bill Clinton's itinerary. And every night Vijay lay awake, haunted by the image of Jalauddin smiling as he moved in for the kill, striding smoothly through the loophole in their security plans.

In the end nothing happened. There wasn't even a hint of the presence of a terrorist anywhere near Clinton.

Then Clinton was gone, using decoy planes as he arrived in Islamabad for a five-hour stopover, where he delivered a speech to the Pakistani people that could have been drafted by Indian policy-makers.

That evening an exhausted Vijay Kaul met John Cassell for drinks at the Maurya Sheraton's Jazz Bar. They clinked glasses, and then Vijay said wearily, 'So what was that all about?'

John drained his glass in one gulp and grinned as he signalled for another. 'Sure this Jalauddin business wasn't a product of your fevered imagination? Just kidding,' he added hastily as he saw the flush on Vijay's face.

'Haider Ali wasn't lying. Jalauddin is here, somewhere,' Vijay said fiercely. 'I'd give my pension to know what he is doing.'

At that moment Jalauddin was lying comfortably on his bed in the Paharganj guest house, tucking into a plate of tandoori chicken that Karim had brought up from a dhaba down the road. None of them had moved from Paharganj in a fortnight; they had spent their time eating, and watching TV, chuckling softly as they watched the security men run back and forth trying to protect Bill Clinton from a nonexistent threat. The wait had heightened their sense of anticipation, and Jalauddin gave his men a daily pep talk to keep their morale high.

The policemen had all moved away from Nangal Deri. The farm and its surrounding areas were completely deserted once again. The Stinger was still carefully hidden behind the false wall in the basement. It wasn't time to use it just yet.

Chapter Twenty-seven

THE SHOURA

Several hundred kilometres north-west, eighteen men had gathered in the small house on the outskirts of the Markaz-ul-Dawa complex at Muridke, and they were kneeling on their mats to offer communal namaaz.

Dates and curd were brought into the room, and Abu Fateh gestured to the others to help themselves.

After they had eaten, the men settled back on their cushions with some anticipation. They could sense that Abu Fateh had called them here with a purpose. Most of them were Pakistanis, but there were also four Afghans, three Arabs, and three Kashmiris. All were dressed in the comfortable shalwar kameez that was the de facto uniform in these parts, and most carried on their faces the thick bushy beard of the committed Islamic hardliner.

Abu Fateh dragged on the suspense for a couple of minutes, and then spoke softly, as always, so that the men at the back of the room had to strain to hear him. 'You all must have heard the message of the American President.'

The portly figure of Maulana Aziz snorted. He was the top ideologue for fundamentalist Islam in Pakistan, and a man who had been calling for jihad at every possible gathering for several years now. 'This age will not reward those who redraw borders with blood,' he mimicked, bringing smiles to the faces of those sitting around him. 'He will learn his lesson when, inshallah, we plant the flag of Islam on the roof of the White House.'

Then he looked straight up at Abu Fateh. 'Pardon me, my brother. But I was under the impression that he would not be allowed to leave this region. Did something go wrong?'

The room was silent, as seventeen pairs of eyes looked at Abu Fateh. This was the *shoura*, or supreme council, of the front that had been created by Abu Fateh, a front that he had termed the sword arm of the jihad, and in particular of the fight against the immediate hated enemies—India, the US, Russia and Israel.

He had formed the shoura in imitation of a practice that he had learnt from his hosts for several years, the Taliban in Afghanistan. He needed all the men at this council, he needed them to stand united behind him in the decades of struggle that would lie ahead.

Abu Fateh knew better than most that the storm troopers of the jihad would have come from Pakistan and from Afghanistan, countries that possessed an almost inexhaustible supply of young men willing to offer themselves up for martyrdom. It was necessary to offer them a triumph, a bait that would lure the next generation into the jihad.

Slowly, with a touch of thespian artistry, Abu Fateh rose to his feet. 'My brothers,' he began. 'Nothing has gone wrong. All our plans are on schedule, and, inshallah, victory will soon be ours.'

His eyes roamed the room, locking into the eyes of every man present, searching for the smallest sign of scepticism. He saw nothing but complete attentiveness, and continued, 'My brothers, you have watched the infidels scurry to protect Clinton from our wrath. Many of you, like our revered Maulana Aziz, may have felt that Clinton was the target of the special mission we have launched, the mission we discussed at our last meeting.'

'If I gave you that impression, then I must apologize.' There was just a hint of a mischievous twinkle in his eyes.

'Because Clinton was never our target. And the Stinger missile which you all know about is not the weapon with which we will strike the first blow for Islam.'

There was an excited stirring in the room, and then

complete silence, and full attention again.

'My brothers, we have recruited a man. A member of the press, a TV cameraman. One week from now there is a gathering of Indian state ministers. The Indian Prime Minister will be present, and the press has been invited as well. That is the day when the cameraman will detonate a bomb, killing the flag bearer of *kufr*.'

Abu Fateh crossed his arms, watching the smiles of pure delight blooming on the faces of the Pakistanis who were present in the room. One or two of them began to clap, and he raised a hand to silence them.

'As the Indians go into shock and run around like headless chickens, all their leaders will gather in Delhi to mourn their so-called leader. All their politicians will rush to Delhi, as will their puppet in Kashmir, Farooq Abdullah, the man who has presided over the genocidal actions of the brutal army of occupation. He will use, as always, his private plane with which he shuttles to Delhi to pay homage to his masters. That is when our mujahideen will dig the Stinger out from the basement of the farmhouse at Nangal Deri where it is hidden. And they will use the missile to slay the traitor.'

This time there was concerted applause, and he let it run on for several minutes before speaking again, a shrill note coming into his voice. 'With the symbols of Indian power crushed at the hands of the jihad, the people of Kashmir will rise again. They will take to the streets, and, inshallah, this time the kaffirs will not be able to restrain them. Kashmir will be free, inshallah.'

The men at the shoura were beginning to rise to their feet. Maulana Aziz tottered forward unsteadily, tears shining brightly in his eyes as he embraced Abu Fateh. The man in white looked a little startled, and then returned the embrace, before turning to the other men who were clustering around him.

'*Allah-o-Akbar*, God is great,' he said, and the cry was taken up by the others, and it echoed through the trees in that little corner of Muridke.

Chapter Twenty-eight

THE MESSAGE

There was one man among the seventeen clustered around Abu Fateh who wasn't quite so filled with joy, even though his eyes also brimmed with tears of feigned delight as he enthusiastically joined the others in praying for the success of the mission.

He was one of the three Kashmiris in the room, a man who had been part of the insurgency for more than a decade, first as a member of the Hizbul Mujahideen and then as a senior leader of the Lashkar-e-Taiba. He wore his beard long, and his shalwar short; and he bore scars of bullet wounds and cigarette burns on his body to demonstrate the full extent of his dedication.

For the last four years he had organized the sending across of armed Lashkar bands into the Kashmir valley, giving them their targets and talking to them every day on the sophisticated wireless sets that the ISI had provided. Through the airwaves he had pumped up the morale of his men as they wandered on the Himalayan heights, always on the move, always with the Indian army one step behind. But even as he mouthed the invocations to martyrdom and jihad, there was a deep corrosive emptiness scalding him from inside.

Even before he had fled the Valley to come to Pakistan, he had heard the anti-Pakistan tales of disillusionment from his associates in the militant movement; stories of how that country had repeatedly let down the Kashmiris, how Pakistan had backed down from its promise to invade in 1990 in support of the men and women who had taken to the streets, how it had betrayed the pro-independence groups like the JLKF to ensure the supremacy of those who wanted merger with Pakistan.

During his years in Muridke, he saw, all too clearly, that for Pakistan the goal was to bleed India in Kashmir, a death by a thousand cuts. He saw that for Pakistan its national objectives would always be far more important than any ideals like the well-being of the Kashmiri people. But he soldiered on. What options did he have?

The final straw came during the Kargil war. He had been asked to send his men to the icy mountain heights to fight alongside the Pakistani army—to add authenticity to the claims that the heights above Batalik, Drass and Mushkoh had been captured by militants and not by Pakistani soldiers. Then he had sat and heard the wireless messages as his men died one by one on Tololing top, denied the dignity of a proper burial or the honour of recognition by the country they had given their lives for.

He had switched off the set, tears pouring down his cheeks. And he had sworn revenge.

The Indian intelligence agencies never did find out how that mysterious man in the highest councils of Abu Fateh's shoura sent his message to Srinagar. It must have been a dangerous business, surrounded as he was by a group of fanatical hardliners who were all sworn to secrecy.

But the message got through.

*   *   *

Four days before the Prime Minister's meeting with the state ministers, the phone rang in Vijay Kaul's apartment. It was 2:30 in the morning and he had just gone to sleep, but he sat bolt upright and grabbed the receiver.

It was the voice he had been waiting to hear. 'It's me— Haider Ali. Don't say anything right now. Be on the plane to Srinagar tomorrow morning and come to Regal Chowk at 3 p.m. sharp.'

Before Vijay could say anything the line was cut. He stared at the handset, and slowly reached across to the bedside table for a glass of water. Then he consulted the list of numbers that were written on a sheet of paper pasted next to the telephone, and began to dial.

'It's a trap,' was the immediate reaction of the special secretary. 'They will kidnap you, and torture you to find out how we learnt about the Stinger plot in the first place.'

'Perhaps, sir,' replied Vijay evenly. 'But I don't see that we have a choice. I think we just have to trust this man.'

'What if he was lying in the first place? There's no Stinger-winger, it's just an attempt to pick up one of our senior men.'

Vijay shrugged in the darkness of his room. 'Perhaps, sir. That is a possibility, but I don't think so. I'm prepared to take the chance, if you will authorize it.'

There was a sigh from the other end. 'Wait for some time, Vijay. I'll have to check with some of the others. I'll call you back in a few minutes.'

Vijay climbed out of bed, switched on the light, and went to the bathroom. Then he returned and sat down on the edge of the bed. He looked at his hands and noticed the slight tremor in his fingers. He clenched his fist and stared at the black phone on the side table.

It rang half an hour later, the shrill tones shattering the silence. 'Vijay? Go ahead. Make whatever arrangements you think best. And be careful.'

Vijay smiled grimly. 'What a bloody idiotic thing to say,' he thought to himself, as he rose to get his things together. He knew that he should try to get some sleep, but he also knew that sleep would be impossible.

At six in the morning Vijay eased the latch on the front door open. Then he paused, and returned down the corridor to the room where his parents were sleeping. He gently drew the curtains apart and looked at Papa, lying on his back in his blue pyjamas, snoring softly through his open mouth. Beyond him, Amma was curled up in a semi-foetal position, breathing evenly and smoothly. He drew the curtains together again, and left the house quietly. There were still several hours for the plane to take off, but he had to first make a quick trip to the office.

* * *

Vijay walked with unhurried steps down Residency Road at 2:45 in the afternoon. There was, of course, no question of any security cover, and he had decided to make the approach in civilian clothes. He had on the ubiquitous phiran, and plastic shoes; inadequate disguise, but if Haider Ali was about to spring a trap, then no disguise would be enough.

As he turned into Regal Chowk, Vijay stole a quick glance at the cheap watch he was wearing on his wrist: 2:55. Five minutes to go. He walked into the general provision store that dominated the Chowk and asked for a soft drink. Then he leant on the glass counter and sipped at the Coke through a plastic straw, casually surveying the area. A number of taxis stood a few metres away, and there were a large number of shoppers taking advantage of the superb weather. Right next to Vijay a young woman who seemed to have come from the plains, perhaps from Punjab, was haggling with the shopkeeper over some authentic kahwa tea leaves and some saffron.

His eyes drifted to the right, and he stiffened slightly as he saw a blue Ambassador parked fifteen metres away with no driver inside. 'Car bomb? No, I don't think so. They'd hardly waste a car bomb just on me—they can easily pick me up and do what they want.'

A gurgling in the straw told Vijay that his drink was over, and he asked the shopkeeper looking at him quizzically for another. It was 3:05. Perhaps he wasn't coming. No, that must be him. A white Maruti van, cruising gently down the road from the direction of Ahdoos Hotel, came straight to where he was standing.

The door slid open and Haider Ali said, 'Get in quickly.' Vijay threw some notes onto the glass counter and clambered in. There were three other men there with Haider, and it was with a swooping feeling of dread in his stomach that Vijay noticed the telltale bulges of the revolvers under their shirts.

The van moved off, darting into the alleys of downtown Srinagar, heading north towards Nagin Lake. Vijay opened his mouth to speak to Haider, but the young Kashmiri held up a forefinger to his lips in an unmistakable command.

The van reached the banks of Dal Lake and raced on over a concrete bridge. Vijay suddenly realized that they were heading for Hazratbal, and he didn't know whether that was a good sign or not.

They drove through a couple of side streets and came to a halt near the back gate of the Hazratbal shrine. Vijay and his escorts climbed out, and the van moved away as quickly as it had arrived. Then they walked towards a building that Vijay knew was often used by militants as a base.

Within minutes they were seated comfortably inside, and Vijay felt the tension ease as Haider gestured to the other men to go into an inner room. Then Haider grinned impishly at Vijay, 'Sorry about all that, we couldn't risk being seen with you publicly. A lot of people know you too well in Srinagar.'

Vijay smiled back, with more than a touch of relief. 'That's okay, although I must admit you had me a little frightened. Now, Haider, please tell me what you know.'

Haider looked at the floor for a few seconds, and then took a deep breath. 'It's far more serious than you can imagine. And the threat is not from the Stinger, that is purely incidental. You face a threat from a cameraman in one of the TV networks. He is going to kill your Prime Minister.'

He spoke on, leaving out none of the details: Abu Fateh, his new council for the jihad, the man inside his shoura who had sent the message across the border, and the double strike that was being planned. Vijay listened, his face ashen.

But when Haider fell silent, there was a slight note of disbelief in Vijay's reply. 'Haider, don't get me wrong. I appreciate what you are telling me, but you must understand if I find all this a little hard to accept. In the first place, I thought that you had originally heard about the Stinger from Jalauddin, in Delhi. Now you say there is a mole in this man Abu Fateh's council . . .'

Haider interrupted him. 'I lied. When I came to you in Badami Bagh, I lied. I only knew about Jalauddin's plans because there had been a message from Muridke; in actual fact, I've only seen Jalauddin once, and that too from a distance.'

Vijay didn't say anything, waiting quietly for Haider to go on. The young Kashmiri rose to his feet. 'I came to you because I had been ordered to do so, as I have been ordered this time too.'

'Ordered?' Vijay sounded bewildered. 'Ordered by whom?'

'Come,' said Haider, 'I will lead you to him. He said that you might want proof, and that I should take you to him if required.'

They walked down the wooden staircase and out of the main door. About fifty yards away, down the street, was the back entrance to Hazratbal, and Haider led the way towards the gate. They walked through the lawns that fringed the side of the shrine and crossed the courtyard that lay between the mosque and the marketplace just outside its boundary. Then they passed through another small gate and reached the small lawn that lay between Hazratbal and the stone steps which led down into the Dal Lake.

To their left the white reflection of the mosque shimmered gently in the cold waters of the lake; taken together with the green expanse of the Nishat gardens on the far bank and the snow which tipped the mountains beyond, it was a classic picture-postcard scene.

But Vijay had eyes only for the man who sat alone on the banks of the Dal, his chin resting lightly on the palm of his hand. 'I'll leave you now,' whispered Haider, but Vijay wasn't listening, as he stumbled down towards the lake.

'Habib,' he said, half in wonder and half in amazement.

Habib Shah didn't turn around; he kept staring out across the Dal. Then he spoke in a conversational voice, 'Do you remember the last time we met? Right here, at this spot, the day after Chrar-e-Sharief was burnt down.'

'Yes, I remember,' replied Vijay carefully. He lowered himself down to sit close to Habib, waiting to hear what he would say next.

Habib swung around suddenly, and Vijay's eyes widened as he saw the changes that time had carved on the other man's face in just a few years.

'Vijay,' said Habib, tasting the unfamiliar word on his tongue, and moving on quickly as if he didn't quite like the flavour, 'you now have the information you need. Go back to Delhi and save your Prime Minister.'

'Why?' croaked Vijay.

'Why what?' Habib raised an eyebrow. 'Why save the PM or why have I told you this?'

'Why did you ask Haider to come to me?'

Habib looked out at the Dal again, following with his eyes the progress of a shikara-wallah as he headed for the algae-covered canal that lay behind Hazratbal. When he replied, his voice was soft, but confident.

'In Muridke Abu Fateh's Jihad Council believes—or pretends to believe—that if they kill the Indian Prime Minister and Farooq Abdullah, then the people of Kashmir will take to the streets again. They claim that azaadi will follow.' He turned his haunted eyes at Vijay. 'Tell me, Vijay. How would your government react?'

Vijay didn't hesitate for a second. 'With force. They would clamp down as hard as necessary to maintain order; the government will not allow terrorists to use assassinations to break up the country.'

'Exactly. With force. If my people take to the streets again—which I doubt—there will be shootings and massacres. Even if they stay in their homes, the oppressive grip of the army will tighten. Is that what Pakistan wants? Perhaps. Is that what my people want? No.'

Habib fished in his phiran for a cigarette, and Vijay bent forward to light it for him, in a gesture that was so achingly familiar that it almost choked him.

'I thought for a long, long time before I sent Haider to you in January. I still don't know whether I did the right thing; perhaps till the end of my days I will have to live with the feeling that I may have betrayed all that I once believed in.'

'Once believed in?' enquired Vijay diffidently.

Habib looked at him straight in the eye. 'I have resigned from the JKLF and the Hurriyat Conference—I communicated my decision to Yasin Malik and the others in the Jodhpur jail several months ago, although they asked me not to make it public yet. All of them have in any case abandoned the gun and are waiting for some sort of talks with the government—though I'm not sure how much use that is going to be.'

'Come with me to Delhi,' urged Vijay, reaching out to touch Habib's arm. 'You know that you can help in a breakthrough, you can help bring peace back to this land.'

'No,' snapped Habib. 'I didn't tell you all this to get some reward from New Delhi; my feelings towards Delhi haven't changed, and they never will.'

'So what will you do now?'

Habib stood up, and dusted the back of his phiran. 'I don't know. I have enough time to find out.'

Vijay rose as well, and sensing the conversation was at an end, he began to walk towards the front of Hazratbal. Then, impulsively, he stopped and turned back to where Habib was standing, reaching out with his hand and with his voice. 'Habib. We were once closer than brothers . . .'

Something moved, very briefly, in Habib's eyes. 'Yes, Vijay. We were. But that was a long time ago, and a lot of water has flown under the bridge. So has a lot of blood.'

Vijay gazed at Habib for a few seconds and then nodded once, before swinging back towards the main road. He walked briskly, and then broke into a fast trot. He knew he could get a taxi at the market square, and he calculated that it would take him less than half an hour to reach the airport, where a special air force plane was waiting for him on standby. There was lots of work to be done; he knew that his information would ensure that there was very little sleep in Lutyens' Delhi that night.

Vijay didn't look back again at Habib, who stood by himself staring emptily at the naked expanse of the Dal Lake.

Chapter Twenty-nine

A CALL IN THE NIGHT

The basement below the Turquoise Cottage restaurant in south Delhi houses one of the most popular bars in the city, and Varun Mathur was enjoying himself. It was 11:30 at night, the next day was a holiday, the huge speakers were booming with 'Nights in White Satin', and the beer was cold and freshly drawn from a keg of Kingfisher.

He was leaning down to whisper something to his wife when the mobile began to beep in his pocket. 'Oh shit,' he said. 'What now?'

In a resigned fashion he pulled out the phone, and then his brow furrowed as he looked at the unfamiliar number on the screen. He pressed the answer button. 'Yes? Who is this?'

'Is that Varun Mathur?'

'Yes.'

'This is Major Vijay Kaul. I don't know if you remember me, we met outside Chrar-e-Sharief some years back. I'm sorry to disturb you, but this is something really urgent. We have to meet right now.'

'Now?' said Varun incredulously, threading his way through the crowd to a quieter spot. 'Just hang on a second, I can hardly hear you.' He scampered up the stairs to the restaurant, where diners were tucking into their Teppen-yaki and their Nasi Goreng. Then he walked out onto the road outside and pressed the phone to his ear again.

'Go on now, Major Kaul. What on earth are you talking about?'

'Mr Mathur, I'm calling from North Block—we got your mobile number with some difficulty from your office. I'm afraid we need you here right now. I'm sorry, but this is an emergency. We'll send a car for you, wherever you like.'

Varun ran a hand through his hair. 'Umm, no, that won't be necessary. Okay, I'll be there soon. Give me half an hour, I'll have to drop my wife home. On second thoughts, send the car; it could save some time. I live in Panchsheel . . .'

'We have your address, Mr Mathur. We'll send the car right away.'

The mobile phone went dead and Varun stared at it in amazement before going back inside the restaurant to fetch his wife, who was beginning to look a little worried. 'Come on, hon. I'm afraid we have to go.'

'Go? What about dinner?'

'Sandwiches at home. Come, come, we have to leave right now, I'll tell you about it on the way.' He cast a last longing look at the tall glass of beer luring him frostily from the counter, and then took his wife's hand and led her out of the restaurant.

The home ministry vehicle was waiting for him outside his flat, a white Ambassador complete with flag pole and red light. 'Here, you'd better park,' said Varun, sliding out of his car. 'They seem to be in a real hurry.'

'When do you think you'll be back?'

'God knows. I'm carrying the mobile, so you can check in a while.'

The drive to North Block barely took twenty minutes; without traffic, the roads of New Delhi at night were like Dr Jekyll to the Mr Hyde that they were during the day.

A young man who introduced himself with an incomprehensible bureaucratic acronym was waiting at the entrance of the home ministry to lead Varun down the corridor and then up a wide, almost majestic staircase. Varun's bemusement intensified as he realized that they were heading straight for the office of the Home Minister. A few minutes later the young bureaucrat knocked on the door, and Varun was led in to where Vijay Kaul was sitting. But there were others in the room as well. The Home Minister himself, looking as perturbed as Varun had ever seen him looking. The top officials from the IB, NSG, and RAW. The home secretary. And a distinguished looking gentleman whom Varun recognized as the head of the SPG, the organization responsible for the security of the Prime Minister.

'Ah, Varun. Sorry to drag you here at this time,' said the Home Minister, a wan smile on his face.

'That's okay, sir. Pardon the curiosity, but what on earth is going on?'

'I thought you'd ask that. First of all, I must make it clear that you are not here as a journalist, but in your personal capacity. A couple of your colleagues will also be joining us, and I'm going to ask—or rather, request—all of you not to let a hint of this ever get out.'

Varun thought for a moment, and then inclined his head. 'You have my word.'

'That's enough for me,' said the Home Minister. 'Major Kaul, will you please fill Mr Mathur in. I think we can trust him with all the details.'

'Sir,' said Vijay, and he repeated all that he had been told. Varun listened to him in silence, stirring once or twice in disbelief.

By the time Vijay finished, Varun was looking quite stunned.

'How did this information reach you?'

Vijay looked a little uncomfortable. 'I'm afraid I can't give you those details.'

The Home Minister cleared his throat. 'Varun, you must have guessed why you have been called here. Now that we have been forewarned, we can, of course, protect the Prime Minister at this meeting day after tomorrow. We can also throw a security net over all occasions where TV cameras are to be present. But how long can that continue? It's much better to find out who this man is, and to grab him. Now, you've covered Kashmir extensively. You know all the cameramen who have worked there. Who could this man be?'

Varun buried his face in his hands, as he trawled his brain

for half-forgotten memories and possible clues. He sat up and shook his head. 'I have absolutely no idea.' Then it suddenly struck him. 'There's no proof . . .' he said slowly.

'There won't be proof,' said the head of the Intelligence Bureau gently. 'Just some possible names.'

Varun debated with himself for a couple of minutes, and then made up his mind. 'Gopalkrishnan.'

Pens went into action immediately across the room. 'Who?' said the Home Minister.

'If I had to pick a name—and please remember that I have no evidence whatsoever to back this with—it would be Gopalkrishnan. He's a cameramen with KTV. I've often met him. His views are extreme, and his behaviour has often been . . . well . . . uncertain.' He told them about his encounters with Gopalkrishnan in Srinagar.

'Does he have Press Information Bureau accreditation? He would need that if he hopes to get close to the PM.'

Varun shrugged. 'I guess most of the cameramen who work in Kashmir are senior enough to have PIB cards.'

The press information officer got up to leave the room. 'I'll start checking on his details. Incidentally, the executive editor of KTV is also supposed to join us in a few minutes, I'll ask him to get along some information about this man.'

There was suddenly a flurry of activity in the room. 'Someone check with the airlines as to when he's travelled to Kashmir.' 'There must have been a police verification done when he applied for a passport.' 'Does anyone know his home address?'

Varun looked a little appalled. 'Look, this is just one possible name. Let's not get too excited over this one guy.'

'Don't worry, son,' a senior policeman patted Varun on the shoulder. 'It's a starting point. Let's see what we get.'

Two o'clock at night in India is hardly a time to get any work done. But computerization and a determined thrust by the home ministry can work wonders. Peons, busy counting their overtime, were clearing away the umpteenth cups of coffee from the smoke-filled room they had all shifted to, when the KTV executive editor arrived, together with a couple of other TV journalists. The Home Minister had just left, asking to be woken up if any concrete information came out. Varun wasn't really required any more, but wild horses couldn't have dragged him out of the room, and no one asked him to go.

Fifteen minutes later the KTV editor sighed heavily. 'Gopalkrishnan. You know, I have to say that it is possible. He's a strange man. Very good at his work, and completely without any nerves; you must have seen the footage we got during the Kargil war—it was all his. But he's never been very good with people, and he's given to strong views and beliefs. And as Varun said, he has a bee in his bonnet about Kashmir— which is why we've taken a decision that he will not be sent there any more.'

Aman Singh, the special secretary in charge of the S-squad, spoke: 'Any references that he came with? Someone we can check with?'

The KTV man almost leapt out of his seat. 'Yes, of course. Why didn't I think of that immediately? The superintendent of police in Warangal, Andhra Pradesh. That's where Gopalkrishnan comes from, and the SP had recommended him to us. Several years back, of course, but I'm sure you can track him down. Madhav Shetty, I think that was his name.'

Aman Singh barked some instructions and a junior ran out to get a copy of the Andhra Pradesh official directory. Half an hour later, a bleary-sounding Madhav Shetty was on a phone line with the home secretary of India, trying to rack his memory about a cameraman whose career he had propelled forward half a dozen years ago.

'He's a distant relative, sir, married to a cousin of mine. He seemed quite harmless to me, though he did have strong leftist leanings once upon a time.'

'Mr Shetty, please try and think over any connection that Gopalkrishnan could have had with any Islamic fundamentalist organization.'

'No, sir. Well, actually . . .'

'Yes, Mr Shetty?'

'Now that you mention it, I had once gone to his house

for dinner, and Shoib Siddiqui had shown up. But he didn't stay for long.'

'And who is Shoib Siddiqui?'

'Sir, he was general secretary of the Student Islamic Movement of India. You will recall that he was arrested in 1997 for alleged links with the ISI.'

The others had been hearing the conversation on a speaker phone, and a murmur ran across the room, like autumn leaves rustled by a fading wind.

The home secretary put down the phone and glanced at Varun. 'Well, Mr Mathur. It looks as though you could be right.'

'Should we pick him up right now?' asked the commissioner of police.

There were several minutes of silence, then some consultations over the phone with the Prime Minister's office. Then the home secretary shook his head. 'No. We don't know who else could be involved, and where he has kept the battery. Let him go to work as usual. We should catch him red-handed, with all the equipment.'

Chapter Thirty

THE CAMERAMAN

By six in the morning most of the senior officers had left. So had all the TV journalists. Vijay and a few others still sat slumped around a big table, checking all the arrangements that they had worked out. The SPG would be mounting its largest ever operation; just about every second person at the state water ministers' meeting would be either a SPG man or a NSG commando. They had decided to funnel the TV cameramen who would come to film the meeting into a special area. The commandos would wait till Gopalkrishnan put his camera down on a table to walk through the metal detector. Then they would grab him.

'Do you think he could have a remote-control detonation device?' asked Sheetal.

'He almost certainly will have one, unless he is planning a suicide attack. My own guess is that he is ready to die, but would prefer not to. That means he may set up his camera next to the PM's podium and then walk out of the room, pretending to get a cable or something. He could then detonate the bomb from outside. Let's go see what the engineers feel,' replied Vijay.

KTV had sent across one of their DVC pro cameras, and a couple of technical engineers were tinkering with it in an adjoining room. In response to Vijay's question, they pointed to a small flat device with an antenna that was stuck to one side of the camera, with a cable running into one of the jacks behind the camera, just below the battery. 'That's the base set for a remote mike. If it can receive broadcast-quality audio signals from thirty metres away it can certainly receive a signal to detonate a bomb.'

Vijay turned to a SPG officer who was glaring at the camera sourly. 'Tell me something, won't all your vapour sniffers detect the Semtex right at the front gate?'

'If the bomb comes from Pakistan, and we must assume that it isn't something that has been assembled in a basement somewhere, then the fake Anton Bauer battery would have been carefully sealed by expert technicians. Where would the vapour escape from? Normally, we keep an eye open for cables and detonators; but in this case the explosives are integrated inside an airtight case with the battery cells right there. Pretty neat,' the SPG man said, prodding the battery that was mounted on the camera in front of him. 'Anyway, not to worry. The commandos will grab this bastard at the point when his arms are outstretched, before he can get his fingers anywhere close to a detonating device.'

Vijay yawned and looked at his watch. 'Breakfast anyone? Otherwise I suggest we pack it in for a while and get some sleep. We have about thirty hours to go.'

He walked down the stairs, and climbed into his car. At the back of his mind there was a terrible nagging feeling that he was missing something really important. But he couldn't figure out what it was.

* * *

Varun was equally restless. He walked into office well after lunchtime—he had to edit a story, and then was supposed to anchor the 8 p.m. bulletin. But he couldn't focus his attention on the words on his computer screen; his mind kept wandering to bombs and batteries.

He knew he was sitting on the biggest story of the decade. But he also knew that this was a story he would never be allowed to tell; all the TV journalists who had attended the North Block meeting had been sworn to complete and absolute secrecy.

He walked to a window and looked out at Delhi. He knew that somewhere out there commando teams were moving into position to stake out all the possible buildings near Nangal Deri where the Stinger could be buried. Once the cameraman was stopped, Jalauddin would be unable to recover his missile.

He turned back and returned slowly to his desk. 'Back to work,' he told himself sternly.

* * *

It wasn't till six in the evening that Vijay's nagging feeling moved from his subconscious to the front of his mind. He had returned from surveying the arrangements being made at the Vigyan Bhawan annexe, and had just sat down with a cup of tea, when the cup fell from his fingers.

'Oh shit,' he shouted, grabbing the phone. Seconds later he was speaking urgently. 'Sir, one loophole that has struck me. We know that Abu Fateh told his council that the attack on the PM was to be at the water ministers' meeting. But sir, he lied to the council earlier, pointing to the Clinton visit. What if he has another card up his sleeve, and the attack is at some other location?'

'My God! The wedding!'

'Exactly, sir. The wedding. It begins in a couple of hours. TV cameras will be present, and so will the PM.'

The son of Jaydev Rawat, one of the country's top politicians, was getting married that evening, and the who's who of the country had all been invited. Rawat was the leader of a political party that was a coalition ally of the Prime Minister's party; it was almost mandatory for every senior minister to attend.

'Sir, can the PM be asked not to attend?' asked Vijay.

'No, he will insist on going; Rawat would be insulted if the PM didn't come. Start dialling all the numbers. I'll speak to the SPG director right away.'

* * *

At the KTV office in central Delhi, a correspondent collected her tapes from the tape library.

'What's the story?' asked the young girl behind the desk, positioning her pen over a huge ledger.

'The Rawat wedding, what else?' she said with a smile. 'Where else would I be going at this time? That's if I can get through all the traffic jams en route.'

'Wedding,' said the other girl, concentrating hard as she made the entry in the ledger. 'Correspondent: Supriya Khanna. And who is your cameraman?'

'Gopalkrishnan.'

* * *

Ten kilometres away, in the Vision TV office, Varun had abandoned his attempts to try and edit his story. He wandered aimlessly through the office, before ending up at the business section. It was the one oasis of relative peace amidst all the hysteria that accompanied the putting together of the evening bulletins.

He sat down before the bank of Reuters terminals, and began to click on the various links there. 'Jesus, I see the stock markets took a real beating today,' he said conversationally to the business editor, Sridhar Saxena, who was scribbling figures on the sheet of paper that would be handed to the graphics department.

'Tell me about it,' replied Sridhar with a wry smile on his face. 'And to think that just a couple of weeks ago everyone was expecting that the Sensex would soon hit the 7000 mark. I blame the Nasdaq for all this.'

Varun laughed. 'No wonder there are so many gloomy faces all over the newsroom.'

'Yeah. But I guess one or two people should be relieved.'

'What do you mean?'

Sridhar paused as he completed the list of figures and handed it over gratefully to the girl from the graphics department who had appeared at his shoulder to hurry him along.

Then he pulled his chair a little closer to Varun's. 'I've been meaning to talk to you about this; I don't know if I should drop a hint to the bosses.'

'What is it?'

'There is a guy in the office who is playing the markets in a big way, and I mean a really big way. You know that's something we are not allowed to do. But this guy really seems to have gone nuts. I've told you that my brother has a brokerage, haven't I? Well, this chap has been sitting in his office for months, doing something that I can only describe as large-scale gambling. He's been short-selling infotech shares, hundreds of them, thousands of them. For nine months he has been gambling that these share prices will come down—but in fact, as you know, they've shot up sharply.'

As the markets fully realized India's strengths in producing computer software—after all, half of Silicon Valley seemed to be run by Indians—all infotech shares had risen through the roof, many doubling in weeks, and then quadrupling. Anyone moving against the market, by selling shares he didn't possess, was bound to have made a huge loss.

'Poor sucker,' said Varun. 'He must have been wiped out.'

'Wiped out? The bugger's losses must be running into crores of rupees. And on a Vision TV salary? My brother refuses to deal with him any more, but I believe that he's now gone to other brokers. So what should I do? Should I tell someone?'

Varun's attention was beginning to wander. The movement of stock prices wasn't uppermost on his mind right now. 'Tough one to call,' he replied absently, 'Who is this idiot?'

'Raju,' replied the other man. 'Raju, the cameraman.'

Varun froze. Strands of memory, loosely floating around in his brain, began coming together, to knit themselves into a blinding flash of realization.

The daily ritual on their shoots. The news bulletin in the evening. Once there had been a story on a farmer committing suicide in Andhra Pradesh, and Raju had made a stray remark: 'I guess when people are pushed to the wall in debt, they can do anything.'

Varun rose slowly from his chair, his face devoid of all colour. Sridhar was saying something, but he couldn't hear him.

Their hotel room. One day before Republic Day. Raju had gone down for a minute, and Varun had tried to tidy the room. Raju had entered just as Varun was arranging all the batteries neatly on the desk. He had shouted at Varun, telling him to leave all the equipment alone. Varun had been shocked; they had never, ever, quarrelled before.

As if in a dream, Varun walked slowly to where the rosters and assignments were pinned on a wall. He looked to see where Raju was at the moment. The entry against his name read, in small crabbed handwriting, '3 to 11 shift. Gone for the Rawat wedding.'

Republic Day in Srinagar. The look on Raju's face as he walked towards the security cordon. 'Is everything all right? You aren't looking too well,' Varun had said. Raju had forced a slight smile onto his face and said, 'I'm not feeling very well.'

Then the spell broke, and Varun began to run for the door, pushing aside all those in his way, his fingers pounding on the buttons of his mobile phone.

EPILOGUE

T. Raju died of gunshot wounds at Delhi's Safdarjang Hospital shortly after midnight. Three bullets from a silenced H&K machine gun had hit his left arm and chest, as he reached for the detonation button on the side of his camera.

In response to Varun's phone call, a semi-convinced SPG commander had ordered his men to surround Raju as he walked towards the bungalow where the wedding was being held. Raju had glanced at the wedding pandal, 200 yards away, and then at the armed men closing in around him. Then he had turned to run, fumbling with the camera as he did so. The Black Cat commando closest to him had been left with no choice but to shoot.

The fatally injured cameraman was rushed to the hospital, where the doctors soon announced that there was nothing they could do.

The guests at the Rawat wedding never even realized what had happened.

The funeral was held the next day at the Nigambodh Ghat. Most of the press corp turned up; Raju had been a popular man. The obituaries in the newspapers noted that he had died in his sleep of a massive heart attack.

After the funeral, Varun Mathur drove back to the Vision TV office, where he still works, occasionally writing columns for the leading newspapers on possible solutions to the Kashmir problem.

As soon as the S-squad was disbanded, Vijay Kaul returned to his unit in Badami Bagh. There was to be another visit to Delhi for him in a few months time—on 15 August, when the

President would pin the Shourya Chakra on his chest. That evening the Prime Minister invited Vijay for a private dinner at 7 Race Course Road—only the family was present.

The police recovered the Stinger missile from the basement of the Nangal Deri farmhouse. A discreet nationwide manhunt was ordered to try and locate Jalauddin, but there was no trace of him.

Habib Shah lives a semi-retired life in Srinagar. He can be seen every morning at a small graveyard, not far from Maisuma, sitting quietly next to a tiny headstone.

Two weeks after his information saved the life of the Indian Prime Minister, Habib walked slowly down the pathway that ran alongside the canal, heading towards the graveyard. His solitary security guard followed a slight distance away, an AK-47 hanging from his shoulder.

Habib had listened to the news bulletins with unusual interest during the past fourteen days. But there had been nothing out of the ordinary, and in this case no news was definitely good news.

He reached Yasmin's grave, and bent down to clear the dust that invariably gathered on the headstone. Then, as he straightened, he sensed that he was being watched.

He turned around and found Jalauddin standing there, watching him silently. The two men stared at each other, as the seconds lengthened into minutes. Then Jalauddin took a step forward. 'It was you, wasn't it? It was you who betrayed our plan.'

Habib said nothing. He kept looking straight into Jalauddin's eyes, and then, in a slow and deliberate gesture, he turned his back on the other man and knelt down beside the grave.

When he looked up again, Jalauddin was gone.